# SON

## AND

# HEIR

RICHARD I.H. BELSER

# SON

## AND

# HEIR

For Suzie & Rob

Richd JM Behn

4 Dec 2014

# PREFACE

MY GREAT-GRANDFATHER, Ritchie Hugh Belser, was born in Summerton, South Carolina in 1848. He served two years in the War Between the States and later attended Washington College, where he earned a certificate in English signed by the college president, General Robert E. Lee. Ritchie Hugh Belser managed Woodlands, the family plantation, and died in a hunting accident in 1896.

Irvine Furman Belser, my grandfather, was born in Summerton in 1889. He graduated first in his class at the University of South Carolina in1910. His accomplishments as an athlete and student leader were extraordinary. He studied for one year at Yale University, and was then awarded a Rhodes Scholarship to Oxford University. A student of law at Christ Church College, Irvine Furman Belser earned a first class placement in the Honors School of Jurisprudence, graduating in 1914 with a Bachelor of Civil Law degree. While at Oxford, he rowed on the crew and played rugby. He married Mary Campbell Heyward, whose father, Duncan Clinch Heyward, served as governor of South Carolina from 1903 until 1907. May Heyward and Irvine Belser had eight children.

From 1954 until 1964, I was blessed to spend a considerable amount of time with my grandfather. He owned large tracts of land in various parts of South Carolina and often invited me to accompany him on trips for fishing or hunting. Occasionally, he attempted to further my education by asking my opinion on some topic and then questioning my answers. The Socratic method required more maturity than I possessed, but I learned a great deal about my mentor and myself as we hunted quail or ducks or fished for bass in one of my grandfather's ponds. I realized that my grandfather had high expectations for himself and for the members of his family. It was also clear to me that my father, Irvine Furman Belser, Jr., and all seven of his siblings, had struggled from childhood with their father's standards, all of them producing impressive evidence of success, but many of them admitting to deep inner wounds. I have no doubt that there was affection in the family, and often occasions of understanding and forgiveness, but I believe the experience of grace, undeserved, freely given love, was rare for my grandfather and for his children.

When, as a college student, I read St. Paul's descriptions of life under the Law, I immediately identified with the Apostle's quandary. My own struggle to meet family expectations had left me with little confidence, and my mediocre performances in the realms of academics and athletics did nothing to improve my self-esteem. Reading the gospels introduced me to Jesus Christ, whose standards for living exceeded even my grandfather's and whose compassion extended even to failures like me. God's grace-filled love changed my life, and the desire to share that love with others continues to grow as my weakness and God's strength unite day by day.

This book is my attempt to relate the remarkable chronology of my grandfather's life as an encounter between the human struggle for success and the divine offer of grace. I have embellished the story with many fictitious characters, changed dates, altered events and developed subplots that are outright inventions and not at all part of my grandfather's biography. In the composite character of Nicholas Bower I have blended aspects of my grandfather's personality with elements of my father's life and with my own spiritual struggle. I am proud of my human ancestry, just as St. Paul was of his Hebrew heritage. But like the Apostle, I know myself to be a son and an heir of a Heavenly Father by adoption and grace. I pray that the human hunger for accomplishment and the universal longing for grace come together in this book in a way that honors my grandfather and gives glory to God.

**Richard I.H. Belser**

# CHAPTER ONE

## Winter 1900

ENTHRONED ON THE BACK of his father's best horse, fifteen-year-old Nicholas Bower squared his stocky shoulders and tugged his cap tighter over his curly brown hair as he waited for the race to begin.

"Steady, Caesar, steady!" he growled, his lowered voice sounding, he thought, too much like a boy and not enough like his father.

The big bay gelding snorted steam into the February air and edged nervously into the confusion of animals and riders jockeying for position on the sandy road that ran between the clapboard store-fronts of Riverton. Having been born and raised in the small South Carolina town, Nicholas knew all the other competitors, and he had a good idea of the capabilities of their mounts. His brother, Philip, younger than Nicholas but taller and thin-faced, had ridden the aging quarter horse, Cherokee, in last year's race, and even though he'd done poorly, he had asked for the same mount again.

"She's a sweet old gal," Philip grinned, swinging his leg out of the way as Nicholas' much larger horse shouldered the buckskin mare aside.

Reining to the right, Nicholas almost unseated Abel Simmons, the chubby boy from the farm next to the Bower's place, who once more had entered the race on Blue, a gaunt plow mule with devious eyes.

"Hold on there, Claus!" laughed Abel. "You do right to be scared of my mule, but that's no cause to knock me out'a the race!"

"Riders to the mark!" Standing on the ruined foundation of the old church, the Rev. Asa Turnbull, the Episcopalians' pastor, tried to shout over the voices of two hundred spectators, each of whom seemed to have a word of encouragement or a disparaging comment for the competitors. Shawl-wrapped women and jacketed men shivered with excitement while chattering, cherry-cheeked children ignored the icy air. The noon hour starting time had come and gone, and still the riders struggled to maneuver their mounts into position. A pinto pony reared and deposited its rider into a forest of legs and tails. The winter wind condensed the breaths of excited animals and eager riders into a rising cloud of steam.

"Gentlemen, please!" begged the minister.

Billy Battle, a skinny lad with wild red hair that had never encountered a comb, whooped in response to the jeering crowd and, with a grin, dug his heels into the sides of an uncooperative billy goat. "Out'a my way!" he bellowed.

The other riders paid him little attention, as each tried to steady his own mount with gentle pressure on the bit and whispered words of inspiration. Several of the boys sat on the same horse that had drawn their family's farm wagon to town. A few, like Nicholas and Philip, had saddle horses, but for the race all rode bareback, relying on a combination of horsemanship and steady nerves.

In the rural hamlet of Riverton, the Winter Race had been an annual event for more than 30 years. Now, in the second month of 1900, there were still plenty of local citizens who had witnessed the beginning, and they told how, on the 12th of February, 1865, a boy named Simeon Wilson had ridden alone from Orangeburg to Riverton to bring the news that Orangeburg had fallen to the Union Army and that General Sherman's men were headed for Columbia. Legend insisted that Simeon had made the thirty-mile ride in two hours, swimming his horse across the Santee River to avoid Union pickets. Locals bragged that the boy's heroism had given farmers and town's people time to hide their valuables and escape the invaders' approach.

"Just like when the British came for Boston!" reminded the generation of grandparents, and the Winter Race had been the community's attempt to hallow the memory of their own Paul Revere.

For the first few years, the Winter Race riders actually traced the rutted road from Orangeburg, but the troubles spawned by the Reconstruction government left citizens, black and white, understandably nervous. In 1875, the race had been shortened, first, to a five-mile course around Riverton, and then a few years later, to a one-mile sprint from the old church, through the town, around the cotton gin, and back. The abbreviated race gave the people of Riverton a satisfying reminder of their history and left the afternoon free for a community-wide celebration, simultaneously observed by whites and blacks in separate parts of town.

Captain Maximilian Bower, the father of Nicholas and Philip, had won the Winter Race at the first three runnings, refusing to let his war wounds keep him out of competition. The Captain had angrily opposed the shortened race.

"We can carry pistols!" he had argued when his neighbors worried about civil unrest, and for twenty-four years he shunned both the race and the festival. Only in 1899 had he begun to allow his sons to ride in the brief cross-town sprint, yielding to their pleas when they told him that a neighboring farmer had dared to disparage the family's patriotism and the boys' horsemanship.

On the ten-mile ride in from the family farm, Capt. Bower's iron gray eyes pierced each of his sons in turn as words exploded like bullets through his full, black beard.

"Look at me! And pay attention!" The boys drew their horses closer to their father's wagon. "This year, one of you will win the race, or you will both walk home. I will not have the family disgraced." Riding in silence, Nicholas showed no emotion, while Philip struggled to conceal a smile.

"You have the best horses," bellowed their father. "You have the best heritage. You will win! Do you understand me?"

Nicholas felt his face flush with anger. "Yes, sir," the boys said together, and their father's mandate echoed in their ears while they rode into Riverton to uphold the family's honor.

As Nicholas jockeyed to bring his mount to the starting line, he felt his father's eyes following him, judging his posture, critiquing the movement of his knees on the gelding's warm ribs and his application of the reins to the animal's proud neck. Captain Bower rarely rode the big Plantation Walker any more. The old wound in his leg made mounting by stirrup difficult and bareback riding all but impossible. Other men in the community of Riverton would often come to town in the family's farm wagon, but Captain Bower refused to be seen in anything but a neat little surrey, a conveyance he deemed suitable for a man of his standing.

Now seated in the surrey, Maximilian Bower stretched his injured leg and stared beneath the brim of his Confederate officer's hat to study his sons. Both showed promise, he'd decided, but each exhibited flaws that often left the highest level of accomplishment just beyond their reach. Nicholas was too serious, the Captain concluded. The boy tried too hard and caused his own blunders. And Philip was too casual about his responsibilities. He could shrug away failure and shed most criticism with a smile.

"But one of them will win today!" breathed Captain Bower.

From within the jostle of horses, Nicholas looked past his father and caught the eye of his mother, Sophie Bower, blanket wrapped and seated in the surrey next to her husband. Pushing back the rim of her bonnet, Sophie waved a gloved hand at her sons and winked to acknowledge Nicholas's smile. For a moment, Nicholas felt a weight lift from his heart. The next instant, tears warmed his cheeks. Looking quickly away, Nicholas cursed in frustration and angrily swept his shirtsleeve across his face. It was a weakness that had embarrassed him for as long as he could remember, and he hated it. Any expression of kindness or sympathy made him weep.

Now, in full view of the whole community, Nicholas wiped his face again, straightened his back, and took a deep breath. His mother's smile assured him that if he walked back to the farm a loser that night someone would welcome him home. But he would not let his tears betray him. Nicholas looked at his father, gripped the reins, and with his free hand, pounded his leg until the anger returned.

"Are you ready, boys?" yelled the Preacher, tentatively lifting a borrowed pistol for the starting shot. "Lord God Almighty, do thou watch over these young men," said Rev. Turnbull.

Nicholas was deaf to the rest of the prayer as he fixed his eyes on the rusty tin roof of the cotton gin that was the turn-around point. Reaching forward to stroke his horse's trembling neck, Nicholas suddenly felt his concentration collapse as two unexplainable impressions captured his attention.

The first was a momentary glimpse of January Wilson, a tall Negro boy about his own age, standing with others of his race behind the throng of white spectators and holding the bridle of a truly magnificent chestnut hued horse. For several months, Nicholas had seen the boy around the community and, with the other white residents, had speculated how a colored boy came to own such a fine animal.

"That's a thoroughbred stallion, you can be sure of it," observed Captain Bower when a neighbor mentioned the unlikely pair. "I suspect the horse is descended from some Union officer's mount and one of the Aiken racers that strayed, or more likely, was stolen, when Sherman came through."

Nicholas didn't have to ask why January Wilson, the owner of such a fine riding horse, didn't compete in the Winter Race. No black resident of Riverton had ever asked and none had been invited to compete. But in the seconds before the starting gun, Nicholas Bower couldn't dismiss the impression that his family and all of Riverton would one day have to come to terms with January Wilson and his chestnut stallion.

The second involuntary impression that assaulted Nicholas's concentration was the striking image of Conner Mayfield, the only rider without a hat, his long blond hair tied back with a string, now mounted just ten feet away and leaning over the neck of a big, well-muscled gray mare. Only a year older than Nicholas, Conner came from a family that had moved to Riverton about the time the opportunists whom local people referred to as carpetbaggers and scalawags had infiltrated communities all over South Carolina. The Mayfield's had bought a farm outside of town and, largely because of the natives' suspicions, Conner's people had stayed mostly to themselves. Conner had gained entrance into Riverton's two-roomed school over the objection of Captain Bower and other leading citizens, but because locals wielded little legal power, Conner and the other Mayfield children were allowed to attend classes.

Speaking to no one at first, Conner soon demonstrated a quick mind with his lessons and impressive skills with all of the physical pursuits that mattered to the boys of Riverton. In addition to having the best grades in his age group, the tall and sinewy boy was also the fastest runner. He could throw a ball or a stone farther than anybody his age. He rode his horse with an easy confidence that made him the secret envy of the other boys and the whispered fascination of all of the girls. Just that morning, when Nicholas' father had issued his edict about a Bower boy winning the Winter Race, Nicholas had thought instantly about Conner Mayfield.

"The race won't be between Philip and me, or Abel and me, or anybody else and me. It will be up to one of us to beat Conner Mayfield," lamented Nicholas.

The Preacher's pistol shot startled Nicholas out of his reverie, and he fought for balance as the broad-backed horse lurched forward with the rest of the field.

"Now, Caesar!" he screamed, his voice lost among the shouts of others riders, the thunder of hoofs, and the cheers of the watching crowd.

Squinting through a shower of sand, Nicholas realized he had made a bad start. Philip was already three yards ahead of him, shouting something unintelligible and flailing the old quarter horse with his hat. Two lengths ahead of Philip galloped Conner Mayfield, crouched low and leaning left to keep his face out of the big gray's flowing mane.

Wiping sand out of his face, Nicholas kicked his own mount hard and shouted, "Damn you, Caesar! Run!"

The easy rocking chair gait of the Plantation Walker became a tooth-rattling chop as the heavy hoofs stretched well beyond their natural reach. Nicholas gripped tighter with his knees and lashed his horse's flanks with the reins, alternating sides with each stroke. Most of the noise was behind him now, and he focused his attention on Philip, who was galloping only a few feet in front and to the left. As Nicholas kicked Caesar again and reined right to pass his brother, he felt the big horse stumble and heard a shriek near his shoulder.

"Look out, Claus!" yelled Able Simmons, whose reluctant plow mule had been inspired to run like he was headed for the barn.

Nicholas cursed aloud and wrenched Caesar's head left, realizing with a flash of shame that Philip and Conner were pulling away and that he was being overtaken by a fat boy on a mule.

Back by the old church, the crowd of spectators exclaimed to each other about the start of the race and all tried to catch a glimpse of the front runners, the women stretching on tip-toe and lifting their daughters, the men standing on wagon beds or rising in their stirrups, and the boys scampering into the magnolia tree to shout the names of the leaders as the horses neared the quarter mile mark at the general store. As they passed the Negro shanty settlement at the end of town, the thundering riders scattered chickens from the road like red and brown leaves. A fat, white-faced steer, which had been passing its final moments tied in front of the abattoir's shed, panicked at the sudden turmoil, jerked loose its tether, and ran bellowing with the last rank of horses.

Nicholas heard Abel Simmon's squeaky voice fade behind him as the boy's lanky plow mule began to tire. Ducking a new shower of sand, Nicholas realized he was gaining on Philip, and in the same instant he understood why. His brother's old quarter horse was limping badly.

"Pull up, Philip! Pull her up!" shouted Nicholas as he urged his own mount ahead.

Philip already had the mare angling toward the rutted wagon yard in front of the cotton gin, where he quickly slid to the ground. Nicholas glanced back in time to see Philip grin and wave him on.

Facing forward again, Nicholas leaned around Caesar's plunging neck in time to see Conner Mayfield turn behind the cotton gin. The tall boy drove the gray horse forward urgently but without a word, offering neither shouted exhortations nor whispered promises. His yellow hair stood out against his faded blue coat and made him an easy mark for the race watchers to follow.

"It's Conner!" trumpeted a black boy who had managed to clamber to the roof of the general store. "Mr. Mayfield come round de gin!"

As he followed the lead horse behind the long building, Nicholas hoped to catch a glimpse of his opponent, but Conner's ten-length advantage had already taken him around the gin and fifteen yards toward the finish line. Nicholas felt the excitement of the race drain from his body. Nearing the corner, he allowed his horse's strides to shorten, and as they slowed, the memory of his father's rage-darkened face suddenly resolved itself into an image of inevitable defeat. For an instant, Nicholas felt his anger dissolve and peace sweep over him.

"It's over," he told himself. "I'll be dead to him. No need to try anymore!"

The end of effort. It was a freedom he'd seldom known before. At once, he felt his tears begin to come, but what he saw in the next heartbeat removed his momentary feeling of relief and restored his desperate desire to win.

When Nicholas reached the front of the cotton gin, he lifted his head and watched, as if in a dream, as Conner Mayfield's gray horse suddenly lurched sideways, whinnied in terror, and rearing desperately, threw its blond rider to the ground. Some part of Nicholas wanted to hurry to help the crumpled figure, but fear spoke first.

"Leave him! It's my chance. I will win!"

As he bent low and flogged Caesar's sweating flanks, Nicholas saw a big yellow dog snarling circles around Conner Mayfield's frantic gray horse.

"Thank you, sir!" yelled Nicholas, smiling as he remembered the times he'd seen that dog sleeping under the statue in the Confederate Veteran's Memorial Park, oblivious to everything, waking only to bite fleas and come home for supper. Nicholas let out a victory whoop as he hurried Caesar toward the crowd gathered at the finish line.

Conner was down. Philip had dropped out with an injured horse. Poor Abel Simmon's mule had quit well before the cotton gin. Only Eddie Carter and Benjamin Baker were close enough to hope for second and third. Nicholas could hear the cheers of the crowd growing louder as he neared the end of the street. It would be easy to rein Caesar back and trot across the finish line, but he wanted to win pulling away, and he kicked his horse to a still longer stride.

Just ahead and to the right, Nicholas could see the top of his father's surrey, and he tried to recall, "What does my father's smile look like? Is it lost in his beard?

Nicholas never could remember what happened next. One moment he was racing home on the broad back of a reliable horse ten strides from victory. The next minute Nicholas fell off. There was no other way to explain it. The big Plantation Walker hadn't stumbled. Nobody threw anything from the crowd. Nicholas Bower, who had grown up on galloping horses, simply lost his balance and fell to the ground. As he began to slip, Nicholas gripped the reins with both hands and held on with all his strength. It was a purely instinctive reaction, as though his body could not accept what was happening. Now with his heels scraping grooves in the sandy street, Nicholas twisted dangerously close to the startled horse's hooves, the weight of his body pulling Caesar's head cruelly to the side.

"Whoa, now! Whoa!" croaked Nicholas, his voice carrying even less authority than at the start of the race.

In the crowd, women screamed. Several men rushed to reach the frantic horse's bridle, then retreated from the street as the approaching horses thundered toward them.

"Let go, boy! Turn him loose, Claus!" came the shouts.

But Nicholas held on. As Caesar wheeled in confusion, Nicholas could see the finish line a few yards ahead of him. The hoof beats of the other racers grew louder every second. Nicholas closed his eyes. Then came a sound that mastered every other noise and froze the boy's pounding heart.

"You will hold on!" roared Maximilian Bower.

Nicholas's cheek collided sharply with the unyielding ribs of his horse as heavy hoofs slashed just inches from his head. A sudden pain in his right leg brought a grimace to his face and a new chorus of screams from the horrified crowd. The leather reins cut into his hands as Nicholas clung to the gyrating horse, and swinging sideways for an instant, he looked up into the branches of the ancient magnolia tree that marked the end of the race. The finish line! How close was he? "Hold on," his father had ordered. Would he be named the winner if his horse stumbled across the finish line with him still attached? Anger tightened Nicholas' grip on the reins, and he shut his eyes hard, clenching his jaw against the pain. He would hold on!

"Jesus! Please, Jesus!" he begged as fire surged down his twisted arms and pain throbbed up his trampled legs. "A little longer! I can still win!"

In the seconds before he lost consciousness, Nicholas realized he no longer felt the impact of his body being slammed to the ground, nor could he hear the shouts of the crowd. But there was a voice, not angry and insistent like his father's, but words charged with a different kind of authority.

"Let go."

With the voice came a sensation of peace that was like nothing Nicholas had ever known. He felt tears on his face.

"I'm dying," he thought, surprised that he felt no fear.

"Let go."

The words came again, urgent but calm, an invitation, not a de-mand. Nicholas never remembered making the decision, but as he rolled again between the horse's pounding hoofs, he allowed his hands to relax on the reins and felt the leather begin to burn its way between his aching fingers. Then he let go. While Caesar bucked his way unburdened toward the end of town, the other riders galloped past Nicholas's crippled form, lying unconscious and bleeding three feet short of his family's honor.

# CHAPTER TWO

"JESUS, WON'T CHA COME BY HERE! Oh, now is a needin' time. Jesus won't cha come by here."

When Nicholas began to regain consciousness, even before he opened his eyes he recognized Ruby's voice. From infancy, he'd heard his mother's servant fill the Bower house with spirituals, and, without paying attention to the words of her songs, he'd been comforted by her gentle spirit.

"Ruby?" whispered Nicholas. The tall, black woman abruptly stopped her song, clutched her handmade broom to her chest, and hurried to his bedside.

"Do Jesus! He's awake! Miss Sophie! Miss Sophie!" exclaimed Ruby, first leaning over him, then turning to shout her excitement through the open door of Nicholas's room and down the central stairs. "Come quick, Miss Sophie!  Claus is awake."

Two hurried steps took Ruby to the window, where she flung open the curtains and let the morning sun flood the boy's bedroom.

"Claus! Where you been, boy? Three days we been praying and takin' turns sittin' up with you. Your momma done worried herself sick!"

"What happened?" croaked Nicholas, pushing his elbows into the mattress in an effort to sit up, and immediately falling back on his pillow, groaning from the pain that seized his right leg.

"What happened? Boy, you nearly got killed, that's what happened! You fell off Caesar right at the end of the race, but you wouldn't let go the reins, and that horse mashed you up somethin' awful and busted your leg."

Nicholas felt dizzy as Ruby's face floated above him. He heard hurried footsteps on the stairs, and when he opened his eyes again, he saw his mother bending down to kiss him.

"My son! My boy! O God, thank you, thank you!" She pressed her cheek close to his, and he felt her tears fall on his neck. When Nicholas grimaced in pain, Sophie Bower pulled her hands away in dismay.

"Oh, son, I'm so sorry. We've been so worried. Lie still! Lie still! Doctor Melton said you're to stay quiet. Oh!" she exclaimed, suddenly looking up. "We need to send someone to let the doctor know Nicholas is awake. Ruby, hurry and send Thomas to the doctor! Tell him to take any horse and go right now! Tell him to bring the doctor back!"

As Ruby rushed from the room, Nicholas tried to focus his eyes on his mother's face. When she leaned to reach a damp cloth on the bedside table, the sunlight through the window splashed across Nicholas' face, and he winced in pain.

"Mother," he groaned. "Mother, I can't see! Everything's blurred!"

"Claus, you've had a bad blow to your head," explained his mother. "Dr. Melton thinks the horse kicked you, and he said that you might have some dizziness for a while. A concussion, he said, but he thinks you'll be all right! I know you will! Ruby and I…"

"What about Father?" said Nicholas, turning to meet his mother's eyes.

Sophie Bower looked away for an instant, then smiling, replied, "Your father has been worried, like all of us. He'll be very glad to know you're awake. You must be famished! Ruby!" called Sophie Bower, feeling the weight of worry lift from her as she called instructions to the kitchen. "Ruby! Bring our boy some of your soup and cornbread!"

Sophie stayed with Nicholas through the afternoon, allowing only short visits from Philip and Ruby.

"I got some things to tell you," said Philip, awkwardly shaking his brother's hand.

"Not now!" ordered their mother. "You can talk later! Right now he needs rest!"

Philip shrugged at his mother and grinned at Nicholas. "Get better!" he growled, imitating their father's voice before he went whistling down the stairs.

Nicholas slept often throughout the afternoon, waking briefly when his mother applied a cool cloth to his forehead. About suppertime, Ruby's boy, Thomas, returned with instructions from the doctor.

"Dr. Melton say if Claus awake, he don't need to come today. He be comin' tomorrow to see 'bout his leg." Holding out a small bottle of purple liquid, Thomas continued importantly, "Doctor say give him this first thing when he wake up and last thing 'fore he sleep at night."

Long after dark, Nicholas woke to the sound of his father coming home. He heard the front door slam and felt fear pulse through his veins as he listened to his father issuing instructions to the household. Nicholas held his breath and waited for the sound of his father's boots on the steps. Only when the first floor conversation moved from the hall to the parlor to his parents' bedroom did Nicholas finally let out a long sigh. Captain Bower would not be visiting his convalescing son that night.

+ + +

"I wish I could be unconscious again," said Nicholas the following morning, as his mother and Ruby bathed him and dressed his wounds. The pain when they moved his leg was bad enough, but the anguish of having two women tend to his naked body was even worse.

"After the race, Dr. Melton came as quickly as he could," explained his mother, attempting to mask the embarrassing situation with talk. "He was in Sumter at the hospital. The telephone at the general store didn't work, so one of the men rode to bring him to our place. Lift up your arm! We put you in the back of the surrey as best we could and covered you with coats. It's a blessing you were not awake for that bumpy ride home. Philip caught Caesar and rode with us."

Caesar! Hearing the horse's name released in Nicholas a sudden whirlwind of impressions. The race. The sound of the crowd. The fall. His father's command. It all came back to him. But the tumbling images orbited an emptiness.

"Who won?" whispered Nicholas.

"The doctor was fixin' to splint your leg," said Ruby, glancing at Mrs. Bowers, "and he sent me to find the sticks. I brung him three tomato stakes from the barn, and that's what holding your bone together right now!"

"Roll over to the right," instructed his mother. "That's good! Dr. Melton said you could get up on crutches to use the chamber pot when you could stand it, but you're not to put any weight on that leg for two weeks."

"Who won the race?" insisted Nicholas, pushing aside his mother's ministering hands.

"I don't remember," came the exasperated response. "It doesn't matter, anyway. What matters is you're going to be all right."

"Go away!" shouted Nicholas as tears covered his reddened cheeks. "Leave me alone! I don't need anybody in here!"

Without a word, Sophie Bower folded her towel, nodded at Ruby, and the two women walked out of Nicholas's room, quietly closing the door on a wound they could not heal.

Nicholas angrily rubbed the sleeve of his nightshirt over his face and glared at the ceiling. With the missing piece in place, the events of the Winter Race now painfully assembled themselves in his mind. He remembered his excitement at the start. He recalled his alarm over Philip's injured horse and his delight at Conner Mayfield's embarrassment. He heard again the cheering crowd, relived the sudden horror of his fall, and clenched his jaw at the echo of his father's heart-stopping command. "You will hold on!" Nicholas fought against tears as he deliberately invited new pain, forcing himself up on both elbows until his splinted leg throbbed unbearably and he collapsed in agony. He had disobeyed. He had let go. He had lost. Nicholas felt the fingers of his right hand trace the muslin-wrapped stiffness of his splinted leg. Finding the tenderest place, he pressed slowly until a cry escaped his lips, then he formed a fist to pound harder and harder over the fractured bone. He would not let go again! Ever! He would not, but his pain gave him no choice, and Nicholas felt mercy embrace him as consciousness slipped away.

+ + +

"You gonna sleep all day?" barked Philip as he pushed open the door to Nicholas' room. "Mother said to bring you this plate. Look here. Pecan pie! Maybe if I broke my leg she'd feed me like this."

Nicholas looked at the food without interest. "Not hungry," he said, turning to stare out the window.

"Well, thank you, too." grinned Philip, pulling a chair close to his brother's bed. "Suit yourself. But listen, I do have some things you need to know about."

"What?"

"Well, first of all, Cherokee's dead." Nicholas turned quickly to look at his brother.

"What happened?"

"Father shot her. After the race, he was in a rage like I've never seen him in before.

Mother was helping some of the men load you into the surrey when I came walking up with

Cherokee. Don't know if you remember she pulled up lame…"

Nicholas nodded.

"Well, Father met us right in front of the crowd and without even feeling that right fetlock, he took his pistol to her head and put her down."

"It was me!" said Nicholas. "He wanted to kill me, so he killed her."

"Oh, I don't know," said Philip, "I think…"

"I hate him! Damn his soul! He's evil!"

"He was angry, for sure, but let me tell you what else."

"I don't want to know!" said Nicholas, shaking his head.

"Well, you're 'gonna find out soon, anyway. After the race, when Father saw your broken leg, he went right over and hired January Wilson to go to work for him. Said you were useless and with plowing coming on, he needed some help."

"So I'm replaced with a nigger."

"Just 'til you're well, I guess. But, there's one other thing."

"If it has to do with Father, keep it to yourself."

"No, it's about Conner Mayfield. Day before yesterday, he rode into town and shot that yellow dog that used to sleep in the Veterans' Park. Bunch'a people saw him do it."

Nicholas shook his head as he remembered his race day salute to the dog. "He's getting even for that dog getting him bucked off in the race. Anything happen to Conner?"

"Don't know of anything. Turns out the dog belonged to old man Huckabee at the general store, and he went and buried him by a cotton field. Huckabee's talking about going out to the Mayfield place and raising a stink with Conner's father."

"Won't do any good. Those people from off stick together."

"Well," laughed Philip, "The Bower boys need to stick together, too. Eat your supper, and relax. Father's gone to a political meeting in Manchester."

As Philip left the room, he passed Sophie Bower, blond hair pinned high, arms heaped with towels, her long dress sweeping over her high button shoes as she hurried in to hover over her injured son.

"I see you boys had a visit," she said, straightening the quilt on Nicholas' bed.

"He told me what Father did to Cherokee," said Nicholas, his voice bitter as poison. "Mother, how do you live with him? He's full of hate, and I hate him!"

"Don't hate him, son. Please don't hate your father! You have to remember what he's been through, things you and I could never understand."

"I understand that he wants Philip and me to be perfect, like we could do for him things he never could do on his own."

"Son," said Sophie Bower, "try to imagine what it was like for your father during the war. He was only fourteen when it started, and since his father was dead, he was the only man in the Bower family to fight the Yankees. His mother tried to keep him busy on the farm, but when the South Carolina 24th went off to join General States Rights Gist in Tennessee, your father lied about his age and marched with them. You've heard him talk about General Gist. Well, the General took a liking for Father, and made him, not a military aide, I guess, but kind of a stable boy, an orderly. Your father would never admit that, but I've found out about it from some who were with them."

Nicholas looked in surprise at his mother. "You mean Father really wasn't a soldier, not a captain, not a cavalry officer?"

"I shouldn't be telling you this, Nicholas, but if you're not to hate him, you need to know why he's like he is."

"My father's a liar and a fake!" exclaimed Nicholas, trying again to sit up in bed.

"Your father's a brave man, but a wounded one," said Sophie Bower. "When General Gist died in battle in the defense of Atlanta, your father stayed with the South Carolina troop, and those who knew him say he fought better than many of the regular soldiers. He got his wound during a raid on one of Sherman's columns on the way to Savannah."

Nicholas sat quietly, trying to reconstruct his image of the violent, black-bearded man who'd raised him in fear. "It's true, what you're telling me?" he asked looking hard into his mother's blue eyes.

"It's true," Sophie replied, "and the wound in his leg was only part of what the war did to him. The worst hurt was in his heart. When the war ended and the South was helpless in the enemy's hands, your father swore he would never lose another battle again."

Nicholas instantly recalled his own adamant pledge, sworn just hours ago, never again to let go of any struggle. He felt his face flush as the similarity between his own sick spirit and his father's wounded heart stood out with undeniable clarity. Nicholas closed his eyes and heard his mother's testimony continue.

"I know you've heard that after the war General Robert E. Lee himself became president of a college in Virginia and dedicated his last years to educating leaders for the fallen South. Your father was one of those students. He finished in 1869, just before General Lee died, and then he came back here."

"Where did you meet him?" said Nicholas, his voice no longer angry and defensive.

"We met at a dance in Charleston," smiled Sophie, looking away as she brushed a strand of hair from her face. "I thought he was so handsome! Although he certainly was no dancer, with his bad leg and all. My family lived in Beaufort, but I had an aunt in Charleston who gave me art lessons, and while I stayed with her, your father would ride down to visit. We were married in St. Helena's, and then I joined him here on the farm."

Nicholas and his mother sat quietly for a long time. "Do you think he will come up to see me?" Nicholas finally asked, instantly aware that he sounded like a much younger boy.

"Father's asked about you, son. I'm sure he'll visit soon. He certainly knows he needs you after school hours in the fields. You know, he's often told people what a fine way you have with horses."

"He won't say that again," said Nicholas, tenderly flexing his hands to feel the raw wounds left by Caesar's leather reins. "Mother, how can I ever please him? I try, honestly, I do, and all he sees is my failures. Philip doesn't seem to care so much. He just shrugs away, Father's curses. I can't! Mother, I really tried to hold on! I swear to you, I did! I heard him shout and I was ready to die under that horse. But ..." Nicholas stopped. He wasn't sure if he could describe what happened in those last terrifying seconds.

"But what?"

"I heard another voice, or I had a feeling, a strong sense that said, 'Let go.' And there was a peaceful feeling like I never had before."

"Yes?" said Sophie.

"I don't know. It was as if Father wanted me to win by holding on and this other voice, this other feeling wanted me to win by letting go."

"Nicholas," said Sophie, placing her hand over his and looking at him intently, "Under the horse, did you pray?"

"Yes M'am, I did," said Nicholas, remembering his desperate plea for strength. "I prayed to be able to hold on."

"Do you suppose?" said his mother. For a while she was silent. Then she spoke again. "Son, I believe God answered your prayer. You didn't win the race, but he gave you back to us. And I've been thanking him ever since!"

+ + +

Three days later, Nicholas, assisted by Ruby and Philip, made his way down the stairs and out to the side porch swing. While the household waited for supper, Nicholas surveyed the clean swept yard that lay between the farmhouse and the outbuildings. He watched the barn door open, and saw his father's hired hand, the boy January Wilson, emerge and look his way. Nicholas expected the black boy to avoid his glance, and was surprised when January turned and walked purposefully toward the porch.

"Good evening, Mr. Nicholas," the boy said. "It appears you're feeling better."

Nicholas could not have been more surprised if January Wilson had flown down from a chinaberry tree. The young man spoke with perfect diction and his words reflected not a trace of Negro dialect.

"Yes, thank you. I am much better," said Nicholas, staring in astonishment at his visitor.

"That was a nasty fall you took. I was impressed at the way you held on."

"Thank you," gulped Nicholas again, looking away nervously as he tried to think what to say next. An idea emerged and Nicholas seized it. "I saw you in town with your horse that day. He's a beautiful animal."

January Wilson nodded and smiled. Then, tipping back his head, he lifted his voice and said, "When I bestride him, I soar, I am a hawk: he trots the air; the earth sings when he touches it; the basest horn of his hoof is more musical than the pipe of Hermes."

Nicholas choked on his next breath. "What," he blurted. "I didn't catch that."

"Shakespeare," grinned the black boy. "Henry the Fifth. One of my favorite lines."

"Oh, mine, too!" lied Nicholas, his mind straining to comprehend what had just happened.

"I'm glad you're better," said January. "Perhaps we can talk again. Now I need to bring in your father's cows."

# CHAPTER THREE

"WHERE'S THAT TRIFLING NIGGER?" roared Captain Bower from the farmhouse porch. "January! You get out here!"

The captain paced the porch impatiently, his gray eyes bitter as the black boy came running from the barn. "Didn't I tell you to have the wagon ready after breakfast?"

"Yes, suh." answered January, his eyes focused on the dirt at his feet.

"And the wagon's not here, is it?" snarled the bearded mouth.

"No, suh."

"And now my son is going to be late for school! What do you have to say for yourself?"

"Nothin', suh."

"Look at me when I'm talking to you, boy! Until Nicholas' leg mends and he can ride his horse to school, you will be taking him in the wagon. Is that clear?"

"Yes, suh," nodded the boy, his eyes emotionless as he stared through Captain Bower's face.

"Well, by damn, do it!" The captain drew his long coat around him angrily as he stalked back into the house.

The other farmers ordinarily wore overhauls on workdays, but Captain Bower set himself apart with a frock coat, vest and necktie whenever he left his home.

Nicholas made his way down the stairs, demonstrating rapidly improving skills with his crutches. Hurrying past without looking at his son, Captain Bower barked, "Tell your teacher our nigger made you late."

"Yes, sir." said Nicholas.

+ + +

"Mr. Nicholas, the wagon's ready," called January a few minutes later. He watched as Nicholas hobbled down the porch stairs, and then helped him climb aboard the farm wagon.

"Come up!" said January to the harnessed mules, and Nicholas winced as the wagon bumped its way toward the rutted road that led to town. "How are you feeling?" said January, turning to smile at his passenger.

"I'm alright," said Nicholas, looking at the passing cotton fields. Smoke from the farmhouse chimney hung low over the newly plowed land. Nicholas shivered, turned up the collar of his jacket, and allowed himself to be warmed by the anger inside. He'd heard his father's words to the black boy, and found that the criticism he was accustomed to hearing sounded much worse when it was directed at somebody else.

"I'm sorry about what my father …"

"He doesn't bother me," said January. "I'm used to that kind of talk. I just let it pass right through me."

Nicholas felt a heartbeat of hope as he imagined what that freedom must be like, but he'd lived too long with his father's criticism to believe he would ever find such peace for himself.

The boys rode without words, both of them listening to the rattle of the wagon and the muffled clop of the mules' hoofs, while each of them silently rehearsed what he might say next.

"Where did you learn about Shakespeare?" said Nicholas.

January laughed out loud. "I knew you would wonder about that!

Since my family came to Riverton, I've kept pretty much to myself. My background is still a mystery to the white people who know my name."

"You're not from South Carolina, are you?"

"I grew up in Philadelphia," explained January. "My mother's people moved there right after freedom came, and my grandmother went to work for a very prominent family. They had a daughter my mother's age, and when the girl's tutors came for lessons, the family invited my mother to learn along with their daughter. You might say, mother had a classical education, even though she never went to any formal school. And what she learned, she passed along to me."

"Including the way you talk," said Nicholas. "You don't speak like colored people here."

"Unless I'm talking to your father," smiled January, his eyes bright with mischief.

"But don't you go to school here?"

"Unfortunately, the colored school in Riverton doesn't have much for me. Most children learn to read a little and then drop out before my age. They don't see much reason to continue."

"But what about you? You're way ahead of most boys our age at my school."

January nodded. "I expect so. I do go to the colored school most days when I'm not working, and I usually help the teacher with the younger students. Who knows what's ahead for me?"

The two boys traveled in silence again until January called. "Come up!' and urged the mules to a faster pace.

"I hear that you're a Latin scholar," he said glancing at the white boy. "Is that true?"

"I'd hardly call myself a scholar," said Nicholas. "But the language has come easily since I began to learn it in school, and I've memorized more of Miss Abernathy's wise Latin sayings than anybody really needs. You ever study any Latin?"

January chuckled. "Not a word! Mother said in Philadelphia they didn't think girls needed Latin, so she didn't have any to teach me."

As the wagon passed through the fields on the outskirts of town, January nodded toward a mound of earth between the road and the plowed ground. "See there? That's where Mr. Huckabee buried his dog after Conner Mayfield shot it. He's a mean one, Conner is! I'd steer clear of him if I were you," warned January.

"Ut sementem feceris ita metes," said Nicholas almost instantly. "As you sew, so shall you reap."

January nodded at the translation, "That boy's got a big harvest of trouble coming, believe me!" Smiling, he turned to Nicholas. "Poor old dog! Everybody's talking about him. 'Nothing in his life became him like the leaving of it!'"

"Shakespeare?"

"From Macbeth," January said as the wagon stopped in the schoolyard. "I'll see you this afternoon for the ride home. Learn a lot today!" Climbing from the wagon, Nicholas realized he'd already learned a great deal.

+ + +

When Nicholas limped his way into the classroom, the other students, a dozen of them, were bending over their copybooks transcribing a name which their gray-haired teacher had written on the blackboard.

"Benjamin Ryan Tillman, governor of South Carolina and United States Senator," proclaimed Miss Abernathy. "Next to John C. Calhoun, he is by far the most important figure in the history of our state."

Turning around, the teacher greeted Nicholas. "Do come in, Mr. Bower. Your brother told me about your accident, and all of us have been anxious for your recovery. I'm glad to see you are making progress. Please take your seat. And tomorrow, do make an effort to be on time. 'Tempus neminen manet' 'Time waits for no one.'"

Nicholas remembered the excuse his father had ordered him to give, but he said simply, "Yes, ma'am."

"Now," continued Miss Abernathy, "who can tell me what we've learned about Senator Tillman?"

"He carried a pitchfork instead of a pistol!" blurted Abel Simmons. Laughter swept over the class.

"He was a friend of the farmers!" said a girl in braids.

"He started a college," added a boy whose wispy beard made him look far too old for the group.

"He made the blue-blooded aristocrats eat humble pie," said Conner Mayfield.

Nicholas turned toward the voice and found Conner smirking at him. Conner widened his eyes, as if to say, "And what are you going to do about it?" Nicholas remembered his father's frequent tirades about Benjamin Tillman.

"He's no friend of the farmer," Captain Bower had thundered. "Takes the side of upcountry bean pickers and turns his back on the agricultural people who made this state! I mean the low country rice and cotton planters!"

Nicholas glared at the blonde haired boy. "You think Tillman's a friend of people like you, Conner? Did you bring your lunch today in a carpet bag?"

Conner Mayfield lunged from his desk, upsetting the bench and scattering books across the room as girls screamed and boys ducked. Nicholas tried to stand in self-defense, but before he managed get to his feet, Philip had rushed between Conner and his brother.

"That will be all! Sit down!" ordered Miss Abernathy. Conner shoved Philip hard before turning away. "Conner! Nicholas!" said Miss Abernathy. "You will both remain when class is dismissed today, and you will stay until you have memorized and recited a poem that I shall assign. Now, let us continue!"

+ + +

When school was over and the other students had departed, Nicholas and Conner sat on opposite sides of the classroom, Nicholas hunched forward in apprehension and Conner casually leaning back against the desk behind him.

"I'm very disappointed in both of you," said Miss Abernathy. "You are my best students, and I expect you to be examples to the other members of your class. You might not care for each other, but you will be respectful while you are in this school. Is that clear?"

"Yes, ma'am," grunted Nicholas. Conner merely shrugged assent.

"Now, the verses I want you to memorize are from 'The Merchant of Venice,' by William Shakespeare."

Nicholas sat up quickly. "How curious," he thought, "that I've encountered Shakespeare twice in as many days!" Conner sat back and studied his fingernails.

"I want both of you to come up and take a copy of the upper level English book and turn to the page I've marked."

Nicholas and Conner came forward. Glancing out the window, Conner spotted January outside in the wagon and said to Nicholas, "Look, your nigger is waiting for you!"

"Now," continued Miss Abernathy, "you will memorize the lines that begin, 'The quality of mercy.'" Conner shook his head in disgust, while Nicholas began to study the appointed verses. Memorizing Latin vocabulary and quotations from famous Latin authors came easily to him, but he struggled with English verses.

"The quality of mercy is not strained," he read. "It droppeth as the gentle rain from heaven upon the place beneath. It is twice blest: it blesseth him that gives and him that takes."

"Mercy," thought Nicholas. "It might not be strained, whatever that means, but in my life it's a rare thing."

He pictured his mother's face as she bent over him, anxious for his every wound. And then, from nowhere, came a hint of that extraordinary feeling of peace he'd known in the seconds before he released his horse's reins and lost the Winter Race. He felt moisture welling in his eyes.

"I'm ready to recite," announced Conner, shattering Nicholas's reverie and surprising the teacher.

"Are you quite sure, Mr. Mayfield?" said Miss Abernathy.

In answer, Conner stood, and in three breaths spat out the playwright's words.

"Accurate, Mr. Mayfield, but without the slightest appropriate sentiment. You have an impressive memory! And you may be excused."

Nicholas watched Conner gather his books and stalk toward the classroom door. At the last step, he turned to stab Nicholas with angry eyes.

Half an hour later, after struggling against his embarrassing tears, Nicholas successfully recited the verses and was released by his teacher.

"We'll have no more such disturbances, Nicholas," warned his teacher. "Verbum sapienti sat est. A word to the wise is sufficient."

As he climbed awkwardly into the farm wagon, Nicholas couldn't wait to tell January about the memorization assignment. "Have you heard this?" he said, and immediately began to recite. January smiled and nodded as he urged the mule home.

When Nicholas ended the monologue, January sighed. "The dread and fear of kings. Is that the power your father has over me?"

"Yes, and me, too. He's not a king, but he sure acts like one, and all of us are afraid of him."

"But mercy is stronger," said January.

"That's what Shakespeare says, anyway," nodded Nicholas. "And my mother, too. She says mercy's from God."

"You always go to church?"

"Ever since I can remember. All of us. Except for Father. I think he gave up on God in the War."

"Winners and losers," said the black boy. "My grandmother tells me the War is what brought her closer to God. Who can say?"

They rode without further talk for a while, and Nicholas found January's cryptic phrase replaying in his thoughts. "'Winners and losers.' I wonder what he means?"

+ + +

The idea still preoccupied Nicholas on Sunday morning when he dragged his splinted leg into his father's surrey. Captain Bower generally spent Sunday at his desk managing the farm's accounts, so for the trip to church, Nicholas sat next to his mother while Philip held the reins. January Wilson had harnessed the tall, white-footed roan the family called their "church horse" because of the animal's practiced ability to draw the surrey to the place of worship without guidance from any of the passengers. Nicholas had explained to his mother the reason for his late return from school on the previous day. On the way to church, Sophie Bower reminded both her sons that Miss Abernathy had a responsibility to preserve order, and she chided Nicholas for his outburst against Conner Mayfield.

"But he is a troublemaker," she conceded, patting Nicholas on his un-splinted knee.

"Would you like to hear the poem Miss Abernathy made me memorize?" asked Nicholas. Sophie listened as her son described the quality of mercy as an attribute of God himself. She was silent when he finished, only looking up when he asked if she liked his recitation.

"Oh, yes, very much indeed," she said. "I only wish ...," and tears interrupted her words.

"I copied it in my book," said Nicholas, "just in case I start to forget it."

"Oh, Son," said Sophie Bower, "Son, do remember!"

+ + +

A congregation of carriages already ringed the open yard in front of St. Matthias Episcopal Church when the Bowers family arrived.

"Gracious, look at the crowd!" said Nicholas' mother. "This little church is too small for us these days. I just wish our congregation had money to build a bigger one, bigger even than the one the Yankees burned during the War."

As his family joined the service already underway, Nicholas glanced furtively toward the pews on the opposite side of the church. Sally Hemphill always sat there with her family, but in recent months, Nicholas had begun to take particular notice of her presence. Philip noticed his brother's wandering eyes and jabbed an elbow into Nicholas' ribs.

"Pay attention!" whispered Philip, feigning a frown.

Vested in black cassock and while surplice, the Rev. Asa Turnbull invited the congregation to turn from the opening hymn to the responsive reading of the Ten Commandments.

"God spake these words and said, 'Thou shalt have none other God's but me.'"

With all the congregation, Nicholas replied, "Lord, have mercy upon us and incline our hearts to keep this law."

"Mercy," thought Nicholas. "There it is again." His mind wandered to Shakespeare and to Conner Mayfield and to his mother as the rest of the congregation responded to the first four Commandments.

Then the minister read, "Honor thy father and thy mother, that thy days may be long in the land the Lord thy God giveth thee." Nicholas could feel himself stiffen at the words. "Honor thy father." How could God expect him to do that? Nicholas found it easy to honor his mother.

"She's an honorable person," he said to himself. "But Father!" The rest of the worship service was lost on Nicholas. His leg hurt. He could not free himself from recurring memories of his father's angry countenance at the Winter Race, his obvious indifference to Nicholas' injuries, his demeaning words to January Wilson and his prideful obsession with family honor. After church, Sally Hemphill smiled his way, but Nicholas was too preoccupied to notice.

On the long ride home from church, Sophie Bower tried, as she did every Sunday, to coax her sons to join her in a hymn sing. Her voice trembled when the surrey bounced from one wheel rut to another. Nicholas croaked out the few verses they knew, and he attempted unsuccessfully to harmonize with his mother's clear soprano voice on the Latin chorus, "Dona nobis pacem." Between songs, Philip tried to brighten his injured brother's mood with voice caricatures of people they knew.

"This is Mr. Turnbull!" he laughed, imitating the singsong inflection of the minister. "Who's this, who's this?" Philip continued, mocking the precise diction of Miss Abernathy. Nicholas easily identified the teacher's voice and just as quickly recognized his brother's parody of Dr. Melton's deep drawl.

"I will not have you boys being disrespectful," warned their mother, hiding her smile behind her scarf.

"How 'bout this one?" laughed Philip, hanging his head and affecting a Negro accent. "Yes, suh. No, suh." Before Nicholas could reply, Philip supplied the answer. "It's January! All that boy ever says is 'Yes, suh!' or 'No, suh!'"

Nicholas started to say, "You might be surprised," but he chose instead to keep secret his friendship with the educated farm hand. "Potest ex casa magnus vir exire," Nicholas murmured, confident that neither his mother nor Philip could understand his coded prophecy. "A great man can come from a cabin."

When they reached the house, Nicholas crutched his way up the porch stairs while Sophie spoke to Ruby and Philip unhitched the horse. As he entered the front hall, Nicholas saw his father standing by the dining room table with a book in his hand. Nicholas felt his face flush with fear as he realized what Captain Bower was reading.

Looking up from Nicholas' copybook, the bearded man in the black frock coat opened the last page toward his son, and pointing to a hand-written paragraph, demanded, "Did you write this?"

Nicholas's anger shaped a quick response that was instantly canceled by habitual restraint. He wanted to snap at his father, "Who else would write in my copybook?" He wanted to sniff sarcastically, "No, any half educated person would know Shakespeare wrote that!" But what he said was, "Yes, sir."

"Look at me when I'm talking to you!" ordered Captain Bower. The big man turned back to the book and was silent for a moment. When he looked again at Nicholas, his voice was softer. "It's a noble sentiment," said Maximilian Bower. "But you will discover that it's rarely true, Nicholas." The boy realized he could not remember the last time his father had spoken his name. "You cannot go through life counting on mercy. You must be strong."

The captain's eyes struggled with the image of his oldest son propped up on crutches. He let out a deep breath and said to Nicholas, "Go tell January he can have the afternoon off."

Nicholas ignored Ruby's call to Sunday dinner in order to go searching for January Wilson.

"Something's got hold of my father," said Nicholas when he found the black boy repairing the chicken coop. "He told me you don't have to work the rest of the afternoon!"

"Well, what about that?" smiled January, laying down his hammer. "I know he didn't go to church with the rest of you. What's made him so generous?"

"He read where I wrote down what Shakespeare said about mercy. That's all I can figure."

"I guess I'll go home, then. I just hope your father is merciful tomorrow when he sees I haven't finished fencing in these chickens!"

# CHAPTER FOUR

## Spring 1900

THE COTTON PLANTED on the Bower farm during the first two weeks of March budded near the last of April, and by the time school closed for the children of Riverton, the first fragile cotton flowers had formed. Little girls skipping rope in the schoolyard chanted the blossom's brief life.

"First day white, next day red, third day from my birth, I'm dead!"

With classes ended, Nicholas and Philip rode to the fields with their father each morning, where the boys joined the farm's hired hands in the backbreaking labor required for a good crop. Nicholas' still-healing leg disqualified him from plowing, so he often found himself hoeing a row next to January Wilson, and the two continued a daily conversation that covered a wide range of topics.

"Tell me some more about your family," asked Nicholas one day. "You said your mother had tutors in Philadelphia, but you never said how she came to bring you down here."

"After my father died," said January, and Nicholas realized with remorse how little he really knew about his friend. "My mother married a man from here. You know him, I believe. Name's Isaiah Adams. He inherited some land over near the Richardson place. That's where we live."

"I know him. Did he give you your horse?"

"No, Isaiah never had any horses like mine. That horse came with me from up north."

"From the people your grandmother worked for?"

"That's right. When they gave him to me to ride south, they called him Freedom, and I figured it was too good a name to change." January rested on his hoe and straightened his back. "Now you tell me," he said, "Is it true your grandfather ran off and married an Indian woman?"

Nicholas looked up in surprise. "Where'd you hear that? That's the craziest thing I've ever heard!"

"You know, people talk," said January. "Some that belonged to your family before the War have their stories."

"Well, it's a lie, and you can tell them!" said Nicholas, even as he realized he'd never heard anything from his own family about his grandfather.

+ + +

At mid-day, Captain Bower drove his surrey to the field edge and called Nicholas to his side. "I don't want you distracting my hired workers," ordered the Captain. "You and that January boy have been an hour on one row! Now I want you to ride home and bring lunch for Philip and me."

Nicholas propped his hoe against a tree and hurried to his horse. "I hope it will be all right if I bring lunch for me, too!" he grumbled under his breath.

The short canter home produced a cooling breeze through his sweated shirt, and by the time he returned with his mother's packed lunch basket, Nicholas felt much relieved. As he tethered his horse and started toward the big tree where his father and Philip were waiting, Nicholas noticed that January Wilson's stallion, Freedom, was not tied where he'd been just half an hour before.

While Captain Bower unpacked the nested food containers and served warm plates of chicken, rice and gravy, Nicholas said, "Where did January go?"

"What do you mean?" said Philip. "He's right there with the other hands."

Nicholas looked where his brother was pointing, and immediately spotted the tall black boy. "Then who's got his horse?" said Nicholas out loud.

Captain Bower and his sons turned toward the grove of trees where the workers' horses were tied and their wagons parked. The big, chestnut thoroughbred was not there.

"I'll be right back," said Nicholas, hurriedly setting his lunch plate on the ground and running toward the shady spot where the farm workers gathered for their mid-day meal.

"January," he said, ignoring the assembly of dark, staring faces, "Where's Freedom?" The black boy leapt to his feet, his expression changing from confusion to shock when he realized his horse was not where he'd tied him. Nicholas and January sprinted together to the hitching place.

"He was right here, not an hour ago!" said January.

"Was he tied up tight?"

"Of course! And even if he'd pulled loose, he wouldn't stray. Somebody's taken him!"

The missing horse brought a sudden end to everybody's lunch as the Bowers and their hired hands gathered at the scene of the disappearance.

"Captain, will you get the sheriff? Please hurry, sir!" begged January.

"Just hold on!" thundered the captain. "We have no reason to think somebody stole your horse. It's the middle of the damn day, and twenty-five people have been in this field all morning. It's most likely the horse pulled himself loose and wandered off."

"No, suh!" insisted January. "I tied him tight, and he wouldn't wander. Somebody sneaked in and stole him!"

While Captain Bower tried to explain how hard it would be to steal a horse in broad daylight in front of a crowd of people, Philip wandered away from the hitching area and ventured into the edge of the woods. When Nicholas looked in his direction, Philip motioned him over.

"Look here," said Philip, pointing to a muddy place between the leaves. "See that boot print? Who wears boots like that?"

Nicholas looked and gasped in recognition. There in the wet earth were the still fresh impressions of pointed, western style riding boots. "Conner Mayfield!" he said, looking up to see Philip nodding in agreement. "Nobody wears those cowboy boots but Conner! And these are fresh tracks! Let's get Father!"

The discovery of boot prints brought the angry assembly of farm hands to even greater outrage. "Them's Conner's tracks, all right," declared a cousin of January Wilson. "You ought'a go right now and find that thief and 'cuse him to his face!"

"Hold on, all of you!" shouted Captain Bower. "You can't go around accusing somebody of stealing a horse because he wears a certain kind of boots! A big, blond-headed, white boy couldn't sneak in here unnoticed. There needs to be an investigation by the proper authorities." The black field hands exchanged glances, and several frowning men mumbled unintelligible replies.

"I want you to get back to work!" said the captain. "Nicholas and I will ride the area and look for the horse. I still think he's just wandered. And if we can't find him before long, we'll report this to the sheriff."

"Captain, can I ride with Nicholas?" said January.

"You do your work! I'll find your horse. Nicholas, come with me!"

For the next half hour, Nicholas rode his horse to scout the woods while his father drove the surrey to investigate the two-rut roads that bordered the Bower farm. They lost the distinctive pointed boot prints after a few hundred yards and had no way of recognizing the tracks of the missing horse from the other impressions in the sandy road.

Captain Bower pulled out his pocket watch and cursed. "Damn it all! I don't have time to do this, but I promised that we'd report to the sheriff if the horse didn't turn up. We're going to town."

Nicholas took a deep breath. "Thank you, Father."

The Captain frowned and glanced up at his son. "I don't want you to be too friendly with the nigras. It's not good, not for you or for them."

"I just want to get January's horse back, that's all."

"You're right to have a concern for them. They're a simple race, and they need us to organize and explain things to them."

"Maybe not all of them," thought Nicholas, wondering if he should reveal his secret about January. But he said nothing more.

+ + +

When the Captain and Nicholas reached Riverton, they found Sheriff Caleb Harvey and reported the missing horse. The sheriff wrote down the name of the horse's owner, a description of the animal, and the time and location of its disappearance. Nicholas waited for his father to describe the distinctive footprints they'd found near the hitching place, but the captain made no mention of that discovery.

"Father," said Nicholas, but he caught the captain's sudden glare and remained silent. Outside the sheriff's office, Nicholas tried to control his frustration as he asked about his father's important omission.

"I'm not a policeman," said Captain Bower, "and neither are you! We don't tell the sheriff how to investigate. He doesn't tell us how to run our farm."

"But Father, those boot prints are evidence!"

Captain Bower stopped and turned toward his son. "Listen," he said. "Those prints could implicate a white boy for the theft of a nigra's horse. It could be true, but that idea will not come from our family!"

As Nicholas and his father rode back to the farm, the boy seethed with indignation. He knew what his father meant. He also knew it was wrong. Nicholas hadn't thought much about justice, but as he pictured January Wilson seated proudly on a horse named Freedom, he understood that justice should not work one way for people with power and another way for those with little voice or influence. He wondered if Sheriff Harvey would actually anything do to find January's horse. "Winners and losers." His black friend's cryptic observation came back to Nicholas.

He thought, "So January ends up a loser and my father pushes me to be a winner. I'm a lot closer to January than to him, and I don't care if he knows it!" Nicholas' anger with his father now dissolved his normal fear-born restraint. He wanted to punish this man who was thoughtless to so many others.

"Did your father marry an Indian woman?" said Nicholas abruptly. He meant the insulting question to hurt and expected to receive his father's fury. Instead, Captain Bower popped the surrey horse with his whip and snorted with indignation.

"Who the hell told you that lie?" growled his father. "Married to an Indian! I've heard that slander all my life! Of course it's not true."

"What happened to him, then?" asked Nicholas, disappointed that the pointed accusation had not shocked his father.

"Listen to me! Your grandfather was an adventurer, not a misogynist," said Captain Bower. "That's the truth about him. People will tell you he was weak and unreliable because he left the farm and my mother and me when I was three years old and rode to California for the gold rush. But I tell you it took a brave man to cross this country and risk everything for the sake of his family."

"Did he find any gold?" asked Nicholas, feeling shaken as the idea of a grandfather in California suddenly expanded his small South Carolina world.

"Not enough," said his father. "The rush was mostly over before he got there. Your grandmother told me that he worked his claim a year. Didn't find a damn thing! Some that were with him said he died of yellow fever on the way home. They wrote to my mother about it. I never really knew him. But you must remember that your grandfather tried! And nobody can prove that he ever married any Indian!"

"No Indian relatives, then," thought Nicholas, silently wondering if a failed adventure and death by common disease was nobler than finding comfort in the arms of a savage.

+ + +

The next Sunday, on the wagon ride to church, Nicholas told his mother about the conversation with his father. "I'm surprised he told you about that," said Sophie Bower. "He's always gotten angry when people mention his father."

"He told me my grandfather was a brave man for going to California."

"You know how your father hates failure. He can't deny the fact that his father found no gold and died before he could redeem himself, so he's decided that courage is what really matters."

"I wonder what Father would think if I hopped on my horse and headed west," said Philip.

"You might as well just keep on going," said Nicholas, "and don't plan on coming back until you've accomplished something big."

"Maybe I will," grinned his brother.

"There's no reason why both my sons can't do important things," said Sophie Bower, smiling at the boys in turn. "But wherever you go and whatever you do, I am proud of you!"

Nicholas' mother hugged him as the surrey pulled into the churchyard, and he experienced a sudden warmth that had nothing to do with the morning sun. The sensation swept over him for an instant, and then it was gone, just the way he'd known it at the end of the Winter Race.

"Claus, are you well?" asked his mother pressing her hand against his cheek. "Your face is flushed!"

Before Nicholas could answer, Philip said, a little louder than necessary, "He's all right! He just saw Sally Hemphill!"

When Mr. Turnbull pulled the bell rope to call the congregation to prayer, the first to respond were the women and girls. Sophie Bower chatted busily with other planters' wives, strolling toward the church door while catching up on the news that everyone always brought to the Sunday gathering. As she entered the family pew, Mrs. Bower observed the devotional custom of her church and fell silent, kneeling to pray while she waited for her sons to join her.

Out under the trees, a different set of customs kept the men and boys at their own gossip until well after the morning worship had begun. The farm owners exchanged opinions about the developing cotton crop, the likelihood of rain, and the prospects of a reasonable price per pound at harvest time. Nicholas reported to the boys that he'd heard no more news about January Wilson's missing horse. Each of the young men offered his opinion about what might have happened and what the sheriff should do to solve the mystery. They were evenly divided about Conner Mayfield's role in the horse's disappearance. And since Conner and his family never came to church, all the young detectives felt free to speculate out loud.

"I heard a man saw Conner in Orangeburg the day the horse disappeared," said Abel Simmons. "What business do you suppose he had over there?"

"Well, I know there were four men buying livestock that day at the railroad yard," said Eddie Carter, whose come-from-behind victory in the last Winter Race gave weight to his opinions.

"You all don't know nothing!" scoffed Billy Battle. "I heard a man at the general store say he saw Isaiah Adams riding toward Charleston on a big handsome horse just about that time."

"You're all forgetting the boot prints I found right where the horse was hitched! Conner's boots!" said Philip.

Nicholas listened to the discussion and said nothing. One of Miss Abernathy's sayings came back to him, "Culpam poena premit comes." "Punishment closely follows crime as its companion." He offered no opinion as the boys slowly preceded their fathers and uncles into the church.

During the minister's sermon, Nicholas found himself thinking less about his friend's vanished horse than about the extraordinary warmth that had touched him on the way to church. It was not just the product of his mother's kind words and her hug, he decided. The feeling came from somewhere deeper. He remembered that he felt it under Caesar's hoofs when something had urged him to let go of the reins that were dragging him toward victory or death. His mother hadn't used the words, but her promise to be proud of her sons no matter what they accomplished was another way of saying, "You can let go of what's crushing you. Failure won't kill you, nor will it destroy my love."

Nicholas's face flushed again as the possibility of unqualified love began to embrace his mind. "She's willing to be proud of a loser," thought Nicholas, and as the concept continued to expand, he straightened himself in the pew and for the first time that morning paid attention to the order of worship.

While his thoughts turned inward, Nicholas had missed the entirety of Mr. Turnbull's sermon, and he had failed to notice the offering plate as it passed in front of his face from the usher to Philip to his mother and back. Now, he realized, the Communion prayer absorbed the rest of the congregation as the minister read on.

"And though we are unworthy, through our manifold sins, to offer unto thee any sacrifice; yet we beseech thee to accept this our bounden duty and service; not weighing our merits, but pardoning our offenses, through Jesus Christ our Lord."

"Not weighing our merits." Nicholas had grown up with the Book of Common Prayer, and he was familiar with its stately language. Many times at worship some previously unnoticed liturgical phrase had captured his wondering thoughts and focused his imagination, and on such mornings, those unexplainably memorable words were what he took home from church.

"Not weighing our merits." Nicholas had heard the phrase hundreds of times, but now the seeds so patiently sewn began to sprout. The minister's voice faded as Nicholas' own memory took up the theme.

"The quality of mercy is not strained. It droppeth as the gentle rain from heaven upon the place beneath." The recitation from Shakespeare momentarily thrust itself into the tumbling vortex of impressions in Nicholas's mind, only to be eclipsed by the image of his mother's face and the sound of her voice.

"Wherever you go and whatever you do, I am proud of you."

"Winners and losers." The voice of January Wilson, his black philosopher friend, captured his consciousness, and Nicholas closed his eyes as all the images began to merge into a single overwhelming thought.

"Let go! Let go! Lose! And win!" came the whispered invitation.

Nicholas felt himself somewhere immeasurably high, surrounded by a vast emptiness. He leaned forward and felt his cheeks burn with welcome warmth. As he began to let go, he heard a familiar voice.

"Wake up," whispered Philip. "It's time for Communion!"

Nicholas stumbled his way through the rest of the service, returning to his pew to fan himself vigorously with a wood-handled funeral home advertisement. After church, he ignored the roadside baseball game that Philip and the other shouting, shoving boys had hurried to organize, and while Sophie Bower visited with her neighbors, he stood alone under a magnolia tree. Nicholas wanted to cry. He believed something important had almost happened to him that morning, but he wasn't sure if he had missed an opportunity or dodged a disaster.

"Does your leg still hurt?" Sally Hemphill's voice brought Nicholas back to the churchyard. "You should be in the game. I've seen you pitch," smiled Sally. Nicholas pushed the hair from his face and stared absently at the other boys.

"Not much," he shrugged. "I just didn't feel like playing."

"Are you coming to the picnic at the river today?" asked the girl.

Nicholas knew about the church-sponsored event that marked the end of school and celebrated the progress of the cotton crop. Rogation Sunday, Mr. Turnbull called it, ever ready to explain the venerable tradition to his Baptist and Methodist friends. The whole community gathered near a wide bend on the Santee River, with tents providing shade and shelter from afternoon showers, and tables spread with the best edible offerings from farms across the county. Just downstream from the white citizens' picnic, the Negroes from the surrounding farms enjoyed their own celebration of summer with music and an unforgettable meal.

And on most years, the citizens of Riverton observed Rogation Sunday with a horserace. Everyone knew it wasn't a serious contest, like the historic Winter Race. There was no tradition behind it and no real accolades to be awarded to the winner, but the Summer Race, as it had come to be called, usually made room for younger, less experienced riders to join the bearded elders of the town in a wild gallop around the picnic ground.

"Are you coming, then?" repeated the girl.

"Maybe," said Nicholas, fumbling to find and open his pocketknife.

Sally Hemphill watched in silence as the boy concentrated on cleaning his fingernails. Finally she said, "Well, I'm coming. Maybe I'll see you there."

# CHAPTER FIVE

SUMMER TRAVELERS ON THE WAGON ROAD from Riverton to the Santee River at Blackford's Picnic Ground sweltered through sun-crushed cotton fields before descending gratefully into the cool shadows of the cypress swamp. The Bower family joined the afternoon migration of local citizens on their way to the Rogation Sunday picnic, with Nicholas and Philip spurring their horses ahead to catch up with friends and Captain Bower driving his surrey through boggy puddles at a pace which left Mrs. Bower's picnic dress splattered with mud. The captain had made no pronouncement to his sons about the Summer Race, leaving them to understand that their participation was optional.

"He doesn't care about this one," said Philip. "It's for children and old men and everybody uses saddles."

Nicholas had felt an enormous sense of relief when he realized that this outing would be about fun and not about family honor, and as he guided Caesar over the wooden bridge to the Picnic Ground, he enjoyed a rare sensation of peace. He heard singing at the south end of the forty-acre field and realized that the black residents of Riverton had already begun their celebration. As he dismounted and hitched Caesar near his father's surrey, Nicholas saw January Wilson arrive with his mother and his sisters. The boys exchanged a wave, and Nicholas walked casually across the unmarked boundary between the races to speak to his friend.

"You falling off today?" asked January, teasing Nicholas with his smile.

"Haven't decided if I'm racing or not," said Nicholas, realizing that he actually hadn't settled the thing in his own mind. Nicholas thought again how easily January's missing horse could win any local race if a black boy were allowed to compete. "You heard anything about Freedom?"

"Nothing. I'm afraid he's gone."

"Nothing from Sheriff Harvey?" asked Nicholas, receiving in response January's incredulous look.

"Anyway," said the black boy, "what did your mother bring for your picnic?"

"Same as always," said Nicholas, already eager for the contents of his mother's basket. "Fried Chicken, rice and gravy, some kind of pie. It'll be great! What about your mother?"

"Same as yours" laughed January, "but by the time she'll let me eat it, I won't care what it is!" His brown eyes brightened. "Remember this from 'Taming of the Shrew?' 'I prithee go and get me some repast; I care not if it be wholesome food.'"

"You are amazing," exclaimed Nicholas. "How do you do it?"

The boys' conversation ended when Mr. Turnbull mounted the steps of the planked platform that served as a bandstand and called the Picnic Grounds to order.

"Before we have the Summer Race and enjoy our picnics," announced the minister, "Miss Agnes Abernathy, our devoted School Mistress, has asked to present some awards. Miss Abernathy!"

Most of the white picnickers applauded, while some who didn't think much of the teacher, and all of the blacks, reserved their responses.

"My friends," said Miss Abernathy, "now that the spring term is over at Riverton School, I want to commend several of our students for outstanding academic achievement over the past school year. In the lower school, Ellen McFadden had highest honors and William Richardson had second best in all subjects, and I'm happy to present them with their certificates."

The crowd applauded politely as the honorees came forward to receive their awards.

Nicholas whispered to January, "That's the shortest speech she's ever given. I'm hungry."

"Now," continued the teacher, "for the first time I can remember, we have a tie for highest honors in the upper school. Will Conner Mayfield and Nicholas Bower please come forward?"

Nicholas cursed under his breath. He hated to be in front of people, and he particularly loathed the idea of standing next to Conner Mayfield.

"Go on, genius!" teased January, poking Nicholas in the back. Nicholas hung his head and shuffled toward the teacher, ignoring the applause of the crowd.

"Where is Mr. Mayfield?" asked Miss Abernathy, lifting her head to survey the expectant assembly. After a brief pause when Conner Mayfield failed to appear, the teacher proceeded with her announcement. "Mr. Mayfield, who has not joined us today, and Mr. Bower have earned exactly the same final grades on their year-end reports. Mr. Bower is highest in literature and Latin, while Mr. Mayfield scored best in mathematics and science. I'm sure you will want to congratulate both of these young men as I present them with their certificates of highest honor! Nicholas Alexander Bower and, in absentia, Connor …"

Suddenly, from the edge of the crowd, a boy's voice shouted, "There he is! There's Conner!"

The startled Miss Abernathy paused and looked up from the second certificate as every head in the assembly turned to where the boy was pointing. A few of the picnickers who had begun to acknowledge the winners now clapped harder while most quickly stopped their applause. Conner Mayfield rode slowly from the swamp road and onto the picnic ground seated on a tall, chestnut colored stallion.

"He's got Freedom!" shouted someone in the Negro gathering, and Nicholas felt his heart skip a beat when he realized it was true. Conner reined in the big horse at the edge of the crowd and casually slid to the ground. Those in the assembly who knew about the missing horse quickly whispered their surprise to the few who hadn't heard, and silence fell over the picnic field.

"When's the race?" said Conner, coldly meeting the stares of his neighbors.

Suddenly, a dark figure pushed through the silent circle around Conner Mayfield.

"Conner, you have my horse!" said January Wilson.

The blond boy's face shaped a long sarcastic smile as he stroked the stallion's neck.

"I have my horse," said Conner Mayfield, "and I can prove it."

"Hold on, hold on there!" ordered Sheriff Harvey, shouldering his way through the crowd. "Let's have no trouble here!"

The white community crowded around the combatants, while on the Negro side of the picnic ground, the mood had already become volatile, as black men muttered their disapproval and black women whispered their prayers.

"Conner," said Sheriff Harvey, "Where did you get that horse?"

"Bought him," said the blond boy. "Bought him from Isaiah Adams. I have his paper right here!"

Nicholas saw January's face fall in disbelief. He looked toward the Negro assembly where January's sisters were already weeping and hugging their mother. Conner pulled a folded paper from his shirt pocket and handed it to the sheriff, who studied it for a moment and then announced to the people of Riverton,

"His paper's good. It's a bill of sale with Conner's full name and Isaiah's mark on it and it's witnessed by the magistrate in Manchester."

Turning to January Wilson, Sheriff Harvey spoke softly and said, "Young man, I'm afraid Conner's bought this horse fair and square."

"But it wasn't Isaiah's horse! It was mine! The people my mother worked for in Pennsylvania, they gave him to me. Isaiah can't sell him! He's mine!"

"Boy," said the sheriff, his voice resuming a tone of authority, "You're living in South Carolina now, in Isaiah's house. Living there and feeding Isaiah's hay to this horse means the horse belongs to him. You're not of age to have title to this horse, no matter who gave him to you." Sheriff Harvey turned away while January stood stunned in front of the crowd and Conner Mayfield grinned in triumph.

"No, wait!" said January. "I'm as old as Conner! Why can't I …?" Before he could make his case, two black men squeezed between the white spectators and, while January shouted and struggled to go back, they forcefully led the weeping boy back to the Negro gathering and to his mother.

As the encounter ended and people in the crowd began to whisper their opinions, Nicholas walked directly to stand at arm's length from Conner Mayfield.

"You didn't buy that horse from Isaiah."

"Hell yes I did! Isaiah's been doing some gambling over in Manchester, and he's been asking all over town to borrow money to pay his debt. I found him and said I wouldn't lend him a nickel, but I'd buy this horse for the right price."

"How much did you give for Freedom?" said Nicholas, barely able to speak.

Conner laughed out loud. "Nobody would believe it, but it's right here on the bill of sale. Isaiah was drunk, and he sold this horse to me for five dollars!"

Nicholas felt his face flush with anger. He lunged forward and felt Philip's restraining grip on his arm.

"Let me go!" he yelled at his brother, struggling to break free.

"Come on, if you like," taunted Conner. "I'm ready!" The blond boy began to unbutton his shirt. "Oh yeah! There was one other thing I paid Isaiah for the horse. He wanted five dollars and my cowboy boots!"

"That's enough, both of you!" commanded Sheriff Harvey, stepping quickly to stand between Nicholas and Conner. "There'll be no trouble here. We already have the nigras stirred up, and the reverend's ready to start the race. You boys are both gonna act like gentlemen!"

Conner spat at the ground by the sheriff's feet, and Nicholas thrust himself forward against his brother's restraining grip.

"Stand aside!" roared Maximilian Bower, shoving spectators out of his way as he pushed in from the edge of the crowd. Ignoring the angry boys, Captain Bower planted himself in front of the sheriff and leaned into his face, his long beard brushing the badge on the lawman's coat.

"Let them settle it now," said Nicholas' father, grabbing the collar of his son's shirt and shoving him toward the Mayfield boy. "Let them settle it like men! Don't coddle my son!"

"Whatever they have to settle, they can do it in the race," said Sheriff Harvey. "If they can both ride fair."

"My boy will, I promise you that," said Captain Bower, turning to glare at Nicholas..

"So, my mind is made up about the race," thought Nicholas, struggling to hide his frustration and contain his rage. Conner Mayfield saw the exchange between the father and son and taunted Nicholas with a sarcastic smile.

"It's already settled," said Conner as he sauntered toward where Freedom stood waiting. "Just let me get my horse!"

The crowd at the center of the picnic grounds quickly scattered as people found shady spots along the edge of the racecourse and the riders moved toward the horses tethered near the bandstand. Captain Bower limped angrily toward his surrey, with Nicholas and Philip scurrying to keep up with him.

"You'll ride Caesar," ordered the captain. His eyes burned briefly toward Nicholas. "Maybe with a saddle you can stay on this time!"

Nicholas stopped and looked at his mother. Sophie Bower blessed her son with a nod that said, "Do your best," and a smile that said, "I love you."

Turning from his parents, Nicholas felt neither rage toward his father nor gratitude toward his mother. A chilly resignation settled over him as he walked slowly toward his horse.

"I'll ride," he told himself," but I don't care." He heard someone running behind him.

"Wait," called Philip as Nicholas climbed aboard the tall horse "Well, now we know!"

"Know what?"

"The cowboy boots! That explains the tracks we saw. Isaiah had Conner's boots on and nobody paid attention when he slipped in and took the horse."

"It doesn't matter," shrugged Nicholas. "Conner's got the horse and nobody's going to do anything about it."

"So beat him today! Wipe that grin off his ugly face!"

"Fat chance! You think any horse here can outrun Freedom?"

Nicholas gestured toward the restless assembly of unlikely animals and even more improbable riders taking positions by the Band Stand. There were horses trained for pulling heavy wagons and mules that spent their lives in front of plows and ponies accustomed to children on their backs. One ancient, sway backed mare carried old man Huckabee, the eighty-year-old proprietor of the general store. The Singleton sisters, ten-year-old twins dressed in identical frocks, sat together giggling on their father's Morgan horse. Billy Battle was there with his cantankerous goat. Conner Mayfield sat smugly on Freedom.

Nicholas reined Caesar toward the opposite end of the starting line and waited indifferently for the race to begin. He remembered the intensity he'd felt at the Winter Race. Then he had a chance to win. This time, even without falling off, he'd certainly lose again.

Nicholas kicked Caesar half-heartedly at the starting gun and loped along with the other riders toward the first corner of the race grounds. When Conner Mayfield and Freedom rounded the turn they were already well ahead of the next horses. The cheers of the crowd were subdued when the thoroughbred easily extended his lead beyond the halfway point, and as the blond boy in the saddle drove the chestnut stallion across the finish line, only a few supporters offered their cheers. Nicholas and Caesar finished third, right after Daisy Thigpen, a girl in his class. Philip, riding the church horse, took eighth place.

As he watched his sons' defeat, Captain Maximilian Bower swore aloud and sat down heavily on the seat of his surrey. He pushed away his wife's restraining hand, climbed awkwardly to the ground, and stalked toward his sons.

Philip saw him coming and said, "Well, Father, if we'd raced from here to St. Matthias, the church horse and I would have won easily!" The captain closed on them, scowling in disgust. Nicholas sat in silence, waiting for the explosion.

"Get down!" ordered Maximilian Bower. The boys slid from their saddles and stood gazing at the ground. "Tie your horses to the surrey." His voice was trembling with rage. "You will walk home and you will start now!"

"But Father," protested Philip, "It's seventeen miles to our house! And we haven't had lunch!"

"I don't care if it's seventy miles. You've disgraced me again, and you deserve no lunch. When I get home, I expect to see you both cleaning the stalls." Nicholas felt his face redden. Suddenly, he stumbled back as the impact of his father's hand stung his cheek.

"You! Look at me when I'm talking to you! You are a constant embarrassment! Now, go home!"

Nicholas stood up straight, his right hand forming a fist, and, for a blazing moment, he felt his fear begin to melt away. Then the moment passed, the impossible thing retreated, and he wheeled abruptly, tugging Caesar toward the surrey.

"They'll probably pass us on their way home," whispered Philip, pulling the church horse. "By then, maybe Father will have cooled down. I'm sure Mother will tell him to pick us up." Both boys scanned the crowd for their mother, finally recognizing her blue picnic dress among a group of women. Sophie Bower had heard her husband's hard words to their sons, as had many of her friends, and she was busy making excuses for the captain's behavior.

"He can't stand for the boys to lose any kind of competition," Sophie explained. "But he has a big heart, and he loves them." She looked away and saw her sons tying their horses to the surrey.

"Excuse me," Sophie said to the ladies of Riverton, as she hurried to the boys. "I am so sorry about the race. And I think it's disgraceful what that Mayfield boy did to January. He might have won the race, but he has lost favor with a lot of people in this community."

"As if he cared," said Nicholas.

"Son," said Sophie Bower, "honorable behavior is always rewarded and deceit is always punished. Don't let the success of evil men tempt you to give up. Always do your best!" She smiled at Nicholas and Philip. "You don't have to prove yourselves to me. You are the finest young men I know, and you make me proud just by being mine."

"We better go," said Philip. "Father's coming!"

Nichols and Philip submitted to their mother's hug and trudged away toward the road to Riverton. "I sure could use some fried chicken about now," said Philip as they crossed the bridge into the cypress swamp. "It's gonna be a long walk home."

Nicholas said nothing, his mind still replaying his mother's words. "You make me proud," she'd said. He felt his eyes begin to shine with tears. The confrontation with his father had filled him with bitter feelings and then left him numb. His mother had once more touched that place in his heart that was vulnerable to the slightest act of kindness.

Philip was offering his opinion about Sheriff Harvey's judgment on the ownership of Freedom, and Nicholas was pretending to listen when they heard footsteps and a voice behind them. "Do slow down! This basket is heavier than it looks!"

The boys turned in surprise and saw Sally Hemphill hurrying up the swamp road bending sideways with a large picnic basket in her hands. Nicholas quickly wiped his cheeks to remove any trace of tears. Philip just grinned.

"I heard what your father said," gasped Sally, trying to catch her breath, "and after you left, I asked your mother if she might give me just a taste of her picnic."

"You are an angel!" said Philip.

"Well," Sally continued, "your mother looked all around, and then handed me this basket and winked at me and said, 'I'm sure you won't be able to eat all of this by yourself.' You have a wonderful mother!"

"Yes, we do," agreed Nicholas, lifting the heavy basket.

"Here's a place," called Philip, pointing to a shady clearing just off the swamp road. Sally watched as the boys sat down and eagerly unpacked the picnic treats and began to help themselves.

"Yes, I would," she said, gathering her skirt to sit down by them and choose a piece of chicken for herself.

"Oh, sorry," said Philip. "We are so rude!"

"We're just hungry," said Nicholas, taking another bite of chicken and avoiding Sally's eyes.

"I'm sorry about the race," said Sally as they finished their meal. "Conner is a horrible boy!"

"I heard all the girls are in love with him," said Philip.

"Certainly not all of them," frowned Sally. Then she turned and, with a napkin, wiped a trace of chicken from Nicholas's blushing face.

After eating, they walked the two-rut road toward Riverton until evening came and Sally's parents collected her in the family wagon.

"Thanks for saving us," said Philip. "You were an angel from heaven!"

"Yeah, thanks," repeated Nicholas, blushing over his unoriginal words and silently cursing his stupidity.

Before long, Captain and Mrs. Bower overtook the boys on their long walk. As the surrey rattled past, their father said nothing, and Sophie Bower smiled helplessly at her sons. When darkness began to settle over the cotton fields, the boys heard a single horse rapidly approaching them from behind. Conner Mayfield galloped between them in a shower of sand, deliberately forcing them off the road and into the cotton bushes. Both the Bower boys yelled curses, and Nicholas found a cotton boll to hurl in Conner's direction. The tall, blond boy slowed the stallion to a walk and settled into a pace that kept him just beyond throwing distance. Just before the last light faded, Nicholas and Philip saw the chestnut stallion lift its tail and scatter its refuse in the darkened roadway. Conner Mayfield turned and smiled at them, and having waited for his horse to cooperate, now spurred him to a gallop and left the Bower boys stepping carefully toward home.

+ + +

As June sweltered into July and July steamed into August, nobody in the Bower household brought up the embarrassment of the Summer Race. Six days a week, Captain Bower's sons hoed side by side with the hired hands, adding their own sweat to the afternoon thundershowers that watered the cotton bushes. Nicholas looked forward to the rare moments when he and January could work together. Their conversations made the backbreaking work almost a pleasure.

The other bright spots in Nicholas' life were his brief Sunday morning encounters with Sally Hemphill. He loved the serious look on her face when she listened to Mr. Turnbull's sermon, and it thrilled him to hear her sing. In the churchyard after services, everything she said fascinated him. But each time, Nicholas went away furious with himself, cursing the mental paralysis and verbal stumbling that overcame him whenever they were together. From time to time, Nicholas would offer Sally one of his memorized Latin quotations, but she always seemed unimpressed with his grasp of the ancient language.

"At least I'm trying," he thought, and he said quietly, "Sedit qui timuit ne non succederet." "He who feared he would not succeed stood still."

"What did you say?" asked Sally.

"Nothing," said Nicholas. He was glad when Philip was there to tell a funny story to make Sally laugh.

+ + +

Like the children of farmers all over the county, Nicholas also looked forward to the beginning of the fall term at school. Fall classes at Riverton School never started until after the first picking of the cotton, but the resumption of the children's daily lessons sometimes saved them from having to work into September and October. When the first day of school finally arrived, Nicholas and Philip happily laced up their stiff new shoes and rode to school to greet their friends.

That evening at supper Philip reported that Miss Abernathy was as boring as ever and that Conner Mayfield was absent.

"Conner's dropping out of school," announced Nicholas, with obvious satisfaction. "He told some of the boys a few days ago that he had better things to do."

"Well, I'm sad for him," said Sophie Bower. "Agnes says he's extremely smart and could have a great future."

"He'll be damned lucky to live another year," said Captain Bower. "That boy's got people after his hide all over the county."

"He told the boys he didn't need school because he already had a fine horse and a great job," said Nicholas.

"What job?" said the captain.

"He didn't say, but from what the boys told me, Conner's been spending money like a drunken Irishman."

"I hope you boys don't entertain any thought about dropping out of school," said Sophie. "You are both going to college, even if I have to take in sewing to pay your expenses."

"My wife will not stoop to menial work for any reason!" said Captain Bower. "This farm could provide all we need if I could get a decent day's work out of the lazy slackers who work for me – including my sons!"

Nicholas knew better than to respond to his father's insult, and Philip dared only give his brother a secret smile.

"You don't understand about competition," said the Captain. "I heard today that Hiram Richardson has got himself a steam powered tractor. The damn thing will out pull a dozen mule teams. Who do you think will be first at the gin next summer?"

"And do you know who will graduate first in his class from Riverton School in a few years? Your son, Nicholas!" said Sophie Bower. Nicholas rolled his eyes. He didn't need more pressure, especially from his most reliable source of grace.

"Mother! Please don't make promises that I have to keep!"

# CHAPTER SIX

## Spring 1903

"THIS IS SPECIAL FOR YOU, CLAUS," whispered Ruby as she carried a white frosted cake from the kitchen to the dining room sideboard. Standing behind his chair at the long mahogany table, Nicholas nodded in appreciation as he waited for his graduation party to begin. The too-short sleeves on the black frock coat he had worn to the ceremony made him seem younger than his eighteen years, but his six-foot frame and the high, stiff collar of his shirt and the brand new valedictory watch ticking in his vest pocket clearly identified him as an adult.

"Father promised to be here on time," fussed Sophie Bower, hurrying again to the front door to look for her missing husband.

"I say, 'Let's eat!'" said Philip, snatching up his folded napkin and waving it dramatically before tucking it into his collar.

"Now, Sophie, do be patient with Maximilian," said Asa Turnbull. "After the ceremony, he seemed to be in deep discussion with several of his neighbors. He'll be along soon."

"That roast certainly smells delicious," said Agnes Abernathy, discreetly changing the subject. "And look at that beautiful cake!"

The minister and the schoolmistress were often guests at the Bower family's table, and both had accepted the invitation to dinner in honor of Nicholas's graduation.

"Nicholas," said Miss Abernathy, "may I say again how proud I am of you for graduating first in Riverton's class of 1903?"

"There were only two others, but thank you."

"Do favor us with that quotation from your valedictory address," said the schoolmistress.

Blushing, Nicholas stared out the window and recited, "Non est ad astra mollis e teris via."

"There is no easy way from the earth to the stars," translated Miss Abernathy. "What a noble thought! Was it Horace?"

"Seneca," said Nicholas.

"Well done!" beamed Mr. Turnbull. "May I also congratulate you on your church attendance? I can't remember when you've missed a Sunday!"

"Thank my mother. She got me there."

"Hey, give a little credit to the church horse!" said Philip.

"Oh, thank the Lord! Here's Father coming!" Sophie gathered her skirt to hurry in from the porch. "Ruby! The captain's home! You can serve now!"

Climbing awkwardly from the surrey and limping up the front steps, Captain Bower hurried across the front hall and loudly greeted his family and guests.

"Well, you waited for me! Not a word, Mother! There are things happening in our community that I need to know about."

"What's going on, Father?" said Philip. "Is it about the night raids?"

"Never mind about that," said Sophie. "Here's Ruby with our dinner, and we need to give thanks. Mr. Turnbull, will you?"

"Indeed I will!" said the minister. "Most Gracious Heavenly Father, we, thy humble servants, do give thee thanks for this faithful family and this food, and especially today, do we thank thee for the grace thou hast given to Nicholas to excel in his school work. Bless him, gracious God, and bless us all as we serve thee through Jesus

Christ our Lord."

"Amen" came from around the table, and the graduation dinner began.

While Ruby served, the Bower family and their guests kept up a busy chatter of conversation.

"Nicholas, have you heard from the university?" said Miss Abernathy. "I know you must be on pins and needles to hear if you've been accepted!" Nicholas swallowed hard and cleared his throat.

"Oh, Agnes! I'm sure you would have heard his shouts all the way to town if he'd been accepted," said Sophie. "You haven't heard, have you, Son?"

Nicholas coughed into his napkin. "Yes, Ma'm," he replied, staring at his plate. "I've heard. My acceptance letter came three weeks ago."

"Claus! Son! Why in the world didn't you tell us?"

"Hey, good work, Big Brother!" said Philip reaching across the table to punch Nicholas' arm.

"Your mother's right," said Captain Bower, "You should have told us. Damned inconsiderate!"

"Well," said Nicholas. "Oh, never mind."

"What do you mean, Son?" said Sophie. "You haven't considered turning down the acceptance, have you?"

Nicholas sighed and stared at the ceiling while all eyes around the table studied his face. He hadn't planned to mention his reservations, but now he decided to go ahead.

"Mother, I'm not sure I want to go to college. I've thought about joining the army."

"Oh, dear!" gasped Miss Abernathy. "My best student! I don't know what to say!"

"Well, I do," said Captain Bower. "He is going to the university! He's all caught up in that old drivel about Roosevelt and the Rough Riders. I've seen the adventure stories you read. It's all nonsense! You think you're grown up, but you've got no idea what war is really like."

"But you went to war, Father! You were in the army and then went to college." Nicholas looked down at his clenched hands as he spoke.

"I didn't have a choice. Listen to this. You sit right there!" roared Maximilian Bower as he stood up abruptly, shoved back his chair, and hurried into the parlor. He returned with a folded newspaper. "You think so much of Roosevelt? Listen to what he says, 'The best boys I know, the best men I know, are good at their studies or their business, fearless and stalwart, hated and feared by all that is wicked and depraved, incapable of submitting to wrongdoing, and equally incapable of being aught but tender to the weak and helpless.'" He shook the newspaper in Nicholas's face. "Good at their studies!" he shouted.

Everyone at the table sat in stunned silence. Mr. Turnbull cleared his throat and said, "Well, Captain, I expect Claus just needs to think about college a little more. He is one of the best boys I know, and I'm sure he'll do the right thing, the godly thing."

The minister's efforts to restore order succeeded, and the damaged conversation limped back to a genial pace. Miss Abernathy contributed several additional quotations from President Roosevelt, and Mr. Turnbull cited the Book of Proverbs about the value of wisdom.

Philip waited for a break in the conversation and then announced, "Well, this is Claus's day, and I have a gift to give him!" He hurried from his place, leaping the stairs to his bedroom and thundering back down to stand grinning before the table.

"Ta da!" trumpeted Philip, bringing from behind his back a shiny ukulele. "This is my public debut! I've been practicing for months with a sock in my uke so nobody could hear. But I took the sock out, and here's a song we'll be singing when old Claus has gone either to college or the army."

The tune everybody recognized as "Bill Bailey," but Philip sang, "Won't cha come home, Claus Bower, won't cha come home. We moan the whole day long! We'll do the cooking, brother! We'll pay the rent! We know we done you wrong!"

Philip's musical offering brought applause from everyone at the table except Captain Bower. Nicholas restored the party's festive spirit by reciting a Latin quotation and playfully inviting the others to guess the translation. "Non omnes qui habent citharam sunt citharoedi."

"We give up! What does it mean?" said Philip.

"Not all those who own a musical instrument are musicians," said Nicholas as the rest of the family joined in laughter. Everyone cheered when Ruby began to serve the special graduation cake.

"The first piece is for Claus," announced Ruby, slicing the cake carefully and placing a large helping before the graduate. As all enjoyed their dessert, Nicholas felt something metallic and unyielding in his second bite. Carefully removing the object from his mouth, he discovered, to his amazement, that Ruby had baked a one dollar gold coin into the celebration cake and deliberately served it to him. He knew the money represented a week's wages for the family's servant. Ruby grinned with delight as she watched him quietly pocket the gift.

Leaning close to Nicholas as she cleared the table, Ruby whispered, "That's for the train when you ready to come home! And listen! January needs to see you after this."

+ + +

At the conclusion of the celebration dinner, the Bower family and their guests retired to the parlor and gave gifts to Nicholas. Miss Abernathy presented him with an elegant, leather bound volume containing selected works of Shakespeare.

"I've been so pleased with this young man's interest in the Bard," said the schoolmistress. "As Seneca said, 'Otium sine litteris mors est et hominis vivi sepultra.' Leisure without literature is death, or rather the burial of a living man."

Mr. Turnbull's gift was the Holy Bible. "The words of Jesus are printed in red," he said, displaying for all to see a page from the New Testament. Not to be outdone in the offering of quotations he added, "'Seek ye first the Kingdom of God and his righteousness, and all these things shall be added unto you.' Matthew six thirty-three."

Philip pretended not to have a gift for his brother to unwrap, joking that everyone had missed the significance of his musical offering, but in the end, he handed Nicholas a box containing a straw boater hat with a black band. "This is for after you've had your turn with the freshman beanie!" teased Philip.

Captain and Mrs. Bower presented their son with a new three-piece suit. "You needed this today," said his mother as she tugged at the sleeves of his out-grown frock coat. While Nicholas was trying on the new suit coat, Captain Bower stepped across the hall to his bedroom and came back with a final gift for his son.

"You'll be needing this come Thanksgiving," said the captain as he handed Nicholas a double-barreled shotgun. "It's a Parker," said the big man. "Hammerless. Twelve gauge." He could barely conceal the excitement in his voice.

Nicholas was speechless as he examined the gun. "Father, isn't this your new gun? The one you used last year?"

"Was my gun. Now it's yours," said Captain Bower, his smile hidden in his beard. "I tried it, but I'd still rather use my father's old fowling piece. This modern one suits you better than me."

When the Bowers's dinner guests had departed, Nicholas retreated to his room with his graduation gifts. The books he placed on his desk. He placed the boater and hung the new suit in the wardrobe. But he displayed his father's amazing gift on his bed, gazing at it for long moments and then shouldering it to swing on imaginary targets all around his bedroom. He couldn't believe what his father had done. Nicholas had been hunting with his father and his father's friends since he was eight and he had become skilled with several borrowed firearms. But to have his own gun, and a treasured Parker at that, was beyond anything he had imagined. Nicholas began to remember that he had enjoyed other good times with his usually domineering father. When Nicholas had won the 1903 Winter Race, the last one in which he would be eligible to compete, Captain Bower had praised him effusively. When Nicholas reported that he would be the first honor graduate, the captain had bragged about his son all over town.

Stretching out on his bed, Nicholas allowed the pleasant feeling to embrace the other people in his life. His mother could always be relied on to encourage him when he was down and praise him when he had failed. If she fussed over him too much at times, he didn't really care. Philip was a great brother and a good friend, when he wasn't being a clown. Miss Abernathy couldn't help her annoying voice, but Nicholas knew she really did think well of him. Even Mr. Turnbull, who'd put the congregation to sleep on so many Sunday mornings, revealed a consistent good will toward his flock and especially to Nicholas. And Sally Hemphill. Nicholas felt his heart skip as the afternoon's comfortable feelings suddenly yielded to a surge of anxiety.

Something strange was going on with Sally Hemphill. He'd felt it now and then over the past months, but that day at graduation she had seemed oddly distant. Nicholas had noticed a few years before when Sally, the pigtailed friend he talked to after church, the gingham-clad angel who'd delivered his mother's picnic basket after the Summer Race disaster, had stopped wearing her hair in braids. At the school ceremony, Sally had appeared with her hair pinned high, wearing a stylish hat adorned with feathery plumes, and a dress that was designed for her maturing figure. But most disturbing of all was her coolness toward him. Sally had greeted him politely after the ceremony and wished him well at the university. The warmth Nicholas had always felt from her was gone. And gone with those thoughts was the glow of graduation.

As evening approached, Nicholas lay on his bed, his hand touching the cool steel and polished wood of the shotgun and his mind retracing again and again his recent times with Sally, examining his words and actions for any hint of offense. He was trying for the tenth time to release his anxieties and to reclaim the delights of the day when he heard something strike his bedroom window. A bird, he thought, or a tree branch. Then another, louder tap brought Nicholas to his feet and to the window. In the fading light, he could just make out the figure of January Wilson, his arm ready to throw another pebble. Nicholas remembered Ruby's whispered message at dinner, and he cursed his forgetfulness as he lifted the window sash.

"Where have you been?" came January's hushed voice. "I've been waiting for you all afternoon!"

"I'm sorry," said Nicholas, "I guess I was distracted by the guests, and …."

"Well, can you come down now?"

"Meet you at the barn in a minute." Nicholas turned abruptly to unbutton his dress shirt and change his clothes.

Tiptoeing down the stairs, Nicholas heard his mother talking with Ruby in the kitchen, and he knew they'd heard his steps.

"Going to the barn," he called out. "Back in a little while."

January was waiting for him by the horse stalls, and although the darkness of the barn hid his friend's face, the first words from the farm hand's mouth told Nicholas that there was trouble.

"I can't stay long," said January. "I have to get back to my family, but I wanted you to know what's going on."

"What?" asked Nicholas, already sharing his friend's anxiety.

"It's the Klan," said January. "They've been shooting into houses owned by Negroes. You haven't heard about it?"

"Well, a little. But I thought it was in the up state and not around here."

"It's right here! They did it to my mother's house last night."

"Is everybody all right? What do they want?"

"Not hurt, just scared! And I don't know! Maybe they want us to leave. Maybe they just want to scare us to quit planting our own crops and only work for white people."

"Does the sheriff know?"

"Of course he does! But he won't do anything about it. Nicholas, your father knows everybody around here. Will you talk to him?"

Nicholas was trying to decide how to respond when in the darkness, he heard January gasp, "Good Lord! I never considered! Could your father be in the Klan?"

Nicholas reacted before he thought. "No! That can't be! My father's a hard man sometimes, but he's not in the Klan! Anyway, there hasn't been any Klan around here since right after the war."

As the words escaped his lips Nicholas realized that he wasn't as certain as he sounded. He remembered times when his father had come home late in the evening. Mr. Turnbull had reported Captain Bower meeting after the graduation ceremony with a group of men from the community.

"January," said Nicholas, "I don't know! I don't think he is, but I really can't say. I'll tell him about the raid on your house and ask him to talk with the men involved, if he knows them."

"Oh, you can be sure he knows them! At least one of them is a local boy."

"How do you know?"

"One of them was riding Freedom!"

"Conner!" said Nicholas. "That certainly fits!"

"I promise you," said January out of the darkness, "if he comes again, I'll fit him with a bullet in his head."

"January," said Nicholas, but his friend had already pushed open the barn door and was slipping into the shadows near the chicken coop. "Wait! Don't do anything until I talk to my father!"

"If they raid again, somebody's going to die!" And January Wilson disappeared into the summer night.

+ + +

Nicholas was moody and silent on the way to church the following morning. He hadn't slept well, his thoughts torn between Sally Hemphill's disturbing change and the frightening news from January Wilson. Over his objections, his mother had insisted that he wear his new suit, and as the surrey bounced toward Riverton, Nicholas twisted on the seat and scratched at the unfamiliar garment. He decided not to tell his mother about the raid on January's house, but he'd promised to talk with his father, and the prospect filled him with dread. Philip had his newly revealed ukulele, and while Nicholas drove the surrey and considered strategies for approaching his father, his extroverted brother and musical mother harmonized happily on popular tunes. "Glow, little glow worm" made him smile, but when Philip started on "Mighty Like a Rose," Nicholas found himself caught up for the hundredth time in the dilemma of Sally Hemphill.

He watched her as the church service began, noticing with gratitude that she still had the same joyful expression when she sang and the same serious face when she listened to Mr. Turnbull's sermon. Nicholas wondered if Sally ever experienced the kind of inner struggle that consumed so much of his own energy. She seemed so content with herself, just like Philip, like his mother. In fact, like almost everybody he knew. He tugged at the collar of his stiff new suit and wondered, "What's wrong with me? Why do I worry so much about everything? Why do I always take myself so seriously?" Nicholas was lost in his familiar mental whirlpool when Mr. Turnbull began to read from the First Letter of John.

"By this we know that we are of the truth, and reassure our hearts before him whenever our hearts condemn us, for God is greater than our hearts and he knows everything."

For an instant, Nicholas felt himself tumbling under horse's hoofs at the Winter Race, and the quiet voice he'd heard three years before invited him again, "Let go!"

The experience still preoccupied Nicholas as he spoke to the minister at the church door after worship.

"Well, congratulations again to our first honor graduate!" said Mr. Turnbull. Nicholas looked away as he shook the minister's hand.

"Thanks," he said. And then, leaning close to Mr. Turnbull's mutton-chopped face, he said, "May I come to see you?"

"Of course!" the clergyman whispered back. "My door is always open to you!"

In the churchyard, Nicholas agonized over his impulsiveness. He wondered what he hoped to accomplish. Now he was committed to arrange a meeting he had no real desire to undertake. Wandering lost in thought, he was surprised to find himself approaching Sally Hemphill, who stood framed under the silk circle of her parasol.

"I'm sure you're excited about the university," said Sally. "When does the fall semester start?"

Nicholas struggled to collect his thoughts. "In the fall," he stammered, "I mean in September. I'm not sure of the date."

"I suppose I should wish you well now," said Sally, "because I will be away for the rest of the summer." Nicholas felt as though he'd been punched in the stomach.

"You're going?" he said, "Where?"

"There's a school in Charleston that offers a summer course. If I complete it, Miss Abernathy tells me I might be able to enter the university for the second semester." Nicholas felt his heaviness suddenly yield to an indescribable feeling of hope.

"Maybe I'll see you there," he said. Instantly, he cursed his choice of words. Why hadn't he shown some excitement? How had he failed to congratulate her and wish her success for the summer course? "Maybe I'll see you there." If she came to the university, he would move heaven and earth to see her!

"Well, goodbye." said Sally, and Nicholas watched her walk quickly toward her family's carriage.

# CHAPTER SEVEN

## Summer 1903

AUGUST IN RIVERTON brought mornings of merciless humidity, scorching middays, and cooling afternoon showers. Nicholas worked in the cotton fields with Philip and his father's hired hands, hours of mindless hoe work that left him free to imagine himself into all sorts of exciting situations. For the length of one row, he would be an army officer leading a troop of cavalry to free Clarendon County from the scourge of the Ku Klux Klan. Hoeing back the other way, he would be in a college classroom, astonishing his professor with accurate answers and his own insightful questions.

Captain Bower's graduation day proclamation had overruled Nicholas' uncertainty about attending the University of South Carolina. While Nicholas struggled to digest his frustration, Sophie Bower repeatedly assured her son that he would eventually see his father's wisdom. Hardly a day went by without Sophie reminding Nicholas about some essential item of clothing or equipment that he would need as a college student. Sundays found him in church, although the experience now brought him more anxiety than comfort. He missed seeing Sally, and he dreaded speaking to Mr. Turnbull, who never failed to whisper a reminder about the appointment Nicholas had requested.

From time to time, January Wilson would bring a new report about a midnight raid in some part of the community, and Nicholas would promise again to talk to his father. The opportunity appeared when Captain Bower directed his sons to ride with him to the railroad station in Sumter to pick up a delivery. Nicholas knew that the long surrey ride would give him a rare, unhurried visit with his father, and he made up his mind to inquire about January's concern. As they drove away from the farm, he was glad to find Captain Bower in a rare good mood.

"Well, boys," said Maximilian Bower, whipping the surrey horse into a trot, "today our farm enters the twentieth century! I've bought a tractor! Gasoline engine! Twenty-six horse power! It's a Hart-Parr made out in Iowa,"

"Today?" shouted Philip, "We're picking it up today?"

"I've rented a freight wagon and six mules to haul it from the railroad yard,"

"Will it beat the steam machine on the Richardson place?" asked Nicholas.

"Ten times stronger! Big difference in the way we run our farm!"

Philip, who already had magazine photos of gasoline powered automobiles on his bedroom wall, asked one technical question after another, leaving Nicholas increasingly eager to change the subject.

Two hours into their journey, the Bowers passed Sheriff Harvey riding toward Riverton. The Sheriff exchanged pleasantries with Captain Bower, and when they continued toward Sumter, Nicholas said, "You know, Father, seeing the Sheriff reminds me. People are saying that the Klan has been raiding colored houses."

"The Klan?" said Captain Bower. "Who's been telling you such nonsense? There's been no Ku Klux Klan in South Carolina in twenty years!"

"Some of the boys at church have been talking about it. They say there's been some raids in Clarendon County."

"You can tell them they're crazy," replied his father. "I know about a gang of local troublemakers, just a few from what I've heard. Word is they've been frightening the niggers so they can buy their land cheap. But it's not the Klan. Don't listen to rumors!"

Nicholas remembered the fear on January's face. What his friend had seen was no rumor.

"I'm glad it's not the Klan," he said. "But can't the Sheriff do something about the raids?"

"He's only one man, but some of the other farmers and I are getting ready to help him."

"Is that what the meeting was about last week?" asked Philip.

"We're reorganizing the Clarendon Rifles," said the Captain. "Not really a militia, more like a local defense society. We did some good in the past, and it looks like we're needed again."

"And the Sheriff supports this?" said Nicholas.

"Because we support him! You might say we're his deputies."

"How does that work?" said Philip.

"You don't need to know, either of you, because you're not having any part of it!" Captain Bower fixed each of his sons with a look that said the discussion had ended.

+ + +

The arrival of the tractor at the Bower farm was the milestone event of the summer in Riverton and around the county. Farmers came every day to examine the machine, and when Captain Bower could be persuaded, to watch a demonstration of the powerful, steel-wheeled engine in action. Nicholas allowed the excitement to obscure the fact that his departure for the university was only days away. Sophie Bower had not forgotten, though, and the piles of essential college items in Nicholas' bedroom grew daily.

"You wouldn't believe all the clothes and books my mother expects me to take to Columbia," complained Nicholas one day when he and January worked together. "I don't know where Father found the money to pay for what this is gonna cost."

January smiled. "Captain Bower might sound like Vincentio in *The Taming of the Shrew*."

"I am undone! While I play the good husband at home, my son and my servant spend it all at the university."

"I swear, January! I don't know how you do it! Your brain is like a photographer's plate! Do you go home and read Shakespeare every night!"

"Well, not every night, but many nights."

"I wish I could remember Shakespeare that way!"

"And I wish I knew any Latin at all!" said January.

"Aliena nobis, nostra plus allis placent," said Nicholas. "Other people's things are more pleasing to us, and ours to other people."

"Have you ever thought about going to college yourself?" asked Nicholas.

"Tell me that's not the first time the idea crossed your mind!" said January.

"Of course not! You're the most educated person I know. I just didn't want to bring up something that might, well, upset you." January was silent.

Then he said, "Seems that Shakespeare could imagine servants at the university, even if they went to serve their master. Of course, he didn't live in South Carolina, and Vincentio's servant probably wasn't a black man."

"If you could go to college, where would you go?"

"A few years ago, I could have gone to Carolina, but they changed the law about that. There are good schools in other places for people like me. Mostly up north. Around here my best bet would probably be over in Orangeburg."

"The colored school?"

"Either Claflin, or the new one with the big, important name! It's called the Colored, Normal, Industrial, Agricultural, and Mechanical College of South Carolina. How about that?"

"You suppose they teach anything about Shakespeare?" said Nicholas shaking his head in dismay.

"Doesn't really matter. I can't afford it, and my family can't do without the money I make."

"Maybe I could talk to my father."

"Sure! You do that," said January, his voice heavy with sarcasm. "Like when you talk to him about the Klan raids."

"Listen! I did talk with him! I just haven't had a chance to tell you what he said."

"Is he going to do anything?"

"He swears it isn't the Klan. Says they've been gone a long time. But he did know about a gang of local bullies that have been shooting colored houses."

"And there's nothing he can do to help, right?"

"No! Listen! A bunch of men are going to help the sheriff keep order! The Clarendon Rifles."

"I won't hold my breath," said January Wilson.

+ + +

"Don't be ridiculous, Sophie!" thundered Maximilian Bower. "Why drive the mules two days to Columbia and two days back when we can just put the boy on the train in Sumter and get him to the university the same day?"

"Because he's our son, and I'm proud to ride with him to college!" said Sophie.

"You just want to go make up his bed! Let the boy grow up, woman!"

Nicholas overheard his parents repeat the argument several times in the days before his departure.

He said to Philip, "Bet a dollar I'm going by train!" And he won his bet. Sophie Bower abandoned her plan when she learned that the Garner's Ferry Road, with its fourteen bridges from Stateburg to Columbia, was currently impassible.

On the morning of his departure, Philip and January helped Nicholas load his suitcase on the farm wagon, along with several large woven oak hampers of coats and books.

"See if there's room for this," said January, slipping a leather-bound book into one of the hampers. "Shakespeare's sonnets. Read number 37. "Look, what is best, that best I wish in thee; This wish I have, then ten times happy me."

Captain Bower called to his son when the wagon was loaded and the team hitched in place. "Son," he said, looking down on Nicholas from the front porch of the family home, "I have only one thing to say to you. I expect you to do your best and to make me proud."

"And I expected that's exactly what you'd say to me," thought Nicholas, avoiding his father's eyes. "Yes, sir," he said.

"You have a distinguished family heritage," continued the Captain, and Nicholas pretended to listen while his father recited the familiar chronicle of notable Bower accomplishments.

"Here's some money to hire a porter to haul your things from the station to the university," said the bearded man. "I expect to see you at Thanksgiving."

"Thank you, sir," said Nicholas. As he watched his father climb into the surrey and rattle away toward the cotton fields, Nicholas remembered a maxim from Agnes Abernathy. "Vestros servate, meos mihi linquite mores," "You cling to your own ways and leave mine to me."

+ + +

The train trip from Sumter to Columbia gave Nicholas a few hours to reflect on events of the morning and on the dramatic change he was about to experience. His mother had wept and waved her handkerchief as the train pulled away from the station, while Nicholas tried to ignore the comments from porters who had teased him about his wagonload of luggage. Philip had given him a handshake, followed by a punch on the arm. As he watched the flat fields of the low country give away to the rolling hills of the midlands, his mood vacillated from stomach-knotting fear to heart-racing excitement. It was not his first train ride, nor his first trip to the state capitol, but this time he was on his own. Whenever the train stopped to take on passengers, Nicholas allowed himself to feel more confident, trying to appear as though he had made the journey hundreds of times. He wore his new suit because his mother had insisted on it, but the boater hat from Philip went into one of the clothes hampers as soon as the locomotive had cleared the station.

The train reached Columbia well after dark, and Nicholas felt his anxiety mount when he saw dozens of passengers spilling from the other cars and crowding toward the waiting line of porters and wagons for hire. It had not occurred to Nicholas that there would be other students traveling to Columbia that day. Looking around as he stepped onto the platform and struggled to collect his various bags and hampers, Nicholas had the impression that everybody else seemed to know each other, and that he was the only one wondering what to do.

"Excuse me," he said to a uniformed man who hurried by.

"Porters that way," gestured the man without slowing down. Nicholas looked despairingly at his load of luggage, realizing that he would never be able to haul it all to the porters' loading platform in time to secure a wagon.

"Look at the country boy," laughed a tall young man in a crisp white linen suit.

"Going to a funeral in that black get-up?" said another well-dressed student, and Nicholas noticed with chagrin that this one was wearing a boater hat exactly like the one he'd hidden away.

"Philip would know," he admitted, and he cursed himself for not trusting his brother.

"Can I give you a hand?" Nicholas looked behind him to see a man about his age standing just beyond his mountain of luggage.

"I'm just looking for a porter," said Nicholas, gazing again at the end of the platform.

"I think they only pick up down there," said the stranger. "Let me help you move your things." Nicholas frowned. He wanted to dismiss the boy's offer, and do it quickly. To his utter embarrassment, he felt himself close to crying.

"Name's Richard. Richard Baker. I'm from Walterboro."

Somehow, the discovery that his rescuer came from a town he'd visited allowed Nicholas to relax. Instead of tears, his face managed to produce a smile.

"Thanks, Richard. I'm Nicholas Bower, from Riverton."

"Two farm boys loose in the big city!" grinned Richard, gathering his own small suitcase under one arm and picking up two of Nicholas's extra bags. "What about these electric lights?" he exclaimed, glancing toward the stationhouse ceiling. "Many houses have them in Riverton?"

"Not mine," grunted Nicholas. Together, they managed to carry or drag Nicholas's belongings to the porters' loading dock, only to discover that there were no wagons left. "Now I've made us both late," swore Nicholas.

"I wouldn't worry about it," said Richard. "They keep the dormitories open late on the first day."

"Are you a returning student?" asked Nicholas, impressed with his new acquaintance's knowledge.

"No, first year. I'm guessing my way along like you."

"It's pretty obvious, isn't it? All my stupid luggage, my suit. I'm as green as they get!"

"Well, one thing's familiar to me, and that's my empty stomach," said Richard, looking around at the largely vacant railroad station. "I wonder where we can get something to eat while we wait for a wagon?"

Nicholas paused, and then said, "Look, I told my mother not to pack any food, but of course, she did it anyway. It's in one of these hampers. Hold on a minute!" He rummaged through the basket. " Biscuits! How about fried chicken?" The boys sat on one of the empty freight wagons watching bugs circle the incandescent bulbs overhead and eagerly consuming everything Sophie Bower had insisted on packing.

"My mother thinks I'm still a kid," said Nicholas wiping his fingers on a napkin prudently provided with the fried chicken.

"You mean because she sent food?" laughed Richard. "Listen, friend, it's what mothers do. I ate what my mother packed for me an hour after the train left Walterboro."

By the time a porter's wagon arrived at the station, Nicholas and Richard had exchanged information about their families and both had confessed more than a little apprehension about the days that lay ahead.

As the wagon rattled toward the campus, Nicholas said "Amicus verus est rara avis."

"Is that Latin?"

"Yes. It means, 'A true friend is a rare bird.'"

Arriving late, Nicholas and Richard found themselves directed by an irritable dorm matron to a double room on the third floor of a house owned by the university.

"Looks like we're roommates," said Richard, sliding his suitcase into a corner.

"Fine with me," replied Nicholas. Both boys collapsed exhausted on their unmade beds, and woke only when the morning sun blazed through the un-curtained window.

Their first day on campus began with a futile search for breakfast, standing in line at the student refectory only to be turned away and sent to the registrar's office, and from there to the bursar's counter to pay their fees.

"Somebody said there are nearly five hundred students," said Richard as the boys wolfed down dry biscuits and gulped cold coffee.

Nicholas wanted to appear untroubled by the day's frustrations, but even while mumbling criticisms of the university bureaucracy to his new friend, he was very glad for Richard's presence. As freshmen, they discovered that their class schedule would be similar, with Nicholas taking advanced Latin and Richard registering for second year mathematics.

"I hope you're better at literature than I am," said Richard during a hurried visit to the bookstore. "They didn't teach me much about plays and poetry in Walterboro."

"I know a little Shakespeare," said Nicholas, "but I had a special tutor for that." He realized then how much he missed the familiar faces of Riverton School and his extracurricular lessons from January Wilson.

At the end of a hectic day, Nicholas and Richard shuffled into the university auditorium with other first-year students to hear an address by President Benjamin Sloan.

"Gentlemen," said the President, "and ladies," he continued, smiling at the handful of female students, "It is my pleasure to welcome you to the University of South Carolina. As you may know, this institution has a long history, just over one hundred years now, and although the events of recent years often put our future in jeopardy, I'm happy to say that there are better times ahead for this great school. With the election of Governor Heyward, we can look forward to a friendly voice in the halls of state government." Nicholas realized that he fallen asleep when he felt a sharp blow from Richard's elbow.

"Listen to this," whispered Richard, and Nicholas blinked and nodded as President Sloan said, "You will discover that more is expected of each of you than was required at your schools back home. There will be regular examinations and papers to prepare. You will have to work hard to balance study time with extracurricular activities and social life."

Nicholas remembered his father's final instructions issued not two days before. "Make me proud."

"I've heard this speech already," he confided to his friend.

When classes began the next morning, Nicholas could hardly believe that his life had changed so dramatically in three days. There was little time to think about his family and friends in Riverton. He tried to take his meals with Richard, often using those hurried visits for a few moments of mental escape from the demands of student life.

"Do you have a girl?" he asked Richard one evening at supper.

"No, can't say that I do. Anyway, I'm hoping to meet the kind of women that don't come from Walterboro! What about you?"

"There's this one girl from home. We were friends all the way through school, but she's acting like a stranger for some reason."

"You know that means she likes you!"

"That's an odd way to show it," said Nicholas. "Fallaces sunt rerum species."

"Which means …?"

"The appearances of things are deceptive." Anyway, maybe you will meet her. She hopes to come here for school after Christmas."

"Well, by that time, she'll be the girlfriend of a genuine football hero!" said Richard. "When's your first game?"

Nicholas had surprised himself by signing up to play football with the university team. There had been no organized football in Riverton, and Nicholas confessed to Richard that while he'd played plenty of baseball, he'd never even seen a football game. But he expected that life on the farm had toughed his body and given him stamina to excel in the strenuous game. In fact, with only eighteen men turning out on the first day of practice, Nicholas discovered that his size and physical conditioning mattered more than the football experience of some of his teammates. To his great surprise,

Nicholas heard the coach assign him to the position of quarterback and place him in charge of the team's offense. Having been shoved around for years by his father's cattle, frequently knocked down by plow mules, and occasionally falling from his horse, Nicholas had no trouble absorbing the relatively mild blows inflicted by other football players. His daily practices consumed valuable study time, but they also gave him a new degree of confidence. Richard remained his closest friend, but Nicholas admitted to himself that he enjoyed the level of campus recognition awarded to athletes.

As the Thanksgiving holiday drew closer. Nicholas began to relish the time when he would report personally to his father the details of athletic accomplishments that he'd only hinted at in his letters home. His studies had gone better than he expected, and almost every day he realized what a gift Miss Agnes Abernathy had been to him. At the end of ten weeks of school he had a perfect grade in Latin.

"Assiduus usus uni rei deditus et ingenium et artem saepe vincit," Miss Abernathy had often said. "Constant practice devoted to one subject often outdoes both intelligence and skill."

Sophie Bower wrote to Nicholas each week, newsy letters that described the comfortingly familiar events around Riverton. But the closing paragraphs of each epistle Sophie used to exhort and encourage her son.

"You are an exceptional young man," she wrote. "Man has no control over birth and surroundings, but everyone can cultivate the mind that God has given him, and good impulses of his heart; truth, rectitude, integrity – these no man can excel you in, if you determine to live on a high plane." [i]

# CHAPTER EIGHT

**Fall 1903**

AUTUMN IN THE SOUTH CAROLINA midlands came earlier than in the low country, but Nicholas, who had grown up closely connected to the land, scarcely noticed the capital city's daily transformation. President Sloan's words of warning proved prophetically true as the freshman from Riverton literally ran between his campus residence, his daily classes, and the University's athletic field. Having surprised himself with superior results on the initial round of examinations, Nicholas resolved to maintain top grades in every subject, and after football practice, he often studied until well after midnight. He wore the freshman beanie, as the rules required, but his success on the athletic field gave him a status far superior to most of his first year classmates. Nicholas' farm-toughened body and his natural coordination fully justified the coach's decision to train him for the quarterback position, and after only two games, Nicholas had outclassed a junior and a sophomore to become the starter for the first team.

September and October vanished before Nicholas found any opportunity to explore the big city that surrounded the University. Most of Nicholas' friends had ventured off campus before the end of the first week of school to visit local establishments that catered to students, and several, including Richard Baker, had urged him to come along. Nicholas had grown up in a household where alcohol was enjoyed in moderation, but he'd not had more than a sip of his mother's sherry or a swallow of his father's beer. Under the South Carolina Dispensary system, each county could make its own rules about the distribution of alcoholic beverages. Columbia provided bars where University students could indulge, but in the second week of November, when Nicholas finally found time to explore the city with Richard, he kept the no-drinking promise he'd made to his football coach. Walking the paved and tree-lined streets of the capitol, Nicholas tried not to reveal to Richard the full extent of his astonishment at the buildings they passed.

"That's the statehouse," explained Richard, pointing to the granite walls and metal dome of the seat of government. "You can see places where Sherman's artillery hit."

The boys passed empty lots where houses had been lost when the city burned, but both felt that the mood of the place was progressive and exciting. Electric lights brightened the sidewalks. Electric streetcars, noisy automobiles and gasoline-powered trucks competed at each intersection with horse-drawn carriages and freight wagons

"There's the Episcopal Church," observed Richard, pointing to a gothic building that faced the statehouse.

"Nothing like my church at home," said Nicholas, remembering the tiny wooden building where his family worshipped. But even as he recognized the physical differences between the two church buildings, Nicholas wondered how much similarity he might find in the services of worship. He discovered that the idea of going to church left him heavy with guilt.

"You know," he said to Richard, "soon as I get home, my mother's gonna ask if I've gone to church. And I haven't. How about going on Sunday?"

"Fine with me," replied Richard. "If they'll let Baptists in!"

When the boys approached the big church on Sunday morning, both felt conspicuous and shy. The worshippers who streamed through the open doors wore clothes unlike the simply dressed churchgoers in Walterboro or Riverton. There were gentlemen with top hats and morning coats, ladies with elaborate hats that matched their long silk dresses, and choir members vested in flowing surplices and ruffled collars.

"Are we alright?" whispered Richard.

"Sure," replied Nicholas, straightening his own necktie and adjusting the jacket of his black graduation suit. "Let's find a seat."

An usher with a carnation in his lapel greeted the boys and escorted them down the long central aisle to a pew near the pulpit. The sounds of people entering echoed under the high gothic arches. Then from the chancel came the first booming notes of an organ prelude that made both boys flinch in surprise.

When the service began, Nicholas felt more and more comfortable as he helped his friend find his way through the prayer book. He realized that he knew most of the words by heart, and in the same instant, he felt his tears begin to flow.

"O be joyful in the Lord, all ye lands, serve the Lord with gladness, and come before his presence with a song" intoned the congregation, but Nicholas was unable to make a sound. He couldn't tell whether the feeling that gripped him was homesickness or the reappearance of his old sentimental flaw. Hoping Richard wouldn't notice his tears, Nicholas leaned forward, as if bowing in prayer, for the final verse of the canticle.

"For the Lord is gracious, his mercy is everlasting, and his truth endureth from generation to generation."

"Mercy." There it was again, the word that intrigued Nicholas even while it revealed his embarrassing weakness. "I need to ask Mr. Turnbull about it," he said to himself, and he spent the rest of the service trying to decide how he would introduce the subject. "If I ever make that appointment," he sighed.

After church, Nicholas listened to Richard's impressions of the service and did his best to explain the structure of the liturgy.

"Up and down! Up and down!" exclaimed the puzzled Baptist. "I'm exhausted! Why do you Episcopalians have so much exercise in church?"

"I was always told that worship is more about what we do for God than what God does for us. All that standing and sitting and kneeling is supposed to be part of our offering."

As they walked, Nicholas realized that he felt more peaceful than he had in weeks. He resolved to make a place for Sunday worship in his cramped schedule. As Nicholas entered the university refectory, a student who came from a town not far from Riverton found him and offered him a ride home for Thanksgiving.

"My uncle's car is a Winton!" bragged the young man. "The same kind somebody just drove across the country in sixty-four days! We can drop you off in Stateburg, if your family can pick you up there."

Nicholas had enjoyed brief rides in several automobiles, but the prospect of an extended trip excited him. "I'll send a message today," he promised.

+ + +

The journey from Columbia to Stateburg by way of Garner's Ferry Road turned out to be an exhausting ordeal instead of the adventure that Nicholas had anticipated. The rutted road required Nicholas and his college friend to push the mud-splattered vehicle through boggy places every few hundred yards. Where the ground was firm, the thin rubber tires encountered rocks that caused punctures, each of which required time-consuming repairs. But perched on the high back seat of the automobile, Nicholas enjoyed the exhilaration of speeding past mule-drawn wagons, and he smiled when saddle horses reared at the approach of the noisy engine.

Late afternoon brought the car and its weary passengers to the steep grade that led from the Wateree River Bridge to the high hills of Santee. They sat and swatted at mosquitoes while waiting for the overheated engine to cool, but then they were away on the final leg of their trip. As the Winton bucked and struggled up the long hill, the passengers didn't need to be told to get out and push. Nicholas had his shoulder against the mud-covered fender of the car when over the sound of the engine he heard a familiar voice calling his name.

"Mr. Bower, perhaps I can be of some assistance," said Asa Turnbull. Straightening in amazement, Nicholas saw the minister seated in a mule-drawn wagon just off the public road.

"Keep pushing!" yelled the driver of the car, but when the two students shoved in unison, the driving wheels continued to spin without effect.

"It's a long hill, and the road's in terrible condition," said Mr. Turnbull. "Perhaps if we attached a rope to my wagon, these two good mules could speed your progress and these boys could be home in time for Thanksgiving!"

The owner of the car refused at first to consider the minister's offer, but finally agreed to the embarrassing plan. The mules managed without difficulty to free the car from its helpless situation, and as darkness fell, the travelers reached Stateburg and the road to Riverton. When Nicholas asked Mr. Turnbull how he happened to be in that part of the county, the minister explained that he'd come with Sophie Bower's permission.

"She said you needed a ride from Stateburg, and I offered to come, so here I am."

After thanking his friend and the owner of the automobile, Nicholas tossed his suitcase onto the wagon and took a seat next to Asa Turnbull as the mules plodded toward Riverton.

"I guessed it would be Philip," said Nicholas, "or January Wilson. But I'm sure glad to see you."

The minister turned to smile at his passenger. "I thought, perhaps, this might be a time for that conversation you mentioned to me some months ago."

Nicholas said nothing for a long minute. He felt surprised, and a little bit trapped by the minister's boldness. This was not how he had imagined the conversation would take place. But he made himself remember the strong feelings that had inspired his anxious request, and, taking a deep breath, he said to Mr. Turnbull, "This is fine with me. Let me think about how to start."

They rode in silence for a while as night settled over the countryside. The sandy road unrolled itself like a winding avenue of starlight through the darkened forest. A deer vanished from their path as suddenly as it had appeared, and in the pines an owl called.

"I'm not good at this," said Nicholas, "but I wanted to talk with you because sometimes I'm ashamed at the way I react to things."

"What sort of things?"

"Well, mostly it's good things, pleasant things. When somebody says something nice to me, or does me a favor, I feel like crying. Sometimes I even feel the same way when something good happens to somebody else."

"And this is troubling to you?"

"Of course it is! I mean, a man's not supposed to cry like that! I can take insults from anybody, but why can't I take kindness and praise?"

The minister nodded and said, "Could it be that you don't think you deserve it?"

"No, that isn't it! I know I've done some good things. It's all right for people to give me compliments. But why does it make me cry? And why am I so softhearted when other people are praised? I've been this way my whole life! I'm too old to keep being embarrassed like this!"

"I wonder if it's really such a weakness," said Asa Turnbull. "I wonder if God has given you a special kind of sensitivity for his own reasons."

"I just want it to go away! If God is really merciful, wouldn't he do something about it?"

To Nicholas' horror, he felt the familiar tears begin to dampen his face. Only the darkness saved him from embarrassment. He realized how rarely anyone had really listened to him. The minister's simple act of kindness touched the very place that he was trying to describe.

The two said nothing then, as the wagon bumped along the sandy road. After a long time, Asa Turnbull said, "Nicholas, you've always seemed to me a thoughtful young man. I mean, not just attentive to the feelings of other people, but someone who thinks a great deal before he speaks."

Nicholas nodded in the darkness. "Maybe so," he said.

"And as valuable as that thoughtfulness is," continued the minister, "I wonder if you would be more at ease if you could be more spontaneous. I mean, less concerned with what you will say or with what others will think about you." Nicholas felt himself tighten inside.

"I don't know how to do that! If I speak without thinking, what I say will sound stupid."

"What if you came to believe that it didn't really matter how you sound to other people? What if you were sure that you're loved just the way you are?"

"That can't be," said Nicholas. He shook his head emphatically. "You don't know me! There are things I've done, things I think about that are really bad!"

"And that's true of me, too," said the minister. Leaning forward, he looped the reins around the wagon seat and freed the mules to proceed at their own pace. He leaned back and looked at Nicholas. "Claus, God is merciful! He knows everything about you and me, and he loves us anyway."

"I keep trying to do better! I swear I do!"

"And God is glad when you do your best, Nicholas, but he wants us to try hard because we're grateful for his mercy, not because we're afraid of how we'll be measured in his eyes."

"I'm not afraid of God. I just want to do the right thing! But I never seem to do any better, and sometimes I feel like I want to let everything go!"

Asa Turnbull smiled at the boy. "Yes, Nicholas! Yes! Letting go is exactly what God wants you to do!"

Nicholas sat in silence, his thoughts tumbling uncontrollably as the wagon bounced its way toward the Bower farm. "Let go!" He'd heard the invitation before. Under the horse, three years ago. "Let go!" Win by losing.

Asa Turnbull was wise enough to know when he'd said enough, and while Nicholas tried to organize his own scattered thoughts, the minister chatted casually about current events in Riverton.

+ + +

Thanksgiving Day brought the congregation of St. Matthias Church together for a mid-morning service. Nicholas enjoyed seeing his friends, and he blushed when his parents' contemporaries greeted him and congratulated him on his achievements at the university. More people in Riverton had heard about his heroism on the football field than about his academic success. Nicholas had wondered if Philip would be envious of his new stature, so he was relieved to hear his younger brother boasting about him to friends in the church-yard. He noticed at once that Sally Hemphill had not joined her family for the service.

As the Bower clan began their trip back to the farm, Sally's mother called out, "Oh, Nicholas, Sally sends her greetings! She decided to stay in Charleston for the holiday." The brief comment was enough to leave Nicholas in a mood of silent withdrawal during the surrey ride to the farm.

After the Bower family enjoyed the dinner Ruby had prepared, Nicholas sat in the parlor with Sophie and Philip recounting stories about life at the university while Captain Bower left the house. Before very long, he returned, his face bright with excitement, and announced to his sons, "I turned the dogs loose! You boys! Upstairs and change! We're going hunting!"

Nicholas and Philip needed no encouragement to respond, and in a matter of a few minutes, both joined their father on the front porch as January Wilson brought the farm wagon from the barn, along with saddled horses for each of them. Suzy and Flash, the captain's bird dogs, romped around the wagon, barking with excitement.

"Listen to them!" shouted Captain Bower as he pulled his way up into the wagon. "We feed them all year long, and today they get to earn their keep! Hush, now!"

Nicholas stood holding Caesar's bridle in one hand and his new shotgun in the other.

"In here, next to me," ordered his father, pointing to the gun. "Make sure it's unloaded. Philip, I'm taking my father's old piece, and I've borrowed one for you. And we have a case of shells. Should last us all winter. So don't you plan to shoot them all up today! Remember, meat from one bird is worth about a single shell. If you have to shoot twice, you can't afford partridges for supper! Now, January, you get up here and drive for me."

Philip mounted the church horse and sent Nicholas a quick grin that acknowledged their father's unusually talkative mood. Climbing into Caesar's saddle, Nicholas nodded back. He was always apprehensive when anything excited his father, because Captain Bower had a way of turning an adventure into an examination. His speech about the price of ammunition had effectively put his sons on notice that they were not to miss too often today.

"Just once," thought Nicholas, "just one time I'd like to hunt birds for fun, without making it a test of my value to the family!"

January started the mule team down the two-rut road that led to the river swamp.

"Where we startin', Cap'n?" asked the black boy, affecting the dialect his employer expected of him and making Nicholas smile.

"There's always a covey near the old saw dust pile up from the branch. Let's try there first," said Captain Bower. Suzy, the young, far-ranging pointer, and Flash, the older, close-hunting setter, had already sprinted ahead of the hunting party, busily scouting ditch banks and field edges on both sides of the road.

"They make a good team," said the captain, "at least when we can keep track of Suzy. Where is that damn dog?"

Captain Bower's shouts and whistles produced no response from the missing pointer, but when Nicholas rounded a curve in the road, he pointed quickly and called to his father, "There she is! On point, just off the road by the sawdust pile. And Flash is backing her!"

Captain Bower ordered January to stop the mules twenty yards from the pointing dogs, and with help from Philip, he climbed from the wagon. As Nicholas handed his father the old, hammerlock double barrel gun that the Captain had chosen to use, he saw his father's eyes shining.

"Get your guns! Get your guns!" commanded the Captain, opening and loading his own weapon. As he slid two shells into his graduation gun, Nicholas wished he'd had a chance to try it a few times before going into the field.

"Nicholas, you take this side. Philip, you go round there. I'll go through the middle and walk them up!" instructed the captain. The boys flanked to the sides as ordered, and all three hunters stepped carefully, guns held before their chests, and their eyes on the bushes in front of the motionless dogs.

"Careful, Suzy, careful!" said the captain as the quivering pointer took a step forward.

Twenty quail exploded from the tall grass with a heart-stopping thunder that took Nicholas by surprise. As he shouldered his gun to track a bird escaping to his right, he heard his father shoot twice, and two shots sounded from Philip. The quail he'd chosen vanished behind a pine tree at fifteen yards, forcing Nicholas to pick a new target from the rapidly disappearing covey. As his gun swung past several twisting birds, Nicholas fired the first, then the second barrel of the Parker double. He heard the shot rattle against the trees and watched in frustration as half a dozen unruffled quail sailed over an overgrown ditch to land in the thick woods on the other side of a cotton field.

"First rate!" shouted Captain Bower. "Beautiful covey! Must have been two-dozen birds! I doubled. Philip, I saw you drop one. What about you, Nicholas?"

"Missed," mumbled Nicholas, opening his gun to remove the spent shells. "I saw where they went, though."

"Probably tried to shoot the whole covey," said his father. "I've told you before, you need to pick out one bird!"

"I did. It went behind a tree."

"Well, I've got two down beyond that persimmon tree. Let's pick up these birds and give those singles time to move around. Suzy! Flash! Hunt dead! Dead bird!"

The retrievers pushed eagerly through the bushes, their tails flailing and their noses searching the ground for the familiar scent that would locate the downed quail and bring praise from the man who fed them. The dogs quickly found the captain's birds and minutes later, brought Philip the one he'd dropped.

"Good girl, Suzy! Good dog!" said the captain, rubbing the pointer's head against his knee. "Let's look for those singles. January, fetch that wagon up here! Nicholas, where did you see them down?"

By the time January had driven Captain Bower around the cotton field, the dogs had already scented the quail Nicholas had missed and were locked on point.

"You boys go ahead," instructed the captain. "I'll watch the ones you miss."

Nicholas slid from Caesar's saddle, retrieved his gun from the wagon, loaded it, and with a sigh, walked toward the pointing dogs. "I'll watch the ones you miss!" His father's disparaging comment echoed in his ears. "One more failure, coming up!" thought Nicholas.

This time, he walked to Philip's left, and when a pair of partridges erupted in front of the dogs, both boys fired. Feathers floated from one of the birds.

"Winged one!" shouted their father. "Watch him down! Whose bird was that?"

"Nicholas hit him," called Philip. "I was tracking the other one." Nicholas took a deep breath. He had been aiming at the undamaged quail. His brother was covering for him.

"Good shot, Nicholas," offered Captain Bower. "Bird's gone down into the branch. Dogs should be able to find him. You go ahead."

Nicholas reloaded his shotgun, called for the dogs, and trudged his way through the underbrush and down the slope toward the small stream that watered an unused portion of the Bower farm.

"Wouldn't you know," he mumbled to himself. "I'm looking for Philip's bird in the worst jungle on our property." Ducking under low-hanging branches and edging his way past sharp pointed cat briars, Nicholas made his way to the boggy ground where soaring cypresses supported themselves with knobby knees. The dogs had plowed their way into the bushes and failed to respond to Nicholas's shouts.

"Need some help?" asked January Wilson.

Nicholas looked around in surprise. "Don't I always? Dogs are down here somewhere, but I don't think we're gonna find this bird." The boys pushed farther into the undergrowth, their eyes searching under every bush and clump of grass for the wounded quail.

"Here's Flash!" called January. "Whoa, boy! Hunt dead!" The setter coursed briefly around the perspiring hunters and vanished again into the jungle.

"Gone! Damn his hide!" swore Nicholas.

"Well, look here!" said January. "Here's Suzy with a bird in her mouth! Good girl! Good dog!" January extracted the bird from the pointer's mouth and held it up so Nicholas could see.

"Nothing beats a good dog!" exclaimed the black boy. And then, as Nicholas had so often seen him do, January Wilson lifted his head and said, "'My hounds are bred out of the Spartan kind; so flew'd, so sanded, and their heads are hung with ears that sweep away the morning dew.' Midsummer Night's Dream, Act IV!"

"Don't be calling my father's bird dogs hounds!" laughed Nicholas. "Hey, look at this!"

January scrambled toward Nicholas's voice and soon found his friend standing at the edge of a small clearing in the woods. In front of them they saw an assembly of metal drums connected with copper pipes, and on either side of the open space, they noticed piles of cloth sacks and wooden boxes filled with bottles. The remains of a fire smoldered in the center of the clearing.

"You know what this is, don't you?" whispered January.

"Of course I do," said Nicholas quietly. "It's a still! We better tell my father!"

"No way he can get down here! We better go get the sheriff. And right now, we better get ourselves out'a here!" As the boys slipped back into the woods, they heard voices from farther down the branch.

"Somebody's coming!" said Nicholas. The briars and cypress knees that had been mere inconveniences before now became painful obstacles as Nicholas and January tried to hurry noiselessly through the jungle. When the bird dogs came crashing to their side, Nicholas cursed silently.

Suddenly, a gunshot sounded from behind them, a branch fell

from the tree above their heads, and a voice shouted, "You're a dead man, nigger!"

Nicholas and January gave up any effort to move silently, struggling forward as fast as they could push away the branches.

At the edge of the woods, they turned and sprinted toward the wagon where the captain and Philip waited with the horses.

"Father," panted Nicholas, "there's a still down by the branch. We just saw it and somebody was coming! They must have heard us, because they shot at us!"

"Somebody shot at you?" said the captain. "That wasn't you shooting the wounded bird?"

"No, Suh," said January. "Like Claus say, it be a still and somebody shootin' at us!"

"Did they follow you?" asked Captain Bower, picking up his shotgun and reaching for ammunition.

"I don't think so," said Nicholas. "At least we didn't hear them coming after us."

"They said, 'Nigger you're a dead man,'" said January. "Must be they had a look at me 'fore we ran. But I got this." January brought from the pocket of his overhauls a flat glass bottle, rounded at the top and bottom and formed with the image of a palmetto tree.

"Dispensary bottle! We can show that to the sheriff," said the captain. "January, you get up here, and you boys mount up. We don't know who we're dealing with, and it's foolish to fight when you don't know your enemy. Let's go!"

# CHAPTER NINE

"DAMN YOUR LAZY BONES, BOY!" shouted Captain Bower. "Give me those reins! We need to see the sheriff today, not next week!"

January handed over the leather straps and ducked when his employer drew back the whip to motivate the mules. Nicholas and Philip kicked their horses into a canter behind their father's wagon, and the Bower clan left a dusty cloud over the road to Riverton.

"Did you see any of them?" asked Nicholas, riding close to January's seat on the wagon.

"I was too scared to notice," the black boy replied. "And when they shot, I didn't care who it was. I just wanted out of there!"

"Tell me what you did see," said Captain Bower over the clatter of the wagon.

"I seen the barrels, three or four of 'em, and a stack of feed sacks, like folks use for totin' corn."

"And there were boxes of bottles," said Nicholas. "A bunch of them."

"Old Dispensary bottles," said the Captain, "if they're all like the one January picked up. The new ones don't have a palmetto tree on them."

"Watch behind us!" yelled Philip, struggling to rein in his startled mount as a single rider on a big horse suddenly overtook and galloped past the Bowers's rattling wagon. Caesar reared in alarm, and Nicholas clung to the pommel of his saddle to keep his seat. January Wilson, who was not contending with a frightened animal, had a clear view of the speeding horse and its rider.

"It's Freedom!" he shouted. "And Conner!"

Caesar wheeled around in time for Nicholas to recognize the chestnut stallion and to identify the blond-headed rider.

"Bastard!" bellowed Captain Bower. "Where in hell does he think he's going?"

"He's coming from our farm," said Philip. "And his boots were covered with mud. Did you see?"

"Shore did!" said January. "And his britches was wet to de knee, like he been walkin' in water." He turned and stared at Nicholas.

"It was he!" the black boy exclaimed, forgetting his field hand parlance. "I remember now! In the woods I recognized his voice!"

"That certainly makes sense," Nicholas said. "It all adds up! Him dropping out of school, spending all kinds of money! Father, I think we know who the bootleggers are!"

"You boys are too damn quick to accuse people," said Captain Bower. "You need more than an old grudge and a pair of muddy boots to call somebody an outlaw."

+ + +

When the Bowers reached Riverton and called at the sheriff's office, they found that the lawman was away. "Tell him I need to see him right away," Captain Bower ordered the deputy.

While the mules and saddle horses rested from their hard ride, the boys sat in front of the general store and drank a "Dope," the popular cocaine-fortified cola. Nicholas and January tried to recall more details of their frightening experience as Captain Bower interrogated them.

"I wonder how long it's been going on," said Philip.

"Too damn long," swore the captain, furious that anyone would trespass on his land and use his branch water for criminal purposes.

Suddenly, January exclaimed, "Well, would you look at that!"

The Bowers turned and saw Conner Mayfield riding into Riverton beside a heavily loaded farm wagon, which was driven by his father and guarded by an unknown man with a rifle. A heavy canvass tarpaulin covered the wagon's cargo. Conner twisted his hard face into a grin, which he directed toward Nicholas and Philip.

"How's school, boys? You miss me?"

"Would we miss sitting down with a cottonmouth?" said Nicholas.

"I hear you're a big football hero, Claus. Big college man!"

"At least I know enough to put on clean clothes. Did you wake up wearing mud?"

"Ain't your business what I wear," said Conner, scratching his stringy blond beard. "I see you let your nigger leave the farm. Boy, you enjoy your freedom?"

Conner smiled mockingly at January Wilson and lavishly stroked Freedom's sleek neck. As January cursed and hurried to climb down from the wagon, Captain Bower blocked him with an outstretched arm.

"You stay put! That boy's got more trouble coming than you can give him." The captain fixed Conner Mayfield with an iron expression. "You tell your father and your hired gun that if any of you come on Bower land, you're gonna need more than that rifle to save your hides." The captain popped the mules with his whip. "Mount up, boys. Something stinks around here!"

+ + +

The discovery of the still on Bower land captured the family's attention and mercifully obscured Nicholas' embarrassing performance on the quail hunt. He cleaned his graduation gun and put it away, wishing mightily that the Thanksgiving break could be extended to give him a day to practice wing shooting.

"I hate to go back to school with a fight with the Mayfields coming on," said Nicholas.

"You just put that out of your mind," said Sophie Bower as she folded clean laundry into his suitcase. "There will be no fight! Your father has talked with Sheriff Harvey. They'll be keeping a watch on Conner and his family. And especially on the still you found. You know what your priorities must be! Study, Son! And don't let athletics get in the way of bookwork!"

January Wilson brought the farm wagon around when Nicholas was ready to depart for the train station.

"Just you and me, this trip," smiled the black boy.

"That suits me fine!" said Nicholas. "I can't think of a better arrangement! "Aspirat primo fortuna labori.""

"I feel so stupid when you do that!"

"How do you think I feel when you throw Shakespeare at me all the time? It means, "Joking aside, let us turn to serious matters.""

"And what might they be?" said January.

"I think it's time to let my family know about your background. Around them, you act like a farm hand, but I know you have the mind and the education of a gentleman."

"I am a farm hand!"

"Well, you could be more, if you had the chance. I'm sure of it!"

"You mean if I had the money for college and my family could get along without what I make," said January.

"Exactly! We need to find some sort of scholarship for you. And some help for them. I want to tell my mother about you when I'm back for Christmas?"

"Just don't let your father know about me!"

"He doesn't have to know! Mother knows people, and if she had a chance to talk to you I'm sure she would want to help."

"I don't know. I wonder, after all that's happened," said January.

Then, smiling at Nicholas, the field hand lifted his head and said, "There's a divinity that shapes our ends, rough-hew them as we will."

"Hamlet! Am I right?" asked Nicholas.

"Well, imagine that!" laughed January. "You are learning something at that big university."

+ + +

After Thanksgiving, with the football season over, Nicholas had intended to spend all of his time studying before the university's Christmas break, but he found himself distracted by memories of the encounter by the still. Speculating about possible developments, he couldn't imagine any harm coming to his father. The captain projected an aura of invincibility. But Nicholas continued to worry about January's safety. If Conner Mayfield was part of the bootlegger business, everybody in January's household had reason to fear.

But a week before his semester examinations, Nicholas encountered an even more troubling distraction. Hurrying to the library one morning, he saw Sally Hemphill and her mother leaving the administration building.

"Sally!" he called. "Mrs. Hemphill! It's Nicholas!"

"You've not been gone so long that we don't know you, Nicholas," frowned Mrs. Hemphill. Sally nodded to Nicholas.

"How have you been?" she asked politely.

"I've been well," he said, feeling his face redden as his train of thought derailed. "I mean, I've been home for Thanksgiving, and now I'm back here."

"So I see," said Sally, coolly.

"What are you doing here?" stammered Nicholas. "I thought you were in Charleston."

"I was," the girl replied. "I completed the college preparation course, and they've accepted me at the university."

"Wonderful!" exclaimed Nicholas. "When will you begin?"

"Right after Christmas. Mother and I have just completed the arrangements."

"You know, there aren't many female students," said Nicholas, immediately regretting his statement.

"Not now," said Sally as she adjusted a small broach pinned to the collar of her dress. "But there will be soon." Nicholas squinted at the writing on the broach.

"What's that pin?" he asked.

"The emblem of the National American Woman Suffrage Association. Have you heard of it?"

"You mean the Susan B. Anthony people?"

"In the beginning, yes, but there's a new generation of women in leadership now."

"Perhaps the two of you will continue this conversation in the new year," said Mrs. Hemphill. "Nicholas, I'm pleased to see you, but Sally and I have a train to catch."

The prospect of seeing Sally Hemphill at the university filled Nicholas with as much apprehension as excitement. When he wasn't worrying about bootleggers back home, he occupied himself with analyzing the curious change that had taken place in the girl. His roommate, Richard, observed his growing mental paralysis and finally told Nicholas to get back on the athletic field and run laps.

"You've got too much free time," said Richard. "You need to sweat more so you can study!"

"Amicus certus in re incerta cernitur," replied Nicholas. "A true friend is discerned during an uncertain matter." He followed Richard's advice, and soon regained the ability to concentrate on his studies.

+ + +

It was a visit to church on the Sunday before the Christmas holiday that shook Nicholas' resolve. Sitting with Richard in the big, downtown church as they waited for the service to begin, Nicholas prayed silently for God's help with the situation on the farm and for clarity about Sally Hemphill. Richard interrupted him with the jab of an elbow.

"Wake up and take a look at an actual angel!" he whispered, nodding toward the other side of the central aisle. Nicholas turned, and felt the breath go out of him. There, entering a pew with two other well-dressed young women, was Sally.

"Not bad, eh?" said Richard. "The blond-haired one especially."

"That's Sally Hemphill," said Nicholas. "The girl from home."

"The one you've been losing sleep over?" said Richard, speaking loudly enough to draw disapproving looks from nearby pews. Nicholas nodded silently and stole another glance in Sally's direction.

The morning's liturgy was lost on Nicholas, and after church, he waited, at Richard's insistence, to speak to Sally and the other young women.

"This is my roommate, Richard Baker, from Walterboro," said Nicholas as they approached the girls. Sally introduced her friends, and engaged Richard in polite conversation until Nicholas interrupted and reminded his roommate that he had work to do.

"We're here for a meeting of the National Woman Suffrage Association," said Sally importantly. "Most of the university women belong to it."

"I'd like very much to hear about that," said Richard. "It's a new century and change is everywhere!" Sally smiled his way.

"Did you hear?" she asked. "Yesterday, two men in North Carolina succeeded with a flying machine!" Nicholas felt miles away from the conversation. Sally's presence, her new political involvement, Richard's obvious interest, and his own helplessness overwhelmed him. A Latin maxim appeared in his brain, and he verbalized it.

"Omnia mutantur nos et mutamur in illis."

"Really, Nicholas," said Sally, shaking her head. "You don't have to show off!" Then to her friends, Sally explained, "Nicholas and I made the best grades in Latin at home, but I prefer to speak English. He just said, 'All things change, and we change with them.'"

All three women laughed as Nicholas pulled Richard by the sleeve and led him, protesting, toward their residence.

+ + +

The Christmas holiday seemed to Nicholas much less satisfying than the break at Thanksgiving. Stories from the university were no longer new to his family, and even though he had earned perfect grades for his first semester and gained athletic fame, Nicholas went to bed every night with an unfocused felling of vulnerability. He tried repeatedly to persuade his father to teach him to drive the new tractor, but Captain Bower always seemed too busy to accommodate him. Philip had simply gone out one morning when his father was away, started the massive machine, and drove it around the barn, leaving tracks that brought first an explosion and later, words of praise from the captain. Nicholas tried to protest when his father allowed Philip to climb behind the wheel and operate the tractor for the early plowing of the cotton fields.

"He still works here," said Captain Bower. "He needs to do it. You're a college student. You can learn later." When Nicholas told his mother about going to Trinity Church with Richard, she insisted that he describe the experience to Mr. Turnbull.

"What did you think about that big church?" asked the minister when Nicholas met him at the general store.

"It's just big," said Nicholas. "The service is the same. Except you're a better preacher."

"Mendacem oportet esse memorem," replied Asa Turnbull shaking his finger at Nicholas. "Don't forget, I studied Latin, too! 'A liar must be good at remembering!'"

The holidays passed quickly. Nicholas enjoyed several good conversations with January and was relieved to learn that the night raids on colored houses had not resumed.

"There's a citizen's group that patrols the area," said January. "I think your father's part of it. Please tell him it seems to be working, and we're all grateful."

Captain Bower shrugged off the good report from Nicholas. "The best result of the Clarendon Rifles is slowing down the bootleggers," the Captain said. "We took Sheriff Harvey to the still you boys found and destroyed it. There wasn't any evidence who it belonged to. Just like you thought, everybody suspects the Mayfield bunch."

Bootlegging dominated the conversation Nicholas had with his friends after church on Christmas Day. Most of the local boys agreed that Conner Mayfield was involved in the illegal liquor trade, and they insisted on hearing Nicholas relate yet again the story of finding the still on the Bower farm.

Passing the gathered young men in the churchyard, Sally Hemphill said over her shoulder, "For heaven's sake, Claus! You make it sound like your stumbling over one still saved the country from drunkenness! If you want to be helpful, you should try to influence the legislature!"

"Look out! Here comes the Temperance Union!" yelled one of the boys.

"Make fun if you must," said Sally, "but until South Carolina rids itself of the failed Dispensary system, no one's family will be safe from alcohol!"

Nicholas said nothing as Sally marched toward her family's wagon. Her sympathy with the temperance movement didn't surprise him. It was just another sign of the radical transformation taking place in his school friend. Women's rights. Temperance. As Sally's wagon rolled out of the churchyard, Nicholas noticed for the first time her very modern dress and the stylish, narrow-brimmed hat that all the women in church were whispering about the minute Sally walked in the door.

+ + +

The Bower boys had hunted quail with their farther several times during the holidays, with January Wilson again driving the wagon. Nicholas shot better than he had at Thanksgiving, but anticipation of his father's caustic comments after any miss often caused him to flinch when he pulled the trigger. January listened to Captain Bower's predictable criticism of his son and hid his own feelings behind a smiling face.

When he and Nicholas were searching for a downed bird far from the wagon, the black boy said, "Methink'st thou art a general offence and every man should beat thee."

"Not you, too!" said Nicholas. "Qui debit beneficium taceat." "Let him who has been given a favor be silent."

"A favor? What are you talking about?"

"I told my mother that we wanted to speak with her privately."

"Will she do it?"

"Of course! She already likes you. We'll drive to your house after church on Sunday," Nicholas promised.

+ + +

"Why are we going to January's house?" complained Philip on the Sunday after Christmas.

"Nicholas and I have business with January and his family," said Sophie Bower. "You're welcome to come with us or walk home from the crossroads."

Philip elected to walk the final half-mile to the Bower farm while Nicholas and his mother drove the wagon to January's house. The wooden structure had once been painted white, but years of weathering had produced a façade of warped and faded boards and paper-covered windows. Chickens and guinea fowl pecked about the clean-swept yard. Smoke drifted from the crumbling brick chimney that clung to one side of the house.

As the Bowers' wagon rumbled past the leafless chinaberry trees that surrounded the house, children began to emerge from the sagging plank door. "It's Miss Sophie and Mr. Nicholas!" an excited voice announced. Venus Adams, mother to January and his six sisters, pushed open the door to make room for her rounded body.

"Praise de Lord!" she exclaimed, wiping her hands on her apron. "You, Rachel, hold dem bridle! Zipporah, help Miss Sophie down! Do Jesus, we is glad to see y'all folks! Mr. Nicholas, you is grown so tall! January! Mr. Nicholas be here!"

January hurried through the door, buttoning his jacket as he came. "Welcome, Miss Sophie!" he said softly. "Claus, thanks for coming."

The conversation between Sophie Bower and January Wilson took place in the tiny sitting room of the Wilsons' cabin while the family waited outside. Nicholas provided an introduction.

"Mother," he said, "I'm sure you know that January and I are good friends. It started back when I broke my leg and Father hired him to work for us. I found out things most white people in Riverton don't know about him. I don't know. Maybe you figured it out. It's just that January has an education! His mother had tutors when they were in Philadelphia, and she taught him. January is not just a field hand, Mother. He's brilliant, and he can quote Shakespeare on any subject you can think of."

Sophie Bower raised her hand to halt her son's impassioned speech. "Don't you suppose that I've heard the two of you talking together when Father was not around? January's natural speech is that of a gentleman. I've known it for years. He talks dialect only when white folks are around, especially your father." Sophie smiled as January stared at the floor.

"Young man," she said, "I have you to thank for my son's recent interest in Shakespeare, and, I'm sure, for many other things. I'm grateful, January."

"No, Miss Sophie," said the field hand. "I'm the one who is grateful. Without Nicholas to talk to, my life here would have been a nightmare. I love my mother, but she has decided that it's best for us to hide our background. In our house, we never talk about literature. Or anything but life on the farm."

"Your mother is as good an actor as you are," smiled Sophie.

"Do you see, Mother?" said Nicholas. "January has the background! He's got the ability to go to college! He just needs the money. And if he went off to school, his family would need to make up for what Father pays him."

"And you want me to help him," said Sophie looking again at January's expressionless face.

"It was my idea, Mother," insisted Nicholas. Mrs. Bower sat quietly for a moment.

"Well," she announced, "I think it's an idea worth considering. January, I will say my prayers about what Claus said. I can't promise you anything, but I'll do my best."

"Please, Miss Sophie," begged the black boy, "don't tell the captain!"

"That I can promise," said Sophie Bower.

+ + +

The spring semester began while winter still held the capitol city in its chilly grasp. Nicholas spent most of his time in the library, braving the icy weather only long enough to go for meals and, occasionally, to run a few tension-relieving laps at the athletic field. His football coach had recommended him for the baseball team, and each visit to the locker room brought an impassioned plea from the baseball coach, who assured Nicholas that the spring sport would not demand so much time as football. When baseball practice began, Nicholas infuriated his roommate by trying out for the team.

"What's more important?" asked Richard. "Being a two-letter man, or keeping up your grades?" Nicholas thanked Richard for his concern, but after a single week of practice he had made up his mind. After three games, he won the first base position on the Gamecock squad and had a batting average of .800.

Hurrying in from practice one afternoon, Nicholas found Richard dressed in freshly ironed trousers and a new sport coat.

"Going out?" Nicholas inquired.

"To a women's vote rally!" said Richard. "Sally Hemphill invited me." Nicholas merely nodded and seated himself at his study desk.

"Stay out of jail," he said as his friend hurried down the hall. The book Nicholas opened in front of him might as well have had blank pages. His thoughts tumbled uncontrollably as images of Richard and Sally swirled through his brain. Even with all the changes in Sally, he never imagined her forming a friendship with another man. Yes, she wore controversial clothes. Yes, she was involved in political causes that Nicholas didn't understand or support. But Richard? Another small town boy, who was in so many ways exactly like himself? Nicholas closed his book and stretched out on his bed. He was lying awake when Richard returned, whistling down the hall.

"You wouldn't believe the nonsense those women are talking about," said Richard when he saw that Nicholas was awake. "Not only do they want women to vote, they expect women to run for office and get elected! Serve on juries! It's crazy!"

"Why did you go if you don't like that sort of thing?"

"Oh, I went to be with Sally. I tease her about her causes, and I pretend to be impressed when she lectures me."

"Don't make fun of her!" shouted Nicholas, sitting up suddenly and glaring at Richard.

"Whoa! Take it easy, old friend," said Richard. "If you want her to be your girl, I'll back off. But if you like her, you ought to pay attention to her." Nicholas collapsed back onto his bed, his emotions still boiling.

"Did you know," asked Richard, hanging up his jacket, "she's going to spend the summer in north Georgia with friends of her family? One of us really should go and visit!"

# CHAPTER TEN

## Spring 1904

THE UNIVERSITY OF SOUTH CAROLINA baseball team recorded its best-ever record in the spring of 1904. Nicholas Bower was appointed team captain, posting an unequaled batting average of .550. At the commencement exercises for the class of 1904, Nicholas, a rising sophomore, received faculty honors for excellence in Latin, literature, and history. He was named Outstanding Athlete of the Year, and his face was known across the campus. Sophie Bower and Philip attended the award ceremonies in Columbia, explaining to Nicholas that his father was busy with the cotton crop.

"Father's planted forty percent more land this year," reported Philip. "The tractor is great! Wait 'till you see what it can do!"

Nicholas received the news indifferently. His homesickness for Riverton had peaked in February, when the weather in Columbia was at its worst, his academic load seemed overwhelming, and the presence of the new Sally Hemphill depressed him daily. But by the end of May, Nicholas realized that his world had changed. He had begun to think of the university as his preferred environment. He was respected in Columbia, even regarded as a hero by some students. Most of all, he had escaped the constant pressure of life with his father.

On his first day back on the farm, Nicholas tried to pass up his father's invitation to operate the tractor. "I'll do it if you need me, Father, but since Philip already has the skill, why not let him be your mechanical man?"

"You'll do it if I need you? Boy, what the hell have they taught you in Columbia? You'll do it because I told you to! Get up here and pay attention!"

After supper that evening, Nicholas admitted to Philip that he enjoyed driving the powerful machine. "It reminds me of Father," said Nicholas. "It just runs over anything in the way!"

Cultivating the cotton still involved plenty of hoe work, and Nicholas took advantage of those days in the field to enjoy long conversations with January Wilson.

"Has your mother said anything about our talk?" said January.

"Not yet," said Nicholas. "But don't worry. I'm sure she'll work something out."

Nicholas was glad for sweat on his face, because the thought of his mother helping his friend produced tears that he quickly wiped away with a sweep of his arm. "Why do I do this?" Nicholas agonized to himself.

When Nicholas rode to the fields with Father and Philip the next morning, they found that none of their field hands had come to work.

"Something's going on," said Captain Bower, "and I don't like it!" He cracked his surrey whip over the church horse, and the boys rode behind him to the home of his foreman, Junius Washington.

"Junius ain't home," explained the foreman's wife. "He gone to de Adams's place. Dey burn out las' night!" Nicholas felt his heart sink. It was what he and January had dreaded since the night raids began.

"Let's go!" shouted the captain, and his bouncing surrey led the way to the Adams's home site. The Bowers could see smoke curling from beyond the trees, and as they rounded the last bend in the road, they came upon an assembly of Negro people of all ages standing before the charred and collapsing frame of what had been Venus Adams's house. The crowed parted as Captain Bower drove into the yard, and Nicholas heard a high-pitched wailing. Venus sat weeping on the back of a neighbor's wagon as her sobbing daughters clung to her. January Wilson turned from his mother's grief and walked deliberately toward Nicholas. Sliding quickly from his saddle, Nicholas approached his friend and only the presence of Captain Bower prevented him from wrapping January in his arms.

"They did it," said the black boy, looking at Nicholas with smoldering eyes.

"I'm sorry."

From the surrey, Captain Bower called out, "Venus, I wish to speak with you."

Someone from the crowd said, "Captain, can't you let her be? She done lost everything last night!"

"I can see that. But now it's time to see what can be done."

Venus arose, and surrounded by weeping daughters, shuffled to stand before the surrey.

"It's a shame, Venus," said Captain Bower. "Some of us have tried to put a stop to this, but we can't be everywhere at once."

"Yes, Suh, I knows," said the grieving woman. "I just don't know what will happen to us now."

"We'll be alright, Mother," said January. "I'll see to it."

"January, you come and see me tonight after supper, do you hear?" said the captain. January looked at him and nodded assent.

+ + +

"What can we do, Father?" asked Philip as the Bower men returned to their farm. There would be no fieldwork that day, while the community struggled to sort out what had happened.

"I will talk to your mother," the captain answered cryptically.

Nicholas and Philip were not invited to participate in their parents's conversation, but when Captain Bower hurried from the house, Sophie called her sons into the parlor and, smiling, gave a report.

"It is a terrible thing, of course, but God has a way of redeeming the worst that can happen to us. Father is going to offer Venus and her family the use of the old Hutchinson place between here and town. It's on our land, and nobody's lived there since Esther Hutchinson passed away."

"But, Mother, it's in terrible shape!" said Nicholas.

"It is now, but with some help from us and their own relatives, I'm sure it can be habitable very soon. It will do until they rebuild their own place."

"Well, there goes January's chance for college," said Nicholas.

"Perhaps not!" said his mother. "I've been hoping to tell you something quite exciting, but not until this very morning did I know that it would happen."

"Something about January?"

"Yes. After our conversation about helping him with college, I said my prayers, as I promised, and the Lord gave me a conviction to do something very bold! I presented the situation to my chapter of the Daughters of the Confederacy!"

"Mother, you must be joking," said Philip. "The Daughters of the Confederacy helping the son of a slave?"

"Don't be so quick to judge, Son! I simply reminded the ladies that one purpose of the Daughters is to provide education for worthy former Confederates."

"Mother, January Wilson is…"

"The son of a good Christian woman! Born a slave, yes, but one who devoted herself to helping wounded Confederate soldiers when the war came through our community. I simply named for the ladies a few of their own relatives who had been cared for by Venus Adams."

"And they want to help?" said Nicholas. "I can't believe it!"

"They have offered, together, an amount that will cover one semester at the agricultural school in Orangeburg. If January does well, and I certainly believe he will, the Daughters will continue to help."

"When can I tell him?"

"As soon as I've told your father that he will need to hire another field hand," smiled Sophie Bower.

+ + +

Captain Bower received the news about January Wilson's new opportunity with predictable threats and curses. "I try to help the trifling darkies, and do they ever think about helping me? No, they send my best hand away to a damned trade school! I've a good mind to cancel my offer of the Hutchinson place!"

Given his father's volatile mood, Nicholas realized he would have to wait to ask about time off for a trip to north Georgia. The journey had been on his mind since Richard told him about Sally Hemphill's summer plans, and he had saved enough money to pay for a train ticket. Even though January would continue to work until college courses began in the fall, Nicholas feared approaching his father about taking a week away from the farm. He was much relieved, then, when Captain Bower announced that he had secured a replacement for January.

"Boy's name is Abednigo," he said. "Big, strapping fellow. Comes from Rimini and has never done a lick of farm work, but he can start right away."

On the strength of this news, Nicholas asked for time off and was surprised when his father agreed with only token complaints.

"Where will you be staying?" asked Sophie.

"That's the best part," said Nicholas. "I've become friends at school with two of the Governor's children, Zach and Catherine Heyward. Their family has a big house near Clarkesville, and they've invited me to visit them!"

"Did you hear that, Father?" said Sophie. "Claus has been invited to stay with the Governor's family!"

"Well, boy, you can tell Mr. Heyward that your daddy voted for him, but I might not again if he doesn't settle this liquor business."

"I'll sure tell him, if I see him," said Nicholas, hurrying to pack his suitcase. "Saepe creat molles aspera spina rosas!" he trumpeted as he bounded upstairs.

"What did he say?" asked Captain Bower.

"Something about prickly thorns producing tender roses," smiled Sophie. "But I'm not sure what it means."

+ + +

The train trip from Sumter took Nicholas first to Columbia, where he boarded the Southern line for a nighttime ride to Newberry, Greenwood and Anderson. The sun rose just as the train steamed out of South Carolina and entered Georgia's Habersham County. Nicholas stared in awe at the green, rolling hills that marched toward the horizon and the tumbling river rapids that often paralleled the railroad tracks. Feeling very far removed from the featureless pinelands and the flat, black water streams of his familiar Low Country, Nicholas turned from the window when the train conductor who had punched his ticket in Columbia passed by and asked him, "Howd'ya like our scenery?"

"Mountains are alright," said Nicholas.

"Mountains!" snorted the conductor. "Son, you ain't even begun to be in the mountains! These is just foothills!"

The train station serving Clarkesville lay a few miles south of the tiny town, and Nicholas was relieved to find a cart driver for hire. His plan was to secure a hotel room in town, where he would rest and refresh himself after the trip, and then he would make his way to Lamont, the Governor's mountain retreat. The cart driver recommended a boarding house on the west side of Clarkesville, and, exhausted from his trip, Nicholas paid the proprietor and quickly retired to his room. A cool breeze ruffled the curtains at the open windows, and Nicholas fell asleep rejoicing in his first vacation from the South Carolina sun.

He awoke at the sound of other guests going down for lunch. Hurrying to bathe, his mind was already busy with the afternoon's agenda. He would obtain directions to the Heyward family's house, hire a cart or rent a horse for the trip, make contact with his school friends, the Governor's children, and then discreetly inquire about Sally Hemphill's whereabouts. But moments after he set foot on Clarkesville's Washington Street, his plans collapsed, along with his spirits. A motorcar rounded the curve, and as it sped past him, Nicholas recognized the man at the wheel, behind a pair of driving goggles, as Richard Baker and the passenger, decked in duster and bonnet, as Sally Hemphill. Both heads turned toward him as the vehicle bounced to a stop a few yards beyond where Nicholas stood staring.

"Claus! Is that really you?" shouted Richard, peeling off his goggles and leaping to his feet behind the steering wheel. Sally smiled from under her bonnet and said nothing. "What in heaven's name are you doing in Clarkesville?"

Nicholas hadn't moved. Struggling to settle his tumbling thoughts, he managed to say, "I came to see Zack and Catherine Heyward."

"They're at Lamont!" said Sally. "I know where that is. The Heyward's are just two miles from where I'm staying."

"Oh," replied Nicholas, unable to say more.

"Listen," said Richard, "Why don't you let us drive you to Lamont. We're going that way, like Sally said, and we can all visit with Catherine and Zach."

Nicholas detested the idea. He wanted to retreat to the boarding house and crawl under the bed covers, but he hated even more the prospect of appearing weak in front of Sally.

"If you're sure it's no trouble, I'll get my suitcase," he said, affecting something like a smile.

The car ride along the dusty road to Lamont gave little opportunity for conversation. Nicholas managed to understand that

Richard had learned how to drive just the week before and that the car belonged to his uncle who summered in North Georgia.

"Let's ask the Heyward's if they want to climb Tallulah Gorge tomorrow," bellowed Richard over the noise of the engine.

"What?" Nicholas yelled.

The aborted proposal had to wait until the steaming automobile chugged the final yards to the Governor's hilltop mansion. A servant greeted the travelers, and as they brushed dust from their garments, Zack and Catherine hurried down the steps to greet them. While Richard, Sally, and the Heyward children exchanged news about life around Clarkesville, Nicholas wished he had never asked for this vacation. He listened silently, responded indifferently when asked a question, and wondered if January Wilson's family had moved into the Hutchinson place. Over the evening meal, Richard brought up his suggestion about a trip to Tallulah Gorge, and in order not to appear as miserable as he was, Nicholas agreed to go with the group.

Nicholas slept very little that night. The guest room at Lamont had windows that opened to the north, and the pleasant breeze that had welcomed him to the mountains soon turned uncomfortably cold. But his sleeplessness had little to do with the lack of blankets and everything to do with his sense of Richard's betrayal.

"I'll back off," Richard had promised before the end of school. "Pay attention to her, if you want her to be your girl," Richard had counseled. "She'll be in North Georgia for the summer," Richard had told him. "One of us should go visit!"

"One of us!" Nicholas pounded his fist on the mattress. Richard had taken his own advice and arrived first. Nicholas sat on the edge of his bed and looked out at the star-lit silhouettes of the mountains. He realized that it was not Richard who had wounded him but Sally. Shivering in the night wind, Nicholas gave himself to the memory of other times of emotional distress – the disaster at the Winter Race, the embarrassment of the Rogation Picnic, the destruction of January's house. Those had been terrible moments, but nothing in his experience had affected him as painfully as the girl's fickle behavior.

Nicholas shook his head in frustration. "I should be crying now," he lectured himself, "but of course, people as disturbed as I am only weep when they're happy."

Suddenly, for a fleeting moment, something solid and unmovable interrupted the destructive vortex of his thinking. He held his breath and listened, waiting for a voice from the hall or knock at the door of his room. But there was no one. He went to the window and leaned out into the starlight. Nothing. Sitting again on his bed, Nicholas yielded himself to a new and unexplainable feeling. Whatever had shattered the downward spiral of his misery had withdrawn and left him with a silent invitation.

"Let go." There had been no words, just an impression of hope that coursed through his body with every heartbeat. Nicholas fell back on his bed, far beyond betrayal or embarrassment, aware only of a peace to be welcomed, if not understood. He slept within minutes.

+ + +

Richard and Sally returned after breakfast with the car, and the sight of them traveling together awakened the emotional burden Nicholas had taken to bed the night before. After his transforming moment, he had slept well and rose refreshed, feeling confident about the day. But now the heaviness returned, and he tried without success to maintain a positive outlook. The Heyward's cook had packed a large picnic basket, which Nicholas carried out to the car. Sally Hemphill sat in front next to Richard, while Zach, Catherine, and Nicholas crowded the second seat of the open car.

The road from the Governor's house to Tallulah Gorge began with a nerve-wracking downhill ride, but after the first high speed half hour, the rest of the journey took the heavily loaded vehicle up one winding road after another, and, for Nicholas, it seemed to take forever.

"There's the hotel," announced Sally as the roof of a large Victorian building appeared beyond the towering trees. The long front porch of the Tallulah Gorge Inn overlooked a dramatic notch in the mountains, and the adventurers from Lamont could see dozens of well-dressed vacationers enjoying the view from shaded rocking chairs.

"What a crowd," said Richard. "Is it always like this?"

"Every summer," said Catherine. "But most of them just sit and look. There won't be many on the trail!"

Nicholas thought Richard and Zach would never finish admiring the elegant array of automobiles in the hotel's parking area, but finally, the picnickers followed Catherine along a path that led toward the famous Tallulah Gorge.

"It's the Grand Canyon of the east," she called as the group began to descend the rapidly steepening trail.

"Where's the gorge?" yelled Richard as he waited for Sally to negotiate a long set of stone steps.

"Follow me!" beckoned Catherine. Both the young women wore summer dresses that covered their ankles and slowed their pace. As an experienced hiker, Catherine had put on sturdy boots, but Sally struggled with the same city shoes she wore to classes at the university.

Nicholas waited for the others to descend the path ahead of him. He didn't want to hear the happy interchange between Richard and Sally, and he allowed himself to be distracted by the spectacular scenery. The trail clung to the side of the canyon, winding in and out of steep ravines and occasionally providing a view of the towering waterfalls at the top of the gorge.

He paused at a particularly dramatic overlook. On the path down below him, he could hear Richard and Zach shouting to each other, and as their voices faded, the sound of the distant river reached up to Nicholas. Leaving the trail, he edged his way toward the cliff face, carefully clinging to one tree after another. Grasping the last slender sapling, Nicholas leaned forward over the gorge. His stomach instantly tightened and his heart pounded as he glimpsed the river through eight hundred feet of empty air. He shut his eyes and leaned his forehead against the smooth bark of the slender tree. Then, to his horror, Nicholas felt a familiar invitation.

"Let go!" His fingers tightened around the tree trunk. "I'll die!" he silently pleaded.

"You will live!" promised the feeling. Opening his eyes for an instant, Nicholas glimpsed distant ribbons of white water tumbling down a giant causeway of boulders. He had a vision of his body hurtling toward destruction, and as he struggled to regain his equilibrium, he imagined himself suddenly caught up, as though on an invisible wind, and gently placed on the canyon floor.

"Nicholas!" The sound of his name returned him to the edge of the precipice. Opening his eyes again, he blinked and saw Catherine Heyward standing on the trail, just yards away.

"What in the world are you doing?" she scolded. Nicholas glanced back at the void beyond his feet and felt instantly nauseated.

"Looking," he said.

"Well, we waited a while, and everybody thought you'd gone back."

"No, I want to go to the river," said Nicholas as he cautiously pulled his way back to the path.

"You must be more careful!" said Catherine, turning to lead the way down the steep trail.

"Careful," thought Nicholas. "I'm always careful," he smiled to himself. Then, feeling gravity quicken his steps, he said out loud, "I care so much about everything that I don't enjoy a damn thing!" Nicholas began to run, clutching at trees to keep himself on the winding trail.

"Here I come!" he shouted.

"Beat you to the river!" challenged Catherine. She laughed and scrambled down the path toward the canyon floor.

Nicholas was dripping with perspiration when he reached the river. The trail ended near a broad pool where the water backed up behind house-sized boulders and the interrupted current created a shallow beach. Richard and Zach had removed their shirts and shoes and were swimming with billowing trousers. Nicholas watched Sally gather her skit to her waist and wade knee-deep into the water. She paused a moment, then splashed back to the beach, unbuttoned her dress and pulled it over her head. Shouting something that was lost in the roar of the rapids, she dove into the pool and came up breathless, her camisole and long pantaloons clinging to her body.

Catherine laughed off Sally's invitation to join her. She removed her hiking shoes and sat on a rock cooling her feet in the current while the others splashed and shouted. Catherine's modesty caused Nicholas to wonder again about Sally's new boldness. How could he have been attracted to this woman whose unconventional behavior was the talk of the university? The puzzle came and then disappeared, and Nicholas was conscious of how briefly Sally's bold behavior occupied his mind. A burden had been lifted. Without an instant's consideration, he pulled off his shirt and shoes and, letting out a whoop, he leapt to join the other swimmers in the river. Surfacing to float on his back in the deep pool, Nicholas looked up the canyon wall toward the distant promontory where he'd heard the invitation.

"Yes," he whispered to his unseen advocate.

## CHAPTER ELEVEN

**Summer 1904**

"DEAR GOVERNOR AND MRS. HEYWARD," wrote Nicholas, using for the first time the expensive stationery that had been a graduation gift from his mother. He knew his timely and graciously worded thank you note would make Sophie Bower proud, and he took care to employ the penmanship skills that had often drawn praise from Miss Abernathy. Nicholas' second letter proved more difficult to produce. He looked forward to seeing Catherine Heyward when school opened in September, and he was eager to let her know that the day spent with her at Lamont had been the high point of his visit. Finding just the right words to convey friendship without implying anything more occupied Nicholas for most of his first morning home from North Georgia. He had just rewritten the brief note for the sixth time and was about to ask Ruby about lunch when he heard his father stamp up the front porch steps and jerk open the front hall door.

"Nicholas!" bellowed Captain Bower. "Get down here now!" Nicholas dropped his pen, sprinted from his room, and came stumbling down the stairs. "When did you get home?" said his father, his eyes blazing with rage.

"Last night, late, sir," stammered Nicholas. "January met me at the station. It was three this morning when I got to bed."

"Do you remember what time work starts on this farm, or is that too damn inconvenient for you?"

"I thought I'd rest today and come to work tomorrow."

"You thought? Let me save you the effort! When you're here, you will be in the field at sunrise with the rest of us! Is that clear?"

"Yes, sir," said Nicholas.

"Damn you, boy! How many times do I have to tell you? Look at me when I'm talking to you!"

"Yes, sir," said Nicholas, staring at his father with expressionless eyes.

As Nicholas hurried upstairs to dress for work, he was fuming. "Welcome home!" he said. "I can't wait to get back to Columbia!" He was still angry when he joined January Wilson at the far edge of a hundred-acre cotton field.

"I see you didn't get your rest day," said January. "'The sins of the father are to be laid upon the child.' Merchant of Venice."

"One day he'll lay nothing on me, I promise you that!"

"You're not free yet, my friend," cautioned the black boy. "Better guard your tongue and mind your manners! 'Come not between the dragon and his wrath.' King Lear!"

"That's enough! I can't remember all your Shakespeare. And you can't tell me you're not dying to start school and get off this farm yourself!"

"You're right about that! Mother's not happy about it, though. Neither are the girls. But they're getting older and they can help. April's seventeen now."

"Is my mother still promising some money?"

"Not promising! She already gave my mother some cash to get me ready for college!" Nicholas smiled as he remembered his own mother's elaborate efforts to prepare him for university life.

"When you leaving for Orangeburg?" he asked.

"Week from tomorrow," replied January.

Nicholas leaned on his hoe and looked at his friend. "Amicitiae nostra memoriam spero sempiternam fore."

"I thought you wanted to call a truce!" said January. "What was that?"

"It just means I'll miss you," answered Nicholas.

+ + +

Captain Bower denied his son's request for a day off to drive January Wilson to the Negro college in Orangeburg.

"Nobody else had a week of vacation this summer," said the captain. "That boy I hired to replace January is strong, but he's as stupid as he is black! January's family can take him to school without your help."

The final weeks of summer passed slowly for Nicholas. He missed his Shakespeare-quoting friend, and he longed to see his college contemporaries. The letter he sent to Richard suggesting that they not continue as roommates received no reply. He knew several members of the football team well enough to room with them, but he delayed making any arrangements.

The one bright moment in that final week was a note from Catherine Heyward thanking Nicholas for his letter and expressing her expectation that they would see each other on the Carolina campus. The sentence implied an accidental encounter, but Nicholas was confident that Catherine had written to invite his attentions. After his trip to North Georgia, he had seen nothing of Sally Hemphill in Riverton. Her mother sat alone in church on Sundays, and Nicholas decided not to inquire about his former friend.

Sophie Bower returned from the August meeting of the Daughters of the Confederacy to report that Sally had spent the summer in Columbia working with a group of political radicals.

"I don't know what's happened to that sweet girl," said Sophie. "She's not the same person you went to school with." Nicholas considered telling his mother about Sally's friendship with Richard Baker and her scandalous behavior at college and in the mountains, but he decided to keep that information to himself.

+ + +

When the university opened for the fall semester, Nicholas took the train to Columbia. Watching confused freshmen arrive at the capitol city station reminded him of his own apprehensions just a year before, and he allowed himself to laugh when some of the other returning students teased the newcomers. The registrar's office confirmed what Nicholas had expected. He had not arranged for a roommate, and now was assigned to a small, single room on the third floor of the men's dormitory.

"Doesn't matter," Nicholas told himself. "In fact, it's better, with nobody to disturb when I leave for football or come in from the library." His first post-summer encounter with Richard Baker took place on the opening day of classes.

"You're looking well, old man," said Richard as Nicholas entered the chemistry lab. Nicholas shook Richard's offered hand and tried to assume a pleasant attitude.

"How's Walterboro?" he inquired indifferently.

"I guess you're sore about me and Sally," said Richard. "You just didn't seem interested, and she liked that I was interested in her causes, so I decided..,."

"Forget about it! She's never been my girl. I don't really care what she does. She grew up in Riverton, but she's changed! I don't know her anymore."

"She surprises me, too," said Richard shaking his head. "I was hoping you and I could room together. I guess you'll be staying with somebody on the team."

"They gave me a single room," said Nicholas, struggling to control his feelings as he turned away to end the conversation.

Nicholas saw Sally later that same afternoon. She was standing on the steps of the library with several other female students who wore their hair pinned fashionably high, with campaign sashes over their long summer dresses, most of them holding hand-lettered signs promoting women's voting rights. Sally's hair was cut short as a man's. She wore farmer's overhauls and carried a megaphone.

Nicholas allowed the pressures of schoolwork and football practice to claim his time and energy, competing on the field with unmatched intensity and in the classroom with unequaled diligence. He was named captain of the varsity team, and in the first games of the 1904 season, he set school records for rushing and passing. His Latin professor assigned him to tutor beginning students, and the English faculty recommended him to serve as editor of the school's literary magazine.

Nicholas rarely wrote letters to his family, even though he took great comfort in his mother's weekly messages. On the farm, Sophie Bower seemed to live in the shadow of her domineering husband, but in rare, private conversations with her sons, and often in her letters, she revealed a depth of wisdom and a breadth of charity that set a high standard for Nicholas.

Sensing, as mothers often do, the un-discussed obstacles that confronted her son as he began his sophomore year, Sophie wrote, "Those who have had difficulties to contend with and had to exercise perseverance to obtain a good education then make the most of it when it is obtained." [ii]

After football practice on a cool October evening, Nicholas sat alone in the refectory, gulping his supper in order to hurry back to his studies. He saw Catherine Heyward enter by herself, and watched discretely as she spoke to several female students who were seated together near the center of the room. His heart leapt when Catherine served her plate and carried it to sit alone at a corner table. Nicholas was certain that a quick wash after practice had done little to prepare him for socializing, but a rare and reckless spirit compelled him to speak to the girl. He picked up his own plate and made his way to Catherine's table.

"May I join you?" he said, speaking with all the confidence his dry throat could manufacture.

"Please," smiled Catherine.

"I thought, perhaps, since you were alone you might be reading a book."

"And I thought, perhaps, since you were alone, you might be hurrying to the library."

"I am. I mean, I will later on," said Nicholas. He stood there balancing his supper plate. "How do you like the refectory food?" he said, immediately hating himself for the witless comment.

"It's alright," said Catherine, pushing away her plate. "But when they serve cold stew and hot lemonade like this, sometimes I go to a restaurant."

"Off campus? Which one is it?"

"Blackies. It's just a few blocks from here, down from the statehouse, on Main Street."

"I've heard of it," nodded Nicholas. "People say a lot of politicians eat there."

"How do you think I found out about it? When Father was elected, he discovered all the good places to eat in Columbia."

Nicholas nodded absently as an unthinkable idea began to take shape. Then his mouth opened, and he heard himself saying, "Why don't we walk down there now?"

The incessant chatter and clatter of the refectory seemed to fade as he waited an eternity for her answer.

"Oh, I don't know!" said the girl. "I have a paper to finish, and you said you're in a hurry to get to the library."

Having risked the invitation, Nicholas now dared to imagine that while her words said no, her tone of voice said yes.

"We can eat and be back in an hour."

"Well, thank you," smiled Catherine, standing up and collecting her sweater. "Come on. I'll show you where it is!"

The streetlights came on as Nicholas and Catherine walked from the quiet campus toward the busy commercial center of the city. She was as talkative and funny as Nicholas remembered from the mountain visit, and he realized that she knew the state capitol far better than he.

"That's my father's office," said Catherine, pointing to a window in the state house. "He was sworn in on the steps on the north side. That's the Senate's chamber, and the House of Representatives meets over there."

"How did your father get involved in politics?" asked Nicholas, feeling proud to have such a well-connected guide.

"He didn't really want to," said Catherine. "But he wasn't happy with the Tillman crowd, and some of his friends convinced him that it was time for somebody with low country roots to change things. You know, he's always been a rice planter. I expect that when he's finished as Governor, he'll go back to the plantation."

Nicholas silently tried to recall the little he knew about recent issues of state government. A thought appeared. "Sally would know all about it." Instantly, he dismissed the idea and focused on the state of his stomach.

"How far is this place? I'm starving!"

"I guess you don't follow politics," said Catherine, teasing him with a disapproving frown.

"Not when I'm hungry. But I do like the idea of a farmer in the governor's desk!"

"Is that what you want to do after school? Farming?"

"I suppose so. I don't know. Father's never said what he plans to do with our farm. I think if the cotton prices don't crash I could make a living there."

"What about your brother?"

"Philip? I can see him in some job with lots of people, maybe teaching or selling things. Something like that. Mother says he'd do well in vaudeville! I think he'd be a good politician! He's better at conversation than I am."

"I think you do quite well," smiled Catherine. "Here's Blackies! But look at the crowd!"

When the two students pulled open the doors to the popular downtown restaurant, the din of multiple conversations and the rank odor of pipe and cigar smoke overwhelmed them.

"I've never seen it this crowded," Catherine shouted into Nicholas' ear. "I forgot it's Saturday night!"

They found a table in a back room and had just been greeted by a busy waiter when Nicholas glanced through the haze and recognized a familiar face at a nearby table. Conner Mayfield sat with six other men, all of them tipping back mugs of beer and laughing raucously at each other's jokes. Conner's whispy blond beard was fuller than Nicholas remembered, his hair was neatly cut at shoulder length, and his angular frame seemed at home in a well-tailored suit. Nicholas didn't recognize any of the other men at the table. All of them appeared to be older than Conner, and several displayed the flushed, jowled faces and portly bellies of men accustomed to a life of affluence.

"See somebody you know?" yelled Catherine.

Nicholas leaned toward her. "That blond man is from Riverton. We went to the same school until he dropped out."

"Looks as though he's done pretty well for himself. And he's got some influential friends! The big man with the sideburns is a senator from somewhere. I don't know his name, but I've seen him at the statehouse."

"Well, look who's come to the big city," said a voice behind Nicholas. He turned and found himself looking up at Conner Mayfield, who had stood to leave with the other men.

"Hello, Conner," said Nicholas evenly.

"Well, what about this?" said the blond boy. "A different girl! Stepping out on Sally, are you?"

"That's none of your business," said Nicholas, pushing back his chair to stand up.

"Look here, Gentlemen!" said Conner to his associates. "This farm boy has become a big football hero, and now he wants to fight me!"

"That's enough, Mayfield," snapped the big man Catherine had identified as a senator. "You make a scene here and the deal is off."

One of the other well-dressed men took Conner's arm and pushed him toward the door.

"Ask the dirt farmer if he's ever seen my horse!" shouted Conner. "Get him to speak Latin for you!"

"Shut up, Mayfield," ordered the senator. "You're drunk."

When Conner and his drinking companions left, Nicholas slumped down into his chair.

"Lord help us!" exclaimed Catherine. "Who was that?"

Nicholas took a deep breath. "He's Conner Mayfield. Comes from a family of damn carpetbaggers in Riverton. He's smart, too smart for his own good! And he's crooked. I think he burned some colored houses around Riverton. Father and I are pretty sure he's bootlegging whiskey."

"What's he doing here?"

"Looks like he was doing business with some of the men he was with. The fat one said something about the deal being off."

"I can't wait to ask my father about senator what's-his-name! Maybe he knows something about whatever Conner and the fat man are doing."

"I think both of us ought to stay out of it," said Nicholas. "Conner is dangerous. And if he's got powerful friends, they're probably worse!"

"Do you want to leave?"

"Not unless you want to. They're gone, and I'm really hungry!"

When they finished their sandwiches, Nicholas offered to pay for the meal, but Catherine insisted on buying her own supper.

"I brought you here for something to eat, and you've introduced me to a bootlegger and given me a project," she laughed. "I should buy your supper!"

They took their time walking back to the university. Neither seemed to care about the pressing responsibilities that had troubled them in the refectory. At the door to the women's dormitory, Nicholas took Catherine's hand. He felt wonderfully calm.

"I enjoyed our evening," he said. "Thank you for introducing me to Blackies. Maybe we can go there again?"

"I'll look forward to it," said Catherine.

Nicholas whistled a favorite tune as he made his way toward the men's dorm. Pausing in a pool of light beneath a lamppost, he spoke aloud to the memory of Catherine's face,

"Haply, I think on thee, and then my state, like to the lark at break of day arising, from sullen earth sings hymns at heaven's gate."

"I beg your pardon?" said a young woman who came striding toward him from the darkened street.

"Sorry," said Nicholas. "A quote from Shakespeare. I was just practicing."

The girl shrugged, and he watched as she pulled a printed flyer from a stack under her arm and, with a thumbtack, fashioned the sheet to the lamppost. As the woman hurried away, Nicholas glanced at the posted notice.

"University Women!" the poster read. "Unite For Equality! Take a stand on the library steps on Wednesday at 10:00 AM!"

Under the headline Nicholas saw a photograph of a woman waving a banner, and in the yellow glow of the streetlight, he recognized the face of Sally Hemphill.

The assault on his buoyant mood was instant and irresistible. Nicholas clenched his teeth and cursed his vulnerability. He had believed himself free from his attachment to the girl from Riverton. He was confident that Sally's behavior in the mountains and her outrageous activities at the university had ended his childhood affection for her. Why, then, did the mere image of her face still have the power to spoil a memorable evening with a perfectly wonderful girl?

Fleeing the picture, Nicholas sprinted to the dormitory, rushed to his room, and flung himself on his narrow bed.

+ + +

Since the start of the new semester, Nicholas had allowed the demands of schoolwork and sports to occupy his weekends, and without Richard's company, it was easy to avoid going to church on Sundays. On the morning after his encounter with Conner Mayfield, Nicholas put on his graduation suit and made his way to the big church near the statehouse. He saw other students in the congregation, but he chose to sit alone near the front of the nave.

As the morning sun rose behind the east wall of the sanctuary, light through the stained glass windows painted the pews with slowly moving patches of color. Nicholas welcomed the quiet time before the service began. He thought about Catherine, and almost immediately, about Sally. He pictured Conner Mayfield's drunken face and remembered January's anguish at the burning of his house. He turned his mind to his mother, imagining her in the kitchen with Ruby, and then in her pew at St. Matthias' Church. He smiled at the thought of Philip strumming his ukulele. He envisioned the face of Agnes Abernathy in front of her blackboard and recalled the voice of Asa Turnbull from his pulpit. There was the image of the big horse, Caesar, and the cotton gin, and the liquor still in the deep woods. Recognizing his familiar pattern of unfocused thinking, Nicholas sighed helplessly and silently asked God to let it all be a prayer and to give his uncontrollable mind some clear direction. He wasn't prepared for the disturbing arrival of his next train of thought.

Suddenly, Nicholas found himself confronted by the mental image of Maximilian Bower! The dark iron eyes bore relentlessly into him, and the full black beard trembled as curses flew from the down turned mouth. How had his random memories of Riverton failed to include the man who so thoroughly dominated his life? Nicholas sat in shock, paralyzed by the palpable presence of his father. He slid to his knees well after the rest of the congregation had knelt to pray. Their unified voices invited him out of his confusion, and, for a moment, comforted him.

"Our Father, which art in heaven," they prayed. Nicholas felt himself relax as he whispered the familiar words. "Thy Kingdom come, thy will be done."

"Give us this day our daily bread." The frightening image of his father began to fade as Nicholas gave himself to the prayerful cadence of the congregation.

"Forgive us our trespasses as we forgive those who trespass against us," he recited with the others. Instantly, Nicholas was alone in the church.

"Damn you, boy! Look at me when I'm talking to you!" roared the spirit of the captain. The savage attack took Nicholas by surprise and shook him into silence.

"Forgive." While the congregation prayed for guidance and deliverance, Nicholas cringed at the echoes of a thousand cruel curses and recoiled from the memories of insults beyond number.

"Forgive."

"I can't! I won't!" confessed Nicholas, silently lowering his head to the bookrack in front of him.

"Forgive."

"Sometimes I can forget about him," he realized, "but I can never forgive him. I can't let him win!"

"Forgive."

The message was unrelenting. Nicholas suddenly rose from his knees and stood up.

"Excuse me," he said to the man who knelt at the end of his pew. "I'm not feeling well," said Nicholas, pushing his way into the aisle and hurrying toward the door of the church. As he reached the sidewalk and turned toward the university campus, he began to run.

"Forgive!"

"I don't want him forgiven! I want him dead!" swore Nicholas, sprinting past puzzled pedestrians. In the space of a hundred yards, running began to release him from the impossible task. He knew he could never accomplish what he had no desire to do. Lowering his head and pumping his arms, he ran harder until his lungs burned and his legs ached. He would outrun the demand to forgive just as he eluded would-be tacklers.

As Nicholas approached the tree-lined lawn at the center of the campus, he never really heard the steps of his pursuer, but he sensed the presence of an unseen runner who first matched his stride and then easily pulled ahead of him. Nicholas slowed, then stopped and stood bent over, his hands on his knees, trembling and gasping for breath as the one who had ordered him to forgive now offered him the power to comply.

"Let go," came the invitation. Nicholas felt his legs buckle under him as he fell face down on the sun-splashed grass.

# CHAPTER TWELVE

NICHOLAS ALLOWED HIS sweat-soaked graduation suit to remain crumpled on the floor of his dorm room for many weeks after his embarrassing church experience. The lack of appropriate clothing gave him a convenient excuse for avoiding Sunday worship, and the grass stains on the knees and elbows of the suit served to remind him of what he regarded as a growing and dangerous weakness. He had fled from two disturbing impressions in as many days, first from the photograph of a girl and then from the mental image of his father, and his loss of control infuriated him. Living alone at the university, he found it easy, as days went by, to retreat behind the emotional walls that guarded his heart, and before long, few among his fellow students or teammates expected more from him than distant cordiality. If people described him as driven, and many did, Nicholas reinforced their impression by spending more hours at the library and exerting greater efforts on the football field. Catherine Heyward was among those who sensed the change in Nicholas, and it disturbed her.

"You're working too hard," she told him one day as she hurried to match his determined stride on the way to class.

"I have a lot to do," said Nicholas without slowing down.

"How about supper at Blackies?"

"No time! Maybe after football season and exams."

"Are you going home for Thanksgiving?" said the girl, already breathless from keeping pace with him.

"Can't," said Nicholas over his shoulder. "See you when you get back."

What drove Nicholas to increase his pace and walk away from his friend was not only the desire to get to class on time, but also the awkward appearance of tears on his cheeks. Catherine's accurate observation about his relentless schedule and her gracious invitation to relax touched the very weakness that he was desperate to hide. He wanted to run and concentrate on his responsibilities. He wanted to stop and take her in his arms. As he hurried into class, Nicholas continued to struggle, at one moment remembering her words of kindness and weeping, and at the next, wiping his face and clearing his mind for the study of chemistry.

"Silicon dioxide, Mr. Bower," repeated his professor. "I asked if you would name some common examples of silicon dioxide. I will need your full attention, young man!"

As Nicholas stood, he drew around himself the opaque and rarely opened curtain of his psyche that had always been his refuge.

"Quartz," he said. "And chalcedony. And agate, in different colored rings." Instantly, he was thinking about stained glass windows and Catherine Heyward's eyes.

Nicholas wrote a short note to his mother announcing that he would not be coming home for Thanksgiving.

"Semester exams follow too closely," he explained. Then he added, "If you see January, please ask him to write me a letter. I'll see everyone at Christmas."

Nicholas received no letter from his black friend, but under the pressure of constant study, he never noticed the lack of response. He barely acknowledged Catherine's greetings on campus, choosing to eat alone in the refectory with a fork in one hand and a textbook in the other. By the time Nicolas sat for his last exam of the term, he had pushed himself beyond exhaustion and could barely concentrate. Coughing and feverish when he boarded the train for the Christmas break, he slept in the surrey between Sumter and Riverton, and the moment Philip delivered him home from the station, Sophie Bower sent him immediately to bed. When Captain Bower called for his son's presence in the field, Sophie dismissed her husband's demands.

Two days' rest and regular trays of Ruby's tasty and nourishing food began to restore the boy's strength. When he ventured downstairs for supper, it didn't take Nicholas long to catch up on the news from the insular world of Riverton. He expected Philip to demand verbal replays of the football season, and so was surprised when, instead, his brother greeted his recovery with an announcement.

"I'm applying to Washington and Lee!" said Philip. "Father said he'd always hoped one of us would go there!"

"Good for you," said Nicholas, punching his brother's arm in their customary act of approval. The thought came immediately, "Always hoped one of us."

As he took his seat at the dining room table, Nicholas wondered, "Why did Father never mention that possibility to me?" The aroma of pork chops quickly claimed his full attention and raised his spirits.

"Pork chops! I can't remember the last time I had pork chops! Little brother, you can pass me that platter! Too bad you're gonna be a Mink!! But, of course, not everyone has what it takes to be a Gamecock!"

"A general! We're the Generals!" shouted Philip, grinning as he tossed a dinner roll at his brother.

"Not a bad pass," grunted Nicholas as he reached up to grab the roll. "For a small college player!"

+ + +

January Wilson came to see Nicholas the morning after he returned from his first semester in Orangeburg.

"It's much better than I hoped!" said the black boy when Nicholas asked about the new Negro college. "I'm way ahead of most people in my class. Some of the teachers are amazing. I've never met a black man with a doctor's degree! It's encouraging just to hear them talk!"

"You're gonna be just like them!"

January's face grew serious as he looked intently at his friend. "You really think I could? It's what I always wanted to do!"

"Amor tussisque non celantur," Nicholas said. "Love, and a cough, are not concealed.' You've always loved learning. You are a teacher; it's obvious!"

"But what about you? I'm still wondering what you'll do with your life."

"So am I! All I know is farming. Father hasn't said what he wants to do with this place. And I don't know if I could handle bad weather and crop prices."

"'If you can look into the seeds of time and say which grain will grow and which will not, speak then to me.' MacBeth," said January. "You will know when the time comes."

"Now you're the prophet," said Nicholas. "I'll tell you if there are any developments!"

+ + +

The months of spring passed without new revelations for Nicholas. His schoolwork and baseball schedule absorbed him almost completely, leaving him little time to see Catherine beyond a brief greeting on campus. He was glad when she invited him to visit her family's home in North Georgia during the summer, and he promised to come if his father would excuse him from his duties on the farm. Nicholas broached the subject on his first day home from the university. His father's response went far beyond anything he expected.

"I suppose you should go," said the Captain as he drove his surrey to the cotton fields. "It doesn't hurt to be on good terms with the Governor's family. I expect we can do without you for a week. But remember! You're a farmer, not a damned politician!"

Nicholas smiled from his saddle and said, "Don't worry about that, Father! Philip's your politician. Me a farmer? I don't know if I have the stamina!"

Captain Bower glared up at his son. "Stamina? You can run touchdowns and hit homeruns in Columbia, and you can't grow a little cotton in your own back yard? Who the hell do you expect will run this place when I'm gone?"

Nicholas was stunned. He rode in silence as his mind struggled with the ramifications of his father's question.

Finally he said, "Is that your plan, Father? I didn't know."

"Of course it is!! Aren't you my eldest son? Haven't you done well in school and brought honor to the family? Yes, I mean to leave the farm to you!"

In all his life, Nicholas had received few compliments from his father, and never had he heard anything like this.

"Father…"

"You're afraid you don't have stamina! That's the most asinine thing I've ever heard! Next you'll be telling me you want to keep your hands clean and your boots polished and be a preacher or a teacher!"

"No, sir. I'm proud to work with you! I am! I guess I've seen the farm go through so many bad times, I don't know if I could do it."

"Well, if you doubt you could, then you can't! This business isn't for people who are quick to quit. You need to take hold of the thing! You make it go where you want! Like plowing with a mule! And when it looks like everything's getting away from you, you hold on and you don't let go!"

The words produced in Nicholas a torrent of instantaneous impressions. "Hold on!" "Let go!" He saw himself battered by horse's hoofs, convicted in church, betrayed by a girl, clinging to the edge of a cliff. Each time his struggle to hold on had been interrupted by an invitation to let go. The peace Nicholas remembered now crept over him again, and he looked away from his father and felt tears in his eyes.

"Well?" said Captain Bower. "You have anything to say about this?"

Peace retreated once more into memory. Nicholas brushed his face with the back of his hand. "I can do it, sir," he said, quietly at first. Then, "Father, I can be a farmer!"

"Good," said Captain Bower. "This is between you and me. Say nothing about it to your mother or your brother. Do you understand?"

Turning to meet his father's eyes, Nicholas replied, "Sir, I do."

When he rode home at midday to pick up the lunch basket for his father and Philip, Nicholas hurried up the porch stairs and clomped his way into the kitchen calling for Ruby. His mother met him at the kitchen door.

"Ruby's sick," she said. "She's had trouble with that goiter, you know, and it hurts her a lot. But her niece, April, has come to help us." Looking over his mother's shoulder, Nicholas saw a young black woman about his age holding the lunch basket.

"April is January's sister," said Sophie.

"Yes, Ma'am," nodded Nicholas. "I think we met when their house burned. How are you, April? How is your mother?"

"We are all well, thank you, sir," replied the black girl, looking steadily at Nicholas.

"You sound like your brother," said Nicholas. "None of you Wilson's talk like you're from around here."

"That's because we're not," said April. "Remember, I was raised in Philadelphia, too. Just don't expect me to quote Shakespeare. That's my brother's annoying habit!"

Nicholas watched a smile briefly touch the corners of the black girl's mouth, displaying even white teeth and sparkling dark eyes.

"April is a wonder in the kitchen," said Sophie, receiving the lunch basket from the girl and handing it to Nicholas. "Venus Adams has taught her well!"

"Do you sing as well as Ruby?" said Nicholas. He noticed that April's hair was ironed straight and combed smooth.

"Perhaps you'll find out," answered the girl, straightening her apron over her slender figure. Then she said, "Oh, Mr. Nicholas, January wanted me to ask you to meet him at the stalls after work today."

"Thanks, April. I'll look for him."

+ + +

"Have you heard about Conner Mayfield?" exclaimed January the moment he and Nicholas met outside the barn.

"Heard what?"

"About his new business! Conner's building a cotton gin!"

"What! When did this happen? Where is it?"

"He's bought property on the west end of town, past the old church. He's had a crew working six weeks and the building's half finished."

"How'd you find out about it? Weren't you in Orangeburg 'til yesterday?"

"Orangeburg's not as far as Columbia! Word gets around out here in the country," smiled January. "What I've heard is Conner means to get his gin running before first picking, and people say he's bragging that he'll pay better than Mr. Singleton."

"How in the world can Conner Mayfield afford to go into business?"

"Think a minute! It's obvious!"

"You mean the liquor trade?"

"What else could it be? Conner's made enough illegal money to start a legitimate business You always told me he was smart!"

Nicholas shook his head in dismay. "I'll tell you what! No Bower cotton is going to Conner's gin!"

"Better not make any promises," said January. "You might not have any choice if Conner puts Mr. Singleton out of business!"

"Only thing we need to worry about right now is having enough of a crop to carry to anybody's gin! Whatever happens, we'll hold on! 'Saepe ne utile quidem est scire quid futurum sit.' 'Often it is not advantageous to know what will be.'"

"Hold on? You sound like somebody we both know," said January. "Yah Suh, Cap'n Nicholas!"

Nicholas drove the surrey to church on Sunday, with his mother and Philip singing their weekly prelude.

"I just don't know what I'm going to do next fall when both you boys have gone off to school," said Sophie Bower. "I can drive the surrey to church well enough, but it just won't be the same without you!"

"Tell you what!" said Philip. "You persuade Father to buy us a car, and he'll be so proud to drive you places, he might even take you to church!"

"If we had a car on this farm, you'd stay home from college so you could drive it!" said Nicholas.

"I'll have a car before you!" said Philip, and the brothers spent the rest of the trip arguing about their favorite automobiles.

Nicholas felt apprehensive as he followed his mother into church and knelt in the family pew. His unexplained experience in the Columbia church still disturbed him, and he feared some new challenge from the liturgy. But the familiar words brought neither comfort nor confrontation. Nicholas could not keep his eyes from returning to the place where Sally Hemphill's mother sat alone through the service. He wondered again about Sally, feeling helpless as his early memories of her collided with his current observations of her changed behavior. After the service, Nicholas took the reins and started the church horse on the road to town.

"Where are you going?" his mother asked. "April will have lunch for us in an hour!"

"I just want to look at Conner Mayfield's gin."

"That's Conner's gin?" said his mother. "I heard someone was building one, but nobody told me it was that terrible man!"

"Mother, it's all over town," said Philip. "I heard it from Able Simmons."

"And January told me," said Nicholas.

As they rode, the Bower family discussed the ramifications of a new cotton gin in Riverton, and before long, they reached the construction site.

"It's big!" observed Philip. "Twice the size of Mr. Singleton's!"

"There's a lot of money in that building," said Nicholas. "Conner's taking a big risk. A bad crop this year would probably put him under."

As Nicholas reined the church horse to a stop in front of the building, the sound of hammering came from behind the new board walls, along with the shout of a familiar voice.

"Not there, you idiot! The rafters are on sixteen-inch centers, not two feet! Pull the damn things out and do it over!"

The Bower family watched as Conner Mayfield stormed through the unfinished door opening and stalked down a planked ramp. He stopped abruptly when he noticed his visitors, and Nicholas felt the dull heat of old anger when Conner slowly smiled.

"So, Farmer Claus wants to be first in line at the Mayfield gin!"

"Don't flatter yourself, Conner! Bower cotton's going to Mr. Singleton, like always."

"If you have any cotton to gin," warned the new businessman. Nicholas noticed that Conner wore a high collared shirt, a necktie, and vest with his frock coat, and his boots were polished. Several sweating, black carpenters peaked through the open door behind him.

"We'll have the cotton," Nicholas said. "The question is, will you have the liquor to pay for this place?"

"What does a big football hero know about liquor?"

"Sheriff Harvey is watching you, Conner!"

"Is he, now? Well, you can tell the sheriff we're watching him!

Go on over there and tell him right now! And until you come here with cotton to sell and a better attitude, get the hell off my property!"

Sophie Bower drew herself upright on the surrey seat. "You should be ashamed, Mr. Mayfield, to work those men on the Sabbath!"

"Sorry to disappoint you, sweetheart, but it doesn't bother me at all! Tell your boys to mind their manners, or they'll be sorry!"

Nicholas leapt angrily from the surrey as Conner Mayfield stalked across the rutted gin yard, quickly mounted the tall horse, Freedom, and with a sarcastic smile, galloped away.

When his father confirmed that the Bowers would not being doing business with Conner Mayfield, Nicholas nodded in satisfaction. As the weeks of summer past, he resumed his role on the farm with new interest, for the first time seeing the familiar routine from the perspective of a future manager. He learned to cultivate with the tractor, and often discussed with his father articles he'd read in farm journals. The captain had his own opinions.

"So you think it won't be long before people pick cotton with a machine? Not in my lifetime! No machine can pick as close as a darky's fingers!"

"That's what everybody thought 200 years ago before Eli Whitney's cotton gin!" said Philip. "Somebody already patented a cotton harvester fifty years ago!"

"Not in my lifetime!" repeated the captain. "We'll be picking here next week, so don't go giving our hands any ideas about some damned machine."

When Captain Bower pronounced the crop ready, Nicholas and Philip labored with the farm's regular workers and with a dozen hired hands. The captain refused to employ children younger than eight years old, but he always paid an older black woman to look after the young children and babies whose mothers were busy in the field. The growing season had been enhanced by unusually favorable weather, and the cotton bolls produced an unprecedented abundance of fiber. Captain Bower and his sons accompanied the first wagonload of cotton from their farm to Singleton's gin in Riverton.

"Are we your first customers, Horace? Anybody else begun to pick?" Captain Bower said to the owner of the gin.

"Not just the first, Captain Bower. So far, you're the only ones to show up," said Mr. Singleton. "Looks like my new competitor's paying a few cents more per pound. I expect he'll have a line before long. I just hope some will come over here so as not to waste time. I certainly do appreciate your business, gentlemen!"

Captain Bower grumbled and almost rescinded his earlier promise when Nicholas asked for time off to visit Catherine Heyward in Georgia.

"The best crop we've had in ten years, and you want to take a vacation! I wonder if I've made the right plans for you!"

Nicholas pacified his father by hiring, with his own money, an additional worker to pick cotton on his behalf. The train trip to Clarkesville relaxed him after weeks of backbreaking labor, and he thoroughly enjoyed his days with Catherine and her family. He found the Governor to be a man of refined manners, humble wisdom, and gentle humor, with a tranquil temperament very different from his father's volatile nature. As much as he enjoyed hiking the countryside with Catherine, he appreciated even more the opportunity to talk about life and farming and government with her father, who dignified Nicholas simply by listening attentively and responding patiently to a young man's unsupported opinions.

Nicholas learned, with considerable relief, that Sally Hemphill would not be returning to Clarkesville that summer. He went to church with Catherine on the last full day of his visit, commenting to her that the simple wooden building of Grace Church reminded him of St. Matthias' Church at home. He didn't tell her that thoughts of Sally visited him several times during the service.

The end of his holiday coincided with the end of the first picking, and therefore, the end of summer. Nicholas teased his brother when Sophie Bower made Philip the target of her relentless pre-college preparations.

"Don't let her pack more than you can carry," warned Nicholas. "I don't know how it'll be in Lexington, but when I arrived in Columbia, all the taxis were taken before I could get all my stuff together."

Nicholas said goodbye to January when the black boy drove him to the train station.

"It's been a good summer," Nicholas said. "We had some good talks. The crop was great and the price wasn't bad. I only had one run-in with Conner. I spent some time with Catherine. It's been a good summer. And you can tell April her fried chicken is the best!"

"I'll tell her. She's always talking about your jokes, saying 'Mr. Claus this' or 'Mr. Claus that.'"

"Why don't you write me sooner this year? I'll try to do better, as soon as I find out about my classes and how football practice goes."

January nodded and smiled. "'Now go we in content to liberty, and not to banishment.' As you like it, good friend! What about one of your words of wisdom? And a translation?"

Nicholas thought a moment, then recited, "Ora et labora. Pray and labor. Advice from St. Benedict, and from me!"

# CHAPTER THIRTEEN

**Winter 1906**

ON THE DAY AFTER CHRISTMAS, 1906, Nicholas woke up early. His bedroom in the Bower farmhouse faced east, and the rising sun silhouetted a massive pecan tree that stretched its limbs toward his window. Nicholas remembered the times when, not many years ago, he and Philip had quietly raised the window sash at night and used the pecan tree as a secret escape route. Studying the leafless branches from the comfort of his pillow, he realized that the distance from the window to the tree seemed shorter now than when he'd last taken that route.

"Tree's grown," he thought. "But now that's it's easy to climb down, I don't need to go that way anymore."

He turned over and lay still for a long time, allowing himself to relive some of his own growing experiences. His years at the University of South Carolina had taught him both the value of self-discipline and the hazards of a driven life. The Dean of Students had advised Nicholas that, barring any unforeseen developments, he would be valedictorian of his graduating class, and the Athletic Director reminded him that, for the third successive year, he would almost certainly be named Most Valuable Athlete in football and baseball.

Nicholas had received their congratulatory comments with little satisfaction. Like an alcoholic downing his tenth drink of the evening, he no longer derived much pleasure from a new award. Captain Bower listened to the frequent reports of his son's successes with apparent indifference, and Nicholas had stopped looking for hints of his father's approval. Study and sports so thoroughly consumed his time at school that Nicholas made few friends, even though everybody on campus knew his name. Since the first summer visit to North Georgia, he had continued to see Catherine Heyward, but even as their friendship grew, and she patiently hoped for a deeper relationship, Nicholas kept her on the fringe of his life. Once, on a hike in the Georgia mountains, he had kissed her, and they had talked about their plans beyond college, but when school resumed, Nicholas withdrew into the impenetrable worlds of the library and the practice field. He saw Sally Hemphill on campus and occasionally had a class with her, but their conversations were brief and, to him, upsetting. None of Sally's causes made sense to Nicholas, but several times he surprised himself by defending her from another student's criticism. With each passing year, his visits to Riverton took on a predicable rhythm: home for the summer to help with the crop, and home for Christmas to eat and hunt.

The sound of activity downstairs in the kitchen ended Nicholas' morning reverie, and he bathed and dressed for the day with uncharacteristic enthusiasm. First, there would be April's breakfast, not prepared the way Ruby had always done it, but spiced with a quick-witted dialogue that Nicholas loved. Ruby had been his mother's friend. April was his. Nicholas pulled on his hunting boots. After breakfast he would be setting out with his father and brother on what would be his first quail hunt of the season. Bounding down the stairs, Nicholas kissed his mother good morning and pushed open the door into the kitchen.

"Oh, April," he said, "That platter of pancakes on the table.

They look like footballs! Why don't you make them round?"

"Don't complain!" said the girl without a second's hesitation. "I made them that way for you because most of the time you're not 'round, either!"

Nicholas withdrew from the kitchen shaking his head. "That girl is so quick!" he said to his mother.

"She's very bright and a delight to work with," said Sophie. "But Son…" Mrs. Bower paused, and then glancing over her shoulder, she said in a low voice, "Don't let your father hear you joking with April. I'm afraid he would not approve!"

Captain Bower came to the table in a buoyant mood. "Perfect day!" he boomed. "A little frost. Moist ground. No wind. The dogs'll find plenty of birds! You boys ready?"

Nicholas and Philip assured their father that they were prepared to leave when he did, and after breakfast, they gathered guns and shell vests, hurried across the porch, and met January Wilson waiting in the farm wagon.

"Mornin', Cap'n!" said the black boy. "Yo' dogs is plenty 'cited t'day!" Even though January had been a student at the Negro college for three years, he continued to speak dialect to his employer, and Captain Bower never noticed the contradiction. With Captain Bower and January leading the way in the wagon, and the Bower boys riding behind, the hunting party set out for a field where the remnants of harvested feed corn lay scattered between the rows. At the junction of the wagon track with the public road, they saw a single horse and rider plodding slowly in their direction.

Sheriff Harvey saluted the captain and greeted the Bower boys. Noticing their guns and dogs, the Sheriff said, "Looks like a perfect day for partridges, Captain!"

"Expect so," the captain replied. "What brings you to these parts so early in the morning? Hope it's not trouble!"

"Well, not trouble for anybody else but me, at least for now. Did you know I'm being opposed in the next election?"

"Hadn't heard that. Can't imagine why anybody would want to run against you. Who's your opponent?"

"Taylor Mayfield," the lawman answered. "I expect you know him."

"We all know him!" said Nicholas, his eyes blazing. "He's one of the Mayfield clan that had a still on our land! Isn't he under investigation? How can he run for office?"

"He can run because I can't find enough against him or any of his family to bring charges. And truth be known, the Mayfields have been spreading plenty of money all over the county. They've told people it's profit from their gin, but it's certainly bootlegging money. I just need to prove it."

"It'll take more money than those carpetbaggers have to buy votes in this county," said Philip. "You've done a great job, and nobody likes the Mayfields!"

"I appreciate that," said the Sheriff. "And I'd be glad for your support when you talk to your neighbors. And for your vote come the election. I'll be visiting around a lot until then."

The Bower men enjoyed a memorable quail hunt, with impressive work from the dogs and better-than-usual shooting from each of the hunters. Using his ancient, double-barreled fowling piece, Captain Bower downed most of the birds he shot at, and twice refused offers from Nicholas to try his graduation gun, the new, hammerless Parker.

"If I shoot any better, there'll be no birds left on our place!" said the captain. "But you boys could use some practice!"

When they returned to the farm, Nicholas trudged wearily upstairs to bathe and change his clothes, and on entering his room, he found a garment bag from a Sumter clothing store lying across his bed. It contained a black tailcoat, white tie and vest, and formal black trousers.

"Mother," Nicholas yelled in the direction of the stairs. "What's the fancy outfit doing in my room?" He heard his mother's shriek and her rapid footsteps in the hall. Her emphatic words reached him before she did.

"Son, Son," she said, "Please tell me you haven't forgotten Catherine's debutante ball in Columbia!"

Nicholas grimaced and silently swore. "When is it?" he mumbled.

"You have forgotten! It's this Saturday! I don't understand how can you keep up with all your school responsibilities and be so indifferent to your friends!"

"Mother, I'm sorry! It's been a hectic semester, and I just forgot! I don't remember when she asked me, but it was probably months ago."

"It was Thanksgiving," said his mother.

"Well, I'll go," said Nicholas.

"You certainly will! And first thing tomorrow, you will go to Sumter and buy a formal shirt that fits you. Honestly!" said Sophie as she turned and stormed downstairs.

Nicholas made it his business to stay out of the house for the rest of the afternoon. He went looking for January, but couldn't find him. The prospect of attending a formal dance with the Governor's daughter and scores of socially prominent and politically influential people weighed heavily upon his spirits. It wasn't a major crisis, he decided, just something he would have to endure. As he rode slowly across the farm, Nicholas realized that his life for many months had been mercifully clear of dramatic events. It occurred to him that with the passage of one routine semester after another, he had not been troubled again by the soundless invitation to let go. He resolved to examine each memory of stress and pain, all the times when he'd felt desperate and sensed the welcoming voice, to see if he could discover any common denominators. Instantly he remembered the profound feeling of peace that always followed the call to surrender, and he knew that he missed it. Routine living avoids costly choices, he decided, and the resulting comfort invites a feeling of self-suffi-ciency. "But it's not peace," Nicholas reminded himself.

Early the next morning, Nicholas saddled Caesar and rode to Sumter. He followed the public road except where there were short-cuts across neighboring farms, and he arrived at the clothing store not long after it opened. The clerk had just selected a formal shirt for Nicholas to try when Sally Hemphill and her mother entered the store. Nicholas looked twice to be sure he recognized the girl, be-cause she was dressed like the friend he'd once known in Riverton and not like the campus activist she'd become in Columbia.

"How do you do, Mr. Bower?" said Mrs. Hemphill stiffly.

"Very well, thank you," said Nicholas, still looking at Sally. Then the girl smiled, and layers of distance vanished from between them.

"Hi, Claus!" she said. "Wouldn't you know! We live a block apart in Columbia, but we have to go to Sumter to see each other!"

"I hope you're well," replied Nicholas, not really sure how the conversation would unfold.

"I beg your pardon, Nicholas," said Mrs. Hemphill. "But Sally has a fitting for a ball gown, and we've arrived just a bit late." Nicholas struggled to comprehend the information.

"When's the ball?" he asked.

"This Saturday," called Sally as she followed her mother toward the back of the store. "In Columbia." She stopped and turned to-ward Nicholas. " I'm not a debutante," she announced defensively. "I'm going as a guest of Conner Mayfield."

Nicholas paid for the formal shirt and rode back to Riverton in shock. Nothing was right about what had just happened! Sally appear-ing in a dress, hat, and gloves and shopping for a ball gown. She had campaigned against just such symbols of traditional femininity! And Sally in the company of Conner Mayfield! She had gone to school with Conner before he dropped out, and she certainly knew of his recent reputation. It was more than Nicholas could comprehend.

"So much for my uneventful life!" he thought as he watered Caesar and led him to the barn. Sophie Bower noticed her son's depressed condition when he handed her the formal shirt and hurried upstairs without a word. She breathed a short prayer, and followed him.

"Are you alright, Claus?" she asked.

Ordinarily, Nicholas would have brushed off his mother's concern and buried his distress under a cheerful response, but this time he simply said, "No, Ma'am." Sophie sat on his bed and listened while Nicholas described the bizarre encounter with Sally.

"I'm glad she's dressing like a regular girl, but going out with Conner?! How could she do that? Why would she?"

"I don't know. But perhaps she's grown tired of the causes you've told me about. Every girl thinks sooner or later about marriage, especially if her mother is pushing her in that direction."

"But Conner Mayfield! She could go out with the best men at the university if she wanted to!"

"I expect Sally's mother has told her that Conner has become a rather prosperous business man in Riverton. And I hear he has high-level contacts in Columbia, as well. A mother wants her daughter to have a secure future."

"I don't know if I can be at that ball and see her with him," said Nicholas.

"It won't be easy, but I know you will do the right thing. You'll give Catherine a wonderful evening and make your father and me very proud."

Nicholas didn't sleep much that night. The next day he told January about his dilemma, and the black boy just whistled.

"Some women are too easy to fool," said January. "But Sally's smart. She won't have to spend much time with Conner before she realizes what she's gotten herself into."

"I hope you're right," said Nicholas. "I can't tell you how much

I dread this weekend!"

"Just give yourself a little Latin encouragement! You can do it!"

Nicholas concentrated for a moment, then smiled and said, "Stultum est timere quod vitare non potes." "It is foolish to fear that which you cannot avoid."

"That's more like it," said January.

+ + +

The black boy's prophetic utterance about Sally's swift awakening came true before the Columbia Ball was halfway over. Nicholas had taken the morning train to the capitol city and changed into his formal attire at the university. He arranged for a motored taxi to deliver him first to the Governor's mansion and then to transport him and Catherine to the hotel ballroom. As she descended the stairs of the stately residence in a white ball gown and elbow length gloves, her dark hair pinned high, Catherine seemed to Nicholas completely unlike the North Georgia friend who preferred country clothes and hiking boots. But her smile and her warm greeting reassured him. Nicholas exchanged pleasantries with the Governor and Mrs. Heyward, who were themselves preparing to leave for the ball, and he promised the Governor that Catherine would be free for the traditional father/daughter dance.

In the taxi, Nicholas and Catherine immediately relaxed and both admitted that they found it very difficult to feel comfortable in formal attire. Nicholas became nervous again as they entered the elegant ballroom and searched for their dinner table seats. Everyone else seemed perfectly at home in the refined atmosphere of crystal, candlelight, and orchestral music. Nicholas suppressed a moment of panic when the orchestra struck up a new tune and he suddenly remembered that what people called a "ball" was, in fact a dance. Catherine would expect him to dance with her, and the daily practice sessions Sophie Bower had required for the last few days now seemed totally inadequate preparation for the task.

Nicholas was so anxious about the prospect of dancing that he tasted very little of the elegant seven-course dinner that began the ball. He was working hard to make conversation with Catherine and the other diners at his table when he heard Conner Mayfield's coarse laugh over the sound of the orchestra. Turning quickly, he located Conner, and in the next second, Sally, seated several tables away. Sally saw Nicholas recognize her, and her anguished expression told him that she had seen him first and had been trying to catch his attention.

"Is that Sally Hemphill?" said Catherine, looking past Nicholas. "That's a surprise! Did you know she was coming?" she asked, turning expectant eyes his way.

Nicholas sipped from his water glass and nodded.

"I suppose she's a guest," said Catherine looking again toward Sally's table. "And, Lord help us! She's with Conner Mayfield!"

Nicholas took a deep breath and said, "I knew about that, too. I saw Sally in Sumter, and she told me he had invited her."

"But what's he doing here?"

Nicholas shrugged. "I don't know. Sally's mother must think Conner's a good catch. That's what my mother said."

"That's crazy! I know Conner's made influential friends in Columbia, but everybody knows he's a small town bootlegger!"

"Not everybody. And I hope for Sally's sake that she realizes what a mistake she's making."

At the conclusion of the dinner, Catherine and the other debutants excused themselves to prepare for their formal introduction and the grand march with their fathers. Nicholas found a place near the ballroom door and stood there watching the crowd and listening to fragments of conversation. He felt a sudden tug at his sleeve and turned to see Sally Hemphill standing behind him, her eyes wide and urgent.

"Come on," she whispered, "I have to tell you something."

Nicholas glanced back at the ballroom and saw the debutants

gathering to make their entrance. "Can I see this first?" he whispered back. "I came with Catherine, and I want to…"

"No!" said Sally. "I'm getting out of here and you have to listen now!" Nicholas looked once more at the ballroom as the orchestra played a fanfare, then he ducked around a potted palm tree and followed Sally out into the portico.

She led him behind one of the parked automobiles, glanced around her, and said, "Conner Mayfield is setting a trap for Sheriff Harvey! You have to tell him before it's too late!"

"Wait a minute! What kind of trap?"

"Conner's uncle is running against the Sheriff in the next election," said Sally, trying hard to calm herself and speak slowly.

"Yes," said Nicholas, "but nobody in Riverton will vote for any of the Mayfields."

"They will if Sheriff Harvey is scandalized!"

"Scandalized? How?"

"Listen! I just heard one of Conner's political friends tell him that they had it all set up. Some woman is going to say that the sheriff had made advances toward her!"

"Nobody would believe that! Caleb Harvey's been married to Sara for at least forty years!"

"I don't have time to argue with you," Sally replied. "My mother insisted on me coming with Conner, but I've never been able to stand him, and after what I heard tonight, I'm not about to let him take me back to my hotel! Claus, please tell Mr. Harvey!"

Behind him, Nicholas heard the voice of the Master of Ceremonies. "Miss Catherine Ann Heyward, escorted by her father, the Honorable Duncan Clinch Heyward."

"Yes, of course!" he whispered. "But I've gotta go in now! Will you be alright?"

"I can take care of myself," said Sally as she drew her wrap around her and hurried off into the night.

Nicholas made his way to the ballroom in time to finish the

dance Catherine had begun with her father. "Your face is all flushed," she said. "Are you feeling well?"

"I'm fine," said Nicholas. As he struggled to remember the waltz, he looked over Catherine's shoulder to locate Conner Mayfield. The tall, blond boy stood laughing with a group of distinguished looking gentlemen. "He doesn't even know his date has left him!" thought Nicholas. "He'll go crazy when he finds out that Sally's gone!"

"You're doing very well," said Catherine, nimbly avoiding her partner's feet.

"Fancy footwork is a quarterback's specialty!" laughed Nicholas, as he tried to release Sally Hemphill from his thoughts.

+ + +

Sophie Bower drove the surrey to meet Nicholas at the Sumter station on Sunday afternoon. "I couldn't wait to hear about the ball!" she said as Nicholas slid his suitcase under the seat.

"It was alright," shrugged her weary son.

"That answer will not do, Claus, and you know it! Tell me about Catherine! What did she wear? Did you have a good visit with the Governor? What about the dinner? How was your dancing? We have a long ride ahead of us, and I expect a full report!"

"Yes, Ma'am," sighed Nicholas. "I'll try to talk about all that, but, please, may I drive by Sheriff Harvey's house on the way home?"

"You need to see the sheriff? Why in the world?"

"Just let me find him, and you'll know why I need to talk to him." Sophie Bower sensed that whatever was troubling Nicholas didn't need to be repeated twice, so she rode in silence, praying for God's resolution of her son's dilemma. Nicholas hitched the surrey horse in front of Sheriff Harvey's house and hurried up on the porch. To his relief, the sheriff himself answered the door.

"Sir," said Nicholas, "I have something important to tell you, and I'd like my mother to hear, if you don't mind."

"As you wish, son," said the sheriff. When they stood by the surrey, Nicholas hurriedly described the plot that Sally Hemphill had reported to him. The lawman's eyes revealed a range of reactions as he listened to what Nicholas was saying.

"You say you heard this from the Hemphill girl?" Sheriff Harvey asked. "Isn't she the one who's gone a little crazy over at the university?"

"Yes, sir. But she's never been one to lie, and I know she has no use for any of the Mayfield's, especially Conner."

"Well, I thank you for telling me about this, Son. I don't exactly know what I should do about it, but at least I can warn Sara that somebody might invent some dirt about me before this election is over." Sheriff Harvey watched from the porch as Nicholas and his mother drove away.

"What a horrible thing to do to that man," said Sophie.

"It's incredible," agreed Nicholas. "But what worries me now is what Conner might do to Sally for leaving him at the ball!"

# CHAPTER FOURTEEN

**Winter 1906**

WHEN NICHOLAS RETURNED to the university, he went look-ing for Sally, but found Catherine first. "I want to thank you again for a marvelous evening," said Nicholas as he walked with Catherine to the refectory. "Your dress was the prettiest one at the ball, and you were so forgiving about my dancing."

"And you are such a storyteller," said the girl. "I didn't mention it during the ball, but some of the girls told me that Sally Hemphill had gotten sick and left early. Did you know that?"

Nicholas squirmed and admitted that he had heard the same story.

"Probably got sick of Conner," said Catherine, looking hard at Nicholas.

"Who wouldn't," Nicholas quickly agreed. "But it makes no dif-ference to me."

Catherine took his arm as they stood in line and waited for their supper to be served. Nicholas ate hurriedly, giving only partial atten-tion to Catherine's commentary about the ball while he tried to de-cide where he might find Sally.

After supper, Nicholas excused himself and made his way across the darkened campus to a small café where university students often gathered. "Anybody seen Sally Hemphill?" he said as faces looked up from a nearby table.

"Hasn't been in here since the Christmas break," replied a voice. "Somebody said she stayed home."

The report did not come as good news to Nicholas. Sally staying in Riverton would make it easier for Conner to find her and take his revenge. "But she would know that," Nicholas assured himself. "She must have gone someplace else." He wrote to his mother, asking her to look into Sally's whereabouts, and then, having done all he could think of to help his former friend, Nicholas immersed himself in the demands of his final college semester.

Shortly before Easter, he received a summons from the Dean of Students, and at the appointed time, he anxiously appeared in the administration building.

'I have a proposal for you, Mr. Bower," said the Dean. "To come right to the point, and the president agrees with me, we want you to apply for a Rhodes Scholarship. You know, of course, that it would mean rigorous competition, and if you are successful, some years of study in England at Oxford University. I expect no answer until you've had time to think about the idea and to discuss it with your parents."

Nicholas felt his face burn. The most troubling challenges and the most appealing benefits of the proposal began to tumble through his mind. "I would miss my family. And Catherine. And Sally," he admitted to himself. "The work would be harder than anything I've experienced here. I'd be a week at sea!"

"But what an adventure!" whispered his imagination. "And I wouldn't have to pick cotton!" He reveled in that thought until a much greater prospect overwhelmed him.

"I'd make Father proud!" Nicholas dreamed. In the same moment, he felt tears begin to dampen the corners of his eyes. The Dean of Students cleared his throat.

"Sir," Nicholas said, trying to regain his composure, "Your suggestion honors me more than I can say. I appreciate your confidence in me, and I will most assuredly think about it and discuss it with my parents."

"Excellent," smiled the Dean. "You will not have to decide until fall, which is when the Rhodes Committee begins interviewing candidates. Good day to you, Mr. Bower, and congratulations!"

+ + +

When Nicholas returned to Riverton for the Easter holiday, he asked his mother about Sally even before mentioning the potential Rhodes Scholarship.

"Nobody's seen her," Sophie Bower said. "Harriet Hemphill is always in church, but Sally's never with her. People tell me that Conner is around. He wears expensive suits these days, and he's helping his uncle campaign against Sheriff Harvey."

"How does he do that?" said Nicholas. "Does he ride around handing out money?"

"Nobody will admit taking any, of course, but people have told me that Conner is making accusations about the sheriff's suitability for office."

"Mother, they're going to set him up, just like Sally said! When is the election?"

"It's the first week of June. I just don't know what any of us can do to help him, except to challenge the rumors the Mayfield's are spreading."

Feeling helpless and angry, Nicholas rode out to January Wilson's house and was delighted to find his friend home for the holiday.

"Let's take a walk," Nicholas said. Sensing his friend's urgency, the black boy quickly joined him.

"I can't find Sally," said Nicholas. "Nobody's seen her in Columbia since Christmas, and Mother tells me she's not in Riverton, either."

"It's alright, Claus," said January, grasping his friend's shoulder.

"I promised Sally I wouldn't tell anybody, but I can tell you."

Nicholas stopped short. "What's happened?"

"Sally's in Charleston. She was in Riverton the day after the ball and came looking for me. She had a suitcase packed, and she asked me to take her to the train."

"Where's she staying?" said Nicholas, already enjoying a feeling of relief.

"She has an aunt there. I don't know her name. But Sally seemed pretty certain that the lady would put her up for a while and maybe find her a job."

"I wish I knew how to get in touch with her," said Nicholas.

"And I wish I could figure you out," said January, shaking his head. "You have these summertime romances with Catherine. Then you worry yourself sick over Sally!"

"It's not so hard. I've known Sally all my life! Catherine's only been around for a few years. Why can't I call Catherine my girl and still be concerned for my friend?"

January smiled at Nicholas. "'But love is blind and lovers cannot see the pretty follies that they themselves commit.' Merchant of Venice. Sally's all right, Claus. Just be glad for that."

Captain Bower listened closely as his son described the Dean's suggestion about the Rhodes Scholarship application. "Well," he said when Nicholas was finished, "That reflects great credit upon you, and it pleases me very much. I expect you to accept the proposal and compete for the scholarship."

"Thank you, sir," said Nicholas, feeling a troublesome mixture of delight and dread. "I'll do my best."

Sophie Bower hugged her son. "If you are chosen, when will you go?"

"Not if," said her husband. "When he is chosen!"

"Not until Christmas. They do the interviews in the fall. If they pick me, I can begin at mid term."

"You will begin at mid term," said the captain.

"My goodness! What do people wear at Oxford in the winter?" said Sophie, already anticipating the logistics of international study.

"I'll find out, Mother, if I am to go."

+ + +

Nicholas graduated first in his class in the spring of 1907. He worked hard on his valedictory address, and no one was surprised when he began with a quotation from the Roman author, Horace.

"Est modus in rebus, sunt certi denique fines, quos ultra citraque nequit consistere rectum. There is a middle ground in all things," translated Nicholas. "In short, there are fixed limits, beyond which on either side truth and right cannot be found."

Nicholas understood the words and recognized their timeless validity, but even as he delivered the speech, he felt convicted. "Why can't I find a happy medium?" he asked himself. "Why do I push myself and never feel satisfied?"

Captain Bower had consented to accompany his wife to the commencement exercises in Columbia, and after offering token applause for the speech, he sat stoically as his son received one honor after another.

"Nicholas Alexander Bower," said the president of the university. "Bachelor of Arts in Literature. Summa cum laude. Rhodes Scholar Nominee. President of the Euphradian Literary Society. Editor of *The Garnet and Black*. President of the Senior Class. Chosen by the student body as Best All-Round College Man, Best Student, Best All-Round Athlete, Most Influential Man, Best Football Player." [iii]

Catherine had stayed in Columbia for the graduation, and at Sophie Bower's invitation, had joined Nicholas and his parents for lunch after the ceremony.

"I'm very proud of you," she said as they took a last walk around the central campus. "You're certain to be accepted at Oxford, and when you go, I don't know what I will do with myself!"

Nicholas put his arm around her. "You have your senior year

coming up, and if you have any spare time, you can write me letters. They deliver to England, you know!"

They took a taxi to the governor's mansion, and in the garden, Nicholas embraced her and, with a kiss, promised to visit in North Georgia before the end of summer.

+ + +

When Nicholas and his parents arrived at the railroad station in Sumter, Philip was waiting for them with the surrey. The boy handed Captain Bower a newspaper. "You need to see this, Father," he warned. Looking at the paper over his father's shoulder, Nicholas saw a front-page photograph of Sheriff Harvey printed next to a picture of a woman he'd never seen. The headline announced, "School Teacher Accuses County Sheriff."

Captain Bower handed the sheet to his wife. "Read it to us," he ordered.

Sophie read, "Miss Annabell Spann, newly arrived in Manchester as Mistress of the Community School, has charged Caleb Harvey, Sheriff of Clarendon County, with assault following the school's commencement exercises last Wednesday evening."

"They've done it!" swore Nicholas. "Who is this woman? How does anybody know she can be trusted?"

"It's just what Sally warned you about, and what we told poor Sheriff Harvey," said Sophie.

"Who'd the woman tell?" said Captain Bower.

"It says, 'Miss Spann reported the alleged assault to Mr. Taylor Mayfield, Sheriff Harvey's opponent in next week's election.'"

"People will see right through that!" said Philip. "It's such an obvious set-up!"

"Some people will," said Captain Bower, "but many will not. And with the election coming so soon, Caleb won't have a chance to get his defense in print. Her charges won't stick, but she's really hurt him politically."

As the Bower family rode through Riverton, they saw a crowd in front of the general store. Taylor Mayfield had positioned himself on the wooden steps and was delivering what was obviously an impassioned speech.

"You know how it is, my friends! You think you know somebody, and then one day you realize that he's been keeping secrets from you. Hasn't that ever happened to you? Of course it has! And we thought we knew Caleb Harvey all these years, didn't we? Seen him as our friend and protector! But he's been hiding something from us! Hiding his sins behind that shiny badge we've entrusted him with. But now we know what he was so good at hiding! We know because a brave young woman has had the courage to speak out and tell us about what this man has done. Should she be ashamed because of what's she's suffered? No! Caleb Harvey should be ashamed! And every God-fearing voter in Riverton should stand against his lust and brutality when they vote on Tuesday!"

"Stop the horse!" said Captain Bower. Gripping the back of the surrey seat, the captain pulled himself to his feet and shouted to the crowd. "Enough of those damned lies!" He paused while heads turned. Most in the crowd would not look at the captain's face. His voice boomed again. "Listen to me! Caleb Harvey has nothing to hide! Most of us have known him all our life, and he's done nothing but good to this community. But tell me this! Do you know his accuser? This brand new teacher who is living in a house on the Mayfield farm? Yes, it's true, even though most people haven't heard about that. She's living at the Mayfield's! Truth be known, how much do any of you know about what goes on over at the Mayfield place? Any other farms have a six-foot hog-wire fence? Taylor Mayfield's place does! Anybody ever seen the first hog come from that farm? Any of you been invited in there? One of the Mayfield boys is always at the gate with a shotgun. Now you tell me, people! Who has something to hide? It's not Caleb Harvey! You remember that on election day!"

Captain Bower snatched the reins from Philip and cracked the buggy whip over the startled horse. "Git!" he yelled.

On Tuesday afternoon, Nicholas and his father rode again into town and hitched the surrey near Mr. Singleton's gin. The sandy main street of Riverton was crowded with wagons and automobiles and tethered horses lined every hitching rail. In front of the post office, most of the white men of the community had gathered to await the local results of the election. Nicholas and his father pushed through the crowd and made their way into the small lobby.

"My oldest son means to be a voter," Captain Bower told the poll manager. "He's of age and can read and write."

While his father quickly marked his own ballot, Nicholas paid the poll tax and added his name to the list of qualified voters. He had just completed and deposited his own ballot when he heard voices from the crowd outside. Looking around, he saw January Wilson pull open the post office door.

"I'd like to register," said the black boy to the man behind the desk. The man looked confused, and glanced quickly at other men in the room.

"What's your name, boy?" called one of the men.

"January Wilson, sir."

"You got your birth certificate?"

"Yes, sir," said January, unfolding a paper from his shirt pocket and handing it to the man behind the desk.

"Pennsylvania!" said the poll manager. "Boy, in case you haven't noticed, this is South Carolina! You want to vote, go on back to Pennsylvania!"

"Sir, I've lived in South Carolina much longer than the required time. My mother is Venus Adams, and I live with her."

"Boy, you think I know your mother or where she lives?" said the official. Nicholas had been watching the interrogation and was surprised by a voice close to him.

"I know him," said Captain Bower, "and his mother. He's lived here for nearly four years and worked for me most of that time."

The poll manager looked again at the men gathered behind his table. He cleared his throat and said, "Well, since Captain Bower certifies your residence, I guess you just need to show us you can read!" He turned over a sheet of paper and thrust it toward January. "What's this say, boy?"

January quickly scanned the sheet and smiled. "It's the preamble to the United States Constitution, Sir. And it reads, 'We, the people of the United States, in order to form a more perfect union, establish justice, insure domestic tranquility, provide for the common defense, promote the general welfare, and secure the blessings of liberty …'"

"That's enough! That's enough!" said the sweating man. "You got money for the tax?"

"Yes, sir," said January, placing the coins on the table. The official looked again at his colleagues. One of them stepped forward and whispered something in his ear. The poll manager smiled.

"Well, gentlemen, I've just been reminded! This boy can't register on the day of the election! There's a two-week deadline!" In a heartbeat, Nicholas stepped forward.

"Excuse me, Sir," he said. "You just allowed me to register and vote on the same day. You can't take my ballot back because you don't know which one it is!"

His challenge led to a heated debate among the poll manager and his assistants. Finally, the official turned to Captain Bower. "Captain, rather than disqualify your son, we're going to allow this nigra to register. If the votes are close, I'm telling you, somebody's gonna contest this election!" Shoving the registration book toward January, he barked, "Sign your name in the book and take a ballot."

After January had voted, he walked from the polling place behind the captain and Nicholas. There were ugly comments from the crowd as January mounted his horse and the Bower men climbed into the surrey.

"Thank you, Father!" said Nicholas as they rode out of town.

"There aren't many coloreds I'd want to have the vote," said the captain. "You're too young to remember what it was like after the war, when the Radicals were in power and anybody breathing could cast a ballot. Most of the state legislature was made up of black men who could barely speak the English language. It was a disaster! The rules you faced today were the only way to restore sensible government to our state."

"More reason for me to say thank you for helping January," said Nicholas.

"I like that boy," nodded the captain. "He's a good worker." As the surrey rattled toward home, the captain turned and looked at Nicholas. "You did a good thing, too, challenging that business about the deadline. Courage is one of the highest virtues, and I'm proud of you."

"How brave am I now?" Nicholas asked himself as he looked away to conceal his tears.

The Bower family's newly installed telephone rang early the next morning. After three years in Columbia, Nicholas was familiar with the wall-mounted instrument, but the jingle of the telephone bell was still a novelty to the rest of the family. Sophie Bower hurried to answer the call.

"Yes, Mr. Huckabee? Say it again, please! You don't mean it! The captain will be fit to be tied!" When she hung up the earpiece, she turned to her sons at the breakfast table. "The call was from Mr. Huckabee at the general store. It's distressing news! Caleb Harvey has lost the election! Taylor Mayfield is the new sheriff!" April heard the report as she emerged from the kitchen with a plate of biscuits.

"That's a bad family," she said. "I didn't like Sheriff Harvey when he said that Conner had bought Freedom, but most of the time he's been fair to my family and other black folks. Black and white, we all need to watch out with a Mayfield as sheriff!"

As soon as Captain Bower came downstairs and heard the news, he waved off his breakfast and called for his sons to hitch up the surrey. The pace was fast and horse was sweating heavily when the captain reined it to a stop in Caleb Harvey's yard. Caleb and his wife came to the front porch, and listened as Captain Bower expressed his disgust with the voters of Clarendon County and his deep appreciation for the sheriff's years of faithful service. Nicholas and Philip added their own condolences. As they rode slowly home, Nicholas treasured some unfamiliar feelings toward his father. For all the captain's bluster and his ironclad ways, Nicholas had begun to discover that his father was a man of real substance and great integrity.

"I just need to remember this the next time he explodes at me," thought Nicholas.

He didn't have long to wait for another clash with Captain Bower. When he presented his request for a week's visit to the Heyward estate in Clarkesville, his father raged about his son's ingratitude and faulted Nicholas for his selfish desire to study in England. Nicholas was about to say, "You told me to enter the competition! If you wanted me home, you should have said so!" but he had the wisdom to keep his mouth shut and allow his father's verbal hurricane to blow itself out.

The trip to North Georgia found both Catherine and Nicholas in a melancholy frame of mind. They could hardly enjoy their time together because both were imagining what their lives might be like if Nicholas were chosen to study in England. On his last day at Lamont, Nicholas and Catherine sat together on the porch swing. "I can't do it!" the boy finally said! "I won't enter the competition! It makes me too sad to think of being gone for three years!"

"Nicholas," said Catherine. "You can do it, and you must! It's the best thing for your future!"

"It's our future I'm thinking about! The only way I'll try it is if you're sure it's right for us."

+ + +

The Rhodes Scholar Committee met in Columbia and for three days quizzed Nicholas and two other South Carolina applicants on the whole spectrum of their academic careers. The better part of one day involved discussions not about information but about the candidates' motivations and their personal characteristics. Nicholas felt completely drained when the examinations were over. He took a streetcar from the university to the governor's mansion and spent a quiet afternoon walking in the garden with Catherine and talking about the prospects for his scholarship.

"How did it go?" asked the governor when Nicholas stayed for supper that evening.

"I did my best, but there were topics I didn't know much about."

"I hope you noticed that they were looking not only for academic knowledge, but also for personal qualifications. I was happy to send them a letter on your behalf."

Nicholas looked up in surprise. "They asked you for a recommendation?"

"They did indeed," smiled Governor Heyward. "I told the committee that you have been a well behaved guest in my house and, I hope, an equally well behaved friend of my daughter's!"

While he waited for a reply from the Rhodes Scholarship Committee, Nicholas poured his energies into the family farm. Philip teased his brother when he departed for Washington and Lee. "Now you'll know what it's like to be the only Bower boy under Father's scrutiny!" he laughed.

The cotton crop had matured late that year, with the final picking delayed until the first of October. Captain Bower had gone to Singleton's gin with a wagon of cotton, and Nicholas was eating lunch with some of the farm hands when he saw a rider galloping toward the field. As the horse slowed, Nicholas suddenly stood up.

"It's Mother!" he said, his surprise quickly turning into appre-hension.

"Claus! Claus! The letter came! A letter from England!"

Nicholas held the horse's bridle as his mother slid to the ground and pulled an envelope from her apron pocket. The boy had a brief memory of his mother describing her early tomboy days and boast-ing of her riding skills, but now for the first time, he had seen a demonstration.

"Open it, for goodness sake," said Sophie Bower. The farm hands circled Nicholas and his mother with smiles as the boy care-fully opened the envelope. He read the first sentence, lowered the letter, and immediately hugged his mother off the ground.

"I've won!" shouted Nicholas. "They're awarding me the schol-arship!"

Some of the farm hands knew about the Bower boy's applica-tion, and all of them celebrated. "Praise de Lawd!" one shouted, and another followed with a song. "God is so good! Amen! Amen!"

"I've got to tell Father! He's gone to the gin. Mother, thank you for coming to bring this. I'll see you at supper!"

Nicholas ran to where Caesar was tied, hurriedly saddled the an-imal, and began a swift canter toward Riverton. He found his father waiting in line for his wagon's turn at the gin.

"Father, I've won it!" said Nicholas. His eager eyes searched his father's bearded face for some evidence of excitement. Captain Bower never looked at his son.

"When will you leave? I'll need to hire someone to work in your place."

The mules hitched to the wagon just ahead of the Bower load suddenly backed up, causing the captain's team to stumble in the traces.

"Move those damn animals!" roared the captain. "I don't have all day!" Nicholas sat on his horse, the life-changing letter still in his hand. Then, without another word, he turned Caesar's head and started toward home. As he rode despondently past the general store, someone called his name.

"Hello, Claus!" Sally Hemphill, dressed in a country dress and apron, stood on the steps with a broom in her hand. Nicholas looked twice to make sure it was true. He hadn't heard from Sally nor had anyone seen her since Christmas.

"What are you doing here?" asked Nicholas, swinging down from the saddle.

"Working. I expect you know I've been in Charleston, hiding out. But a week ago, I decided that I wasn't going to let Mr. Conner Mayfield run my life. So here I am, Mr. Huckabee's new assistant clerk and janitor!"

"Does Conner know you're here?"

"Probably. Word gets around fast in this town. But so what? I can take care of myself!"

"Everybody's missed you in Columbia," said Nicholas.

"Everybody? Even you? But you've probably been busy graduating! Congratulations!"

"I've been worried about you! I did what you asked and warned Sheriff Harvey."

"You mean 'Former Sheriff Harvey.' I know about the frame up and the election," said Sally. "Well, it's over anyway. And you're out of school! I suppose you're running the farm?"

"Helping. But I'm about to go to England to study."

"England! Imagine that! A boy from Riverton in merry old England! And I've been feeling good that they're letting me back at Carolina."

"You're going back?" said Nicholas.

"I am. And maybe Catherine Heyward and I can be best friends," said Sally with a mischievous grin.

# CHAPTER FIFTEEN

**Fall 1907**

SOPHIE BOWER WEPT INTO HER APRON when she learned that Philip would not be coming home for Thanksgiving. "It just won't be the same," she said. "All these years I've tried to help my boys grow up, and now that they are, I miss them constantly!"

"Yes, Ma'am," said April as she added sticks to the cook stove fire. "We feel the same at our house with January off at college. Mr. Philip is always so much fun, with his jokes and his ukulele and all. But Mr. Nicholas is here, at least until he goes to England. And he always has something clever to say, even if it's in Latin!"

In order to compensate for Philip's absence, Sophie invited Asa Turnbull and Agnes Abernathy to join the family for Thanksgiving dinner. When the day came, the talkative guests more than filled the conversational spaces that would have been taken by Philip.

"Captain Bower," said the minister, "I must confess that I've been very close to coveting your son's opportunity to study in England! All my life I've considered myself an Anglican, but the Lord has not provided a way for me to visit my spiritual roots."

"Never been inclined to go there, myself," said the captain. "Give me good South Carolina soil under my feet, not three thousand miles of ocean!"

"Well, of course you know how I feel about Nicholas' honor," said Miss Abernathy. "In all my years of teaching, there have been just a few students who won college scholarships, but until your son, none of my pupils has ever received international recognition!" Nicholas blushed and concentrated on his dinner.

When the Bower family and their guests had enjoyed all the delights of their traditional Thanksgiving meal, Sophie made an announcement.

"Everyone, we have a surprise today! In honor of Nicholas' upcoming stay in England, April has made us a special dessert. A plumb pudding!"

On cue, April came in smiling proudly and holding the flaming dish high in front of her. As she leaned in front of Nicholas, she stumbled slightly, and the pudding, lubricated by an overly generous libation of brandy, slid from the platter and spread flaming liquid across the tablecloth. In the confusion that followed, everyone at the table leapt to their feet, shouting instructions and sloshing glasses of water in Nicholas' direction. The fire lasted only a few seconds, burning no one and leaving the soggy dessert smoldering in front of the astonished diners. April burst into tears and rushed into the kitchen.

"It's all right, April!" called Sophie.

"Never liked that stuff anyway," said Captain Bower.

"Perhaps it's still edible," said Agnes Abernathy, reaching tentatively with her fork to loosen a bit of pudding.

"And, praise the Lord, not one of us was burned," added Mr. Turnbull.

"Mother, let me go see about April," said Nicholas, pushing back his chair.

April Wilson sat slumped over the kitchen table, weeping, her face buried in her hands. Nicholas put his hand on her back. "Please don't be upset, April," he said softly. "I really do appreciate what you made for me."

"But I ruined everything," sobbed April. "I wanted it to be special for you!"

"It was special! The thought of it was the best present of all," said Nicholas. Realizing he had never touched April, he quickly withdrew his hand from her shoulder. The girl turned and looked at him.

"I would do anything for you," she said, her face still wet with tears.

"And I would for you. Your family has always been part of my family, especially January."

"But not especially me," murmured April, turning away.

"Yes, now especially you," said Nicholas, not knowing what else to say. "Look, when everything's cleaned up and you're ready to go home, let me take you in the surrey."

"You would do that?" said the girl.

"Of course! It's a long walk, and you've already gone out of your way for me today."

In the surrey, on the way to the Adams's homestead, Nicholas managed to make April smile, and finally, to laugh about the plumb pudding disaster. "Did you see Father's face?" he grinned. "His jaw dropped so far I thought he was going to try to blow the fire out!"

"I didn't see anything but the flames on that table! I thought the whole house was going to catch fire."

"Just think! You might make a thousand plumb puddings but you'll never forget your first one! 'Aspirat primo Fortuna labori.' Fortune smiles upon our first effort."

"There you go!" said April. "You and January! Always quoting Latin or Shakespeare!"

"Who do you quote?" said Nicholas, as he reined in the surrey horse in front of April's house.

"You," said the girl as she jumped to the ground. Nicholas sat speechless as April ran toward her porch steps. The door opened, and as April ran in, Venus Adams came smiling out.

"That girl's sure in a hurry to come home, Mr. Nicholas! I hope your mother didn't put too much on her today!"

"April made quite a hit at the Bower house this afternoon! Ask her to tell you about it! We all appreciate your daughter very much, and I just wanted to give her a ride home."

"This certainly seems to be the day for giving people rides," said Venus. "January got a ride from Orangeburg this morning. They carried him as far as Riverton, and he was intending to walk here to the house, but look who came to his rescue!"

"Happy Thanksgiving," smiled Sally Hemphill, as she and January joined Venus Adams on the front porch. "Your boon companion here had to walk right past our house," the girl explained. "We had finished our dinner, and he was about to be late to his."

"Couldn't let that happen!" laughed January, hugging his mother. "When it's cooked by this lady! Sally got me here just in time."

"And just in time for me to eat my second feast of the day," said Sally.

"A horse, a horse! My kingdom for a horse!" quoted January. "Or if not a horse, then even Richard the Third would welcome Sally Hemphill with a wagon!"

As Nicholas visited with his friends and the Adams family, he noticed that April remained strangely quiet, refusing to talk about what happened with the plumb pudding.

+ + +

On the day after Thanksgiving, January Wilson arrived early at the Bower farm, and by the time Nicholas and his father had finished breakfast, he had hitched up the farm wagon and turned lose the captain's frantic bird dogs.

"It's gonna be a perfect day," said the captain as he climbed into the wagon. "Too bad Philip isn't here, but you can shoot his share of the birds." January drove the mules for the captain while Nicholas rode behind on Caesar.

"Make for the road by the branch," ordered Captain Bower. "We'll try that saw dust pile covey first." As they followed the two-rut road under moss draped oaks and down toward the thickets of the swamp, they buttoned their coats against the morning chill. The dogs ranged back and forth in front of them, with Flash investigating each clump of grass within a hundred feet, and Suzy scouting field edges a hundred yards away. The wagon had just emerged from a tunneled cane break when the hunters heard both dogs bark.

Suddenly, four men on horseback materialized out of the trees. Nicholas recognized two of them. "Well, well!" said Conner May-field. "If it isn't the big football hero!" He glanced at the wagon. "And the famous Captain Bower! And I'll be damned if it isn't the only nigger in the county who thinks he can vote!"

"Get off my land!" growled the captain, lifting his shotgun from his lap and opening it to load a pair of shells.

The man on the horse next to Conner pulled back his jacket to reveal a shiny badge.

"It might be your land, Captain, but this star gives me all the right I need to go where I please!"

"I believe you all know my Uncle Taylor," said Conner. "That's 'Sheriff Mayfield' to you!"

"This here's official business!" said the sheriff, turning to grin at Conner and their two companions. "We're out here looking for boot-leggers! Isn't that right boys?"

"Yes, indeed!" said Conner. "Dangerous business. Could be any-where. You citizens need to be very careful where you go hunting in these parts."

"I'm looking at the only bootleggers around here," said the cap-tain.

"Now, old man," warned the sheriff, "don't say nothing that would make me lock you up for interfering with a posse doing its duty!" Nicholas watched his father's face redden and his grip tighten on the shotgun.

"You heard my father," he said. "Finish your business and get off our land!"

"Mind your tongue, boy!" snapped the man with the badge. "We'll leave when we're ready!"

Nicholas heard a loud click as Captain Bower pulled back one of the hammers on his ancient shotgun. Conner Mayfield heard it, too.

"Come on, boys! We've wasted enough time with the dirt farmers. Let's go!" He spurred his horse to a gallop, the others followed, and the forest quickly swallowed the sound of hoof beats on the sandy road.

Captain Bower cursed as the Mayfield gang rode away. "Looking for bootleggers, hell! I wouldn't be surprised if they weren't here to rebuild the still Sheriff Harvey busted up!"

"Why would they do that?" said Nicholas. "It's common knowledge they make all the liquor they can sell on their own farm."

"Mus' be them mens lak the taste ob your branch water, Cap'n," said January. Still furious, Captain Bower turned sharply to face January on the wagon seat.

"Enough of that!" he shouted. "I'm tired of your deception! Don't you talk nigger to me! I can hear you when you're talking to my wife and my son!" January sat still, staring at his feet and saying nothing. "Boy, look at me when I'm talking to you!" bellowed the captain. Nicholas was stunned by the sudden turn of events and the unexpected challenge.

"Father…"

"It's alright," said January. "Claus, your father's right. We both know I have been deceiving him." The black boy sat up straight and turned toward Captain Bower. "Sir, I've talked that way because I thought that's what you expected. I thought you couldn't imagine a black man speaking correct English. But that's because I couldn't imagine a white man accepting someone like me."

"You don't talk down to Nicholas!" said the captain.

"No, sir. I took a chance that he would let me be who I am, and he did."

"But I'm not to be trusted?"

"Sir, you're the captain! You're the Confederate hero! There's not a Negro in Riverton who hasn't been terrified of you! At least, until recently."

"Tell him, January!" said Nicholas.

"Captain, you became a different man when you came to my house after the fire. You found us a place to live, but even if you hadn't been able to do that, just your coming to see my mother would have changed everything."

"Well, I've known Venus a long time. And I didn't want the night riders driving you off your land."

"And, Captain, you stood up for me when I came to vote. You took a risk for me, and I should have stopped talking down to you from that day."

"Well, I don't want to hear any more of it!" said the captain. "We can expect deception from the Mayfield gang, but we don't have to lie to each other."

"No, sir," smiled January, taking a deep breath.

"Just don't expect me to be impressed when you quote Shakespeare! You've got my wife and my son talking like English teachers!"

"Here's one he just taught me," said Nicholas. "What's gone and what's past help should be past grief."

"A Winter's Tale," said January. "Captain, if you'll forgive my past deception, you won't hear any more quotes from me!"

"We're here to hunt, not talk all morning!' said Captain Bower. "Where are those consarned dogs?"

With a pop of the whip, January urged the mules forward while Nicholas stood in his stirrups to look for the missing dogs. "There's Suzy," he called. "Just to the right of the saw dust pile! And Flash is backing her!" Nicholas slid from his saddle as the wagon rumbled to a stop.

"Take the guns! Take the guns!" ordered Captain Bower.

Nicholas saw his father's eyes flashing with excitement as he watched the trembling dogs creep forward.

"Whoa, Suzy!" called the captain. He leaned down and passed the graduation gun to Nicholas, and then held out his own gun as Nicholas reached up. The blast of the shotgun and the captain's scream were almost simultaneous. In the deafening silence that followed, Nicholas saw the smoking gun fall and land at his feet. His father pitched backward against January, his eyes wide with shock and his right hand clutching his thigh as blood pulsed from a ragged wound.

"My God," shouted the captain. "You've killed me!"

Nicholas heard the covey of quail burst from their hiding place twenty yards away. The dogs ran barking in pursuit, and the startled mules jerked nervously at their traces.

"Father!" screamed Nicholas. He climbed frantically to his father's side, his boots slipping on the bloody wagon step. January held the captain in his arms, his own eyes wide with horror. Nicholas tried to lift his father's hand from the wound, but the captain's groans stopped him.

"I need to look at it, Father!" he begged.

"Use your belt," gasped the captain.

"I don't understand!"

"A tourniquet!" said January. "He means to use your belt as a tourniquet! To stop the bleeding!" Nicholas quickly stripped loose his leather belt and tried to thread it under his father's leg.

"Higher!" ordered January. "Up by his groin!" Nicholas heard his father groan again, and then felt the big man's body relax as he lost consciousness.

"We've gotta hurry!" he said to January. "Back to the house! We can call the doctor from there. Drive!" January turned the mules through a stand of broom straw until they were headed in the right direction, then he cracked the whip repeatedly over the reluctant animals. Nicholas sat holding his father's unconscious form in his arms as the wagon bounced and banged toward home.

"I can't tell if this is doing any good!" muttered Nicholas as he tried to pull harder on the bloody belt. The frantic ride to the Bower farm seemed to take forever, and Nicholas found himself reliving the terrible moment. January had the same thoughts.

"Did he drop it?" asked the black boy?

"I don't know. Maybe he did. But I might have let it slip. I don't know!"

"But it had to be cocked!"

"It was!" said Nicholas. "He loaded it and cocked it when the Mayfield's stopped us!"

"It's not like your father to keep a loaded gun in the wagon, specially one that's cocked."

"He forgot! In the argument, he must have forgot! But now I don't know!" Nicholas looked in agony at his friend. "He said, 'You've killed me!' Did I drop the gun? Did I kill him?"

"He's not dead! He's just unconscious! If we can stop the bleeding he'll be all right! Git up! Git up! Git up, you hear?" yelled January, turning again to apply his whip to the tiring mules.

Nicholas began shouting for help as the wagon rumbled into the yard. "Mother!" he yelled. "April! Hurry! Father's been shot!" Sophie Bower ran down the porch steps, her apron flying. April followed close behind.

"God help us," said Sophie as she saw her husband's limp form lying in the arms of their son.

"He's lost a lot of blood," said January as he and Nicholas lifted the captain from the wagon and carried him into the house.

"Maybe you should take him on to town," said April, staring in terror at the trail of blood across the porch.

"No, it's too far," said Sophie. "We need to stop the bleeding now! April! Get some water and towels! Nicholas! Go telephone Dr. Melton. January! You hold the belt!"

Nicholas told the operator that there was an emergency, and he listened anxiously as the woman searched the telephones of Riverton inquiring about the doctor. Everyone who answered the phone call offered to spread the word, but for the moment, the doctor could not be found. After Sophie had cut the trousers from her husband's bleeding leg, she cleaned and dressed the wound, picking out the shot pellets she could see and compressing towels under a tightly bound strip of bed sheet.

Nicholas hurried back to his parents' bedroom and saw his mother sitting beside his father's prostrate form. Sophie beckoned to him. "Take my hand," she whispered, reaching out to Nicholas on one side and January on the other. "April, you too," she said to the frightened girl.

As April completed the circle around the captain's bed, Sophie prayed, "Lord Jesus, we plead for the life of this man, Maximilian." Nicholas realized he had never heard his mother call his father by name. "Show us what we can do to help his healing. But Lord, we know his life is out of our hands and completely in yours." She released the boys' hands, then bent toward her husband and brushed damp strands of hair from his eyes.

Softly, she began to sing. "Jesus, won't 'cha come by here! Now is a needin' time, now is a needin' time." Nicholas remembered Ruby singing the same words over him, and he whispered the song with his mother as January and April added their voices.

In the hall, the telephone rang. Nicholas bolted from the room and snatched up the receiver. Dr. Melton listened as Nicholas blurted out the circumstances of the shooting and described the nature of the wound.

"You're doing all the right things," said the doctor. "Keep pressure on the wound. I have someone to drive me, and I should arrive within the hour." Nicholas felt an immeasurable burden lift from him as he rushed back to the bedside. His father's desperate prophecy would not come true. "I haven't killed him! I haven't!" he repeated to himself.

Nicholas found Sophie Bower collapsed across her husband's chest, her face buried in his beard, her shoulders pulsing with sobs. "Mother!" he exclaimed. For a long minute, Sophie didn't respond, then she sat up, turned her tear-streaked face to Nicholas, and said quietly, "Your father is gone."

"No!" shouted Nicholas, shaking the captain's jacket-clad shoulder and looking desperately into the unblinking eyes. January placed his hand on Nicholas' back.

"The captain just stopped breathing," he said quietly. "There was nothing the doctor could have done. I'm sorry, Claus."

Sophie and April held each other and wept openly, their sobs the only sound in the room. Nicholas felt nothing. Then, slowly, he stood up and wandered into the hall. In the silence of the house, he heard the shot again and the echo of his father's words, "You have killed me!"

Stepping onto the front porch, other memories assaulted him. His own voice shouting, "I hate him! I want him dead!" As if in a nightmare, Nicholas descended the steps and walked to the bloody wagon. His horse, Caesar, had followed the mules home and now stood near the wagon waiting restlessly to be unsaddled, brushed and fed. Nicholas caught the horse, took the reins, and swung himself into the saddle.

He heard January call from the porch, "Claus, wait!" Nicholas ignored him. The bird dogs had also found their way home, and when they saw Nicholas mount, both rushed from under the house to cavort around Caesar's legs. Nicholas ignored them, too, and urged the big horse into a canter. Looking neither right nor left, he retraced the wagon road to the sawdust pile and rode directly to the scene of the shooting. His father's gun lay on the ground, and a few feet away, he saw a still-glistening pool of his father's blood. Nicholas swiftly dismounted, grabbed the gun and hurled himself back into the saddle. Now he spurred the horse into a gallop, thundering down the river road toward the picnic grounds. The grassy field was empty as he crossed it. Nicholas pulled Caesar to a walk when they reached the Santee River, then he urged the horse down the bank and into the water. When the big horse was close to swimming, Nicholas gripped the gun, drew back his arm, and threw the weapon as far as he could into the swirling water.

# CHAPTER SIXTEEN

NICHOLAS RODE SLOWLY on his way back to the farm. Slumped in the saddle, he draped the reins across the pommel and allowed the weary horse to find its own way home. Shadows crept across the picked over cotton fields as the cold winter sun dropped below the trees. Nicholas saw nothing until the lights from the farmhouse interrupted his tortured thoughts. Several saddled horses and a mule-drawn farm wagon stood in the darkened yard, silent reminders that the nightmare was real. Captain Maximilian Bower was three hours dead, and the first mourners had already arrived.

Nicholas led Caesar to the barn, lit a lantern, and took a long time rubbing down the sweating animal and providing the proper amount of food and water. He was in no hurry to engage the serious faces and lingering handshakes that awaited him. Sitting on a hay bale in a dark corner of the barn, Nicholas tried again to clear his mind of the relentless images that assaulted him. He saw his father's face as an ever-changing mask, scowling in sarcasm, swelling with rage, glowing with pride, suppressing a smile, eagerly watching the dogs, grimacing in pain. He remembered words from that bearded mouth, exploding in anger, cursing in frustration, murmuring in praise, screaming over and over, "You have killed me!" Nicholas rehearsed it helplessly until he felt nothing.

"Claus, where are you?" called January Wilson from the barn door. Nicholas saw his friend silhouetted by the lantern light.

"Over here," he replied from the darkness. January felt his way toward the voice and sat on a nearby bale.

"Your mother is worried about you," said January. "She really needs to see you."

"Who else is here?"

"Caleb Harvey and Mister Huckabee. And Reverend Turnbull. Doctor Melton left a little while ago."

"Does Philip know?"

"Your mother asked the doctor to send Philip a telegram when he got to town, but it's too soon to hear anything back from him."

Nicholas sat in silence. After a long time, he said, "Did I kill my father, January?"

"Look, you have to stop worrying about that! It doesn't matter whether he dropped the gun or you let it slip. What you have to be clear about is that you didn't load it or cock it! It was your father's mistake, and the shot was absolutely an accident."

"That's what I've already told myself a thousand times," said Nicholas, his voice rising in frustration. "Don't tell me I've got to stop worrying about it! For God's sake, I'm trying!" He leapt to his feet, pushed his way past January and stormed across the barnyard toward the house. Stamping up the steps, he yanked open the front door and stood blinking in the lighted hall.

"Thank God you're here!" exclaimed Sophie Bower, hurrying from the parlor to embrace her son. "I didn't know where you were! You should have told me!"

"I should have done a lot of things, Mother. Things would be different if I had."

"Please, please don't talk like that! It was an accident! It wasn't your fault! January saw everything, and he told us exactly what happened!"

"He doesn't know exactly what happened," said Nicholas. "Nobody does! And I will live with it the rest of my life!"

Asa Turnbull rose from the settee and hurried toward Nicholas, his arms spread open in front of him. "Son, don't you believe God knows? He knows what happened out there in the woods, and he knows what is in your heart! You didn't kill your father!"

"What if I did? What if in my heart I really wanted my father dead? What does God think about that?" shouted Nicholas, pulling himself away from his mother and turning his back on the minister. Sophie began to weep again. When Asa Turnbull spoke again, his voice did not carry the comforting assurance of a pastor but the disturbing authority of a prophet.

"Nicholas! When your heart condemns you, God is greater than your heart, and he knows everything!"

Nicholas felt something move inside him as a power vastly bigger than the clergyman's voice shook him into silence. Nicholas felt the tears begin to form while he waited for the whispered invitation he knew would come.

"Let go!" bid the soundless voice.

"Leave me alone!" shouted Nicholas turning his face to hide the tears as he bolted for the stairs.

Sophie Bower collapsed on the settee, and January sat with her as Mr. Turnbull thanked the other visitors and escorted them to the porch. "Please spread the word that Mrs. Bower will receive friends here tomorrow evening, and let them know the funeral will be at St. Matthias on Sunday at two," said the minister.

"Oh, Asa! I'm so worried about Nicholas!" said Sophie when the clergyman returned. "He thinks it's his fault! And he wants to be left alone! What are we going to do?"

"Sophie, he just needs time! And our prayers! Only the Lord can heal the wound that gun inflicted on your son, and I believe he's already at work!" Asa Turnbull took Sophie's hand and smiled. "Do you know, when Nicholas said, 'Leave me alone!' I don't think he was talking to us!"

"You're thinking God is working on Nicholas?" asked January.

"I'm sure of it," said Mr. Turnbull. "I've had some good conversations with Nicholas, and I believe God is calling him to a deeper faith. We can pray that this terrible tragedy will be the way the Lord reaches our boy."

+ + +

The next day brought one emotional earthquake after another to Nicholas. His mother's excessively cheerful sisters took the train from Beaufort and descended on the house before lunch. The women from the church had already bathed and dressed his father's body, cutting the back of the Confederate uniform coat so it would button across his chest. Philip's train came into Sumter late in the afternoon, and Nicholas insisted on driving to meet him at the station. The brothers shook hands awkwardly on the platform and hurried to the waiting surrey. Neither spoke until the horse was trotting through the outskirts of the city.

"What happened?" asked Philip, staring ahead. "The wire from Dr. Melton just said it was a hunting accident."

"That's what everybody's saying," said Nicholas. "And I suppose that's true."

"For heaven's sake! What happened?"

Nicholas took a deep breath and recited, "We had the dogs on point by the saw dust pile. Father handed me my gun from the wagon, then he picked up his. I don't know if he dropped it or I let it slip, but it hit the side of the wagon and went off. Into his leg. There was a lot of blood right away."

"Father had a loaded gun in the wagon? He would never do that!"

"Of course not! But we had a run-in with Conner Mayfield and his gang a few minutes before. Father got angry, and I saw him load and cock his gun."

"Conner! I'm not surprised he had some part in this!"

"Conner didn't shoot him."

"Well, from what you've said, neither did you." Philip put his hand on Nicholas's shoulder. "How's Mother?" Nicholas wasn't sure if his brother's touch or the thought of his mother's pain produced his tears, but he could not answer.

The yard around the farmhouse was crowded with horse-drawn wagons and several automobiles when Nicholas and Philip arrived. Friends from Riverton and across the county spoke solemnly to each other on the front porch before entering the parlor to express their condolences to Sophie Bower. Most brought baskets or serving dishes of food and all took turns filling their plates at the dining room table before returning to the porch steps. Many of the captain's farm hands gathered in the back yard by the kitchen door, and a few family retainers, like Ruby and Venus Adams, made their way into the house to speak to Sophie.

Standing near his mother, Nicholas shook hands and nodded in response to kind words from the community. He had little to say. Most of the visitors had already heard the details of the shooting, and those who spoke to Nicholas expressed the unanimous opinion that the Mayfield gang, and not the captain's carelessness, had caused the tragedy. The earnest faces and reassuring words had little impact on Nicholas. Only the appearance, late in the afternoon, of Sally Hemphill penetrated his emotional armor. He spotted her immediately, noticing that she was conventionally dressed, and that her hair was longer than when he'd last seen her. She said nothing that dozens of well-wishers had not already expressed to him, but as he looked into her face and shook her hand, tears began to flow.

"Excuse me," said Nicholas, turning abruptly and hurrying out of the room.

Nicholas stood alone in the kitchen, furiously wiping his face with his coat sleeve. He felt a hand on his arm, and looked up to see April standing in the pantry door. She made no effort to hide her tears, and Nicholas offered no resistance as the girl pulled him into the pantry and embraced him. He felt himself push the door shut behind him and in the darkness, his mouth found hers as he pulled her body against him.

"Oh, Claus," whispered April, clinging to him as she sobbed against his chest. For Nicholas, the world beyond the pantry door ceased to exist. He held the girl tightly and let his tears come.

The sound of someone calling his name sent an electric shock through Nicholas' body. Philip was in the kitchen looking for him. "Hush!" he whispered into April's ear.

"He's not in the kitchen!" said Philip, and Nicholas heard the dining room door swing shut.

"Go see if the back door is clear," said Nicholas, pushing April away. "Let me know when it's safe to come out!" The girl straightened her apron and smoothed her hair before peeking into the kitchen, then, closing the pantry behind her, she stepped quickly toward the back door.

In a few seconds, she returned and whispered to Nicholas. "It's all right! Hurry!" Nicholas pushed past her, crossed the kitchen in three strides, and leapt down the steps into the yard.

Looking over his shoulder, he walked quickly to the barn, closed the big door, and stood by the horse stalls, his heart pounding. He couldn't believe what had just happened. The emotional numbness of the morning had exploded into a kaleidoscope of feelings that left him shaken and confused. April's boldness had surprised and thrilled him. At the same time, his eager response filled him with terror and shame. He heard movement in the stall behind him and felt Caesar's warm breath on his neck. Grateful for the interruption, Nicholas turned to stroke the big horse's face. He thought for a moment what it would be like to lose the animal he'd relied on for so many years, but quickly dismissed the depressing idea. Before long, his heart slowed and his breathing returned to normal.

"I need to go in now," Nicholas told the uncomprehending horse. He peered through a crack in the barn door, and then walked casually toward the farmhouse, passing beneath the pecan tree and into the front yard.

"Here he is!" called a neighbor from the porch, and Nicholas soon found himself caught up in a new round of heartfelt greetings. Sally was not there.

From across the parlor, he heard Philip say to his mother, "I can't find April. She must have gone home. But I brought in another pitcher of tea."

+ + +

Captain Bower's funeral at St. Mathias' Church brought out more than three hundred citizens of Clarendon County, white and black. The little church contained pews for no more than a hundred, but the open windows allowed other mourners to hear and to sing. Those outside huddled together against late November chill, while on the front pew, Sophie Bower snuggled between her sons, her arms linked with theirs, her long black dress and veiled hat blending with their dark woolen suits. Caleb Harvey led the cadre of pallbearers, carrying the head of the casket on the right hand side, while January Wilson carried on the left. Sophie Bower knew that some people would whisper about January's participation, but she had insisted on it, and Mr. Turnbull had supported her decision. Sophie had also se-lected the hymn, "Amazing Grace," even though Mr. Turnbull re-minded her that it was not in the church's hymnal.

"We can sing it line by line," she explained, "the way some of the colored churches do it." Nicholas and Philip had often sung the hymn with their mother on the way to church, and they remembered most of the words. Nicholas had regained his composure after the previous day's disturbing episode with April, and as the funeral serv-ice began, he stood tall and sang with unusual strength. Asa Turnbull recited and the congregation responded in song.

"Amazing grace, how sweet the sound, that saved a wretch like me." The words flowed from Nicholas's mouth without registering in his mind.

And then the minister began the second verse. "'Twas grace that taught my heart to fear and grace my fears relieved." Instantly, Nicholas felt himself drifting away from the funeral, helplessly re-living the horror of his weakest moments and hearing again the ter-rifying summons, "Let go!" He was being trampled by a horse, humiliated by his father, confused by a liturgy, rejected by a girl, con-victed by a prayer, clinging to a cliff.

"No!" he commanded himself, trying to clear his mind of the disturbing images. But the invitation ignored him.

"Let go!" came the words, stronger and close to his ear. He turned toward his mother, her eyes closed, her face serene, as she sang with the congregation.

"How precious did that grace appear, the hour I first believed." Peace settled briefly upon Nicholas, found no place to land, and just as quickly left him on invisible wings. He stopped singing, and Sophie felt him stiffen at her side. When the hymn ended, he sat with the congregation and listened as Mr. Turnbull read from the Psalms.

"God is our hope and strength, a very present help in trouble." Nicholas realized he was thinking about April, and silently cursed himself as he battled to pay attention.

"Who shall separate us from the love of Christ?" read the min-ister from St. Paul's Epistle to the Romans. "For I am persuaded that neither death nor life, nor angels, nor principalities, nor powers, nor things present, nor things to come, nor height, nor depth, nor any other creature, shall be able to separate us from the love of God which is in Christ Jesus our Lord."

Nicholas was not persuaded. He gazed through the window and studied the throng of solemn faces as Asa Turnbull stepped into the pulpit.

"Dear friends," said Mr. Turnbull. "We gather today to celebrate the life of Maximilian Bower, a true community hero who was widely respected by all who knew him. I was privileged on many occasions, as recently as last Thursday, to dine with his family, and each time I visited and passed through the Bowers's front hall, I beheld a truly amazing, and in my experience, an unsurpassed collection of framed certificates, beribboned awards, and memorabilia from a lifetime of public service.

"I saw the captain's college graduation certificate bearing the signature of Robert E. Lee. There, also, was the document proclaiming him a Son of the Confederacy, and a letter signed by the governor recognizing him for leadership in the Clarendon Rifles. I saw a small silver cup proclaiming him the winner of Riverton's very first Winter Race. There were colored ribbons, most of them blue, given to the captain for horses and cattle he raised on his farm. A pair of cavalry spurs hung there, spurs worn by General States Rights Gist, with a note identifying them as a gift from the general's widow in appreciation for Captain Bower's service to her husband during the war. And there was a medal recognizing the captain for the battle wound he received just before the end of the war, the wound that we saw him successfully overcome every day of his energetic life."

Nicholas pictured his father's wall of honor as the minister spoke. He was certain that as long as the house remained the property of the Bower family, nothing on that wall would be touched, and the captain's memory would be secure. Then an outrageous question pushed its way into consciousness. What would happen to his father's awards and trophies if the house were to be sold, if his mother should die and if he and Philip should move away? He had a momentary image of General Lee's signature and General Gist's spurs tossed into a trunk with the other awards and stored in the attic of some other house.

Mr. Turnbull's voice interrupted Nicholas' disturbing reverie. "Beloved, we are all led by our eagerness for praise." The maxim triggered an instant response in Nicholas, and he said to himself, "That's Cicero! 'Trahimur omnes laudis studio.'"

But the minister continued, "That's what Solomon taught long ago when he wrote, 'I became great and surpassed all who were before me in Jerusalem; also my wisdom remained with me. And whatever my eyes desired I did not keep from them.'"

Nicholas remembered the pride on his father's face the day they went to pick up the new tractor, the first in the county with a gasoline engine. "Ten times stronger than the one Richardson's got!" his father had gloated.

The minister continued to read, "I kept my heart from no pleasure, for my heart found pleasure in all my toil, and this was the reward for my toil."

Nicholas pictured his father standing over him and shouting, "When you're here, you will be in field with the rest of us at sunrise! Is that clear?"

"What's the pleasure in endless work?" wondered Nicholas. "His pleasure was our punishment!"

"And here is what Solomon discovered about a life desperate for praise," said Mr. Turnbull. "Then I considered all that my hands had done and the toil I had spent doing it and behold, all was vanity and a striving after wind, and there was nothing to be gained under the sun."

"Disappointment! The worst kind of disappointment!" Nicholas said to himself. "My father was starved for approval all his life and never gained enough praise to satisfy his hunger!"

"As most of you know," said the minister, "Captain Bower was not a church-going man. I spoke with him now and then about his Sunday habits, and he told me quite candidly that as long as he tried to live a moral life and treated other people fairly, he was sure that God would be pleased with him. And I have no doubt that the good Lord saw in the captain what we all saw – a stern man, always with strong opinions and often with a short temper, but at the same time, a good man, a brave soldier, a faithful family man, a hardworking farmer, a reliable neighbor, a man of his word. But throughout this good man's life, the Lord also saw what eventually became clear to many of us. He saw, I truly believe, the captain's hunger for praise."

Nicholas looked at Mr. Turnbull in astonishment. "Had it been so obvious to him, to so many people, and I never saw this about my own father?" he asked himself.

"What Maximilian Bower almost overlooked was the highest praise anybody could desire – the approval of Almighty God."

Nicholas listened closely. "Almost overlooked? Did Mr. Turnbull know something else that I missed about Father?"

"Most people imagine that God's approval must be earned, the way we earn certificates and awards, and all of us naturally think we have earned enough of God's favor. But the Lord doesn't just weigh our merits. His standard isn't just being 'good enough!' It's perfection! And when we fail, because he still loves us, he pardons our offenses through the sacrifice of Jesus Christ our Lord!"

"Merits! Offenses!" Nicholas instantly recalled the words from the communion service and in the same moment, he remembered his own struggle with them. "If God approves us on the basis of offenses forgiven, then instead of clinging to our accomplishments, we can let them go!" Nicholas realized that his mind was already ahead of the minister's words.

"So we try to live a good life not for gain, not to win God's approval, but for gratitude, to thank God for the sacrifice of his Son!" said Asa Turnbull. "In the Gospel according to St. John, we read that Jesus said, 'No man comes to the Father but by me!' And, my friends, I believe Maximilian Bower had recently begun to understand that promise, and to believe it!"

Nicholas frowned. What possible reason could the minister have for such a claim?

"Have you not seen it yourselves?" said the preacher. "There has been a softening in Maximilian Bower's heart!"

208 | RICHARD BELSER

Nicholas struggled to sort out a flurry of memories. There was his father intruding into his private notebook and bitterly discounting the divine qualities of mercy. And there he was hurrying to console Venus Adams on the loss of her family's home and quietly arranging for a temporary residence on his own land. Nicholas pictured his father's rage at his sons' slightest mistakes and his indifference to their greatest honors. He recalled the humiliation inflicted by his father at the Rogation Day picnic, and also his father's thrilling gift of the graduation gun. He remembered his father publicly vouching for January on Election Day and on the very day of his death, insisting that the black boy stop playing the role of an ignorant farm hand and start speaking like the educated man he was. It was true! The evidence was inconsistent, but his father had begun to change!

"Could it really be God?" wondered Nicholas. The minister's voice softened, and heads outside the windows leaned closer to hear.

"The Lord has been inviting this strong man to let go of his relentless pursuit of praise and to trust his Savior's mercy. God has been saying to Maximilian Bower, 'Cling to the cross! Let go of your trophies! And I believe the captain had begun to do just that!"

The minister's gentle words stung Nicholas like a hard slap. "Let go!" It was the invitation that had been haunting him.

Suddenly, the possibility of change in his father didn't matter. Nicholas felt personally pursued! He wanted to get up and run from the church. In desperation, he summoned his father's voice. "You've killed me!" accused the dying man again and again. Nicholas forced himself to listen, sitting rigidly, holding his mother's arm with his left hand and staring straight ahead while he pressed the fingernails of his right hand into his palm until he could think about nothing but the pain.

## CHAPTER SEVENTEEN

THE BODY OF MAXIMILIAN BOWER was laid to rest in Riverton's community cemetery, just below the grave of his mother and the empty plot that had been saved for his adventuresome father, whose mortal remains had long ago been buried at sea off the coast of Chile or interred somewhere on the plains of Kansas. Nicholas responded with mechanical politeness to scores of neighbors and distant relatives who shook his hand and expressed their admiration for Captain Bower and their dismay over his death. He discovered, to his own dismay, that successful control of his thoughts and feelings depended on his relationship with the person consoling him. Sally Hemphill's gentle smile and graveside words of condolence suddenly gave way to the disturbing memory of her anxious face on the night of the debutant ball and her urgent message, "Come on! I have to tell you something!"

A succession of greetings from the Adams's family, beginning with the matriarch, old Venus Adams, and continuing with January and each of his sisters, brought Nicholas almost uncontrollably close to tears. Venus swallowed him in a ponderous embrace. January's eyes conveyed his own deep grief for his friend.

"We will have better days, Claus!" said the black boy. "If after every tempest come such calms, may the winds blow till they have waken'd death."

"Hamlet?" smiled Nicholas.

"Othello," said January. "But it was a good guess!"

The oldest of January's sisters, April Wilson, stood at arms' length from Nicholas as she briefly shook his hand and carefully avoided looking at his face.

"I am very sorry for you, Mr. Nicholas," she said formally. Nicholas could not deny the electric sensation of her touch, and he silently reproached himself even as he released her hand to speak to the other members of her family.

Nicholas had not seen Catherine Heyward at the church service, and her appearance at the graveside filled him with a new whirlwind of feelings.

"God bless you," she said, leaning forward to kiss his cheek. "Mother and I arrived late and stood outside the church. I am so sorry for your loss. But all these people! What a tribute to your father!"

Nicholas found it hard to speak. "Thank you for coming," he finally said, looking through Catherine's face to observe the memories of their times together. Instantly, they were hiking in the mountains, eating at Blackies, dancing at the Ball, walking on campus, kissing in the governor's garden. The girl was saying something when Nicholas regained control of his thoughts.

"What will you do now, Claus?" asked Catherine. "This is so terribly sudden! Do you think you'll go to England like you planned?" The questions penetrated Nicholas's emotional armor and allowed a host of unresolved issues to escape into consciousness. He took a deep breath before answering.

"I don't know," he said. "Mother and I haven't had a chance to talk about it. We've just been trying to get through the funeral."

"I hope you will go when the time is right," said Catherine. "But until then, I'd like to see you. Will you visit me in Columbia?" Nicholas felt his heart leap at the prospect. To be beyond the daily reminders of his father's death, to be away from Riverton, to be with her! Perhaps January was right. There would be better days.

"Of course you will go to England!" said Sophie Bower when Nicholas raised the subject of Oxford at breakfast the next morning. "Father would have insisted on it. He was so proud of you!"

"But what about you?" asked Nicholas. "With Philip off in Virginia, who'll run the farm?"

Philip responded immediately. "That's easy! I'll run the farm. I can take time off from school while you're away."

"You certainly will not!" said Sophie. "We will hire a farm manager. I'm sure that among your father's friends there's a capable and trustworthy man to help us. Maybe not even someone from Riverton. South Carolina has lots of good farmers who need work."

"It's not gonna be that easy," said Nicholas. "There's no way we can hire somebody in time to do the spring plowing and get the crop in the ground. I can't go to England at Christmas! I'll wire them and explain the situation and arrange to take up the scholarship later."

Sophie Bower began to weep. "Your father was so strong! He could be hard sometimes, but none of us knew how much we all relied on him!" Both boys embraced their mother.

"We have each other," said Philip. "If we have to, we can rent out the farm until we can run it ourselves."

Nicholas' strong reaction to his brother's suggestion surprised him. "Don't say that! We should never talk about renting our land!"

Since the day his father announced his plans about leaving him the farm and swore him to secrecy, Nicholas had begun to think of the land in a different way. The prospect of inheriting the farm had dispelled the vocational fantasies of his boyhood, and Nicholas had become comfortable with the idea of finishing school and spending the rest of his life as a farmer.

"This has been the Bower farm for three generations, and for Father's sake, and for yours, Mother, we need to keep it that way!"

+ + +

In the weeks that followed his father's funeral, Nicholas felt January's hopeful prediction of better times slipping away. His own emotional state vacillated between brief moments of optimism and long nights of crushing depression. He found it infuriating when other people's moods conflicted with his own, resenting Philip's unfailingly cheerful outlook and hating equally his mother's daily bouts of weeping. When his brother returned to school, Nicholas secretly celebrated. Despite Sophie Bower's frequent reminders, Nicholas did nothing to look for a farm manager.

The morning after the funeral, he assembled his father's hired hands and announced that, for the present, he would be running the farm. He tried to sound confident, but the workers' sluggish response made it clear that they didn't believe him. On a particularly discouraging day, Nicholas rode to Riverton and sent a cable to the representatives of the Rhodes Scholarship Committee informing them of his new situation and asking for a postponement of his matriculation at Oxford.

At breakfast every morning, and sometimes at supper, Nicholas saw April. She tried to encourage him with her smile and to lighten his mood with the clever comments they used to share, but his gruff manner and curt responses pushed her away and increasingly left her in tears.

"Poor April!" said Sophie one morning after the girl had served them and hurried, sobbing, back into the kitchen. "She's so distraught these days! I never knew she thought so much of your father." Nicholas said nothing.

When Philip returned from Virginia for the Christmas break, Sophie Bower rode to Sumter with Nicholas to meet his train. On the way home, seated in the surrey with both her sons, she made an announcement.

"We have a letter from Charles Haynesworth, Father's solicitor.

It's about the will. He wrote us the week after the funeral, but I asked him if we might wait to read it until Philip was home." She paused to collect herself. "And so Mr. Haynesworth is coming tomorrow morning at 11:00."

"Now we can decide how to spend Father's millions!" laughed Philip.

"I'm certain it will be nothing like that! All we have is the land, the farm equipment and the house and furnishings, and a little money saved for emergencies. I don't know how much it might be after any debts are paid."

"The money's yours, Mother! The farm, the house! Everything! I'm sure that's what Father wanted," said Nicholas. He turned to frown at Philip. "Show a little respect," he said, popping the whip to hurry the horse toward home.

As Philip helped his mother from the surrey at the porch steps, Nicholas let his eyes sweep across the house, the yard, the pecan tree, the barn and the chicken house. He gazed at the gray, unplowed cotton patch that lay just beyond the cow pasture and mentally marked the perimeters of the larger fields beyond the pine trees. It would be a big responsibility, he knew, but he would accept his father's legacy and manage the farm. He would decide about Oxford later.

Nicholas felt unusually relaxed the next day when the lawyer arrived. Mr. Haynesworth greeted the family, took his seat in the farmhouse parlor, and began to read the Last Will and Testament of Maximilian Bower. After the usual preliminaries came these words.

"All of my possessions, including land, property, and liquid assets, I bequeath to my beloved wife, Sophie Bower." Nicholas nodded in complete agreement. But the next part of the document struck him like a kick in the stomach. "For use during her lifetime, after which the title to the land and all such real property as she may accumulate shall pass to my son, Philip Bower, and such liquid assets as may then remain shall pass to my son, Nicholas, for the furtherance of his education in the study of law."

"That's a joke, isn't it?" said Philip, grinning weakly.

"Merciful heaven!" said Sophie. "We talked about it, but that's not what I thought he was going to do! Did he change the will, Charles?"

The lawyer looked up from the papers. "Yes, a few months ago. It's dated the last day of October."

"Damn him! Damn it all!" shouted Nicholas. "It's no joke! You know what this is? You know what this is? It's the captain shooting back from his grave!"

He leapt to his feet and stormed from the parlor. Philip followed him onto the porch, begging him to return, but Nicholas ignored him and stalked behind the house toward the barn. He passed April returning from the chicken coop, an empty feed bucket in her hand. The girl's eyes widened and her mouth opened in surprise when she saw the fury in his face.

"Claus? What's wrong? What's happened?"

"Nothing," he yelled as he hurried to the horse stalls. "Just leave me alone!"

In the house, his mother and brother apologized to the solicitor, who read the rest of the will and tactfully excused himself from the parlor. The lawyer was just going down the steps when Nicholas rode Caesar into the front yard and kicked the big horse into a gallop down the farmhouse avenue. Sophie and Philip heard the hoof beats and rushed to the porch in time to see Nicholas turn on the road toward town.

"I'll go after him," said Philip, starting toward the barn.

Sophie held his arm. "Let him go. He's so troubled! You know he still thinks he killed his father. We must pray, Philip. Claus could so easily hurt himself, but we can't protect him."

"Why did Father change the will? He never said anything to me about inheriting the farm. I'm sure Claus was expecting to get it!"

He pounded his fist against a front porch column. "Mother, I don't want this house! I love it, but I don't want to live here! I want to finish school and get a job in the city. I want to sell automobiles. Father knew that. Claus is the farmer, not me!"

Sophie embraced her son and placed her cheek against his chest. "We need to pray now. God will help us sort it out. He will see to it that both my sons are blessed."

A cold December wind burned Nicholas's face as he flogged the horse toward Riverton. He had no idea where he was going, but the rough ride and the icy air distracted him from the furious thoughts that thundered inside him. As he cantered through the Negro shanty quarter on the edge of town, he saw a black man he knew, made an instant decision, and reined Caesar to a sudden stop.

"Samson, can we do a little business?" he asked the startled man.

"Why, Ah don' rightly know what you talking 'bout, Mr. Nicholas," said the Negro.

"Yes, you do! I want to buy what you sell to almost everybody else in town."

"Why, Ah never knowd you to indulge, Mr. Nicholas, nor none of the Bower men!"

After a lengthy and embarrassing discussion, Nicholas paid the bootlegger and rode away with a jar of corn liquor. He had tasted alcohol before, some of it sips of fancy, refined whiskey and some just samples of the local product. But now, not being a connoisseur, he simply opened the jar, tilted it back in time with Caesar's steps, and began to swallow one burning mouthful after another.

"Probably some of Conner's stuff," he told his horse. "But, hell, it doesn't matter!" Caesar sensed the lack of decision in the saddle, and plodded routinely toward the Bower farm. Nicholas warmly greeted the few people he passed, responding effusively to their offers of condolence.

As Nicholas neared the farm, he saw someone walking the field edge behind the house. Turning the horse's head, he rode closer. April Wilson stopped when she saw him coming. His outburst at the farm had left her worried about his state of mind, and she felt greatly relieved when Nicholas smiled broadly and called her name.

"Be of good cheer, Lady April!" he said. "Your prince has come to rescue you! 'Salus populi suprema lex!' 'The safety of the people is the highest law!'"

April's eagerness to restore her friendship with Nicholas allowed her to ignore his exaggerated movements and elaborate speech.

"Perhaps my prince will bear me to my castle on his noble steed?"

"Let my charger be your chariot, fair princess!"

Nicholas reached down to grasp the girl's hand and pulled her onto the horse behind him. April giggled and wrapped both arms around Nicholas' waist.

"You're alright, now," said April. "I was so worried about you!" She rested her head against his back. "You haven't talked to me in weeks. So tell me now. What happened at the farm this morning?"

"A quarrel with my father! 'Aliquando et insanire iucundum est!'"

"Now stop that, or at least tell me what it means! How can you quarrel with your father, anyway?"

"It means, 'It is sometimes pleasant even to act like a madman,'" the boy said mysteriously.

The short winter afternoon dissolved into darkness as Nicholas and April rode toward the Adams house. They passed a small, tin-roofed structure closely surrounded by a grove of chinaberry trees.

"That's where my family stayed while we rebuilt our house," said April.

"I know. The old Hutchinson place. I need to get off and go behind the house for a minute. You just wait here." Nicholas slid down from the horse and walked unsteadily into the darkness under the trees. When he had relieved himself, he staggered into the front yard and saw Caesar tied to a tree, and the saddle was empty.

"April," he called quietly. "Where are you? What are you doing?"

"In here," said the girl, appearing at the front door of the house.

"Come see what I found!"

Nicholas pulled himself up the crooked porch steps and followed April into the front room. Suddenly, a flame pierced the darkness. In the flickering light, he saw April holding a match, and behind her on the floor, a lantern and a makeshift pallet.

"Somebody's been staying here!" whispered the girl as she lit another match.

"This is not your family's stuff?" said Nicholas, steadying himself against the wall.

"No, we moved everything out and cleaned the place up when our house was ready. Maybe your father's been renting it to somebody."

"He would have said something. Looks to me like a squatter!"

"We should go!" April's voice was urgent. Nicholas replied with a different kind of urgency.

"In a minute!" he said. He felt dizzy.

The match began to flicker, and as April reached for another, Nicholas whispered, "No. Let it go. Come here!"

She embraced him eagerly, and in the darkness, they found the lumpy bed and hungrily undressed each other.

Nicholas and April lay together for a long time. For Nicholas, the turmoil of the past days completely dissolved in the warmth of the girl's body. For April, the impossible dream seemed momentarily real with the man's arms around her. Outside in the starlight, they heard Caesar whinny.

"Somebody's coming!" said April, sitting up and clutching her clothes around her.

"It's nobody! Lie down! That was just Caesar."

"I heard another horse!" insisted the girl, hurrying to dress herself.

"I'll go see," said Nicholas. He pulled on his pants and shirt and crept toward the door. "Like I said, it's nobody!"

"I need to go home!"

They said little as they rode the final mile to the Adams house. April clung to Nicholas' back, and when they saw the lights of the house, he felt her shudder and squeeze him tightly. Venus Adams and several of her daughters came out to greet them.

"Thank you, Mr. Nicholas," said the woman. "I've told April to leave your house so she won't be after dark coming home."

"Mother needed her. So I thought the least I could do would be to give her a ride home."

April slid down from the horse and stood looking up at Nicholas.

"Bye, Claus. I'll see you tomorrow."

The headache that pounded Nicholas' temples when he awoke hurt him much less than the agony that assaulted his stomach, and his physical pain couldn't begin to match the massive weight that burdened his spirit. He forced himself to dress for work, cursing himself as he splashed water on his face and yanked on his boots. At breakfast, he exchanged cautious glances with April, and he noticed that behind her apron, she was wearing a new dress.

"Doesn't April look nice this morning?" Sophie asked cheerfully as the girl cleaned the table. Nicholas grunted and sipped his coffee.

"Is that dress an early Christmas present?" said Sophie.

"No, Ma'am," said April. "It's my church dress, and I wore it because I just felt special today!"

Nicholas tried all day to forget her face. When he rode back to the farmhouse after a tortuous morning in the fields, he saw a saddle horse hitched by the front porch. Climbing the steps, he heard a conversation from the parlor, and as soon as his mother saw him, she called him to come in.

"Nicholas, I want you to meet Millard Brunson. Mr. Brunson, this is my son, Nicholas. Claus, I believe you will be amazed by what Mr. Brunson has come to say to us!"

Nicholas thought instantly of April and terror gripped him as he turned to shake hands with the bearded stranger. Had they been discovered?

"Pleased to meet you, Son," said Mr. Brunson. "What your mother means is that some friends of your family told me about the tragic loss of your father. I didn't have the honor of knowing the captain myself, but he was a great man, for certain! And your friends thought that maybe with him gone and both his sons in school, your mother," he smiled at Sophie, "your mother might need some help running this place. So I came to see if I could be of assistance."

Nicholas felt his face redden as his anger flared. "You have a lot of nerve!" he said. "My father's not cold in his grave and you've come to replace him? Mother, I can't believe you would actually…."

"Son, do be patient!" said Sophie. "Mr. Brunson isn't forcing himself on us! Friends sent him! Weren't we talking just yesterday about hiring a farm manager?"

"Who sent you?" said Nicholas, glaring at the visitor.

"Some of your friends from college! People who knew you in Columbia."

"What are their names?" insisted Nicholas. "Who are your references?"

"I'm ashamed to say I don't remember their names. I met them at a tavern. Blackies, I think it was called. And we got to talking about you and your father, and when they heard my background, they said I should come and offer to help!"

"We want it in writing! You tell your anonymous friends to write me a letter about you. And then I plan to have some of my friends ask around about your friends!"

Sophie Bower thanked Millard Brunson for coming and promised to consider his offer. "Where are you staying?" she said as the visitor mounted his horse.

"I've just checked into Mrs. Moore's boarding house in town," he said with a broad smile.

At first light the next morning, Nicholas awoke to the sharp sound of an ax. Peering from his window, he expected to see January working at the woodpile and was surprised to recognize Millard

Brunson busily splitting logs. He dressed quickly and stormed downstairs. Hurrying through the kitchen, he passed April.

"Who's that?" asked the girl, nodding her head toward the woodpile.

"Some man who wants to work for Mother. I told him yesterday that he needed references."

"Looks like he intends to be his own reference! He rode up and told January he was the new foreman. Took the ax from my brother and sent him straight to the fields. I don't like that man, Claus!"

The confrontation between Nicholas and Millard Brunson was brief and ugly.

"I'll thank you to leave our property until you are invited here!" said Nicholas. Millard Brunson gave the ax a final hard swing and smirked at Nicholas.

"You'd best be polite to me, boy! I can be a help to you or I can be trouble. You listen to your mamma!"

Nicholas struggled to keep from punching the intruder, and he stayed in the yard until Brunson had ridden away.

When his mother came downstairs, Nicholas reported the incident with Brunson.

"Well, you must agree that he has initiative," said Sophie. "Perhaps he was just upset because he thought we would be glad to have him volunteering until we receive his references."

"But he threatened me! I don't trust him, Mother!" said the boy.

"Neither do I," said April as she came in from the kitchen. "And neither does January!"

"Maybe you're all right, but I can't help thinking that God might have sent Mr. Brunson in response to our need. I do feel so strongly about my boys finishing school, and here is a man who can see to the plowing and get the crop in on time. Nicholas, you said yourself that we could never expect to hire somebody so quickly! Why don't we let him work by the hour so we can observe him and decide if we want to employ him as our manager?"

"It's too big a decision! Mr. Turnbull warned us about making any important decisions while we're still upset about Father."

"Sometimes Mr. Turnbull doesn't understand that life doesn't allow us to follow the rules. We have a crop to plant, and we don't have time to wait! I think Philip would agree." Nicholas bristled at the mention of his brother's name.

"Of course," he said bitterly. "I forgot! It's Philip's farm."

Sophie gripped her son's arm. "It's our farm, but for now, it's mine to run. We will certainly talk to other candidates, if we can find any, but for now, I plan to give Mr. Brunson a chance."

# CHAPTER EIGHTEEN

THE TWENTY-FIFTH OF DECEMBER brought nothing but gloom to the Bower farm. Sophie and her sons tried to encourage each other, setting up the cedar Christmas tree where they had always placed it and decorating the fragrant branches with traditional ornaments. But their artificial cheerfulness only made them more aware of the enormous void in their lives. Sophie wept when Philip topped the tree with a tinsel star. Nicholas declined to go to church with his mother and brother on Christmas Day. Sophie had remained adamant about employing Millard Brunson, and Nicholas resented her stubborn rejection of his warnings.

As soon as Sophie and Philip turned the surrey toward town, Nicholas walked to the barn, opened a rough trunk full of old saddle blankets, and dug under the pile. The jar of corn liquor he'd bought after the reading of the will remained half full, and Nicholas sat on a hay bale, sipping the fiery liquid until his anger dissolved into indifference.

"If she won't listen, and she wants Brunson to ruin everything, it's no business of mine!" he told himself. "It's Philip's farm, anyway!" His anger returned when Sophie and Philip came home from the morning service, with Millard Brunson riding his horse beside the surrey.

"Everyone missed you, Nicholas," called Sophie as they rode

toward the barn. "It was lovely! And look who was at church!"

"Merry Christmas!" said Brunson, giving Nicholas a crooked smile.

On the day after Christmas, Nicholas insisted that his mother and brother sit down with him and talk about their plans for the farm.

"I think Mother's right," said Philip. "We don't have time to look all over for a farm manager. Since she's decided that you and I are going back to school, I think Brunson's a godsend!"

"You actually trust him?" said Nicholas. "On the strength of so-called friends of mine? Look, I've asked Caleb Harvey to find out what he can about Brunson. At least wait until we have his report!"

Sophie interrupted him. "Caleb isn't sheriff anymore, Claus. What can he do?"

"But he still knows people!"

"I'm sorry," said Sophie, shaking her head. ""Until I have reason to suspect him, I need Mr. Brunson on the farm!"

Nicholas leapt to his feet. "Then you don't need me!" he shouted, rushing from the room and slamming the front door.

"What are we going to do, Mother?" sighed Philip. "Something bad's wrong with Nicholas! He keeps running away!"

"We're going to pray, Son! God isn't finished with Nicholas yet!"

Nicholas swallowed two big gulps of whiskey as he saddled Caesar, and his face was flushed as he rode into Riverton. At the general store, he sent a wire to the Rhodes Scholarship Committee and another message to a steamship company in Charleston.

"Please reply with information about the next available passage to England," he wrote. He asked Mr. Huckabee to telephone the Bower house as soon as an answer arrived.

When Nicholas returned to the farm, Millard Brunson had joined Sophie and Philip in the parlor. "Mr. Brunson has agreed to work, at least temporarily, as our manager," said Sophie.

Brunson smiled. "I'm so pleased to be of help to you at this difficult time. I promise you the best crop that ever came from your land!" Nicholas barely restrained himself from striking the grinning face.

"Perhaps you will help me do my best work by granting me a small favor?" said Brunson. "As I rode across the farm, I couldn't help noticing a modest little house just off the road toward the Adams's place. It's in rough shape, but I could fix it up, and I would be happy to live there while I'm working for you. It would save me from riding back and forth from town!"

Nicholas felt panic race through his body, and he worked to control the expression on his face. The Hutchinson place! Could this be the unknown rider April thought she heard?

"Yes, that will work out well," said Sophie. "You may live there rent free, so long as you work for us, but any repairs will be at your own expense."

When Mr. Huckabee telephoned, Nicholas asked him to read the steamship company's message. At supper, Nicholas made an unemotional announcement to Sophie and Philip.

"I've told the Rhodes Scholarship Committee that I can come for the spring term, and this afternoon I learned that a ship will leave Boston on January 4. The passage takes seven days. If I took the train day after tomorrow, I could be in England by the eleventh or twelfth."

"Good gracious, no!" said Sophie. "I'm glad you've decided to go, but we could never get you packed in one day! You'll need a new wardrobe for England! It's not South Carolina, you know."

Nicholas shrugged. "I'm not a kid going off to college. I can pack on my own, Mother, and if I need anything, I would rather get it over there, anyway."

Nicholas had his suitcase mostly packed before he went to bed, and the next morning he saddled Caesar and rode through the community saying his goodbyes. He found January in the field with the other farm hands.

"I'm leaving for England tomorrow. Philip is taking me to the train early."

"Good for you! I was hoping you'd decide to go. Don't worry about your mother. I'll look after her, and if Brunson is doing damage to the farm, well, I know who to tell. Your father still has friends in this community."

Nicholas slid from the saddle and shook his friend's hand. "I'm going to miss you," he said, feeling his tears begin and making no effort to hide them.

"And I'm the same," replied January. "'When sorrows come, they come not single spies but in battalions.' But I do believe the Lord has us in his hands."

Forcing himself to remount, Nicholas put the most difficult departure behind him.

In the town of Riverton, he spoke to Mr. Huckabee at the general store and Mr. Singleton at the old cotton gin. He visited with the manager of the Riverton Bank while a clerk withdrew a substantial sum from the account Nicholas had inherited from his father. Taking a different route home, he passed several farms and spoke briefly to school friends who were at work in the fields. He surprised himself by riding down the lane leading to the Hemphill Farm, and when Mrs. Hemphill reported that Sally already returned to Columbia, his disappointment was mixed with relief. As he rode home, Nicholas mentally composed and repeatedly revised a letter to Catherine. He tended to Caesar, then hurried to his room and penned the full message on his first attempt.

"Dear Catherine: At my father's funeral, you asked about my plans for England. I'm writing to tell you that because of certain developments on the farm and after much deliberation, I have determined to take up my scholarship at Oxford right away. I will travel to Boston tomorrow by train and board

an Allan Line ship for Londonderry on January 4.
It is my intention to return to Riverton for the summer, and with that prospect in mind, I will look forward every day to spending time with you. I will
come to Columbia, if that is suitable, or should you
be at Lamont with your family, I will take the first
available train to Clarkesville. I shall miss you, and
if you think of me while I'm away, I do hope you
will remember me before God."

Nicholas debated about requesting the girl's prayers. "It makes
me seem weak," he told himself. But to his surprise, he wrote the
words. He closed the letter, "Affectionately, Claus."

Before daylight on the morning of his departure, Nicholas
bumped his bulging suitcase down the stairs from his bedroom and
returned to collect his overcoat along with a smaller satchel of books
and the letter to Catherine. Sophie had been a whirlwind the previous
day, taking the surrey to town for an emergency shopping trip and,
on her return, repeatedly hurrying into Nicholas' room to add new
items to the growing mountain of essential items.

Nicholas had finally announced, "That's all, Mother! They have
shops in England! I can buy what I need."

While he waited for Philip to bring around the surrey, Nicholas
noticed April beckoning from the kitchen door. Not knowing what
to say to the girl, he had avoided her. Now as he approached, he saw
that her eyes were red, and he could tell she'd been crying.

"Take this!" she said, thrusting a small, cloth-wrapped package
into his hand. Nicholas pulled back the fabric and recognized the
shiny brown contours of a buckeye.

"It's for good luck," whispered April. "I brought it from Pennsylvania when I was a little girl. Claus, don't forget me!"

There was no opportunity to risk an embrace. The two simply
shook hands at the kitchen door, and Nicholas turned quickly to hide
his tears. On the front porch, he regained his composure, only to

lose it again when Sophie Bower hugged him and pronounced a benediction.

Not until the train to Columbia had cleared the Sumter station did Nicholas allow the feelings of the past thirty-six hours to over-take him. His mother's unalterable decision to hire Millard Brunson sickened him. His parting moments with her and January and April and the others wrenched him. And his own angry decision to turn his life upside down in a single day terrified him. From the train win-dow, Nicholas watched men with mule teams turn gray, picked over cotton fields to rows of fresh brown earth. He thought with disgust about his mother's new farm manager driving the Captain's big gaso-line tractor.

"Father would run him off in a minute," thought Nicholas. As he watched the flat, low country fields give way to the rolling hills of the midlands, Nicholas found himself thinking about England. He had read about the English midlands and seen pictures of Ox-ford's medieval colleges, and after receiving the scholarship, he had imagined himself visiting those picturesque places. Now, with the distant prospect about to become reality, he felt excitement mixed with dread. What if the committee had made a bad choice? What if he were not really prepared for the rigorous academic challenge of Oxford? What if the other students sneered at his clothing or his ac-cent?

"If I had not pursued this scholarship, none of this would be hap-pening, and I would be home running the Bower farm." Nicholas felt certain that his father had changed his will because of the scholarship.

"I won't let you waste that education growing cotton! You will be a lawyer!" He could imagine the captain's emphatic pronounce-ments over the rhythmic rumble of the train.

While Nicholas waited to change trains in Columbia, he stood on the platform with his belongings gathered around him and heard a familiar voice call his name.

"Claus Bower! Do you always bring more baggage than you can carry?"

Looking behind him, he recognized Richard Baker.

"Seems to me you had the same problem when we met right here four years ago!" said Richard.

"How are you, Richard?" Nicholas asked coolly.

"I'm well enough. But let me guess! You're coming back to Carolina to coach the football team? Baseball?"

Nicholas eyed his former roommate with disdain. "Actually, I'm traveling to Boston, and from there I'm taking a ship to England."

"Oh! The Grand Tour! Small town boy sees the world!"

"I have a scholarship at Oxford," said Nicholas evenly. Then without waiting for a reply, he continued, "What about you? You're a long way from Walterboro."

"Law school," replied Richard. "I mean to stay away from little towns, too. Oxford! Well, I say, Old Chap!"

The young men endured an awkward silence.

"You see anything of Sally?" Richard finally asked.

"Not much. She came to my father's funeral, but she's still here in school, from what I've heard."

"Sorry about your father, Claus. I didn't know."

"What about you and Sally?"

"Oh, she dropped me two years ago! I got tired of her big political campaigns," said Richard. Then smiling mischievously, he added, "That girl's gone a little crazy, if you ask me. She's a hundred percent Republican! I heard she was sparking some black farm hand!"

The remark stunned Nicholas. He instantly recalled Sally and January together on the Adams's front porch.

"I wouldn't trust the source of that information. Tell the truth, I decided she was crazy when she started hanging around with you."

Richard's eyes blazed as he searched for a response.

"Good luck in law school," said Nicholas. "I have to go. They're calling my train."

Richard Baker's gossip haunted Nicholas as the northbound train pulled away from Columbia. "Sally might do something like that," he admitted to himself. "Even though it would shock people, she might pursue a friendship with a Negro man. It would be a campaign for her, like women's rights and temperance laws. But not January!"

Nicholas decided that there could be nothing to Richard's rumor, because if it were true, his friend would have told him. He worried about Sally, wondering again what had happened to turn a sweet farm girl into a strident social reformer. But very quickly, his concern shifted to January. Nicholas knew what his Negro friend's fate would be if certain men in Riverton heard Richard's gossip.

"I'll write to him," Nicholas promised himself. "He needs to be very careful."

With a sudden jolt of fear, Nicholas remembered his relationship with April and the danger in Millard Brunson's mocking innuendo. He was leaving the country, but what would happen to April if people began to gossip about her?

As the train rattled through communities in North Carolina, Nicholas realized that he had already traveled farther from home than he'd ever been before. He pawed through the contents of his satchel and found the letter from the Rhodes Scholarship Committee with a separate sheet of unsettlingly vague enrollment instructions. Rereading them, Nicholas felt quite certain that he was not up to the adventure before him. He could not remember why he'd said yes to the journey, and casting about for some positive thought, he realized that nothing about his life gave him comfort. As he sat in misery, a middle-aged man walked past him in the swaying aisle of the Pullman car and then abruptly stopped and turned to approach him.

"Aren't you Nicolas Bower, the quarterback from South Carolina?"

Nicholas felt his spirits lift as he smiled toward the stranger's face. In college, he had grown tired of being recognized as an athletic hero, but it had been some time since anyone remembered his record-setting performances. "I am," confessed Nicholas, feeling better already. "Class of '07. Are you a Gamecock alumnus?"

"Hell, no!" said the man. "I'm a Clemson grad! I just wanted to thank you for fumbling in the last minute of the '06 game. Won me a hundred bucks!"

The stranger laughed raucously and lurched down the aisle toward the adjoining car. Nicholas made no effort to respond. He stared out the train window and allowed himself to be mesmerized by the lights that streamed by in the darkness. He had not anticipated the early appearance of loneliness or the fragile nature of everything that mattered to him. The train whistle sounded from far away as fragments of Asa Turnbull's funeral homily tumbled through his mind.

"We are all led by our eagerness for praise." "The Lord has been inviting this strong man to let go of his relentless pursuit of praise and to trust his Savior's mercy!"

"Let go!"

Nicholas suddenly pictured a defensive end from the University of Georgia who, every time the two schools played, harassed him from one end of the field to the other. "Appleby! Number 40! I couldn't get away from that damn jersey!" he swore silently.

"Or from God!" came the surprising thought.

He closed his eyes and squirmed uncomfortably as the train passed through a town and picked up speed. "Tick Tick! Tick Tick! Tick Tick!" The rhythm of the wheels soon joined the conspiracy against him. "Let go! Let go! Let go!" they endlessly echoed.

When he awoke at daylight, the train was passing through the outskirts of New York City. Nicholas could not believe the size of the buildings, the thousands of streetcars and motorized vehicles, and the numberless throngs of people on the streets. The city was nothing at all like Atlanta, and it made Columbia look like a rural village. Nicholas stared through the window until his neck ached, then turned his attention to the newly boarded passengers.

"They're all so well dressed, so sophisticated," he thought, looking with disgust at his own threadbare graduation suit.

One of the young women who boarded in New York reminded him of Catherine, but when she smiled at him, Nicholas retreated into the thick book he held on his lap. Listening to conversations around him, he realized that the men and women his age were discussing plays and concerts, automobiles and fashionable resorts, topics about which he knew nothing. He recognized the frequent appearance of French phrases and agonized again about his cultural ignorance.

As the train headed north through the snowy Connecticut countryside, Nicholas paid grateful attention to the passing farms. He recognized preparations underway for the planting of several different crops and even identified the manufacturers of familiar farm machinery. The cows and mules he passed seemed like old friends.

"Look at the thick coats!" he silently wondered. "Those fellows are dressed for the climate!"

"You certainly are interested in cows!" said a girl who suddenly peered over the train seat. "Do you think the poor things are freezing to death?"

Nicholas swallowed hard when he saw that the speaker was the dark-haired young woman who looked like Catherine.

"Actually, I was just thinking how well adapted they are," he replied. "They have much thicker coats than the cows where I live."

"Well, you are a cow expert, then! What kind are those? I think the brown and white ones are the nicest!"

"Those are Herefords," smiled Nicholas. "We have them in South Carolina, too."

The girl had removed her hat, and Nicholas noticed that her brown hair, even pinned up, was longer than Catherine's.

"I've been to South Carolina! At least, I've passed through it on the way to Florida. From the train, I didn't see anything there but farms."

Nicholas admitted that much of his home state was rural, and even confessed that he had grown up on a farm.

"What's your name?" asked the girl. Nicholas told her and asked her the same.

"Jenny, Jenny Flagler. I live in Palm Beach. But you haven't told me where you're going!"

"England," replied Nicholas, feeling proud that he could name an international destination.

"So am I! I can't believe it! I'll bet you're sailing on the Allan Line's *Laurentian* on the forth!"

"That I am," smiled Nicholas. "Are you going to tell me you're on the same ship?"

Jenny squealed with excitement. "I am! I am! My parents have sent me and two of my friends on the Grand Tour of Europe. That's Ellen and Daisy across the aisle! Wait till I tell them we have a gentleman planter as a traveling companion!"

The long trip to Boston seemed only a matter of minutes after Nicholas and the girls began telling stories about themselves and describing the adventures they hoped to experience in Europe. When they arrived at Boston's South Station, Nicholas stared in amazement as porters unloaded steamer trunks, hatboxes, and several bulging suitcases for each of the girls. He smiled when they pointed to his single suitcase and valise and laughed when they chided him for packing too lightly. But his most welcome discovery on arrival in Boston was the freight wagon and spacious touring car Jenny's father had provided for his daughter's transportation to the dock.

"Of course you will ride with us!" insisted Jenny. "We can board the ship this afternoon and have the rest of the evening to explore Boston!"

Nicholas discovered that when conversing with Jenny and her friends, he quickly expended his list of useful topics. They showed no interest in the University of South Carolina football team or in learning how to grow cotton, and they displayed only momentary curiosity about his invitation to Oxford.

When the car dropped them off at a fashionable restaurant, Jenny whispered to the matre d'hotel, and the travelers quickly found themselves seated at an excellent table. Nicholas knew nothing about the popular cocktails, but with the first sip of the smooth and tasty drink Jenny ordered for him, he understood that corn whiskey played no part in the recipe. He was delighted with how clever he became after a few more drinks. By the end of the evening, the girls were laughing at everything he said.

Sometime after midnight, Nicholas staggered up the ship's gangway, gave his name to the steward, and wound his way below decks to his third level room. He gripped the sides of his bunk as the whole cabin swayed, "Oshford!" he said to the gimbaled bedside lamp. "I'm going to study at Oshford! In England!

When Nicholas awoke, the ship had already cleared the harbor and was steaming into the gray North Atlantic. Donning his overcoat, he made his way to the promenade deck and stood there breathless as the icy wind showered him with spray. He retreated inside, and bracing himself against one wall or the other as the ship rolled, he explored the lavish public areas of the giant liner. He found Jenny and her friends sipping tomato juice in the aft salon.

"Our farm boy's up!" announced Daisy.

"I bet he's not having any breakfast this morning," said Ellen.

"You two, leave Claus alone!" said Jenny, beckoning for Nicholas to join them.

He accepted a glass of juice, but quickly realized that while the girls chattered away, easily generating non-stop conversation about one topic after another, his own mind had lost the ability to concentrate and his tongue felt thick. His stomach was in turmoil, and he began to sweat. A jazz band took the stage at the end of the salon and soon filled the room with ear-shattering sound. Nicholas let his mind drift and felt his spirit plummet.

"I hope you don't feel as bad as you look!" said Jenny.

"I think I killed my father," Nicholas heard himself say, and lurching to his feet, he staggered from the salon and bent far over the ship's leeward rail.

# CHAPTER NINETEEN

## Winter 1908

AFTER A DAY AT SEA, Nicholas' physical condition began to improve. He regained his appetite and enjoyed sharing meals with Jenny Flagler and her friends. Their high-spirited banter entertained him, and as long as he walked the promenade deck with them or allowed them to teach him to play bridge, he managed to avoid the inner enemies that had followed him from Riverton. At night, alone and sleepless in his cabin, Nicholas suffered terribly. He imagined his mother innocently agreeing to damaging agricultural advice from Millard Brunson. He thought of Philip's distress over the prospect of farming for the rest of his life.

"If Brunson is as crooked as I know he is," thought Nicholas, "we'll lose the farm and Philip won't have to run it!"

He worried about January and Sally, agonizing over the consequences of a real relationship between them, and dreading the equally destructive effects of fabricated gossip. He rubbed April's smooth, brown buckeye between his hands, and cursed himself for allowing his selfish hunger to put her in jeopardy. His efforts to picture himself hiking mountain trails with Catherine yielded only brief comfort, because beneath his conscious thoughts lay a festering wound that infected every wholesome image. He had failed his father. In life, Nicholas was certain that he had disappointed the captain. In death, he had touched the gun that killed him.

"We missed you at lunch," said Jenny on the fifth day of the voyage. "You've become an absolute hermit! What are you reading, anyway?"

Nicholas had discovered that immersion in study worked effectively to mask his inner anguish, and as the day of his arrival at Oxford drew nearer, he buried himself in books, re-reading the texts he brought from his courses at Carolina and delving into others he found in the ship's library.

"I'm entering the college at mid-term," said Nicholas, rubbing his weary eyes. "So I'm trying to stimulate my brain."

Jenny snatched the book from Nicholas and scanned a page. "*The Satires of Horace*. Good Lord! It's in Latin! How stimulating is that?"

"It is for me!" Nicholas grabbed the book and placed it protectively in his satchel. "You don't seem to understand! I'm about to face the toughest competition of my life, and I need to be ready!"

Jenny stared at him, and finally smiled. "Are you going to school, Claus, or to war? You sound like it's your life on the line, not your education!"

"It is!" he said angrily.

"It is which? I don't think you know!"

Nicholas picked up his books and hurried to his room. From far away he heard again Asa Turnbull's convicting maxim, "Beloved, we are all led by our eagerness for praise."

The Laurentian docked at Londonderry, Ireland, at noon. Preparing to go ashore took Nicholas all of ten minutes, while his traveling companions folded and packed late into the night, and still kept the porters waiting. Together, Nicholas and the girls took a taxi to the pier where they were to meet the Liverpool ferry. Their baggage followed in a heavily laden lorry.

"Are you sure you can't come with us to London?" begged Jenny when the ferry neared the west coast of England. "We can all take the train from Liverpool and explore London together!"

"I'm afraid Liverpool has to be the end. It would be fun to explore together, but I'm due at Oxford tomorrow."

Jenny crossed her arms and pouted. "Maybe Father could send them a cable and get you excused for a week! He knows people in England!"

Nicholas smiled. "I don't believe your father's influence can reach this far!" And instantly he realized, "But my father's influence can!" He gripped the icy deck rail and squeezed until his fingers ached.

The pitch and roll of the Liverpool ferry left Nicholas feeling queasy again, and at the dock, he struggled to send the girls off with a cheerful farewell. As he searched the quay alone for directions to the Oxford trains, Nicholas felt overwhelmed by the enormity of what lay ahead. Having American companions on the train ride from New York and the ocean voyage from Boston had allowed him to forget about the cultural tidal wave that was about to sweep over him. Now standing on British soil, he couldn't comprehend the hurried answers people gave to his questions, and he often nodded as if he understood before wandering away in complete frustration. He found a shop and changed some money, wondering throughout the transaction if he were being cheated. Even buying a rail ticket to Oxford confused him, and he ended up extending a handful of coins so an impatient clerk could pick out the proper amount.

+ + +

As the train rumbled southeast toward Oxford, the rolling hills of the English midlands fascinated Nicholas. Rock walls and hedgerows defined plots of land much smaller than the cotton fields of the Bower farm. Stone cottages with thatched roofs seemed ancient and alien to him, and only fleeting glimpses of cattle and plow horses made him feel comfortable.

238 | RICHARD BELSER

"I guess farmers are at home around the world," he decided.

On the high street of each passing village, Nicholas noticed the slate-shingled spire or the turreted tower of one parish church after another, and he thought about Mr. Turnbull's longing to visit his Anglican home. Nicholas smiled. "I have my prayer book. Maybe liturgy will give me as much comfort as livestock!"

"Going up to Oxford, are you?"

A crisply accented voice interrupted Nicholas' study of the scenery. The speaker was a man about his age, very neatly dressed in a smart brown suit, vest, high-collared shirt, and contrasting neck tie, with his hair smoothly parted in the middle.

"Yes, I am," replied Nicholas, suddenly feeling self-conscious about his about his own wrinkled jacket and trousers.

"And a Yank, at that! I guessed as much! You looked quite a cabbage as you entered the compartment," smiled the stranger.

Nicholas blushed. "I suppose you mean lost. Am I really so obvious?"

"It's quite elementary! Foreign-looking kit, all a mess from travel. Your haircut. Your bulging trunk. Your books, including the one you're holding, but not reading, which appears to be in Latin. And your preoccupation with scenery that most Englishmen would find familiar."

Nicholas shook his head and smiled back. "Is there anything about me you haven't figured out?"

"Quite a lot, I'm sure. But I can add that you work with your hands, and are therefore not a businessman. And you're not married," replied the traveler.

"You don't miss a thing, do you? I thought Sherlock Holmes was a fictional character!"

"Bad luck he is! The police could use someone like him these days. I take it you've read Conan Doyle?"

"It's been a while," said Nicholas.

"I'm something of a student of Sir Arthur," said the stranger. "Oh, by the by, the name's Middleton, Charles Middleton."

Nicholas shook hands with his traveling companion. "I'm Nicholas Bower. I'm from America. But you already figured that out!"

Having recognized Nicholas as a visiting student, Charles Middleton quickly assumed the role of mentor and guide to all things English. Nicholas sometimes had to interrupt his new friend's non-stop monologue to request translation for some British colloquialism, but with each passing hour, his knowledge of language and customs grew dramatically. When the train stopped in Birmingham, Charles helped Nicholas purchase lunch from a vendor's cart.

"Care for some nosh? There's a take-away! Let me recommend a couple of pasties and a glass of bitter."

"Pasties?"

"Meat pies. Call them oggies in Cornwall. You'll like it! And bitter is just proper beer."

Charles' recommendations turned out to be excellent, and as the two young men ate, Nicholas learned more about his benefactor.

"I'm from Liverpool myself," said Charles. "You wouldn't imagine me at Oxford, but my family is well connected and even a prat like me can get in with the right recommendations."

"I should have guessed you were a student," said Nicholas. "Your age. Your clothes. Your analytical mind! And, if I'm not mistaken, that's a scarf from Christ Church College you're wearing!"

"Not bad, Dr. Watson!" laughed Charles. "Not at all elementary! By the by, do you know your college?"

"Christ Church! It was in the registrar's letter. I looked it up and read all about it! How else would I have known about your scarf?"

"Oh, well done! You've copped one of the big four, and Bob's your uncle!"

"What?" asked Nicholas. "Who's my uncle?"

Charles took great delight in explaining each incomprehensible expression to his American friend. "It just means, 'And that's all there is to it!'" laughed the Englishman.

By the time the train pulled into the Oxford station, Nicholas felt that he had already completed a semester of British education. He and Charles hired a porter to cart their baggage along St. Aldate's Street and through the imposing gates to Christ Church College. A few late arriving students waited in queues on Tom Quad to complete the registration process.

"Meet me at the Eagle and Child at half seven," called Charles as he started toward his rooms.

+ + +

Nicholas apologized his way through the administration process, constantly asking for explanations that brought exasperated sighs from the students in charge. By the time he dropped his baggage in the assigned room, Nicholas felt exhausted. He collapsed on his bed and listened to the sound of tower bells chiming the hour. Riverton seemed worlds away, and he had to concentrate to picture his white-painted wooden house and the flat cotton fields of Clarendon County. He allowed himself to remember the day of his departure, years ago it seemed, and saw his mother praying for him on the front porch. He pictured January's final wave and wondered if Catherine had received his letter.

Suddenly, Nicholas sat up and reached for his pocket watch. "Damn!" he swore. "It's already after seven, and I have no idea where the Eagle and Child is, or what it is, for that matter!"

Charles Middleton waved from a corner table when Nicholas finally found the pub. "Why didn't you tell me people call this place the Bird and Baby?!" complained Nicholas.

"Let's have no puckering, Yank! I want to introduce you to some of my mates," said Charles. "We're all Christ Church men, and we know everything there is to know about the town, the university, the entertainment...,"

"And that includes the dollymops!" added a grinning student.

"Mind your cheeky mouth!" said Charles. "Our American friend has higher standards than the rest of you gammy blokes. The College Bursar told me he's a Rhodes Scholar!" The men at the table whistled approvingly.

"Well, I'll be blinkered!" exclaimed a broad-shouldered boy. "By the size of him, I had him figured for a rugby ringer."

"You're off your trolley!" said Charles. "I'll wager this man's never even seen a rugby match!"

"And you'd be right," said Nicholas. "I played football in college. I mean American football. And baseball."

"Ever had a go at cricket?" said another of the young men.

"Unfortunately not. I'd like to learn, but right now I don't know how much time I'll have for athletics."

Nicholas' remark prompted a vigorous debate among his table-mates, with each claiming the superiority of a different sport and all accusing each other of inexcusable laziness. Nicholas listened attentively to the witty repartee of his new colleagues until he had consumed his second pint of beer. At that point he became uncharacteristically talkative, volunteering more information about himself than the others at the table wanted to hear.

"Half a bale of cotton per acre! Half a bale! Do you know how many pounds that is?"

"Take him home, Charles!" one of the men finally said. "It's after nine, and we don't want the Yank to make a bodge of his first day of classes!"

The effects of his hangover only served to magnify the anxiety Nicholas felt the next day as he wandered the streets of Oxford with a map in his hand. The orientation provided by the master of his house had covered so much information that everything became a blur, and Nicholas quickly forgot important university procedures. When the stressful day finally ended, he retreated to his room and forced himself to pen a brief letter to his mother. The circumstances of his train trip and ocean voyage already seemed like ancient history, and Nicholas hurried to describe his most recent discoveries.

"Oxford University is about as different from an American university as one university can be from another," he wrote. "In an American university a student's physical freedom is in large part unrestricted, though he is required to attend classes regularly and to take frequent examinations. At Oxford an undergraduate's physical life is very much regulated and he must be within the college walls by a certain hour, usually ten p.m. On the other hand, his intellectual life is almost entirely unrestricted and he can attend classes and lectures or not as he pleases." [iv]

After a week of classes, Nicholas began to feel more comfortable with his new environment. His second letter home shared this information. "Oxford is composed of some twenty-odd colleges, each of which is largely self-governing, except in the matter of university lectures and examinations. An average undergraduate lives his life largely within his own college. Each college has its own athletic teams, and to some extent the colleges at Oxford take the place of fraternities in a large American university." [v]

The pub visit Nicholas made to the Bird and Baby on his first evening in Oxford proved to be his last for the semester. He was so conscious of the university's standards and of his own responsibility to represent his country that he plunged himself almost completely into his studies. Charles Middleton continued to invite him to join the group of hail-fellows each evening before curfew, but Nicholas politely declined.

Occasionally, after the evening meal, Nicholas would take his books and sit on the grassy banks of the River Cherwell or the Isis, both of which flowed just south of the college. He looked up one spring evening to watch the college crew row smoothly up river in a sleek racing shell and found himself fascinated by the rhythm of the long, varnished sweeps. After some investigation, he learned the identity of the crew's captain and went to speak to him.

When Nicholas impulsively removed his shirt to demonstrate his athletic physique, the crew captain exclaimed, "The Yank's a nutter!" and challenged him to an arm wrestling contest. Three quick victories made Nicholas the only American member of the Christ Church rowing club. Daily practice of the strenuous sport proved to be relaxing for Nicholas, and as he labored in harmony with his crewmates, he remembered finding the same benefit on steamy afternoons on the University of South Carolina's football practice field.

+ + +

Nicholas visited the college's common room every day hoping to find a letter from home, but the spring term had nearly ended before the first communication arrived. He had written weekly to his mother, and when he eagerly opened her first letter, he could not deny feeling some resentment. Sophie began by apologizing for her failure to write.

"I have never been a depressive person," she explained, "but the loss of your father has been much harder than I would have imagined. I have little energy for anything beyond keeping up the house and going to church. Mr. Brunson asks me questions every day about the farm, and I have begun to wonder if he really knows much about growing cotton. With you and Philip gone, I have no one to guide me. Yesterday, Mr. Brunson strongly recommended that we gin our cotton this fall at Mayfield's Gin. I know that Father always did business with Mr. Singleton, but Mr. Brunson is convinced that the Mayfield's will give us a much better price.

"Philip seems to be happy at Washington and Lee. He will soon graduate, as you know, and I do believe things on the farm will improve when he returns next month. Your Aunt Abigail and I will go up for his commencement. My dear April is gone, having been invited to go to Philadelphia by the people who used to employ her mother. Her little sister, June, now helps me in the kitchen, but I do miss April terribly. I don't see much of January. He is usually in Orangeburg and only works on the farm during holidays. June tells me that after the colored college he wants to continue his schooling in the north.

"Dear Claus, as much as I long to see you, I must say that you really do not need to make the long journey home this summer. The trip is expensive and, I'm sure, exhausting, and you would scarcely have unpacked your suitcase before packing again to return to Oxford. From your letters, I gather that your life there is busy but fulfilling. It would please me if you could take a summer course that would hasten the time of your own graduation and speed the day when you can return to Riverton."

Nicholas studied every sentence of his mother's letter, letting her brief comments ignite his imagination. He fumed over Millard Brunson's incompetence, and swore aloud when he read about doing business with the Mayfields's gin. He felt proud about Philip's upcoming graduation, but remembering his brother's reluctant acceptance of an agricultural life, Nicholas could not avoid anxiety about the future of the farm. The news about April worried him. She had never mentioned moving to Philadelphia, and Nicholas pondered several possible reasons, all of them bad, for her sudden departure from Riverton. January's desire to continue his education outside of South Carolina made perfect sense to Nicholas, but at the same time, the prospect of living in Riverton without his friend left him feeling lonely.

Nicholas received his mother's final suggestion with real ambivalence. He had come to England expecting a six-month stay and had looked forward to a summer at home, but having so recently made the long journey and now having found his footing at Oxford, he was reluctant to adhere to his original plan. Nicholas decided to inquire about opportunities for summer study.

The decision became easier a few days later when he received a letter from January. His friend wrote: "You are sorely missed at the Bower farm and in the Adams house. I long for the day when you and I have put school behind us and can once more enjoy swapping quotations and devouring our mothers' fried chicken! But 'How poor are they that have not patience? What wound did ever heal but by degrees?' I'm no Iago, but I do know that 'wit depends on dilatory time.' I believe my wits have gone as far as the state college in Orangeburg can take them.

"During the Easter break, your wonderful mother asked me to your house and told me that she had found me a scholarship and hoped I would apply to a northern university. I didn't ask about the source of the funds, but on the strength of your mother's promise, I applied to Yale. Yesterday, I received my letter of acceptance! They have asked me to enroll for the summer term, and I have eagerly complied! I shall miss you this summer, my friend. But 'I go, and it is done; the bell invites me.' I'm not Macbeth, off to commit a murder, but I do hope to slay the world's limited expectations for men of my color."

January had added a postscript. "Sally has graduated from Carolina and has taken a job teaching at the colored school in Sumter." The news about Sally's new job didn't surprise Nicholas, but he found January's mention of it disturbing.

Philip's letter, a few days later, assured Nicholas that the long trip home would not be necessary. "I have a car!" wrote Philip. Nicholas could see his brother's excitement in the angular shape of the penned words. "It's a graduation present! A Model T Ford! One of the first ones made! I picked it up in Roanoke after exams and drove it home so mother can ride back with me for graduation. You will love it!"

Nicholas shook his head as he imagined Sophie Bower in an automobile bouncing her way over three hundred miles of rough highways with her enthusiastic son at the wheel. "They'll take the train!" he smiled.

Philip continued: "I'm sure you'll be happy to know that I fired Millard Brunson. While I was home, I didn't like the way he had begun to ignore Mother's instructions and to act as though he were the owner of the farm, and not just the manager. He cursed me quite thoroughly before he left and promised to have his friends in Columbia make things difficult for us. I'm not worried. With the crop laid by, I'll be able to go for graduation and get back to the farm before the next cultivation. Our hands know what to do. I can't wait to show you the car! In case you've forgotten, we drive on the right side of the road over here!"

Nicholas breathed a sigh of relief. As much as he had looked forward to visiting Riverton and to seeing Catherine in North Georgia, he also dreaded the trip. With the farm in good hands and with January and April gone, his only concern was for his mother, and she had advised him to stay in England. Nicholas surprised Charles Middleton and the other regulars at the Bird and Baby when he joined them for a drink.

"You've a litsome face, lad!" said Charles. "It's a rare thing to find you with neither book nor sweep in your hands! Let me see! Either you've heard good news from home, or you've taken up with some local Judy!"

Nicholas told them about the letters from South Carolina and announced his plans to stay the summer at Oxford.

"Well done!" said Charles. "Perhaps you'll pop over to Liverpool for a visit!"

"If you'll promise to pop over to South Carolina some time!" laughed Nicholas.

His buoyant mood continued until curfew, and when he returned to the college and found a letter from Catherine, his joy was complete. And then he read her message.

"Nicholas," wrote Catherine. "I have prayed and agonized over how to tell you what I must. The only way is to be straightforward about it. Father told me yesterday that an associate of his had learned of your intimate relationship with a Negro girl who worked on your farm. A Mr. Brunson, who also works on your farm, saw the two of you together. My father's associate sought to investigate Mr. Brunson's story and found that the girl has moved away. I am writing with the most profound hope that you will immediately send me a cable denying Mr. Brunson's allegations. I pray that you will not break my heart." Catherine signed her letter. "Fondly."

# CHAPTER TWENTY

## Spring 1908

NICHOLAS SAT ON THE EDGE OF HIS BED and read the letter again. Far across the quadrangle, the tower bell called Great Tom tolled the curfew hour. For a long time, Nicholas sat paralyzed, and not until the pain of accusing images surrendered to the balm of emotional exhaustion did his tears cease. He got up, stuffed Catherine's letter into his pocket, and hurried, almost running, from the students' residence across the quadrangle to the porter's gate. An elderly porter reminded him of the hour, but Nicholas blurted out a story about securing the boats for the rowing club, and the porter unlocked the gate and allowed him to leave.

With the college walls behind him, Nicholas began to run hard. His footsteps, echoing loudly as he passed the cathedral, were soon muffled by the grass of Merton Field. In one of his secluded study places on the banks of the River Cherwell, Nicholas fell to his knees and then toppled forward to lie face down in the darkness. He was beyond pain and beyond hope. "Jesus!" he whispered into the dew-dampened grass.

Nicholas awoke cold and shivering as the morning sun began to draw mist from the green water of the river. He sat up and clasped his hands around his knees, conscious of nothing but the chill in his limbs and the hunger in his stomach. He had no ideas, no plan about how to reply to Catherine's letter. Staring blankly at the water, he noticed a movement in the reeds a few yards to his left, and he watched without feeling as a swan rose from its evening bed, stretched its elegant neck, shook the dew from its broad wings, and standing as tall as Nicholas, looked at him with bright black eyes. Unfrightened, the bird studied the young man for a long moment, and then slowly eased itself into the water and swam silently to the opposite bank. Nicholas watched in wonder as the swan stepped onto the grassy slope, then turned and fixed him again with its unblinking stare.

"Go across! Just like that! Go to her!"

The idea exploded into Nicholas' consciousness. Instantly, he could picture Catherine again! He could imagine himself frantically packing a suitcase, standing in the bow of a ship, pacing the aisle of a swaying rail car, leaning eagerly forward on the seat of a surrey, and then clasping her hand to pour out a torrent of heart-felt words. Then, as suddenly as the pictured plan appeared, it shattered into disjointed fragments.

"No!" Nicholas groaned to himself. "I could never get there! If I did, she would never listen! Go across! For what? It's a swan, for heaven's sake!" Shivering, he stood and walked slowly back toward the college.

The swan's mysterious crossing had lost every trace of its inspirational power by the time Nicolas returned to his room, but as he reflected on his night by the river, he sensed that something important had happened. He was able to think about Catherine again, and he immediately set himself to the task of composing the cable she had requested. The words flowed from his pen with astonishing ease, and as he walked to the telegraph office, Nicholas read the message to himself.

"My Dearest Catherine: There are broken hearts on both sides of the Atlantic, and I am the cause of both. My behavior with the girl came at a moment of deepest pain following the death of my father. I was drunk and angry with myself, and I acted selfishly toward her, and as I immediately realized, toward you. I do not ask you to understand or excuse my transgression, because it is inexcusable. I can only beg for your forgiveness. Until I received your letter, I had decided to remain at Oxford through the summer and the next term, but if you would allow me to see you and to plead personally for your forgiveness, I will come to South Carolina as soon as I possibly can. If I may see you, please heal my heart and respond by cable the moment your heart allows. With deepest sorrow and fondest hope, I am your Nicholas."

"Them's a bloody lot of words, mate!" observed the telegraph clerk when Nicholas showed him the text of his cable. "Cost a pretty penny!"

"It's alright," replied the boy, hurriedly pulling out his money and hoping that the clerk had only counted words and not read the message.

Leaving the telegraph office, Nicholas visited the refectory for the mid-day meal, and then spent the afternoon attempting to prepare for the examinations he would face the following week. When he heard Great Tom strike five o'clock, Nicholas laid aside a thick volume and entertained an idea that had come to him on his way back from the river.

"Evensong," he thought. He had attended Sunday services only occasionally during his months at Oxford, and while he understood that Christ Church Cathedral enjoyed a celebrated choir, he had never been to a sung evening service. Quickly combing his hair and donning his tie and jacket, Nicholas jogged across the quadrangle and entered the cathedral through the south transept.

The service had already begun when he slid breathlessly into an empty chair. The voices of the men and boy singers blended ethereally in the church's gothic arches, and Nicholas allowed the fine harmonies to quiet him. When his breathing relaxed and his heartbeat slowed, he began to listen to the clearly chanted words.

"Praise the Lord, O my soul, and forget not all his benefits: Who forgiveth all thy sin, and healeth all thine infirmities."

Nicholas leaned back and let his eyes trace the intricate stonework high overhead in the chancel vault. His thoughts began to tumble.

"All thy sin." "All thine infirmities."

Up above him, rough rocks reshaped into delicate arches seemed suspended by nothing but air. The choir continued.

"Who saveth thy life from destruction and crowneth thee with mercy and loving kindness."

Nicholas remembered the voice of Miss Abernathy. "You will memorize the lines titled, 'The Quality of Mercy.'"

He heard himself, from long ago, mindlessly reciting, "The quality of mercy is not strained. It droppeth as the gentle rain from heaven upon the place beneath."

As tears began to fall from Nicholas's cheeks, he realized that they had nothing to do with his estrangement from Catherine. They flowed from a deeper source, and he recognized them as his lifelong response to the near approach of any kindness undeserved.

The promise of forgiveness. Everything in him wanted to believe it, to welcome it, to experience the peace of a liberated heart. Nicholas lowered his head against the chair in front of him and silently wept as the service continued. A group of women seated behind him saw his shoulders shake and exchanged glances with each other. When the congregation stood to begin the final hymn, Nicholas wiped away his tears and walked quietly toward the south transept door. He had not taken ten steps into the evening air when someone called his name. Turning, he saw Jenny Flagler push open the door and wave vigorously.

"Nicholas! For heaven's sake, wait for me!"

The girl rushed to embrace him before he could utter a word, and as he stood speechless, she continued to talk as if they had been in conversation for hours.

"Well, everybody insisted that you would almost certainly have gone home for the summer, but I said, 'He could still be here,' and then I reminded them that we need to hear the Christ Church choir, because if you're visiting England you simply must, and here you are!"

Nicholas greeted Jenny and the women with her. "You remember Daisy and Ellen," said Jenny. "And this is Mrs. Baxter. She's our companion." Jenny winked at Nicholas as he shook hands with the distinguished gray-haired woman. "Mrs. Baxter missed the boat in New York. That's why you didn't meet her on the way over, but Father arranged passage for her on the next ship, and she caught up with us in London. Father says it's not proper for young ladies to travel unchaperoned! Isn't that right, Mrs. Baxter?" The older woman scowled at Jenny.

"It is certainly not proper for well-bred young ladies to lock their traveling companion in a hotel room! I didn't miss the boat in New York, young man! I was deliberately abandoned!"

"But we've been good for four months, haven't we, girls?" asked Jenny innocently.

"Except for that time in Paris," giggled Daisy.

"And the one in Venice," added Ellen.

"But enough about our adventures!" said Jenny. "What about you, Nicholas?"

"I've been working pretty hard. Studying, mostly, and rowing on the crew."

"What about the summer?" the girl asked. "Are you coming home when this term ends?"

"I had decided not to go, but I'm waiting for a cable that could change my mind. I hope to have that answer tomorrow or the next day."

"I am quite sure you will find it difficult to arrange passage on short notice, Mr. Bower," said Mrs. Baxter.

"I know you're right, but if I'm asked to go home, I'd do anything to get there."

"Sounds important!" said Jenny. "Who's the cable from? Is it a girl?"

Nicholas blushed. "Maybe," he conceded.

"Well, you must tell us all about her," insisted Jenny, "But first, we want you to tell us where to find a good supper. Our hotel is terrible!"

Nicholas escorted the girls and their companion to the most reliable restaurant in Oxford. After supper, he took the group on a short walking tour of the university, and then left them at their hotel with a promise to join them for breakfast the next morning at 8:00. Nicholas returned to his room, and after several hours of study, as he was preparing for bed, he heard a knock on his door. A porter stood there with a note.

"It's from a young lady, sir!" beamed the gatekeeper. Nicholas read the note, hurried to the college gate, and found Jenny wrapped in a raincoat, her face bright with excitement.

"Daisy and Ellen and I have talked it over, and we all think you should leave with us in the morning!"

"But I won't know until the cable arrives if I am asked to come!" said Nicholas.

"We think you should forget about the cable! You could be weeks arranging passage, and by then who knows what that girl will be thinking? You need to surprise her! Show her how important she is to you! Don't wait to be invited and show up with your hat in your hand like you're so lucky to be there! Be romantic! Sweep her off her feet!"

"You don't understand the situation. Showing up uninvited could make things worse!"

"But if you show up six weeks after her cable, you'll miss your whole opportunity!"

"How can I come tomorrow? I couldn't possibly find a ticket!"

Jenny drew close to Nicholas and whispered, "You can use Mrs. Baxter's ticket!"

As the astonished boy listened, Jenny Flagler spelled out the plan that she and her co-conspirators had devised.

"We've told Mrs. Baxter that our train to Liverpool is at 3:00 p.m. But really, we're leaving at 9:00 in the morning! After breakfast, we'll send her to visit the Bodleian Library or something, and we'll get on the train! We've already filtched her ticket! And if the Allan Line gives us any trouble, I'll mention my father's name! He's a railroad tycoon, you know!"

"This is crazy! I don't know what to say!"

"Don't say anything! Just pack your suitcase and be ready in the morning!"

Nicholas returned to his room with a battle raging in his mind. There were so many things wrong with Jenny's plan! He would miss four final examinations and the last rowing match of the season. The steamship company might not board him with someone else's ticket.

When he arrived home, Catherine might not want to see him, and the whole bizarre adventure would have been in vain. But he could not deny that the prospect of taking initiative and rushing home unbidden to plead his case with Catherine filled him with excitement. He studied his face in the mirror over his dresser.

"That's the face of a cautious man," he thought, "A man who's always careful to weigh the positive and negative in every situation. When he takes a risk and does something spontaneously, it usually produces a disaster." He paced the floor.

"But what if something is calling me to do this? What if Jenny's unexpected arrival is a sign?" And then he thought about the swan.

"Cross over. Go to her!" the voice had commanded.

Nicholas never remembered making up his mind. As if in a dream, he sat at his desk and penned notes to each of his class instructors and to the crew captain, explaining that an emergency at home demanded his immediate return. Packing his suitcase took no more than a few minutes, and then for long hours, Nicholas lay on his bed, imagining his riverside reverie unfolding just as he had pictured it.

+ + +

Jenny Flagler's plan worked perfectly. After a pleasant breakfast, the girls and Nicholas sent Mrs. Baxter off to explore the university, and as soon as she was out of sight, they signaled to a waiting lorry to load their trunks, hat boxes and suitcases, and finally, all four piled into a motor cab for the short ride to the Oxford station. In Liverpool, the Allan Line agent raised the obvious objections about Nicholas using Mrs. Baxter's ticket, but Jenny Flagler was accustomed to dealing with bureaucrats, and by indignantly mentioning her famous father's name, she prevailed. When the ferry set out for Londonderry, Nicholas and the girls stood on the deck and gave a cheer for Mrs. Baxter, who at the moment was giving a statement to the Oxford police.

The cold wind from the Irish Sea soon chilled Nicholas' buoyant mood, and before the hills of England vanished astern, a cloud of circling doubts dove at the boy like the shrieking seagulls over the ship's wake. Jenny and the girls did their best to encourage him, boasting about his courage and assuring him that any young woman would be thrilled by such a romantic gesture from a man.

After they set out from Londonderry, this time bound for New York, Nicholas soon lost count of days at sea. He spent most of his time in his cabin, half-heartedly reading a book he had packed at the last minute.

"Libenter homines id quod volunt credunt," Julius Caesar had written. "Men gladly believe that which they wish for," Nicholas silently translated, cursing himself again for his inexcusable recklessness.

The girls chided Nicholas for a few days, accusing him of ruining their adventure with his dreary mood, but as they neared the end of the voyage, they left him alone and directed their energies to the enjoyment of everything Mrs. Baxter would have prevented.

When the ship docked in New York, Nicholas rode with Jenny and her companions to the Waldorf Astoria Hotel. The girls had decided to wait in New York for Mrs. Baxter to catch up with them.

"I'm sure they have a room for us," said Jenny. "Father's a friend of the Astor's. And we'll have more fun here than if we took the next train to Palm Beach." She easily arranged a rail ticket for Nicholas, and all of the girls insisted that he leave right away.

"You must write and tell us everything," Jenny said. "I know it will turn out wonderfully! Just wait!"

+ + +

Nicholas didn't know whether to thank Jenny Flagler or accuse her of reckless tampering with his life. As he boarded the southbound train, he said, "I will certainly never forget you! All of you! And if you ever want to get closer to one of those cute Hereford cows, stop in South Carolina the next time you pass through."

As the train rumbled through the rural counties of Virginia, Nicholas stared through the window as though he were seeing American farms for the first time. He had only been gone six months, but many of the farms seemed to be larger and more mechanically advanced than he remembered. There were more tractors at work here than in the rocky fields of England, and Nicholas felt much more comfortable with the shape of the American barns.

Early in the journey, he had designed his plan for the unannounced, and unbidden, meeting with Catherine, and as the day of his arrival drew closer, he had to force himself to leave the plan alone and not subject it to endless revisions. He would get off the train in Columbia and go directly to the Governor's Mansion. Since Catherine's parents knew about his dalliance with the Negro girl, they would be cool toward him, but as cultured people, they would treat him with respect. If he found Catherine there, he would request a private meeting with her and would describe in the simplest words the truth of his transgression and the depth of his remorse. He had rehearsed his speech.

"I could not wait for an invitation that might never come," he would say. "You mean so much more to me than a paper message could ever say, and my grief in hurting you is deeper than written words could possibly express. The ocean could not keep me from coming to beg your forgiveness. And on my knees, I humbly ask you now!"

When the train slowed outside of Columbia, Nicholas hurriedly changed into the clean shirt and suit that Jenny Flagler had the hotel staff press for him in New York. He loaded his bag into a motor cab, and directed the driver toward the governor's mansion. Six months in the sheltered confines of Oxford made South Carolina's capitol city seem larger than Nicholas remembered, and as his cab dodged electric streetcars and motorized vehicles, he was amazed at the crowds of people on the street.

"Going to see the governor?" asked the cabbie.

"No, I'm a friend of his daughter's," replied Nicholas as the mansion's gates came into view.

"Daughter? Boy, Governor Ansel don't have no daughter! I haul people up here all the time, and there ain't no daughter! You must be thinking about the old governor, Governor Heyward."

"The old governor! You mean Mr. Heyward isn't governor now?"

"Son, you must have been in some other country! Mr. Heyward finished his term and left outa here back in January. I expect he's gone back to Walterboro."

Every measure of courage that Nicholas had counted on collapsed in a heartbeat. In the confusion of his father's death and his own hurried departure for England, he had forgotten about the end of Duncan Clinch Heyward's term and the election of a new governor.

"Yes, I expect he has," said Nicholas. "You can take me back to the train. And you're right. I have been in another country."

+ + +

While the long journey from New York had been marked by clarity of purpose and mounting confidence, the short train ride to Walterboro found Nicholas wallowing in confusion and sinking toward despair. He was certain now that the surprise visit would be a disaster. He had no assurance that he would even find Catherine at home. The Heywards always summered in North Georgia, and with the governor no longer in office, there was every reason to expect that the whole family would be enjoying the cool weather at Lamont. Nicholas cursed himself as the train traveled south. He had ruined everything. He had disappointed his father and probably dropped the gun that killed him. He had compromised his Oxford scholarship and with it, the career his father desired for him. He had taken advantage of a woman whom he found physically exciting, but with whom there would never be a future. And in that selfish action, he had betrayed the girl's brother, his dearest friend, and had torn apart generations of good will between the girl's family and his own. Worst of all, he had hurt the woman he loved.

Nicholas got up and walked down the aisle of the Pullman car. He pulled open the door and stepped out onto the creaking iron platform that connected his car to the next. A hot wind blew cinders from the engine's boiler fire into his face, and he squinted as the iron wheels clanked rhythmically on the fast moving rails beneath his feet.

"I could just jump," Nicholas told himself. He leaned forward, clutching the boarding handles on both sides.

"I pray you will not break my heart," whispered a silent voice. Nicholas pulled himself back to the shifting platform and looked quickly into both rail cars. He saw no one.

"It's what Catherine said in her cable," he reminded himself, "but it wasn't her voice." Nicholas felt something heavy and murderous suddenly pass from him. Closing the car door behind him, he swayed back to his seat and sat down, rubbing his eyes with his sleeve.

"Cinders," he explained to the passengers seated across the aisle.

Nicholas left his suitcase with the agent at the Walterboro station. "I'll come for it later," he said. "Can you tell me where Governor Heyward lives?"

Armed with directions, and assured that the house wasn't far, Nicholas walked the oak-shaded streets of Walterboro until he came to the picket fence the agent had described. A quiet confidence filled him as he opened the gate, and he smiled at the thought of seeing Catherine. Whatever she said, no matter how she might react to his surprise visit, he knew he was right to have come.

"Even if she's in Georgia," he said to himself, "I'm happy to be on the street where she lives!"

As Nicholas approached the porch, a black man with a rake called to him from under the moss-draped trees.

"Governor Heyward ain't home," announced the gardener. "They leave out for de mountains las' week." Nicholas stopped and nodded his head.

"Thank you," he replied, manufacturing a cheerful smile. "I expected that might be the case."

He turned and walked back to the gate. He felt like vomiting.

"I can't do this again," he told himself. The spontaneous exchange of buoyant hope for bottomless despair had become too familiar, and with each rapid step, Nicholas knew he would not put himself through it anymore.

"No one's worth it!" he said, slamming the gate behind him. "Not to cross an ocean for! Not to cross the street for! Not even the damn front yard!"

He kicked a magnolia pod into the street and stalked away from the house.

"Claus! Claus Bower!"

Nicholas stopped and turned at the sound of his name. Catherine Heyward gathered her skirt and ran down the front steps and across the yard. Pushing open the gate, she rushed to Nicholas, threw her arms around his neck, and kissed him.

## CHAPTER TWENTY-ONE

AFTER THE KISS, Nicholas and Catherine held each other and wept. For a long time, neither could speak. Then, taking a deep breath, Nicholas grasped the girl's shoulders, gently pushed her from him, looked down into her tear streaked face and began to say, "Catherine, I could not wait for an invitation that might not ever come. You mean so much more …"

"Don't!" said Catherine, embracing him again. "Don't say anything!" She looked up at him with shining eyes. "When you answered my cable, I replied right away and told you that whatever happened didn't need to come between us. I said you didn't need to travel all that distance. But, oh, Claus, how glad I am that you're here!" Nicholas could only hold her and weep.

"I wasn't sure I could find you," he said at last. "I forgot your family isn't in Columbia anymore, and then when I came here, I was afraid you would be in the mountains."

"My parents are, but when you didn't answer my last cable, I wondered if you might try to come here, so I told them to go ahead without me."

"You were waiting for me?"

"I told myself it was silly, but I knew that if you did come, I wanted to be here." Catherine smiled then and took his hand. "Come on," she urged, pulling him toward the front steps. "I have something for you!"

Nicholas waited in the front hall of the Heywards's home while Catherine raced upstairs. She returned with a soft object rolled in white paper.

"I didn't have time to wrap it properly. I just finished it last week."

Nicholas shook his head in amazement as he carefully unwrapped the gift. "I can't believe this!" he murmured. The neatly knitted ends of a soft woolen scarf reached from his hands to the floor, revealing the black, red, white and brown bands of Christ Church College.

"You made this for me?" said Nicholas, draping the scarf around his neck.

"Who else do I know at Christ Church in Oxford?"

Anguish suddenly colored Nicholas' face. "But I didn't bring you anything."

"You brought me you," said Catherine, putting her arms sound him again. "And I want to celebrate! What are your plans? Can you come with me to Lamont?"

"I don't have any plans, other than to see you. At some point, I'll want to go home and see my family, but today, right now, I can't think of anything I'd rather do than go with you to the mountains!"

Catherine sent the gardener to retrieve Nicholas's bag from the railroad station while the Heywards's cook prepared the guest room for the young man. In the morning, Catherine and Nicholas took the train to Clarkesville, and before sunset that evening they were sitting on the front porch at Lamont enjoying the view with Governor and Mrs. Heyward. The days unfolded for Nicholas like the petals of a magnolia blossom, each one more fragrant and beautiful than the one before. In the mornings, he and Catherine hiked laurel-shrouded trails. They explored old Indian campgrounds. To escape the afternoon heat, they swam in a pool of the Soque River just below the Heywards's house. At night, they slipped away with a blanket from Nicholas's room and spread it on a secluded knoll where they kissed and talked and laughed and looked up at the stars. Oxford seemed a distant memory, and the anguish of past months gave way to a peace like nothing Nicholas had ever known.

+ + +

At the end of a week, Nicholas forced himself to think beyond the delightful days at Lamont and to remember his family in Riverton.

"I wish I could be with you forever. I just don't want to overstay your parents's welcome."

"You know you'll always be welcome here. But I know your mother wants to see you, too!"

The following morning at the Toccoa train station, Nicholas and Catherine held each other in a long embrace.

"I am already missing you," sobbed the girl. "But I know you'll be back when you can."

Nicholas could hardly speak. "I pray God will make it soon," he said softly.

"Do you think God has brought us together?"

"There's no other explanation. Since the moment I saw you in Walterboro, I've felt a peace that could only be from God."

"I pray God will keep you safe," murmured Catherine.

"All aboard!" called the train's conductor. Nicholas pressed his lips close to Catherine's ear.

"I love you," he said. And before the girl could reply, he released her and, without looking back, mounted the steps to the railroad car.

Nicholas's late night arrival surprised all the residents of the Bower Farm. Sophie Bower woke to the sound of footsteps on the porch and emerged from her bedroom to see her son smiling in front of her.

"Merciful heavens!" she exclaimed, "I can't believe what I'm seeing! Claus, is it really you? I have to sit down!"

"No one else!" grinned the boy. "May I hug my mother?" Sophie threw open her arms and welcomed her son, wailing loudly as her tears began to pour.

"Why didn't you let us know you were coming?" she said into his chest. Then, pulling away, she looked intently at his face and cried, "Are you well? You're not sick, are you?"

Nicholas led his distraught mother to the settee in the parlor, and when she had begun to relax, he related a shortened version of Jenny Flagler's provision of a steamship ticket and his spontaneous decision to make the journey. He said nothing about his affair with April or about Catherine's heartbreaking cable. He also chose not to mention his missed exams and his unexcused absence from the university.

While Sophie was busy preparing a midnight supper for him, Nicholas talked about life at Oxford. Then he said, "Mother, one of the reasons I decided to come was something that happened in the college cathedral. I went to an evensong service and some of the words really hit me hard. It was a psalm, I think. About forgiveness."

"If the Anglican evening service is the same as ours, that might be Psalm 103," said Sophie. "It's always been one of my favorites!"

"I don't know why it made such an impact, but it left me in tears, and all I can say is I felt free."

"You don't need to understand God's gifts, Son. You just accept them gratefully."

"I am grateful. More than I can say." Nicholas sat silently for a while.

"I think it might have something to do with Father," he said. "I don't know. Maybe I can talk about it with Mr. Turnbull while I'm here."

The following morning, Nicholas managed to make Philip spill his breakfast coffee by surprising him with a plate of biscuits from the kitchen.

"Will there be anything else, sir?" said Nicholas. The boys greeted each other with a hug that quickly became a wrestling match.

"Not at the table!" insisted Sophie. "Honestly! When will you two grow up?"

"He's certainly grown out!" said Nicholas tugging on his brother's belt. "Farm life is clearly treating you well, Farmer Phil!"

"I'd be as skinny as you if I had to live on tea and crumpets, Old Chap!"

Nicholas repeated most of his Oxford stories while the family ate breakfast, and then he joined his brother for a tour of the farm.

"There she is!" crowed Philip, proudly pulling open the barn door to reveal a shiny black automobile.

"So this is the famous Model T!" said Nicholas.

"One of the first ones from the factory! Let me tell you, this is the wave of the future! Hop in. I'll take you for a spin!"

Nicholas grinned as Philip cranked the engine and leapt to the seat to adjust the throttle. "Here we go!" the younger boy shouted. As the car rattled along the roads that traversed the farm, Nicholas looked closely at the passing cotton fields.

"Looks like a good crop!" he shouted over the noise of the engine.

"Price is down," said Philip. "The Mayfields have contracted for almost everybody's cotton, and Mr. Singleton can't afford to pay anything more. I don't know what we're going to do. January's home. You want to stop and say hello?"

When the car rattled into the Adams's front yard, half a dozen children streamed from the cabin door and danced around the visitors. Venus Adams emerged in all her majesty to wrap Nicholas in her massive arms. For a moment, Nicholas worried that in her enthusiasm she might forget to let him breathe.

"All that glisters is not gold," said a familiar voice, "but I'll be The Merchant of Venice if that man you're squeezing to death isn't Nicholas Bower!"

"January!" Nicholas extracted himself from Venus' arms. "I'm sure glad to see you!"

"What? No refined words from the Oxford scholar?" grinned the black boy.

"Fallaces sunt rerum species," Nicholas fired back without a moment's hesitation. " 'The appearances of things are deceptive!' I can still match you one for one!"

"You've used that slogan before!"

"Well, you didn't give me a chance to think!"

After the Bower brothers visited with the Adams family, January asked if Nicholas might stay awhile longer.

"I'll bring him home before supper," he promised Philip. When the Model T had chugged its way out of the yard, January beckoned to Nicholas. "Let's take a walk," he said.

The boys trudged in silence until they could no longer see the house. "There's something I've wanted to tell you," said January. Nicholas felt new rumblings from his old anxiety.

"Is it about Sally?"

"You've known, haven't you? Yes. It's about Sally."

"You love her, don't you?" Nicholas tried to hide his surging emotions.

"Of course I do! What man in his right mind wouldn't? I expect you loved her yourself at one time."

Nicholas nodded. "We were children. But she's changed! I saw it happening at Carolina. I don't really know who Sally is anymore."

"I saw her change, too," said January. "And what I see is a woman of strength and courage!"

"I've seen the two of you together. I guess everybody in Riverton has."

"We've got nothing to hide. I went to see her a few times in Columbia, and she came once to Orangeburg, but we've never really been together."

"I've worried about you both. You know how people are. Even if there's nothing but friendship between you, there could be trouble."

"We're not children, Claus! We know what we're dealing with."

"So what are you going to do?"

January walked without speaking, and finally stopped and looked at his friend. "Nothing," he said. "We talked about moving up north, but we had to admit that things are not much better there. And if we moved away, we'd be giving up things that are important to us."

"Like what?" said Nicholas.

"Like educating black children! Both of us want to teach. And Sally's pretty passionate about getting the vote for women."

"So you'll stay here and be friends? Nothing more?"

"For now," nodded January, looking far over the cotton fields. "But," he said, his face brightening, "Not all the Adams family are unlucky in love!"

Nicholas felt a surge of fear as he thought of April's unexplained absence from Riverton.

"My sister's got herself engaged!"

"April?" said Nicholas, trying to sound only casually interested.

"April!" laughed January. "You know she's been in Philadelphia working for the people my mother used to work for. Well, she's met a young man, a preacher, she says, with degrees from college and seminary! And they're getting married in the fall!"

Nicholas struggled to sort out his feelings. Apparently, April wasn't pregnant. She hadn't gone north to avoid embarrassing herself, and him. Nicholas felt a weight float from his shoulders, and in the same moment, he sensed a jealous longing for the girl.

"Have you met the man?" he asked.

"Not yet. They're supposed to come for a visit in a few weeks. If you're still here, you can help me interrogate him!"

On Sunday, Nicholas sat next to his mother at St. Matthias Church. The tiny, wood frame building would have fit easily in the narthex of Christ Church Cathedral, Nicholas observed, but the sound of the liturgy had a comforting familiarity. Asa Turnbull stood before the congregation and with a broad smile proclaimed, "Grace be unto you, and peace, from God our Father, and from the Lord Jesus Christ!"

All at once the peace that had fallen upon Nicholas in front of the Heyward house in Walterboro found him again. The tears didn't surprise him. He welcomed the feeling, and remained puzzled about the source.

"I'll ask Mr. Turnbull about it," thought Nicholas.

Seeing Sally Hemphill sitting in her old pew next to her mother produced a new mixture of emotions, and after church, he hesitated to speak to the girl. Sally saw him, and hurried across the church-yard.

"You're not going back to England without saying hello to one of your oldest friends!" said Sally, giving Nicholas a bold hug. He blushed as she took his hand and led him to a shady place under the magnolia tree, the same place where they talked when they were children.

"Now, tell me everything," Sally said. "Only do it fast because Mother is eager to go home!"

Nicholas gave his friend an abbreviated account of his travels and his life at Oxford, and was about to add more details when Sally interrupted him.

"I need to be quick. January told me that the two of you have talked."

Nicholas looked at her and nodded. "I think you're doing the right thing."

"We knew you might be worried about us, and we wanted you to know that we're not going to do anything reckless."

"Some of your progressive friends at Carolina would be sur-prised to hear you say that!" smiled Nicholas.

Sally laughed. "I think I still have plenty of surprises in me! So does your friend, January. And I would be surprised myself if there weren't some unpredictable ideas in you, too!"

Before riding home in Philip's car, Nicholas made an appointment to speak to Mr. Turnbull. The following morning, on his way to the church, Nicholas visited the general store and sent a cable to the Allen Line requesting passage to England as soon as possible.

When Nicholas and Asa Turnbull had seated themselves in the minister's study, the boy began with what had become a brief, standard description of his recent travels and his Oxford experiences.

"One afternoon at evensong," said Nicholas.

"Ah! Choral evensong!" said the priest. "I've heard it done beautifully in New York, but how I'd love to hear it sung properly in England!"

Nicholas frowned. "Yes, it's lovely, but the effect of one particular service has stayed with me and I wanted to ask you about it."

"Please do!"

"I think I remember one of the psalms saying, 'Who forgiveth all thy sin and healeth all thine infirmities.'"

"Yes, yes," nodded Asa Turnbull. "Psalm 103! Beautiful!"

"Well, it made me think of a verse from Shakespeare about mercy, and I don't know why but it made me weep."

"Son, God's grace often makes people weep. But then it makes them shout for joy!"

"I don't understand," Nicholas stood and stared through the open window.

"Undeserved love!" said the minister. "It's such rare thing for all of us that when we experience it, all our reservations fall away and we become like little children."

Nicholas thought about Catherine's greeting under the oaks in Walterboro. He had wept like a baby. And he had felt like shouting!

"Could grace come from someone other than God?"

"It always comes from someone!" Mr. Turnbull leaned forward eagerly, his face bright with excitement. "It's from anyone who loves us and forgives us when we don't deserve it, and most of all, it's from Jesus!"

"I must have hurt a lot of people," said Nicholas, "because any time somebody does anything kind to me, or even if I see kindness extended to someone else, I cry!"

"Everybody needs grace, and some of us seem to have a particular sensitivity to it. Apparently, you do!"

"But I hate to cry like that. I don't like to look so weak all the time!"

"What you're calling a weakness might be God's blessing," said Mr. Turnbull. "Our strengths are the very things that keep us from receiving the grace God is always trying to give us. It's when we let go and admit our weaknesses that we become strong!"

As soon as the words, "Let go" emerged from the minister's mouth, Nicholas felt himself far away from the pastor's study. The invitation that had begun to haunt him on the day of the Winter Race suddenly came whispering to him again.

"Let go!'

"Nicholas? Are you alright, Son?" asked the minister. "For a minute there, I thought you'd left me!"

The shaken boy stated at his pastor. "Do you remember, years ago, when I fell off my horse in the Winter Race?"

"I could never forget that! We all thought you had been killed!"

"Do you remember what my father said to me when I was being dragged under the horse?"

"If I'm not mistaken, I believe the captain ordered you to hold on."

"And I tried! But there was another voice. Not a voice, really, but an invitation inside of me that said, 'Let go!'"

"And you did," said the minister.

"And I lived."

Nicholas sat down and faced Asa Turnbull. "Sir," he said, "this talk has been good! Better than I can tell you. Now I want to think about it."

"May I make three suggestions?" asked the minister. "First, pray about what we've been discussing. I'm quite sure that God is speaking to you. Then, when you get home, or after you're back at Oxford, take your Bible and read the Gospel according to Mark out loud, all at one sitting. The whole thing! It only takes an hour. And finally, before you go, I hope you will visit your father's grave. It just might be that you and the captain have some unfinished business to attend to."

After saying goodbye to the minister, Nicholas climbed into Caesar's saddle and cantered toward the farm. The discussion of God's grace had left him with exciting hints of the gift itself, and he wanted to waste no time taking the next steps.

"God," he murmured as the horse rocked beneath him, "I'm not good at this. Please help me."

Nicholas stabled the horse quickly, and as he hurried through the parlor he called to his mother. "When's lunch?"

"About an hour," answered Sophie.

"Perfect!" Nicholas said, thundering up the stairs to his room.

As soon as he had closed the door behind him, Nicholas picked up the Bible his mother always kept on the bedside table, and he skimmed the pages until he found the Gospel according to Mark. Nicholas stretched out on his bed and, in his best Oxford accent, began to enunciate the lofty language from the time of King James.

"The beginning of the Gospel of Jesus Christ, the Son of God."

Satisfied with his sound, Nicholas read on. The very next sentence introduced the ministry of John the Baptist, and Nicholas found himself appreciating an author who got right down to business. By the end of the first chapter, the story had captured his full attention. He read about Jesus being baptized and teaching and healing and rebuking demons. By the end of the second chapter, Nicholas had abandoned the Oxford accent and was simply reading the narrative in his own low country drawl.

But the real turning point for Nicholas came at the end of Chapter Eight, where Jesus told his friends about his own death and res-urrection. A life-long church member, Nicholas had listened to many excerpts from the Gospel story, but he'd never heard the whole saga recounted without interruption. Now he could see where the mira-cle-working teacher was headed. "He's going to Jerusalem to die!" Nicholas realized. He sat up in bed as the story continued, with each chapter hastening toward the end more ominously than the one be-fore. When he read about the disciples abandoning their master in the place called Gethsemane, Nicholas stood up and paced the floor as he half-whispered the final chapters.

"Supper!" called Sophie Bower from the hall below.

"Coming!" yelled Nicholas as he read the last sentences of the story. He closed the book. Jesus was alive. He had sent his followers to preach and win the world with signs of God's power. The boy was strangely quiet when he pulled his chair to the family table.

"Taking a nap?" said Philip, who had come from the fields and had just finished washing his hands and face.

"Reading," replied Nicholas without explanation.

"For school?" asked Sophie, passing the potatoes.

"For me," said Nicholas, smiling mysteriously.

When Nicholas stopped by the general store the next day, Mr. Huckabee handed him a cable from the Allan Line.

"Pretty quick response! I hope it's good news," said the store-keeper. Nicholas read the short document and shook his head.

"I guess it depends on how I look at it. They have a birth for me out of New York in three days, but that means I have to leave tomorrow, and I'm not ready to go!"

Riding Caesar back to the farm gave Nicholas time to remind himself about responsibilities he had set aside during his unplanned visit to Riverton.

"The sooner I'm back in Oxford, the better chance I'll have of completing those final exams and getting my work back on sched-ule."

When he reached the farm, his mind was already racing ahead to the train ride and the ocean crossing. "Mother!" he shouted as he leapt up the porch steps. "Can you help me pack? I need to leave in the morning!"

The announcement sent Sophie into frantic activity, washing and folding Nicholas's clothing as tears ran down her face.

"I thought you would stay through the summer. You've hardly been here long enough to say hello!"

By the next morning, Sophie Bower had resigned herself to her son's departure, and after a long prayer and a quick kiss, she sent him off to the train station with Philip at the wheel of the Model T.

"When we get to the Sumter turnoff, let's go straight ahead to the cemetery. I'd like to visit Father's grave before I go," said Nicholas.

"Will do! To tell the truth, I haven't been back there since the funeral, either."

They parked the car in the shade of a giant oak, and walked together to the burial site. Scattered sprigs of grass had begun to grow in the smoothly packed earth over their father's grave.

Philip stared at the ground. "We ordered the stone. I guess I'd better ask somebody about it. And then I need to come back and cut the grass."

Nicholas didn't respond. The sight of the grave brought back painful memories of the funeral for both of the captain's sons. But for Nicholas, the scene also invited a flood of even more troubling images. He heard the gun shot. He winced at the echo of his father's scream. He shut his eyes at the memory of the ringing accusation, "You have killed me!" Nicholas knelt in the soft earth. Oblivious to the presence of his brother, he leaned forward until his forehead touched the ground.

"I'm sorry, Father!" he whispered. "I can't change what happened. I can only ask you to forgive me."

Philip stood silently, lost in his own private dialogue. When

Nicholas lifted his head and knelt erect, he made no effort to hide his tears. His lips moved silently.

"I hope you can do it, Father. But either way, I want you to know that I forgive you."

Nicholas got to his feet and took a deep breath. Turning back toward the car, he said to Philip, "I'm ready when you are."

## CHAPTER TWENTY-TWO

"I FEEL LIKE I'VE SPENT the last half of my life on a train," said Nicholas to his brother as they watched the massive locomotive pull into the Sumter station.

Philip laughed. "For a country boy, you've sure done a lot of traveling. One of these days, it's gonna be me on the way to merry old England!"

"I wish it were you this time! It's a long way, and my heart's not in it."

"Come on! You're a few semesters away from a law degree from Oxford! You think about me at the end of August and be glad you're not here picking cotton!"

"I hate leaving you and Mother."

"We'll be all right. And so will Catherine. That girl loves you, you know!"

Nicholas nodded, looking away until he could speak. "It might be two years this time," he said.

Philip punched him on the arm. "I'll write, I promise. And Mother's doing better, so she can tell you how everything looks to her."

"I guess it's time," said Nicholas. He took a deep breath, lifted his suitcase, and began the longest journey of his life.

+ + +

The train trip to Boston seemed to take forever, and Nicholas waited in vain for the appearance of a new Jenny Flagler. The fast changing view from the Pullman window revealed nothing of interest, even when the tracks negotiated the busy streets of New York. In Boston, Nicholas had to pay for a cab to deliver him to the Allen Line docks. His brief venture into the city left him feeling lonely, and he returned to board the liner early in the evening. He unpacked his few belongings in the cramped third level cabin, piling the room's small table with books from the Christ Church library and others borrowed from Asa Turnbull.

"I'm not sure any of these will help much," he had explained to the minister, "but when I get to Oxford, I'll be facing some exams that I walked away from. If they'll let me take them late, I need to use the trip to review the material."

Before the ship cast off the next morning, Nicholas had already begun to take notes on the history of English law.

The crossing turned out to be much smoother than his first voyage, and Nicholas had no difficulty with his stomach. He took most of his meals with a group of very friendly people from Michigan, saying little and listening without interest to their tour agenda.

"No, I haven't been to London. I'm a student," he said simply. From time to time, Nicholas visited the aft salon where he had enjoyed spirited conversation with Jenny Flagler and her friends, but most of his waking hours found him in his cabin pouring through thick textbooks. The Theory of Legislation. International Law. Torts. Contracts. Real Property. Nicholas reviewed the semester's reading, only emerging from his cabin to eat and take short walks on the promenade deck.

The ferry from Londonderry and the train ride to Oxford brought Nicholas none of the excitement he'd felt on his first trip. Every mile under cloudy skies increased his apprehension about how the university would deal with his sudden departure. When he stepped onto the platform and picked up his luggage for the short walk to Christ Church, a hard rain was falling. The familiar skyline of the ancient city brought him no comfort. At the college gate, a porter he didn't know examined the student roster and told Nicholas that he would not be admitted without written authorization from the university. Leaving his bags, he trudged to the office of the Dean, only to be told to return the next day. Nicholas walked through the rain to the high street and stood dripping in the alcove of a bookstore, hoping to recognize an acquaintance among the umbrellaed people who hurried by. Their preoccupied expressions left him feeling like an intruder, and he cursed his impulsive decision to drop his courses and hurry home.

Not until Nicholas pulled open the door at the Eagle and Child did his outlook begin to improve. Charles Middleton and two of his friends immediately spotted the soaking wet American and welcomed him to their table.

"What the bloody hell! It's the Yank!" said one of the boys. "Are you done gallivanting, lad? Take off that coat and set your bum here!"

"He'll fancy a pint and some nosh, or I'm a rat's arse! The Yank's jolly well knackered!"

Nicholas collapsed in an empty chair and sat wearily as a puddle formed beneath him. "I'd forgotten that you all speak a foreign language," he said, trying to smile.

"Only in here, mate!" said Charles. "Remember, in class, it's strictly the King's English. You were actually communicating quite well before you disappeared."

"It's a long story," said Nicholas.

"I understand the Dean is eager to hear it! There was a bit of a do when you left. Angry American lady. The Oxford cops. All very confusing."

"All I can say is it seemed like a good idea at the time. Now I can't get into the college! Can somebody have me admitted as a guest?"

Charles Middleton vouched for Nicholas at the college gate and provided a pallet on the floor of his single room. The next morning, Nicholas went before the Dean and received the answer he had dreaded for days.

"I'm afraid you have wasted your first semester at Oxford, Mr. Bower, unless you have an acceptable explanation for missing your final examinations," said the Dean.

"As I wrote in my note, it was a family emergency, Sir."

"Will you reveal the nature of that emergency?" Nicholas could not imagine that crossing the ocean to apologize to a girl would qualify as an acceptable explanation.

"I'm sorry, Sir. It's a private matter."

"Well, then, I must inform you that you will receive no credit for the four courses you failed to complete. And it's a pity, because your grades placed you at the top of your class. Most unusual for an international student. However, since you have shown such promise, the university will enroll you on probation for the Michaelmas term."

Nicholas sipped his beer alone until Charles joined him for supper at the Eagle and Child. "Well, what's the report?" asked the Englishman.

"First term's a total loss," said Nicholas. "But I'm still in. They're letting me back in the fall."

"That's naff! Dean didn't swallow your story?"

"I didn't tell him. It's my business. I believe I did the right thing. No, I'm sure I did!"

"And you've noticed that none of your Bird and Baby mates have pressed you for details."

"I do appreciate that," said Nicholas. "Too bad the men on the crew aren't as understanding."

"Glocky lads! Decided to ding you, have they?"

"If you mean I'm off the Christ Church crew, yes. They lost the final match and blamed it on me."

"No school! No boats! Looks like you've got the summer off,

Old Man!" said Charles.

"I need to do something! Maybe this is my chance to play a little rugby."

"If you're serious about that, I can introduce you to Oliver Courtenay. He's a jemmy forward! The real don of the Christ Church team."

The next morning, Nicholas and Charles walked to Merton Field where the members of the college rugby team held their daily practices.

"There he is!" said Charles. "Ollie! Over here!" As Oliver Courtenay jogged toward them, Nicholas began to reconsider his interest in playing rugby.

"That man's huge! He's bigger than most of the guards and tackles at Carolina!"

"He's a forward, one of the lads who go after the ball," said Charles. "But you'll learn all about it." After shaking hands with the big athlete, Nicholas tried to sound modest about his own athletic accomplishments.

"I was quarterback for my university team. The coach thought I was pretty fast and could throw the ball. I rowed for Christ Church last spring, but I'm probably out of shape now."

"Well, mate, if you've a mind to try rugby, you'll be getting your wind back in short order or be going about on crutches!" said Ollie. "Come along and watch the squad working out. I'll explain the game when we take lunch."

"That reminds me," said Nicholas, looking around for Charles Middleton. "I've got to find some place to stay. The college won't admit me until the fall term starts."

"Plenty of flats for let in the city. Step lively, now! Rugby players don't stop and rest like you American footballers!"

Nicholas stood on the sidelines while Ollie and his teammates resumed their scrimmage, running, passing or kicking the ball, tackling the ball carrier and piling together to form human tunnels. Occasionally, play would stop because of a foul Nicholas couldn't recognize or a rule infraction he couldn't understand. He noticed that the chalked off practice area seemed considerably larger than the football field at home.

"Longer and wider," said Ollie when the players paused for a short lunch break. "And it's called a pitch. You run up and down it for two forty-minute halves and you're ready for a pint and a good night's sleep!" Nicholas listened with growing confusion as Ollie explained the rules of the game.

"Everybody plays offense and defense? How do you score?"

"Any way we can! Touchdown and conversion, penalty kick, drop goal. You could be one of the backs, I'll wager. Fast and agile, like your fullback or quarterback."

By the end of the morning practice, Nicholas had begun to understand the most obvious elements of the game, but he waited to ask Ollie about the mysterious offside rules.

"You've got a lot to learn," said Ollie as the two men walked back to Christ Church. "We can talk some more over supper. Why don't you take my roommate's bed tonight? He's gone back to Wales for the summer." Nicholas accepted the invitation with great relief.

"I'll get my things from Charles's room and be back in ten minutes."

"Make that fifteen, and I'll be dressed and ready to go. There's a group of athletes I meet with each week. Perhaps you'd like to pop in there with me before supper?"

"Rugby players?"

"Some are. But we've also got some footballers and cricket players."

"What do you do?"

"Bible study."

Nicholas took a new look at his tall and muscular friend. "You're active in church?"

"Some of the lads are. Me, I'm chapel. Methodist. But we meet upstairs at the Bird and Baby."

Nicholas smiled. "Well, since we'll already be so close to supper,

I'll be glad to go with you!"

When Nicholas and Ollie climbed the stairs to the pub's second floor, six other men had already taken seats in a circle of chairs. The group members stood as Ollie introduced the newcomer. Nicholas had seen several of the men around the university, but only one had he met before.

"Yes, I know Mr. Bower," said a short, broad shouldered man. "He rowed with us on the crew this spring. For a while."

Nicholas felt his face redden as he shook the man's tentatively offered hand. "Smythe, I just came back yesterday and I haven't had a chance to explain why I left."

"Makes no difference now. But you'd do better to come with an apology instead of an explanation."

Nicholas released the man's hand. "I didn't come here expecting to feel guilty."

"Why shouldn't you feel guilty if you are guilty?" said Smythe.

Ollie Courtenay stepped between the antagonists. "Gentlemen, can we postpone this until after our meeting?"

"It's all right!" said Nicholas, stepping forward and pushing Ollie aside. "Smythe is right! I left the crew with no warning, and they lost the final match. I was thinking about my own situation. He's right. I do owe them an apology!"

Smythe looked steadily at Nicholas. "I'm waiting."

Nicholas took a deep breath. "I acted selfishly and let down the team. I shouldn't have done it, and I'm very sorry that I did. I hope you will all forgive me."

Smythe stood silently for a dozen heartbeats. Then, gradually, the corners of his mouth began to turn upward until his whole face had surrendered to a smile.

"Well, mate, I forgive you! Don't know about the rest of those blokes, but I'm a sucker for real repentance!" He extended his hand again, and the light in his eyes confirmed the gesture. Nicholas kept his guard up as he tried to assess the unexpected development, then he took Smythe's hand and solemnly gripped it.

"Thank you. I wasn't expecting this."

Smythe laughed, and the other men in the room joined him. "You weren't expecting forgiveness from a follower of Jesus Christ? You've just done as pretty a Matthew 18 as I've ever seen!"

Nicholas stood in amazement as the group members each came forward to shake his hand.

"Welcome!"

"So glad you've joined us!"

"Well done, mate!"

When all had greeted the newcomer and he had taken his seat in the circle, Nicholas asked weakly, "Matthew 18?"

"It's where Jesus talked about how to regain a brother who's offended you," explained Ollie.

"It's about accountability among brothers," said Smythe. "Oh, and my given name is Albert."

"You're in good company, Bower," said one of the men. "Smythe gets more than his share of accountability in here! He's a bloody expert in apologizing!"

"I'll be apologizing again if you cobblers don't shut up and stop acting like total gorms!"

One of the men pretended to whisper to Nicholas. "He's got the lesson tonight, and he's nervous because we've a newcomer!"

Nicholas raised his hands defensively. "He's got nothing to worry about from me! I know the Bible about like I know rugby!"

When the group had come to order, Smythe opened the meeting with a short extemporaneous prayer. Nicholas had grown up with the Episcopal prayer book but, with the exception of his mother, he had heard very few people pray out loud in their own words. He joined the others in a concluding amen, and then positioned himself where he could read the open Bible in Ollie's lap. Smythe read aloud verses from the fourth chapter of the Epistle to the Galatians, and Nicholas followed attentively until he heard these words.

"So through God, you are no longer a slave but a son, and if a son, then an heir."

Without warning, the pub's upper room dissolved around him and Nicholas bent forward, assaulted by painful memories of his father. He could still hear the captain's curses. He could feel his own rage at his father's cruelty to him and to others who failed to meet the captain's standards. He could taste the bitterness of his unexpected legacy, a promise broken and his future manipulated. He could hear the shotgun blast and his father's scream.

"Here, Yank! What's got over you! Have you taken ill?" A hand on his shoulder brought Nicholas back to the meeting. He sat up as Ollie turned to search his eyes.

"I'm OK. It was a bad memory. Long ago. It's gone. I'll be all right." The other members of the group looked at Nicholas with serious faces.

"We'll be praying for this lad," said Smythe with a glance around the circle. "That is, if you don't mind."

"I don't! Please pray. Maybe I'll be able to … Well, anyway, it wouldn't hurt to pray." As the Bible lesson continued, Nicholas couldn't help drifting back occasionally into recollections of his father. "Son and heir. Maximilian Bower's son and heir. A son to persecute and an heir to disappoint! What an inheritance!"

"You see, lads, God wants to adopt us as his sons! It's what Paul says right here in four, verse five!" said Smythe.

"And he sent his own Son to take away the things that disqualify us from the family!" said Ollie.

"Accountability!" said another of the men. "We get ourselves snockered, and Jesus has the hangover!"

Nicholas listened and frowned. "That doesn't seem fair! Why would he do that?"

"Because he loves us, mate! And he's wanting us to love him back!"

When an hour had ended, Nicholas shifted self-consciously as the other students gathered around him to touch his back and shoulders while they prayed. Sensing the American's discomfort, Albert Smythe made his petition graciously short.

"Thank you for bringing Nicholas tonight, Lord. Please do for him what will be best, an even better answer than he knows how to ask for."

The other group members agreed and everyone shook Nicholas' hand in turn as they went downstairs for supper.

"The Yank has a mind to try out for rugby," said Ollie as they ordered the meal. "While you're praying, better ask the Lord to have mercy on his weak little American body tomorrow!"

Putting borrowed sheets on the extra bed in Ollie's room, Nicholas let his mind jump between his perplexing visit to the rugby practice field and his equally disturbing encounter at the Bible study group. He felt certain that he could learn the sport, and perhaps even play it well, but the mystery of St. Paul's words filled him with a mixture of excitement and apprehension. He felt good about the way he'd handled the confrontation with Albert Smythe. The genuine friendliness of the other men stood in clear contrast to the competitive attitude of most students at the university. But something about the whole encounter left Nicholas with his emotional guard firmly in place. He sensed the emergence of important, even life-changing issues, and he wanted time to think about what had happened.

"You made a cracking good impression on the lads tonight." Ollie stood at the door holding out a clean towel.

"I hope so," said Nicholas. "I like them all. There's something different about them."

"You know what they have in common is faith in the Lord."

"I saw that. They seemed to come from all over the country, just listening to their accents."

"From all over, and from different backgrounds. Albert's father is a motorman in Chester. Tom's parents own a greengrocer shop in York. Bunny's the youngest son of a solicitor in Manchester."

"How many of them are going back to do what their fathers do?"

"Not a one, to my knowledge. Most people don't take on hereditary jobs these days."

Nicholas sat on the bed and nodded. "That scripture tonight got me thinking. The one about if a son, then an heir."

"You plan to do what your father did?"

Nicholas laughed. "I thought I would, but my father changed all that! He gave the farm to my brother and sent me here to law school."

"You sound brassed. Does your father know?"

Nicholas shook his head. "He died last fall."

"Cor! And left you diddled! I'm sorry for you, Old Man."

"You can see why the part about a son and an heir got to me."

"Aye, and why you need a better inheritance."

"From who?"

"Who do you think? God!" Ollie sat at the other end of the bed and looked closely at Nicholas ."That's what the study was all about, mate! Anybody with faith in Jesus becomes a son of God, and inherits what belongs to Jesus!"

Nicholas frowned. "I thought all people are God's children."

"God's creatures, and he loves us all. But we become his sons when we welcome his real self back inside us."

"His real self?"

"Jesus! We give up trying to impress God and let Jesus be born in us!"

Nicholas lay back on the bed while Ollie's words invited another flood of memories. "We give up trying." What had Asa Turnbull said? "Yes, Nicholas, giving up is exactly what God wants you to do!"

And then Nicholas sensed the whisper of a familiar invitation. "Let go!" The message was not new, but Nicholas realized that the words had lost their terrifying impact. Something had changed.

"I should be crying by now," Nicholas told himself. "But I'm not!" He sat up and looked at Ollie. "How do you know when it happens?"

"You just know. It's different for everybody."

"It's from God?"

"Exactly!"

"A new inheritance?"

"Just what Jesus had."

Across Tom Quad the tower bell tolled the curfew hour. "What about your inheritance?" asked Nicholas.

"You mean from my family?"

"From your father."

Oliver Courtenay smiled. "My dad's the Fourteenth Earl of Devon. He's in the House of Lords, and we have an estate in Dartmoor. I expect it will be mine one day. But the inheritance I'm looking forward to doesn't come with taxes and a leaky roof!" The big rugby player looked at Nicholas and winked. "I'm inheriting a place in Heaven! But look, mate, if you hope to live through rugby tomorrow, you'd best be off to sleep!"

+ + +

On Merton Field the next day, Nicholas discovered that seven months away from football had not seriously diminished his physical conditioning. He impressed the Christ Church rugby players with his speed and agility, even managing to throw and kick the oblong ball with surprising accuracy. The strenuous exercise helped keep Nicholas free from discouraging thoughts, and camaraderie with the other men left him feeling increasingly welcome. Mornings on the athletic field relaxed him for afternoons of concentrated reading. Each evening, he enjoyed supper with Ollie and other members of the team. And at bedtime, Nicholas found himself postponing sleep in order to ask God's blessings on the important people in his life. He felt certain that his mumbled petitions would sound amateurish next to the fluent prayers of Ollie and the members of the second floor Bible group, but he took comfort in the hope that God would hear them anyway.

# CHAPTER TWENTY-THREE

## Fall 1908

CLASSES FOR THE MICHAELMAS TERM had just begun when Nicholas received his first letter from Catherine.

"After you left, I stayed at Lamont with my parents, but I could hardly stand to be there. Everything reminded me of you. I thought that visiting our special places would make me feel better, but the first time I went at night to our hill top, I cried all the way home. Nicholas, I just don't know how I'll be able to stand the months – no, I'll face it – the years we will be apart! All I can do is try to graduate next spring and hope that Mother and Father will send me to England for a graduation present."

Nicholas tried to imagine what it would be like to show Catherine around Oxford. Perhaps they could travel together to see places his busy schedule had prevented him from visiting. The thought delighted him, and he had to force himself to set it aside in order to resume his studies. The new classes plunged Nicholas into material for which he had little preparation. Most of the other students had read much more extensively than he, and having grown up under British law, all of them demonstrated an easy familiarity with terms and concepts that Nicholas found difficult to understand and apply.

He made a place for himself on the rugby team, and just as at the University of South Carolina, he soon gained something of a hero's reputation around the colleges of Oxford.

In the middle of November, Oliver Courtenay came with a request that Nicholas found more intimidating than any university exam.

"How about taking a spot to lead the lesson at the Bird and Baby next week?"

"Not my cup of tea!" said Nicholas. "I know nowt when it comes to the Bible!"

"Listen to you! Been here not a year and you're talking like a Yorkshire man! And you know more Bible than you let on!"

"Don't let a few quotations fool you. In school at home, I memorized some Latin expressions and got myself a reputation as a classical scholar."

"You know Latin?" said Ollie. "Fancy that! I've a bit of it myself! 'Rident stolidi verba Latina.' Fools laugh at the Latin language."

"And everybody will laugh at me if I try to explain the Bible! 'Quid rides? De te fibula narrator!' What are you laughing at? The joke's on you!"

After further banter, Nicholas agreed to prepare a lesson for the study group. "Not next week! I'll need at least a fortnight to get ready. 'Diligentia maximum steam mediocris ingeni subsidium.'"

Ollie doubled over in laughter. "Diligence is a very great help even to a mediocre intelligence," he translated between gasps.

As the days grew shorter and the air colder, Nicholas began to think about the seasonal customs that had always warmed the winter for his family. At supper with Charles Middleton and Ollie Courtenay one night, he admitted that he would miss an American Thanksgiving, with all its associated traditions.

"Ruby would cook a turkey. Mother would fix rice and gravy. And we'd have plenty of sweet potatoes from the hill by the barn."

"I don't suppose a Cornish hen would do?" said Charles. "Or

bangers and mash?"

"A couple of quail broiled with bacon might take the edge off," said Nicholas. "Thanksgiving was when we always…"

Charles and Ollie waited. "Yes?"

"We used to hunt quail at Thanksgiving."

"Would that be the partridge called Bob White?"

"Let's order supper. It was a bad idea to think about Thanksgiving."

Ollie spoke up. "Cor blimey, Yank! You didn't tell me you've shot birds!"

"He'd like to skive the shooting talk, if you don't mind!" said Charles. "I don't think he'd mind you knowing his father was killed in a shooting accident."

"Well, I'm a smashing idiot! Sorry, Old Man. I'd no idea!"

"It's all right," said Nicholas. "It bothers me sometimes, but I'll get over it."

"Then when you're ready, I want you – you too, Charles – to go to Dartmoor with me and have a go at our red grouse."

Nicholas promised he would remember the invitation. "You'll love the moorlands," said Ollie. "Wild and very different from Oxfordshire."

+ + +

The arrival of a letter from his mother only made Nicholas feel increasingly lonely. In her graceful hand, Sophie Bower penned, "Most of the news from your family is good at this writing. The cotton crop exceeded previous years. You would be proud of the way your brother has taken over management of the farm. He hired more pickers this summer and our cotton was the first to reach the gin. I'm sad to report that dear Mr. Singleton has gone out of business. The Mayfields's gin continued to pay a few cents more per pound, and, to their shame, all the other planters in the country sold Mayfield their crop. We intended to keep our business with Singleton, but when he closed his gin, we had no alternative but to trade with the Mayfields. Philip says that Conner spends most of his time in Columbia, and we never see him around Riverton. His family shows every evidence of prospering, and no one here knows why, although several suspicions are widespread.

"Your dear Catherine sent me a sweet note at Thanksgiving telling me how much she and her family think of you and how much you are missed. January stops in when he is home from Yale. He is doing very well, as we all knew he would. I understand that both he and Catherine will graduate in the spring. Miss Abernathy and Mr. Turnbull both send their greetings. Your Christmas present should arrive before long."

Sophie closed the letter with words of encouragement and an exhortation to go to church. "God has great things for you to do," she wrote, "and he wants to help you recognize and accomplish them."

The next day's post contained a letter from January that left Nicholas with new anxieties.

"I'm doing fine at school, and am looking forward to graduation in May. The people here in New Haven have talked to me about staying to teach literature, but I'm not inclined to accept their offer. My calling is to teach young children. If I could get a job like Sally's, that would be all I could ask for."

Nicholas shook his head. He worried each time January mentioned Sally Hemphill, wondering how long they would be able to maintain a platonic friendship and avoid serious trouble with certain elements in Clarendon County.

January continued, "The last time I was home, I rode past the gate to the Mayfield place. You wouldn't believe how they have that road guarded! And the wagon tracks from their farm have the county road all chopped up! Mr. Huckabee told me that the railroad is building a spur from Sumter right into Rimini. Do you realize how close that is to the Mayfields's? It looks to me and to other people who are willing to talk about it, that somebody's been making deals with powerful people in Columbia. You already know what I think is going on!"

Under his breath, Nicholas whispered, "Bootlegging! No more backwoods stills! They're making it into a big business!"

The final paragraphs of January's letter caused Nicholas the most concern.

"I went to April's wedding," wrote January. "Mother and I took the young ones on the train to Philadelphia, the first train ride for them. April's employers bought our tickets. April looked very happy. I like the young preacher she took as her husband."

Nicholas couldn't help the feeling that swept over him. He had never imagined a life with April, but he found the thought of her with another man hard to take.

Then he read, "Mother told me that Taylor Mayfield – that's Sheriff Mayfield, remember – came to our farm and offered to buy it. She said he was very polite, but she had the feeling that it wasn't just an offer. The Mayfield's mean to take our land, one way or another. They have the money, it seems, and I'm afraid they will soon have the power, if they don't already, to force us to sell."

Nicholas' fist scattered books from his desk. "Damn!" he muttered. And then he thought about his father. "Where are you, Captain? This isn't right!"

+ + +

A week before Christmas, Ollie Courtenay extended an invitation to Nicholas.

"You've gone about all watered for much too long, mate! I think a Christmas visit to my home would set you right. Shall I ring my mum?"

Nicholas tried to turn down his friend's offer, but when he learned that Charles Middleton had also been invited, he thought about how lonely he would be without his friends, and he agreed to join them in Devon for the holidays. On the way to the train station, Ollie and Charles walked briskly and kept up an excited banter with each other and with fellow travelers who shared their holiday mood. Nicholas fell behind, burdened by his suitcase and a large satchel of books. He ignored the disdainful stares and critical remarks of several students, but Ollie defended him and put his detractors on notice.

"Don't mind the Yank's books! He's been carrying the Christ Church rugby team all season, and when we get to the platform, he's likely to have the lot of you in a ruck!"

The train trip west through the English midlands proved to be good medicine for Nicholas.

"It's amazing," he said with his face pressed close to the window. "Every city or village has some great event attached to it! I feel like I'm riding through a history book!"

"Look there," said Charles, "Just between those hills. That's the Cathedral in Bath. The Romans built a spa around a natural hot spring."

Shaking his head in amazement, Nicholas whispered, "Divina natura dedit agros, ars humana aedificavit urbes."

Charles translated. "The divine nature produced the fields; human skill has built the cities."

When the train had passed through Bristol and turned south toward Exeter, Ollie joined Nicholas at the window. "Now this is my country! Pretty soon we'll be in the hills of Devon. You'll see steep granite topped hills we call tors. Just there to the west – that's High Willhays, the tallest of the lot."

Nicholas watched the rugged countryside hurry past. "I don't see many houses or farms. Who owns all this?"

"Mostly the Duke of Cornwall," said Ollie. "And the Army uses some of it for training. But this is the River Teign we're crossing! Not far now to Newton Abbot and my family's land."

When Nicholas and his friends stepped from the train at the small Newton Abbot station, a tall man in a tweed jacket waved to them.

"It's my father!" said Ollie, hurrying ahead of the others.

Nicholas suddenly found himself overcome with uncertainty. He had enjoyed frequent conversations with the governor of an American state, but the prospect of an encounter with an English Lord left him speechless.

"What do you call an earl?" he whispered to Charles.

"Try 'Lord Courtenay.'"

As he took the tall man's hand and pronounced the right words, Nicholas felt himself being pulled forward and clapped on the shoulder.

"There's my best American greeting! And I'd be honored if you would just call me 'Bob,'" said Ollie's father. "My son's told me all about you. And for sure, you are a strapping lad! But let's to the car and be off!"

The car turned out to be nothing like Nicholas had ever seen – longer and higher and more elegantly appointed than any American vehicle.

"Where's Simmons?" asked Ollie as he strapped their bags onto the boot.

"Enjoying his day off," said Robert Lord Courtenay. "I wanted to drive you home myself."

The road through Dartmoor wound through shadowed valleys and crested wind-swept hills with a view of forested hillsides and vast heather filled moors.

"What's this town?" asked Nicholas as the car slowed to negotiate the high street of a rural village.

"Haytor! Not far now!" said Ollie.

The tall hedgerows that bordered the lane to the Courtenay estate ended at a sharp right turn, where an avenue of stately trees led to a broad lawn and to the largest private house Nicholas had ever seen.

"Welcome to Moorlands!" said Lord Courtenay.

Nicholas had imagined a country residence on the order of the Heyward family's Lamont, and he stared in disbelief at the acres of sculptured gardens, the sweeping expanse of the gray stone mansion, the rows of third floor dormers intersecting the dark slate roof.

"There's Victoria and Albert!"

Ollie leaned from the window and whistled as a pair of yellow Labrador retrievers galloped down the driveway and leapt enthusiastically around the car. Nicholas smiled.

"You couldn't have picked a better welcoming committee! At my house, they would be Suzy and Flash!"

A servant hurried from the house to open the car doors, and Nicholas stepped down to greet the dogs and, at the same time, to meet Ollie's mother, a distinguished looking woman in her late fifties. Charles had prepared him for the encounter.

"Technically, she's a countess, but you can call her Lady Courtenay."

Nicholas couldn't help bowing slightly as he took her hand.

"Oh, do call me Helen!" said the mistress of Moorlands as she escorted her son and his guests into her home. Nicholas tried not to stare as he passed beneath a crystal chandelier as broad as his family's dining room table. Everything reflected a standard far beyond his experience, and he was glad when Ollie finally brought him to a third floor bedroom suite.

"When Henry brings up your bag, go ahead and dress for dinner. See you downstairs at eight!"

When his suitcase arrived, Nicholas laid out his formal clothes and stretched out on the broad, four-poster bed. He had an hour before supper, enough time to reflect on the day's events and, perhaps, to take a short nap. The car ride from Newton Abbot had brought the rugged terrain of Dartmoor very close, and Nicholas looked forward to exploring the hills and feeling the heather beneath his feet. He understood Ollie's excitement about going home. Natural grandeur and elegant accommodations were the big rugby player's birthright. He wondered what Ollie would think about Riverton and the six-room farmhouse that sheltered the Bower family.

"Ollie would love it!" Nicholas suddenly realized. "He's not as impressed with all of this as I am."

Then he thought, "My lesson!"

The Bird and Baby Bible study group had been reading St. Paul's epistle to the Philippians, and Nicholas had agreed to present an exegesis of chapter three after the holidays.

"It's what Paul was saying! What impresses people really doesn't matter. The only thing that matters is …"

Nicholas knew that verses in his assigned chapter specifically addressed this theme, but he couldn't remember them. "I wish I had …"

Then Nicholas laughed out loud. "What am I thinking?! This is Ollie's house! There'll be a Bible in this room, right over there."

He sat up and without looking pointed to the bedside table. There, beneath the silk-shaded electric lamp, lay a leather-bound Bible.

"If any other man thinks he has reason for confidence in the flesh, I have more," wrote the Apostle. Nicholas read Paul's impressive pedigree and shook his head.

"He's a first-century Ollie! Anybody living in this house has good reason for confidence. Born the eldest son of the Earl of Devon. Physically flawless. Intellectually brilliant. Enrolled at Oxford. Captain of the rugby team!"

Nicholas let the comparison flow. "Fabulously wealthy and destined to inherit even more. A list of powerful friends. Anybody else would think life couldn't be any better! But Ollie smiles and shrugs it off. He says he has a better inheritance. How did Paul say it?"

Nicholas found the verse and read out loud, "'The surpassing worth of knowing Christ Jesus my Lord.'"

Leave it all behind. No righteousness of my own. In the pit of his stomach, Nicholas felt the near approach of his old nemesis.

"He's talking about letting go."

Fear oozed up in Nicholas as he continued to read. "One thing I do, forgetting what lies behind and straining forward to what lies ahead, I press on toward the goal for the prize of the upward call of God in Christ Jesus."

Nicholas stood and walked to the window. Starlight through the passing clouds reminded him of his first view of the North Georgia hills.

"I was afraid that night," he admitted, "but it's where I met Catherine. Jesus! Please take away this fear!"

+ + +

"Are you up for a bit of grindage, Old Man?"

Ollie Courtenay's voice preceded his knock on the door. "Time for supper! Are you dressed?"

"Two minutes!" said Nicholas as he rushed to remove his travel clothes and put on his tuxedo.

He walked with Ollie down the wide central stairs and followed him to the dining room, where Lord and Lady Courtenay sat conversing with Charles Middleton.

"I hope you will forgive my tardiness," said Nicholas.

"Please think nothing of it," said Lord Courtenay. "You've had a long day. I was just about to ask Charles if he might be interested in a day of shooting tomorrow. How about you, Lad? Ollie tells me you've shot partridges at home. Are you up for a go at our red grouse?"

Charles started to speak, but Nicholas interrupted him.

"Yes, Sir, I believe I would. I haven't picked up a gun in over a year, but I'd love to try."

"Are you sure you're ready for this, Nicholas?" said Charles.

"It's time. I need to let go of what lies behind."

Ollie and Charles exchanged glances.

"Well, it's settled, then!" said Lord Courtenay. "Ollie can find you some boots. We'll breakfast at half seven and be away at eight."

Clothed in borrowed Wellingtons, tweed cap, and an oiled cotton raincoat, Nicholas stood inside the stable door with Ollie and Charles. A cold rain dripped from fast moving clouds.

"Here comes Hal," said Ollie as a young man approached in an enclosed caravan pulled by a pair of enormous horses. The boys had just climbed aboard the wagon when Lord Courtenay hurried from the house.

"It looks to be a great day!" he said, stepping through the back door. "Hal, have the beaters and flankers gone ahead? Well, then, let's be off!"

Nicholas settled back in the comfortable caravan seat. He felt perfectly at home. His father's enthusiasm for the hunt had been somehow transferred to Lord Courtenay, and instead of January on the front seat, a young man named Hal drove the team. Even the Labradors, Victoria and Albert, shared the occasion with Suzy and Flash, the Bower's bird dogs.

"Charles has shot grouse before," said Lord Courtenay over the rumble of the wagon, "but, Nicholas, let me explain the process to you. We'll not be walking up the birds today. We'll be in stands. Butts, some call them. And we've sent beaters and flankers out over the property to walk the assigned cover and drive the birds our way. They'll come high and fast, most of them, and you'll be using two guns with a loader to keep you ready to shoot. Just lead the bird farther than you think you should, and you'll be all right."

The rain had stopped when the shooting party climbed from the caravan. Lord Courtenay introduced each of the boys to their assigned loader.

"Nicholas, this is Gareth. He's Welsh and a damned fine loader! Gareth, you take care of the Yank!"

The Welshman shook Nicholas' hand without comment, and

turned to pick up a basket of shells and two cased shotguns.

"After me, then," he said to Nicholas, and started out at a brisk pace. They had just reached the assigned shooting station and Gareth was explaining the guns to Nicholas when the first bevy of grouse sailed overhead.

"Mark, Nicholas!" called Ollie from two hundred yards along the ridge.

"It's OK," Nicholas said to Gareth. "I've hunted birds before. I know how to fire a shotgun."

"Hunted birds, have ye?" snorted the Welshman. "Huntin's what's done with hounds. I expect ye mean ye've shot birds!"

Two more grouse flew high above the butt.

"Mark!" said Lord Courtenay. "Don't let them get away, Lad!"

Nicholas took the loaded gun from the Welshman and turned to watch the approaching beaters. He saw five grouse erupt from a thicket of gorse two hundred yards away and his heart began to pound when the birds caught the moorland wind and rocketed toward him. His hands gripped the gun helplessly as his mind projected the image of his father's mortal agony. He watched his father's gun strike the wagon. He saw the captain fall and the blood splatter. But there was no sound! No explosion! No accusing shriek came from his father's lips.

"Mark, mark!" muttered Gareth behind him.

Nicholas lifted the gun smoothly to his shoulder in the effortless motion he'd practiced hundreds of times. There was no time to make sense of it, but Nicholas felt free. He picked a single grouse from the scattered covey, swung the double barrels past the bird's beak, and squeezed the first trigger. Nicholas never felt the recoil of the shot. He watched without surprise as the grouse folded in mid-air and plummeted to the ground, leaving a trail of floating feathers.

"Well done, Lad," said Gareth. "But there's four got past! Remember, ye've got two shots next time."

"Next time! Next time! I like the sound of that!" said Nicholas.

+ + +

"Well, I'm impressed!" said Ollie when the shooting party assembled at the caravan. "That's the best performance for a first-timer I've ever seen! Look! You've even brought out the first sunshine in a week!"

"Just claiming my heritage," said Nicholas.

"You mean, your partridge shooting experience?"

"There's that. But for some reason I felt free today. I didn't worry about missing. I've recently left behind some things that have been bothering me. And I am glad to see the sun!"

Nicholas received Lord Courtenay's congratulations with no further explanation. He expressed his own appreciation to Gareth, who grudgingly admitted that the Yank had done well. For the trip back to Moorlands, he sat on the caravan seat next to Hal.

"I wish you could meet a friend of mine," said Nicholas. "You remind me of him."

"He's a stableman, is he?"

"That and a lot more. Even your name. My friend loves Shakespeare!"

"Knows about Prince Hal, does he? I've not read that much of the bard, but my name's required me to learn this much. "We few, we happy few, we band of brothers; for he today that sheds his blood with me shall be my brother; be he ne're so vile, this day shall gentle his condition.""

"Now I do feel at home! And this day has gentled my condition!"

# CHAPTER TWENTY-FOUR

## Winter 1908 – Spring 1910

CHRISTMAS AT MOORLANDS provided Nicholas with a much-needed break from the pressures of school. The Courtenay family kept him so busy exploring the estate and sharing their Christmas customs that at the end of five days he had not opened any of the textbooks in his heavy satchel.

"If you've got a wooly jumper, wear it today," said Ollie at breakfast. "On the day before Christmas, we always take the horses to St. Anselm's for a mummer's play."

Nicholas had no idea what a mummer's play might be, but the prospect of riding to church on one of Lord Courtenay's magnificent thoroughbreds thrilled him. At the stable door, he stepped eagerly from the mounting block into the stirrup and smiled at the familiar creak of leather and the musty aroma of the saddle blanket.

"This is Champion," said Ollie, stroking the horse's neck. "He's six and probably our fastest mount."

"I wish you could see my horse. He's named Caesar," said Nicholas. "He's what we call a Plantation Walker. Not fast, but the smoothest gait you ever felt."

Nicholas waited with Ollie and Charles while the grooms brought a pair of matched grays for Lord and Lady Courtenay.

"Everyone up?" said the Earl of Devon. "Then let's away!"

The air felt colder than Christmas in South Carolina and the hilly terrain offered more spectacular views than the flat fields of Clarendon county, but Nicholas felt more at home in the saddle than he had anywhere else in England. He chatted with his friends until the tower of St. Anselm's Church inspired Ollie to instigate a race to the churchyard.

"Who's up for it, mates? Last one to the door's a Nancy boy!"

Nicholas pressed his heels into Champion's flanks, tapped lightly with the reins, and leaned forward as the big horse exploded into a gallop. Ollie and Charles kicked their mounts to a two-length lead and rode neck and neck as the lane rounded the last bend before the churchyard. From the corner of his eye, Nicholas noticed a wooden gate in the stone wall of the sheep pasture. The decision took less than a second. With a shout, he reined Champion to the left and directly toward the five-foot gate. The big horse never faltered, splashing through puddles in the potholed road until he gathered his legs beneath him and sailed across the fence.

"Well done, Lad!" Lord Courtenay cheered from the lane behind, watching in admiration as the American drove the galloping horse across the pasture and toward the churchyard fence.

"He'll do it again! Watch him now!" said Lady Courtenay. As she spoke, Nicholas kicked hard and held on as the brush-covered fence passed beneath the horse's outstretched hoofs. Nicholas reined in by the front door of the church and sat whispering compliments to the excited horse as Ollie and Charles cantered toward the meeting place.

"Bloody brilliant!" said Ollie. "A regular steeplechase! Have you done much hunting?"

"I've jumped a few trees fallen over the road and lots of farm ditches. Never a fence. I just felt Champion could do it."

The crowd gathering for the Christmas play had witnessed Nicholas' shortcut, and as he made his way into the church parish hall, many people smiled and nodded approvingly. The mummer's play turned out to be nothing like what he expected. Instead of an extended nativity scene, the humorous drama included St. George, a sword wielding adversary, and an impossibly inept physician. As they rode back to Moorlands, Lady Courtenay explained the history of the mummer's tradition.

"They go back to medieval times. The stories are all about things good and evil, with hints of resurrection. Oh, and one of the good things you'll see at Christmas is plum pudding. It has a long history, too."

Nicholas laughed, "It certainly has history with my family. Last year, ours nearly burned the house down!" He went on to describe April's first attempt to prepare and serve the brandy-flamed dessert.

"I do hope she put the ingredients together on the Sunday before Advent!" said Lady Courtenay. "Blending everything takes weeks!"

"I expect April used an American recipe – more haste than history! 'In virtute sunt multi ascensus' In excellence there are many degrees."

"Listen to the lad!" said Lord Courtenay. "He shoots well, rides well, excels at rugby, even knows the classics! 'Ab ovo usque ad mala!' It's all there, from the egg to the fruits!"

Two days after Christmas, Nicholas and his friends packed their bags and shared a final breakfast with Lord and Lady Courtenay.

"This has been the most delightful experience I've had in England," Nicholas said to Ollie's mother. "I hope that one day Ollie might visit me in America so my family can share our home with him."

Simmons, the Courtenays's chauffer, drove the boys to the train station in Newton Abbot, and all three students slept on the trip back to Oxford. Nicholas ignored the heavy rain that met them at the station, and he trudged wearily to the Christ Church gate, stopping often to switch hands with his suitcase and his heavy book bag.

"Remember the Bird and Baby tomorrow," said Ollie as they climbed the steps to their rooms. "It's your turn for the lesson."

304 | RICHARD BELSER

Nicholas reread the third chapter of Philippians before he went to bed. He decided that he would begin his lesson with some examples of Jewish law as interpreted by the party of the Pharisees. He would explain the significance of Paul's claim to human confidence and then unpack the meaning of the Greek word translated "flesh." He would bring in the Apostle's teaching from Galatians about sons and heirs. Then, for his concluding point, Nicholas planned to describe the ideas that came to him during his first evening at Moorlands. He would ask Ollie's permission to recognize him as an example of someone whose extraordinary earthly heritage had not obscured his God-given spiritual inheritance.

When classes began the next morning, Nicholas went from breakfast to supper without finding an opportunity to talk with Ollie about his plan. Only as they climbed the steps to the Bird and Baby meeting room did he explain his intentions. Ollie listened and shook his head.

"Me? I'm no example of redemption! Why not talk about your own new start? There's a bit of something different in you, unless I'm a lummox and a loser!"

The unexpected alteration to his lesson plan left Nicholas feeling anxious as the members of the group arrived. He managed to offer a brief and theologically awkward prayer before taking the points of his outline in order. When he finished his commentary about sons and heirs, Nicholas paused, and then set out on unfamiliar ground.

"I must tell you, gentlemen, that this study about sonship and about different kinds of inheritance has come at a good time for me. Most of you know that my father died just over a year ago in a hunting accident. I had a strained relationship with him before his death, and when his will assigned to me an inheritance I didn't want, I became very upset. I had tried all my life to measure up to his standards, and I saw the will as his final rejection of me. My unsuccessful efforts had already made me a self-conscious person, always anxious about how I might appear to others and never able to relax and enjoy my life.

"But for some years now, I've had the feeling that something was inviting me to stop working so hard to measure up and just allow myself to be who I am. It was an invitation that confused and terrified me, because I've never really liked who I am. But over and over, in so many places I can't remember them all, someone's been telling me to let go. I now believe that the one inviting me has been Jesus. I thank my mother for that. And Mr. Turnbull, my minister. And Ollie. And all of you. I think he wants me to claim a gift that I could never earn, and to take hold of it, he wants me to let go of my old standards. I certainly don't have the spiritual pedigree that Paul had, but I know how hard it is to let go of things you've counted on to give you confidence. But, gentlemen, tonight I'm happy to tell you that I am ready to count it all as loss for the surpassing worth of knowing Christ Jesus as my Lord."

The members of the Bird and Baby study group leapt to their feet, clapping as they would at a rugby match and crowding around Nicholas to shake his hand. As he received their congratulations, Nicholas thought about Catherine. Would she understand? And as he tried to imagine her reaction, he realized something was different about his own. There were no tears! Under ordinary circumstances, such an overt expression of love and support would have left him weeping, but there surrounded by a group of bright, articulate men who also believed in God, Nicholas felt perfectly at home. They had each let go of an old life to receive a new inheritance. They were sons of God by adoption and grace. They were now his brothers and with him, heirs to an unchanging inheritance.

Before the jubilant group members filed down to the bar to toast their brother's new beginning, Nicholas had begun to question everything.

"Let go?" he told himself, while pretending to smile. "I haven't really let go! Look at me! I'm still desperate for these men to like me! It's easy for somebody like Ollie. He can play at being religious and still inherit his estate. This whole thing is just a new way to measure up. It's a competition. I've learned the vocabulary and for now I have them fooled."

As they walked back to Christ Church, Ollie kept up a running commentary about the other group members.

"Wait till you hear old Arthur's story! It's pure Damascus Road! Overnight transformation! But Percy! Took the Lord fifteen years to bring him round!"

Nicholas listened without comment. As they crossed Tom Quad, Ollie stepped in front of Nicholas and turned to look into his face.

"Resist him, Nicholas! Don't let the Reasoner change your mind!"

"How did you know?"

"It always happens, especially at first. Most of us find that we're never ever free of it. But when we get weak, we help each other! Nobody can do it alone!"

"I'll remember," said Nicholas. And as his tears began to flow, he knew how God would remind him. He went to sleep thinking, "Paul had his thorn in the flesh. I have my tears. Until God takes them away, his grace will have to do."

+ + +

The Epiphany Term introduced Nicholas to different classes and new instructors who kept him so busy that he had no time to seek another opportunity with the Christ Church College crew. Every day he wore the scarf that Catherine had made for him, and each month, he wrote her a short letter describing his daily routine. At the beginning of Holy Week, he decided to tell her about the changes in his spiritual life.

"As you know, I've been meeting weekly with a group of exceptionally able men from different colleges, all of whom take their Christian faith very seriously. My friend Ollie Courtenay is one of the fellowship. And I've found that through regular study of the Bible, and the prayers of these men, my own understanding of God has grown dramatically. I can tell you that Jesus has become real to me, and I hope that my friends can see some difference in my life. Dearest Catherine, I do pray that my new direction pleases you, and that when at last we are together, you will find me a better man than the self-conscious boy you used to know."

Nicholas's new-found faith received a shocking blow when he received a letter from January Wilson.

"I hope you're well, my friend, and if you have a moment, I ask you to remember my family and me. We have lost our farm to the Mayfield gang. Sheriff Mayfield delivered a delinquent tax notice to my mother claiming that we had paid nothing for ten years. Of course it's a lie! I've carried the money myself to the assessor's office in Manchester every year. But now they say they can't find any record of our payments. When our farm came up for tax sale, the Mayfields bought it and gave us a week to vacate our house.

"Your mother has come to our aid, of course, and has given us use of the Hutchinson place again. She has offered us twenty acres of your land to farm as sharecroppers in addition to the work my sisters do for Philip. Claus, how I wish your father were here! And you, too! I did get a job teaching at the colored school in Manchester. It's what I wanted, and it should make me happy, but nothing brings me much joy these days. This is a very bad time."

Nicholas noticed that January had not specifically asked for prayer, but he lost no time asking God to send someone to intervene and bring justice for January's family.

The monthly letters from Catherine always left Nicholas with both excitement and anguish. She wrote just as she talked, and the drop of perfume she placed on each page brought her so close he could feel her presence. But Catherine was not in Oxford, and unless she received an ocean voyage as a graduation gift, he would not see her for another year. Having lived with the hope of her approaching visit, Nicholas eagerly opened her next letter.

"Dearest Claus, my heart is broken! Today Father told me that he will not be able to send me abroad for a graduation gift. The hurricane last fall destroyed so many of his rice fields that the crop was almost totally lost. Now the plantation is up for sale! I have tried to be cheerful for Father's sake, but every night I think of you and the ocean that separates us, and I cry myself to sleep. I don't know what changes our financial situation will mean for my family, but I do know that nothing will change the way I feel about you. I cried tears of joy when I read about your new commitment to Christ. It means so much to me that we have our faith in common. This year will hurry by as we turn to God in prayer."

Catherine's letter became a grim turning point for Nicholas. Instead of anticipating her visit and happily imagining her presence in all his favorite places around Oxford, he began to see the city as an obstacle course, a devilish collection of wearisome challenges that stood between him and what he most desired. Every day, he said his prayers and, remembering his football experiences at South Carolina, he lowered his head and bulled his way through classes and examinations. He studied late every night and ate most of his meals alone. His friends at the Bird and Baby noticed his sullen mood.

"What's come over you, mate?" asked Ollie. "A joyless friend of Jesus is an oxymoron!"

"I'm ready to finish here and go home."

"It's that bonzer lass, isn't it?"

"She can't come this summer! I was counting on seeing her, and now it'll be a year!"

Ollie laughed. "You'll not likely get much snogging at Moorlands, but if you'd fancy a ride through the hills on Champion, we can pop in on Mum and Dad next week!"

Nicholas accepted the invitation gratefully. "You're a lifesaver, Lord Oliver! It's gonna take your kindness and a lot more to get me through to graduation!"

"I'll not have you calling on the wrong lord, Yank! You give our Master the days one at a time and May will be here before you know it!"

Ollie Courtenay's words proved to be prophetic. The Pentecost Term ended with a relaxing visit to the Courtenay estate, and when Michaelmas courses began, Nicholas established a study routine that kept him at the top of his class and a social agenda that brought many evenings of fellowship and laughter. The rugby team provided afternoons of satisfying physical exertion and widened his circle of friendships beyond his own college. He never missed the weekly Bible study upstairs at the Bird and Baby, and on Sundays, he alternated between the Methodist church with Ollie and the sung Anglican liturgy at Christ Church Cathedral with Charles Middleton.

Over the Christmas break, Nicholas spent two weeks in London with Charles and Ollie. Lord Courtenay maintained a town house in the city, and to the boy's delight, he arranged a private audience with King Edward VII. Ollie had met the King before, and he tried to reassure his friends as they were admitted to Buckingham Palace. "You'll like him, I think. He's done wonders for our relationship with France. The press calls him 'Europe's Uncle.' Personally I think he smokes too many cigars!" Nicholas found the ruler of the British Empire cordial and quite interested in American agriculture. As he answered the king's questions, he couldn't help thinking of how the meeting would thrill his mother and Miss Abernathy and his Anglophile clergyman, Mr. Turnbull.

After many years in the academic world, Nicholas expected that the months between Christmas and Easter would pass more slowly than the rest of the year. But as his final semester of graduate school began, he found the days quickly dissolving into weeks and weeks into months. After saying his morning prayers and before hurrying down to breakfast, Nicholas always planted a kiss on the photograph Catherine had sent him. Dressed for hiking, she sat on a rocky overlook at Lamont with the North Georgia hills marching toward the mountains.

"Soon!" he said to the picture.

+ + +

It was after such a ritual on the first Wednesday in March that a porter at Christ Church gate handed Nicholas a letter. The handwriting was unfamiliar, but Nicholas immediately recognized the initials printed on the flap of the envelope.

"D.C.H.! Duncan Clinch Heyward!" A letter from the former Governor of South Carolina. Catherine's father! Nicholas found a quiet place in a corner of Tom Quad and studied the envelope. He entertained a list of reasons why Governor Heyward might send him a personal letter, and many of them did not involve good news. For a moment, Nicholas thought about saving the letter until the end of the day, anticipating that whatever the message contained might leave him unable to concentrate on his classes. But his curiosity overcame his caution, and with fumbling fingers he opened the letter.

"Dear Mr. Bower:  I hope this letter finds you well, with all your studies approaching a successful conclusion. The Rhodes Scholarship Committee informs me that you have excelled in your work and will in all likelihood graduate at the top of your class. Let me be the first congratulate you. You have brought honor to your already distinguished family and have reflected great credit on the state of South Carolina. As you prepare for your return, I hope you will consider a job offer that will soon be tendered by the United States District Attorney in Columbia. I have recommended you for a position with his office. In that capacity, you will gain considerable trial experience and will, at the same time, help prosecute persons who violate our nation's laws. I trust you will be adequately compensated for your work. Mrs.

Heyward and I look forward to seeing you upon
your return. Our daughter, Catherine, sends her re-
gards. Very Truly Yours, D.C. Heyward."

Nicholas read the letter twice before he could absorb its full significance. He had focused so intently on completing his studies that the
matter of employment had completely escaped him. A job as a trial
lawyer! Recommended by the former governor! He sandwiched the
folded letter in a textbook and hurried to his first class. At lunch, he
showed the letter to Charles and Ollie.

"Smashing!" said Charles.

"Absobloodylootley top!" echoed Ollie. "Well done, Old Man!
The only thing better than a degree from Oxford is a paying job!
And you've got a prospect! Tell me you'll take it."

"I suppose I should! I haven't thought much about working as a
lawyer. But this is handed to me!"

"I wonder what the governor means by 'adequately compensated?' said Charles.

"I expect he means our friend Nicholas will be able to take care
of the governor's little girl!" laughed Ollie.

When the district attorney's invitation came a week later,
Nicholas immediately cabled his response.

"I am honored to accept the offer to join your staff as an assistant U.S. district attorney. I understand I am to meet with the Bar
Association on June 15. If their judgment of me is affirmative, I will
be available to start right away."

Nicholas cabled his thanks to Governor Heyward, and he sent a third
message to his mother and Philip, by way of Riverton's general store.

"Good news! I am to be hired by the U.S. Attorney in Columbia,
starting after the middle of June. I will complete my courses here at
the end of May. Oxford delays awarding degrees until the following
semester, so there will be no commencement ceremony. I will let you
know as soon as my travel plans are complete."

When he left the telegraph office, Nicholas walked past the Christ Church gate and followed the road to Merton Field. Keeping to the edge, he skirted the afternoon cricket match and took a footpath to the river. He sat by the reeds where he had seen the swan and watched the green water slide silently past. Scenes from the past three years chased each other through his imagination.

The scholarship to Oxford. His father's death. The unexpected legacy. Travel by train and ship. Scheming Jenny Flagler. Catherine's crushing letter. The hurried trip home. Charles and Ollie. His rugby mates. The men upstairs at the Bird and Baby. Moorlands. A new inheritance. London and the King.

From the Cathedral tower, Great Tom struck the hour, and Nicholas realized that in a few weeks he would leave Oxford and never hear that sound again. He lay back on the grass and wept.

## CHAPTER TWENTY-FIVE

## Spring 1910

IN THE SPRING OF 1910, Nicholas took the final examination in Oxford's Honor School of Jurisprudence and received the distinction of "First Class," along with a monetary award to be invested in books stamped with the college coat of arms.

He wrote to his mother, "I have come to believe that the object of education is not merely to train one to follow some specialized profession so as to make a living, but to teach one to live a good life among men; to know that man's chief asset is his soul, and achievement his highest instinct. I have come to appreciate the truth of the saying from Psalm 111, 'The fear of the Lord is the beginning of wisdom.'" [vi]

The last evening at the Bird and Baby with his Christian friends produced many toasts and mutual promises to stay in touch with each other. Nicholas wept unashamedly as he embraced Charles Middleton and Ollie Courtenay. The following morning, waiting for the train to Liverpool, tears came again as church bells across the ancient city rang in the new day.

The six-day sea voyage to New York gave Nicholas a much-needed opportunity to study the books sent to him by his new employer. Scott Morris, the United States district attorney in Columbia, had written, "I trust you are prepared to answer the Bar Association's questions concerning general principles of law, but you will need to be conversant with specific statutes and policies that apply in our country and, particularly, in South Carolina."

Nicholas buried himself in one book after another for most of every day, pausing briefly at sundown for a short walk around the promenade deck. Only when he boarded the train from New York to South Carolina, did he begin to realize that his formal education had ended. He had been a student for so long that he had trouble imagining himself with a new identity. Watching the fields of Virginia and North Carolina pass by his window, Nicholas looked forward with growing excitement to his visit to the Bower farm. He tried to prepare himself for the changes that no letter from home had mentioned, but when he switched trains in Columbia, the new construction in the city and the pace of traffic through the streets left him astonished.

As the train pulled into the Sumter station, Nicholas noticed a crowd of people waving from the platform. Then he looked again and began to recognize faces. There was his mother, holding down her hat and waving a handkerchief. Philip swooped his bowler hat back and forth. Miss Abernathy wiped tears with her gloved hand, and Mr. Turnbull clapped vigorously. January Wilson and Sally Hemphill stood side by side, smiling and trying to catch his eye. And at the back of the assembly waited Catherine Heyward and her mother.

Nicholas felt overwhelmed. He had expected someone to be there with a ride home, but nothing like the greeting that awaited him. He stepped from the Pullman car into a flurry of hugs, handshakes, and words of welcome. Every member of the party bombarded him with questions, to which he gave only the briefest answers while brushing away his tears and promising to tell everything soon. While Philip and January carried his luggage to the waiting car, Nicholas quickly expressed his gratitude to the others before crossing to where Catherine stood. Conscious of her mother's smiling presence, Nicholas took the girl's hand in both of his and lightly kissed her cheek. Neither knew what to say.

"Thank you for your letters," Nicholas finally managed.

"I am so happy to see you."

"I didn't know if you would come."

"Nothing could have kept me away. Mother insisted on seeing you, too."

"Will you come to the farm? I couldn't stand to see you here and then not again for weeks."

Catherine squeezed his hand and looked down. "The train to Walterboro leaves in half an hour. I wish we could go someplace. But everybody's waiting for you, and you need to go."

"May I come tomorrow? My family will understand."

"Yes. I'm sure Father wants to see you, too."

Nicholas glanced at Mrs. Heyward, who chose that moment to turn and say something to Sophie Bower. Quickly, he pulled Catherine close to him and brushed his lips against hers.

"Until tomorrow," he whispered.

The car ride with Sophie and Philip gave Nicholas time to answer some of their questions in more detail and also to make inquiries of his own. He admitted that he had completed his courses at the top of his class. They told him that the cotton crop on the Bower farm looked good. He explained what he knew about his new job. They reported that the Mayfield clan continued to operate some secret business on their closely guarded property and that, with Singleton's gin out of business, the Mayfields had announced a reduction in what they would pay local farmers for their crop. When his bags had been deposited in his old room, Nicholas went immediately to the barn and called for Caesar. The big horse whinnied at the sound of the familiar voice, and Nicholas stroked the powerful neck and promised to return soon for a long ride.

After supper, January knocked on the kitchen door, and Nicholas hurried to usher his friend into the parlor. They chatted briefly with

Sophie and Philip until January announced that it was time for him to go.

When Nicholas walked his friend to the waiting wagon, January said, "I really don't need to leave. I just wanted to tell you something." Nicholas felt his anxiety rising. "I'm giving up my job in Manchester and going back to school."

Nicholas took a deep breath. "Wonderful! I think it's exactly what you should do!"

"You know how I've always said I wanted to teach young kids? I finally realized that I could do more for them by teaching their teachers."

"You going back to Yale?"

"No. To Howard, in Washington. They've got a great faculty and, I think, a real future. They don't give doctorates yet, but the day will come."

Nicholas nodded in agreement. "I'm relieved. I didn't know what you got me out here to tell me."

January stood without speaking, then he looked at Nicholas. "Sally's going with me."

It was Nicholas' turn to be silent. "I don't know what to say. Except I'm not surprised. I didn't think you could just be friends forever." Nicholas pulled January into a hug. "God bless you both!"

"We're not leaving till next month, so don't tell even your family about it."

"Does Mrs. Hemphill know?"

"She does. We told her a few weeks ago, and she went crazy. Talked about calling the sheriff! But she's calmed down a little, and we've been able to talk with her about it."

"What about your mother?"

"She took it better. Cried for a while. But she's with us."

"I guess this means you'll get married?"

"Of course! But not here! There'd be a riot! In Washington. Just family. We want you to come."

"I want to come! It depends on how free I'll be with my new job."

January climbed into the wagon. "I know you've gotten closer to God. Please pray. We're sure it's right, but we're not fooling ourselves about the problems."

Weary as he was, Nicholas found it hard to sleep that night. His mixed feelings about January and Sally battled with his excitement about seeing Catherine. In the morning, Philip drove him to the Sumter station, and just before the noon hour, Nicholas sprinted down the streets of Walterboro and knocked on the Heywards's front door. Governor and Mrs. Heyward greeted him warmly, and after lunch, they excused themselves, leaving Nicholas and Catherine alone for the afternoon.

"I've got it all planned," said Catherine as she led the way to the stables. "Father's given us the gig and his best horse and mother's packed us a picnic supper!"

"Where're we going?"

"You'll see! Now hitch up Snowball so we can get there!"

"Snowball? That black horse?"

"My fault. I had the name picked out before I saw the horse. But Snowball doesn't mind!"

Nicholas drove the two-wheeled gig through the shaded streets of Walterboro until Catherine directed him to a lightly used public road. They passed through Canadys crossroad and had just entered a forest of towering cypress when they came to a river and bridge.

"It's the Edisto!" said Catherine. "Next to Lamont, my favorite place in the world!"

They borrowed a boat from a farmer who lived near the bridge, and Nicholas rowed upstream until the cool, black water divided around a large sandbar. As the silence of the swamp settled around them, Nicholas and Catherine unfolded a blanket from the basket and spread it on the sand. They stood holding each other in a long embrace, and as their kisses began, they first knelt together and then slowly lay down in each other's arms.

"Somebody might see us!" whispered Catherine.

"It's all right. I just want to hold you. It's been so long!"

As they settled close to each other, Nicholas experienced a feeling of peace beyond anything he'd even known. He knew he wanted to spend his life with this woman. He wanted to tell her of his love, but he wasn't sure he would recognize the right moment. He closed his eyes.

"Lord, please show me!"

Suddenly he pictured January's face and remembered his words. "Sally's going with me." Nicholas kissed Catherine again, and sat up, gazing down at her face.

"I love you," he heard himself say, "and I hope you will be my wife."

Catherine's sparkling eyes spoke before her lips. She sat up and flung her arms around his neck.

"If I couldn't be your wife, I wouldn't want to live! Yes! Yes! I will marry you!"

Nicholas realized he didn't know what to do next. He looked around at the sandy island.

"I wanted to ask you but I didn't know it would be here!"

"It's perfect! Our own island! Our private world!"

"I don't have a ring. I should have waited and got you a ring."

"No, you couldn't have asked at a better time or a better place! I don't need a ring. I just need you!"

Nicholas and Catherine lay on the blanket talking and dreaming through the afternoon. They considered the best way for Nicholas to ask Governor Heyward for the hand of his daughter.

"Father won't be surprised," said Catherine. "Or mother."

"Neither will my mother. Philip either. He's been prying me for a hint since I got home."

Catherine touched his cheek. "You're crying!"

"I always do when I'm happy!"

As the sun dropped below the cypress trees, they loaded their boat and floated slowly back to the bridge and the waiting gig. The trip back to Walterboro seemed to take no time at all. With the reins draped over the dashboard, Snowball, the black horse, followed the narrow road without guidance while, under the gig's sheltering canopy, his passengers embraced in the darkness.

Nicholas slept in the Heywards's guest room that night, and in the morning, before he took the train back to Riverton, he agreed with Catherine that they should wait before announcing their plans to their parents.

"We don't want to look impulsive. After I'm settled in my job will be better."

The next few days passed quickly, with Nicholas studying hard for the Bar Exam between visits to the many people who wanted to see him. Miss Abernathy insisted on serving high tea while Nicholas described his visit with the Earl of Devon and his audience with King Edward. Mr. Turnbull listened ecstatically to the young man's testimony of faith and opened his Bible to mark the pivotal passages. The priest insisted that they end the visit by entering the church to kneel together at the altar rail. His spontaneous and passionate prayer brought tears to Nicholas's eyes.

Nicholas went next to see Sally Hemphill and found her working in the garden behind her mother's house. When she saw him approaching, she stood and wiped her forehead with her dress sleeve.

"Well, what do you think?" she said.

Nicholas clasped her shoulders and lightly kissed her cheek. "I think it's wonderful! You two are so right for each other."

"We know it's gonna be hard, even in Washington. We probably won't ever be able to come home."

"Things will change. Laws can be amended."

"Isn't that gonna be your job?"

"I'm afraid my job is to enforce the laws. But time is on your side."

+ + +

Nicholas met in mid-June with three lawyers from the Bar Association, answering most of their questions without difficulty and ending the three-day interview with their unanimous endorsement. The district attorney asked him to report for work the next day.

After the briefest greeting, Scott Morris said, "Ordinarily, I'd want you to take some time to get to know the people in this office and meet some of the judges and local attorneys, but I've got a case that we need to move on right now, and it seems tailor made for you. You're from Clarendon County, right?"

Nicholas acknowledged that he was.

"Do you know the sheriff there? A Mr. Taylor Mayfield? Or his nephew, Conner?"

Nicholas nodded as apprehension crept over him. "Yes, Sir. I know the sheriff and I went to school with Conner."

"You've been out of the country, but have you heard anything about a bootlegging operation run by the Mayfields?"

"Sir, everybody in the county knows about it. A few years ago, my family found one of the Mayfield's stills on our property."

"How do you know the Mayfield's ran it? Did you see them operating it?"

"No, but we found them nearby. We believe one of them took a shot at us."

"Believing they shot at you isn't enough! You're new in the law business, but you should know that! We need hard evidence to prosecute these slick operators."

"Do you have any leads?"

The district attorney opened a file on his desk. "We've had a team out of Atlanta from the Bureau of Internal Revenue investigating this case. The lead agent is Carl Reeves. I want you to go see him this afternoon and give him some background about the Mayfield family."

Scott Morris handed Nicholas the file and shook his hand. "This is your first case. I've got high hopes for you! Let's see what you can do."

Nicholas spent the rest of the day pouring over the Federal Government's file on the Mayfields of Clarendon County. He found reports of large shipments of sugar delivered to the Mayfields's farm along with heavy wooden crates with unknown contents.

"Bottles," Nicholas said to himself, remembering the boxes he and January had found in the woods. In the file he also found paperwork documenting the construction of a railroad spur from Sumter to Rimini, with the terminus half a mile from the Mayfields's farm. The legislative approval was there, but Nicholas looked in vain for any details justifying the project.

"Agricultural transportation," he read, shaking his head in disgust. "There are dozens of South Carolina counties with less rail access than Clarendon County. Somebody's been paid off to approve this."

When he met with Carl Reeves the next day, the federal agent immediately agreed with him.

"We've known that for a couple of years, but we can't put our fingers on the operator in your county or the deal maker in Columbia. We've been asking for a warrant to go down there and look around, but most of the judges hate to push things when the legislature's involved. If you know anybody who can get us in, that might help us a lot!"

Nicholas went back to his office, carefully weighing his next step. His main contact in state government would soon become his father-in-law, and he didn't want to complicate his relationship with the former governor by asking him for a political favor. But he remembered Scott Morris' charge, "Let's see what you can do," and, taking a deep breath, he placed a phone call to Walterboro.

"You need a judge who'll sign a warrant?" asked Governor Heyward. "Has anybody approached Clarence Campbell in Florence? He's an old friend of mine. Call and tell him I'd like him to help you. He can call me if he needs verification."

With the governor's endorsement, Nicholas easily obtained the needed warrant to enter the Mayfields's property.

"I'll sign it and have a courier deliver it to your office tomorrow," said Judge Campbell.

Nicholas hurried to break the news to the federal agent, and together, they went to the district attorney's office.

"Your new man works fast!" said Carl. "He's got the warrant coming tomorrow! We can make the raid after dark and catch them off guard."

Scott Morris congratulated Nicholas, and the three men spent the next hours formulating their plan.

"We want papers with names," said the district attorney. "Anything you can find with signatures – checks, orders, receipts. Take a photographer and get some pictures. We need to get this right, because it might be our only chance."


The next morning, Nicholas reported to the federal building and saw six armed government officers waiting by a pair of canvas-topped freight trucks.

"We want it to look like an ordinary delivery," said Carl. "But we've got guns and lights and the camera. You've got the warrant. Take off your tie and suit coat, and let's go!"

As the short convoy headed for Sumter Highway, Nicholas thought about how radically his life had changed in the course of a month. A tooth-rattling, dusty ride in a truck filled with armed men seemed to have no connection with the comfortable intellectual atmosphere of Oxford.

"The principles of the law require enforcement." Nicholas told himself. "This isn't about punishing the Mayfields as much as it is insuring a good life for everyone else."

He smiled as a Latin maxim came to mind. "'Juris praecepta sunt haec: honeste vivere, alterum  non laedere, suum quicue tribuere.' The precepts of the law are these: to live honorably, to hurt no one, to give each man his due." "Justinian," thought Nicholas,  "the foundation of civil law."

"You're awful quiet. You afraid?" asked the federal agent.

Nicholas nodded. "It's hard to put ideas into action."

+ + +

The investigative team had lunch in Sumter, deliberately stopping their trucks in front of two different cafes. They entered the back door of the county courthouse and spent most of the afternoon going over their plans. Just before dark, the agents checked their weapons and lights and the trucks rolled toward Riverton. Nicholas rode in the front of the lead vehicle with Carl.

"Take a left at the next crossroad," he said. "The Mayfields's gate is half a mile beyond. There's a guardhouse. It'll be manned, so that's where we need to show the warrant and get in, if we can."

As the headlights from the first truck swept over the entrance to the Mayfield farm, a bearded man carrying a shotgun stepped from a nearby shack and stood in the middle of the road. Carl stopped the truck and left the engine running. He said to Nicholas, "You approach from the right, I'll come on his left. When you're ready, show him the warrant."

As they opened the truck doors, the gate guard raised his weapon.

"Get the hell off this land. You got no business here!"

"Sir," said Nicholas, trying not to let his voice tremble, "I am a United States district attorney and these man are federal marshals. We have a warrant to search the property belonging to the Mayfield family."

He unfolded the paper and held it toward the man.

"Ain't nobody here to take that. You get the hell out of here!"

"Sir, I am serving you with this warrant and asking you to stand out of the way!"

As the bearded man brought his gun to firing position, six armed marshals jumped from the trucks and aimed their weapons. The guard hesitated, then lowered his gun.

"I told you. Ain't nobody here."

"Just open the gate, Sir," said Nicholas.

When the way was clear, the team boarded their trucks, leaving one man to watch the Mayfields's guard.

"I've never been in here," said Nicholas as they entered the property. "If we follow the road that's had all the traffic, we should find the operations center."

Carl turned off the headlights, and the second truck driver did the same. After a ten-minute drive, they came to a farmhouse that was flanked by a barn and a large warehouse. None of the structures displayed any lights.

"Park by the house," whispered Nicholas.

The members of the team climbed silently from their vehicles, and following hand signals from Carl, they surrounded the house.

"Me first," said Carl.

"No argument from me," said Nicholas.

When everyone was in place, the federal agent knocked loudly on the front door. "I am a federal agent with a search warrant. Please stay where you are. We are coming in."

One of the marshals lit a kerosene lamp and followed Reeves and Nicholas into the building, pistol in hand. Nicholas heard sounds from an adjacent room, and as he turned, a man entered the parlor clutching a rifle with one hand and pulling on overhauls with the other.

"Sir," said Nicholas, "I am a United States district attorney …"

"Don't shoot me! Lord, don't shoot me! I ain't one of them! I just work here!"

"We don't want to shoot you, Sir," said Carl. "We want to see the records of this operation."

"They's all in Mr. Hiram's office. It's locked and don't nobody have a key but Mr. Hiram."

"Show us where it is," ordered Nicholas.

The terrified man led Carl and Nicholas to a back room door that was secured by a large hasp and padlock.

"I ain't got no key," he repeated.

Carl ordered one of the marshals to break the hasp, and when the way was clear, he and Nicholas entered the office.

"Bring another lamp," said Carl.

"Don't need no lamp," said the overhauled man. "They got 'lectricity."

He pressed a wall switch and filled the room with light, "Remember, I'm helping you all!"

As Nicholas began a swift inventory of papers on the desk and nearby filing cabinets, Carl questioned the Mayfields's employee.

"Who else is here?"

"Ain't nobody here but me and the gate man. Mr. Hiram comes this time every week to do business, but I ain't seen him tonight."

"Who's Mr. Hiram?"

"The big boss! The one what sends out the orders and pays us."

"You expect him tonight?"

"Yes, Sir, this night every week. He comes after the rest is gone home and keeps his hat pulled down so nobody will see him."

"Do you know who Mr. Hiram is? Is he part of the Mayfield family?"

"Could be one of you, for all I know. Like I said, he does the book work and leaves. Don't nobody know him."

Nicholas listened to the interrogation and then said, "Looks like he's right. All these orders are signed by a Hiram Mayfield. We've got receipts for sugar, big bottles, small bottles, even six tons of corn! I guess they can't grow enough of their own to operate year round."

"What about orders from customers?" said Carl.

"Got those, too! All of it's going to Mr. Smith or Mr. Jones!"

A shout from the farmhouse yard froze them all.

"Stop!"

326 | RICHARD BELSER

Nicholas heard the marshals running and then the sound of a horse galloping from the barn. He stumbled after Carl to the porch in time to see a single rider flogging a big horse toward the wire fence that surrounded the barnyard.

"He's gonna jump it!" yelled Carl. "Shoot!"

As the marshals tracked the moving target, the rider slid from the saddle and clung to the left side of the horse, shielding himself from the guns as his mount raced toward the fence.

"He'll never make it!" said Nicholas.

In the next instant, the powerful horse launched itself toward the empty air above the highest strand of wire and cleared the six-foot fence with ease. The rider slipped from his precarious position and fell heavily into the rutted barnyard.

"Get him!" yelled Carl.

The marshals quickly surrounded the prostrate rider, who lay writhing in pain. In the light of the marshal's lamp, Nicholas pulled off the fallen man's hat and looked at his face.

"Conner Mayfield!" he said.

"Go to hell!" snarled the man with the broken leg.

# CHAPTER TWENTY-SIX

WHILE THE MARSHALS HANDCUFFED the gate guard and the man apprehended in the house, Nicholas and Carl knelt by Conner Mayfield.

Carl said, "Mr. Mayfield, you are under arrest for violation of the federal statutes concerning the manufacture and sale of alcoholic beverages."

"You've got nothing on me! This is my family's land. I live in Columbia and was here on a visit."

"Where's the rest of your family?"

"How should I know? I told you I just got here."

"You were trying pretty hard to leave just now."

"Hell, people yelling and pointing guns at me! What else would I do?"

"Who's Hiram Mayfield?" asked Nicholas.

"A relative. An uncle."

"Where is he?"

"I told you I don't know where anybody is! You come barging in here scaring my horse and busting my leg! Just shut up and get me to a doctor!"

Carl directed the marshals to splint Conner's leg and put him in one of the trucks with the other suspects.

"Let's go collect what we need from inside," he said to Nicholas.

As they walked toward the house, they heard a horse whinny by the barnyard fence.

"Must be the horse that dumped him. That's a hell of a jumper, though," said Carl.

In the darkness, Nicholas couldn't identify the horse's color, but the animal's size and confirmation looked familiar.

"I think I know that horse!" He walked toward the fence.

"Freedom?" The horse nickered and moved restlessly along the wire.

"It is! It's Conner's horse," said Nicholas, hurrying to open to gate. He took Freedom's bridle as the animal came to him.

"Put him in the barn," said Carl. "Everything here is confiscated till we go to trial."

"You ain't taking my horse!" yelled Conner from the truck.

"He's never been your horse," said Nicholas, "and you've had him long enough!"

Before daylight, Nicholas and the team of federal marshals gathered boxes of records and took dozens of photographs of the distillery they discovered in the warehouse.

"Look here," said Carl. "A kerosene fired still! Less smoke for people to notice!"

They also collected crates of bottles filled with clear corn whiskey. Carl shook his head in wonder.

"How about that? Where'd they get all these old South Carolina Distillery bottles? No wonder it's been hard to catch them. This stuff looks like old but perfectly legal stuff!"

Nicholas went over the office a second time, making sure that no important piece of evidence had been overlooked.

"I think that's everything," he said to Carl. "Let's get some breakfast and head for Columbia."

The federal agent assigned four men to secure the farm and the illegal distillery, leaving instructions to arrest any person arriving for work.

"Take the one with the loud mouth to the hospital in Sumter," said Carl. "Get his leg fixed."

The district attorney received Nicholas's report with excitement. "You really did it! When we organize everything you collected, we'll have a case against the whole family! Congratulations!"

Nicholas tried to share the praise with Carl Reeves and the team of marshals. "I think the man we caught inside the house will be very cooperative. He's already told us that Taylor Mayfield, the sheriff, is part of the operation."

"I hope he'll be as talkative when the Mayfields's lawyers get their hands on him. Did he say anything about their contacts in Columbia?"

"Nothing," said Nicholas. "Conner's the one with that information. Or the mystery man who signed all the orders, that Hiram Mayfield."

"Well, that's a job for tomorrow!" said Scott Morris. "You go on and get some sleep. You've done a real piece of work today!"

Nicholas found his way back to his rented apartment and collapsed on the bed. When he woke, he found a telephone and called the Bower farm to tell them about the raid on the Mayfields.

"We've already heard about it," said Sophie Bower. "Philip said the field hands came to work telling the whole story! They said you had a pistol in each hand!"

Nicholas laughed. "There were guns, but my equipment was a notebook and a pencil. I think we got the evidence we need. I can't reach January on the telephone, but if you see him, please tell him that we have Freedom. Conner tried to jump the fence. Freedom made it over but Conner didn't. He's in the hospital with a broken leg."

Nicholas placed the next call to the Heywards's home in Walterboro. When he spoke with Catherine, she asked questions which he modestly answered. Suddenly, she cried, "Wait! You didn't tell me your job included midnight raids and guns. You could have been killed!"

"We had a regular army of trained men. Last night was the exception to my job. I'm just glad it turned out well."

"You've scared me, Claus! You're going to have to come to visit to make me feel better!"

"As soon as I can. Anyway, it's a good start for me. Maybe we can tell our parents soon!"

+ + +

Weeks passed while Nicholas and Scott Morris worked to develop their case against the Mayfields's bootlegging operation. The man apprehended in the farmhouse continued to provide helpful information, as did others who were employees of the Mayfield family. Nicholas found documents proving that Sheriff Taylor Mayfield regularly paid railroad employees to insure their silence about cargos loaded at the Rimini rail spur.

"I think we've got the whole family," said Scott. "Even Conner. But we still don't know who Hiram Mayfield is, and we don't have any idea about their contact in the legislature. We need to find Hiram!"

"Why don't we question Conner again next week. He's out of the hospital and on bail staying with his family. Turns out they haven't lived in the old farmhouse for years. They built a big place with a view of the river. I can't believe nobody in Riverton knew!"

Conner Mayfield appeared for questioning with his attorney, and when Nicholas entered the room a familiar voice called his name.

"Nicholas Bower! My old roommate and everybody's football hero!"

Nicholas turned to see Richard Baker grinning at him.

"You're representing Mayfield?" said Nicholas.

"That I am! He's not my first client, but he's my biggest so far. How about that?! You and me against each other!"

"Let's just keep it professional."

"Oh, I will! But I can't help remembering that the first time we competed, I won. How is Sally, anyway?"

"Why don't we get started?"

Conner Mayfield provided Nicholas with no new information, and Richard Baker made sure that the key questions were not answered. At the end of the interview, Richard said, "I expected to be more impressed, Nicholas! I mean, with your training at Oxford and all. I'm just from little old South Carolina. Maybe you'll do better when we get to court!"

Nicholas said nothing.

"You handled that well," said his boss as they went back to the district attorney's office. "You were pursuing a line of questioning that makes me think you've got a plan. Think you ought to tell me?"

"I couldn't get him to slip up, but I think Hiram Mayfield is Conner."

"I see what you're thinking! The man you caught in the house said Hiram always came after dark on that night of the week, and Conner showed up on his horse. Interesting, but it's circumstantial. We need somebody to identify him!"

"I'll work on it. I've got a few ideas."

"I hope one of them works! Be a shame to put the family in jail for a few years and let the big boss get away. And the crook in the legislature who's in on it!"

When Nicholas sat down with Scott to go over the prosecution's case before the trial, the district attorney looked at the list of prospective witnesses and asked, "Who is Hattie Mae Mayfield?"

"Conner's grandmother," said Nicholas.

"What in the world could she know?"

"She would know her grandson's full name."

"You think Conner's middle name is Hiram?"

"I do. All the years I went to school with him, I never heard anybody call him anything but Conner. Well, some of the boys had other names for him! But somewhere I believe he's got to be on record with that middle name."

"I'm not sure Granny would tell the truth, and even if she did it might not be enough to convict him of bigger charges."

"Maybe not," said Nicholas, "but he might not know that. And if we can spook him, maybe he'll name the Columbia contact as part of a plea bargain."

"I don't think you learned that at Oxford!"

"I just know Conner! I think if we surprise him, he'll fold."

On the morning of the trial, Nicholas received a letter from Catherine.

"Where are you?" she wrote. "I know you're busy preparing for the trial, but I expected to hear something from you! But never mind! Father's coming to Columbia on business the day you go to court, and I'm riding with him. I won't embarrass you or anything, but I'll be sitting in the back somewhere praying for you."

Nicholas smiled and put the letter into his suit pocket.

The evidence collected by Nicholas and the federal agents filled a dozen large cardboard boxes and made an impressive display in the courtroom. Nicholas showed no emotion as the Mayfield family entered with Richard Baker and several other attorneys. Conner came in on crutches. His suit looked expensive and his hair was neatly trimmed. He stared at Nicholas for a long moment before twisting his angular face into a smile.

After the jury had been drawn, Scott Morris rose to present the case for the prosecution. "Your Honor, the State has filed charges against seven individuals who have been identified as members of the Mayfield family. There is another person whose name we have but whose identity remains unknown. The State believes the unknown person is, in fact, someone present in this court, and we would like to begin by establishing his identity."

The district attorney introduced Nicholas to call the first witness.

"The State calls Mrs. Hattie Mae Mayfield."

An elderly woman, overdressed in an elaborate, lavender gown and wide, feathered hat, came forward, assisted by a black woman in a nurse's white uniform.

Nicholas established the woman's identity, and then he asked, "Mrs. Mayfield, please tell the court your relationship to Mr. Conner Mayfield, one of the defendants."

"Conner's my grandson. And he's a good boy! Smart as a whip and looks after the family."

"Please tell the court your grandson's name."

"You just called his name! He's Conner, Conner Mayfield."

"To the best of your knowledge, is that his full name?"

"He don't have no other name. Just Conner."

When Nicholas finished his questioning of the witness, Richard Baker rose to address the woman. "Miss Hattie Mae, are you a Christian?"

"All my life, since I was baptized in the Santee River June 15, 1842."

"Do you own a Bible, Miss Hattie Mae?"

"Course I do! I got it right here!"

Richard Baker directed the jury's attention to the old woman's white leather Bible. "Now, Miss Hattie Mae, do the Mayfield's have what people call a family Bible?"

"Yes, sir, we do. We keep it on the table in my parlor."

Richard picked up a large book from the defense table and carried it to the witness stand. "Will you tell the court if this is the Mayfield Family Bible?"

The woman opened the cover and pointed to the first page. "It's all right here! All the generations of our people."

"Do you see the name 'Conner Mayfield' in the family Bible?"

Hattie May adjusted her eyeglasses. "Yes, sir! It's right here. The oldest son of my son, Lamar, and Lillian Mayfield."

Richard Baker glanced back at Nicholas, and then bent over the witness. "Miss Hattie Mae, will you read me Conner's full name as recorded in the Mayfield family Bible?"

"It's Conner Mayfield. Just like I said. He ain't got no other name."

334 | RICHARD BELSER

Richard stood abruptly and addressed the jury. "Gentleman, I submit to you that the State has failed to demonstrate their assertion that Conner's middle name is Hiram, or that he even has a middle name. They have admitted that they have found no birth certificate for Mr. Mayfield, or any other legal document with a middle name. I don't know who else they intend to hang the name 'Hiram'" on, but it's perfectly clear that it can't be Conner Mayfield."

When the trial recessed for lunch, Scott Morris looked at Nicholas and shook his head. "We didn't anticipate that family Bible maneuver. A sweet old lady and a big Bible! Who can top that?"

Nicholas frowned. "I have another idea. It might take me till to-morrow to make it work."

"Not a chance! The judge saw all our boxes of evidence and he's determined to move the trial along. If your idea is convincing, we might be able to get him to give us a couple of hours after we go back into session."

"So we have an hour for lunch, and maybe two more. It'll take a miracle to get everything we need by three o'clock, but it might be worth a try?"

Nicholas whispered his strategy to the district attorney.

Scott Morris said, "You get started. I'll move for a two-hour delay when the judge comes back in."

Nicholas found Catherine at the back of the courtroom. "It's not going too well, is it?" she said.

Nicholas grimaced. "I need your help! Come up to my office and telephone my house. I've got another call to make. Tell Mother we need Philip to find some evidence for us and get it to Columbia before three this afternoon."

"Claus, is that possible? How long does it take to drive here from Riverton?"

"Two hours, if nothing goes wrong."

"What do you want Philip to bring?"

Nicholas pulled Catherine close and whispered into her ear the assignment she was to pass along to Philip.

"What if you mother's not there? Or she can't find Philip?"

"We just have to pray that they're all there! We don't have time to talk about alternatives. Let's go!"

Catherine and Nicholas hurried upstairs to the district attorney's office, sat down at different desks and placed their calls. In ten minutes they met each other in the hall.

"Well?" said Nicholas.

Catherine smiled. "The Lord was with us! Your mother answered, and Philip was there for lunch! I couldn't believe it! He said he would leave right then. He wasn't too optimistic about getting here by three. What about your call?"

Nicholas grinned. "Same with me! I got through on the first try and it's on the way! All we can do is pray."


At five minutes to three, the Mayfield family and their attorneys filed into the courtroom. Richard Baker glared at Nicholas. The attorneys for the Mayfields had protested Scott Morris's request for a delay, but the judge granted the motion over their objection.

Scott looked at his pocket watch and frowned at Nicholas. "We're in big trouble if they don't come."

"I believe we'll see them. Maybe late, but they'll be here. Is there some way we can buy a little more time?"

When everyone stood for the judge's entrance, Nicholas looked anxiously toward the back of the courtroom. Catherine had taken a position just inside the door, and every few seconds, she looked out into the hall. She caught Nicholas's eye and shook her head.

The judge called the court to order. "I granted the State their request for a two-hour delay after lunch, and I warned them that no such favor would be granted from this time forward. Now, is the district attorney prepared to call the witnesses he told me about?"

Scott Morris stood. "Your Honor, the State believes the witnesses are on their way. We expect them to arrive at any moment."

Richard Baker leapt to his feet. "We object, your Honor! The Court has already indulged the prosecutor's imagination while my clients continue to suffer the State's unjust accusations. Unless the trial resumes immediately, the defense will move for dismissal of the charges!"

Nicholas heard someone enter the courtroom. He turned to see Catherine waving to get his attention, and in the center aisle stood Philip, smiling and vigorously nodding his head. Nicholas gripped Scott Morris' shoulder.

"Your Honor," said the District Attorney, "Mr. Bower will call the State's next witness."

When Philip took the stand, Nicholas lost no time covering the preliminary questions.

"Mr. Bower," he said, "have you recently visited the Ex Libris Bookstore in Sumter, South Carolina?"

"Yes, I have. Just this afternoon."

"Did you determine if the Ex Libris Bookstore sells large Bibles, the kind often called family Bibles?"

"Yes, Sir, they do."

"And were you able to find out how many of those holy books they have sold recently?"

"The owner, Mr. Harris, told me they have only sold one family Bible this year."

"Did Mr. Harris tell you to whom that Bible was sold?"

"He did."

"Will you tell the court who purchased that Bible and when the sale was made?"

"Your Honor, I object!" said Richard Baker. "We don't have the bookstore owner here!

This is nothing but hearsay!"

"Overruled! The State will have a chance to produce the bookstore owner if the testimony of this witness is relevant. Please answer the question, Mr. Bower."

"The family Bible was bought on June 1, 1910 by Mr. Conner Mayfield."

A loud cry echoed through the courtroom. Nicholas turned to see Hattie Mae Mayfield slump sideways in her seat while the attending nurse tried to cool her with a fan.

"Lord Jesus, have mercy! Have mercy on me!" wailed the frail woman. "I was wrong! I can't help it that I love my family!"

When the hysterical grandmother had regained her composure, the judge reminded her of her oath to tell the truth and then asked her, "Did you lie about the Bible, Mrs. Mayfield?"

"No, No! I swear to God! We do have a family Bible! I reckoned the one that lawyer showed me was the one from my parlor. I don't see too good, you know."

Richard Baker told the judge that Conner Mayfield had given him the Bible and told him that it had been in the family for generations. After examining the book, Nicholas addressed the jury.

"Gentlemen, you'll have a chance to see this yourself, but it is clear to me that this is a new, never used Bible with a little dirt rubbed on the cover, and that all the entries in the family history section are made with different pens but by the same hand."

When the room had quieted, Nicholas excused Philip from the witness stand. During the commotion, his second witness had entered the courtroom. He stood and said, "The State calls Mr. January Wilson."

The tall black man walked quickly to the front and took his seat. When January had been sworn and identified, Nicholas asked him, "Will you tell the Court the nature of your job and where you perform it?"

"I teach at the colored school in Manchester, South Carolina."

"Where is your school located?"

"Right there in Manchester."

"Do you know where the Clarendon County magistrate's office is, Mr. Wilson?"

"Two blocks from my school."

"And do you personally know the man who serves as magistrate in Clarendon County?"

"I do. It's Mr. Kendrick."

"To your knowledge, how long has Mr. Kendrick served in that capacity?"

"Well over twenty years."

"Did you visit Mr. Kendrick today?"

"Yes, sir."

"Did Mr. Kendrick give you anything during your visit?"

"Mr. Kendrick gave me a copy of a bill of sale for a horse."

"Do you have that copy with you?"

"I do."

Nicholas looked at Richard Baker and smiled. He said to January, "Would you read the date of the sale, the description of the horse, the amount paid, and the names of the seller and the buyer?"

"I object!" yelled Richard Baker. "We have no certainty that this paper is legitimate!"

January gestured to get the judge's attention. "Sir, Mr. Kendrick can vouch for the bill of sale himself. He gave me a ride from Manchester, and he's sitting right back there in the third row."

"Objection overruled," said the judge. "The witness will read the document."

January sat straight in the chair. "The date is April 2, 1900. The horse is a chestnut stallion standing sixteen hands, and approximately three years old. The amount paid is five dollars. The seller is Isaiah Adams, and he's signed with an X."

The judge asked, "And the buyer?"

"Conner Hiram Mayfield."

The courtroom erupted in shouts as Conner Mayfield pushed his way toward the witness stand, swinging viciously with one of his crutches as his attorneys tried to force him back into his seat.

When the judge had gaveled the room to order, Nicholas

continued. "Your Honor, the State submits that the bill of sale from the Clarendon County Magistrates' office bears Mr. Kendrick's signature and the seal of his office. We identify this as an official document bearing the legal signature of Mr. Conner Hiram Mayfield."

From the defense table Conner's voice sounded again. "You might have my name, but I know some names you don't have. You want names? Talk to my lawyer! Think I'm lying? I'll give you one for nothing!"

Richard Baker tried to stand, but Conner pushed him out of the way.

"You can start with Alphonse Spann. Senator Spann! Big Al! He's big in Rock Hill. And his good buddy, Garner Bullard. Senator from Aiken. They been backing our operation for five years. We did the dirty work and they took in the money. You want the rest of 'em? Talk to my lawyer! If I'm serving time, I ain't doing it alone."

Nicholas could hardly believe his ears. He looked at Scott Morris. "It worked!" he said.

After some plea-bargaining, the trial came to a speedy conclusion, with Conner Mayfield pleading guilty to charges more serious than those faced by the other members of his family. Before the marshals took Conner away in handcuffs, Nicholas stood and made a motion.

"You honor, since the court has confiscated the property used by the defendants in their illegal operation, I ask for a special order concerning the care of the horse mentioned in the bill of sale, the one formerly ridden by Conner Hiram Mayfield. If it please the court, may that horse be placed in the care of Mr. January Wilson, until such time as the court is ready to award permanent custody."

The judge looked at January. "Mr. Wilson, are you prepared to take good care of this horse, who is now a ward of the state?"

"Yes, sir, I am. I'll look after him as if he were my own."

"The court orders the horse in question to be remanded to the custody of Mr. January Wilson. That will be permanent custody, Mr. Wilson. By the way, what's the horse's name?"

"Freedom, sir."

## CHAPTER TWENTY-SEVEN

AFTER THE JUDGE HAD GAVELED the proceedings to a close, Nicholas stood at the prosecution's desk to receive his boss's handshake.

"You are either very smart or very lucky, Mr. Bower! I figured this case would go on for at least a month, and you've wrapped it up in a day!" said Scott Morris. Nicholas felt his face redden as he fought against the upwelling tears.

"Not just lucky! Dumb luck!" said a voice from the defense table. Richard Baker stuffed papers into his briefcase as he glared at Nicholas. "That business of the missing middle name. You know perfectly well that's no real evidence! You didn't win this case, Bower. My client folded!"

"Your client was guilty! I just gave him a chance to admit it," said Nicholas. "But look on the bright side, Richard. All those names Conner gave us. They're all potential clients for you. Big, important clients. If any of them are willing to hire you!"

"This isn't over, Bower!"

"It's over for today," said the district attorney. "And Claus, you've got some people who are eager to speak to you."

As the courtroom cleared, Nicholas found himself surrounded by well-wishers eager to shake his hand. Philip was the first to reach him.

"Good job, brother!" said Philip, punching Nicholas in the arm before wrapping him in a hug. "Did you see Conner's face when January read the bill of sale? You really got to him! But how in the world did you think to look there?"

"I don't know! It's been ten years, but somehow I kept remembering the Summer Race and something the sheriff said when he looked at Conner's copy of the paper."

"It's a good thing that wasn't stolen from my files," said the Clarendon County magistrate.

"You've had files stolen?" asked the district attorney.

"I've been running my own little investigation," said the magistrate. "Since last year when somebody got into my property tax files."

Nicholas suddenly sat down at the prosecutor's table. "You wouldn't be talking about the taxes on the Adams family farm, would you? The place you sold to the Mayfields?"

"That's exactly what I'm talking about! It never made sense to me that I couldn't find any record of those payments, because I can remember January coming in every year with the money."

"Then why did you go ahead with the tax sale?" said Nicholas.

"Conner's lawyer, that Baker fellow, came in and demanded that since there was no record, I had to put the land up for sale. Made me mad, but there was nothing I could do."

"Have you found anything linking the Mayfields with the missing records?"

"Well, Helen Mayfield, you know, oldest daughter of Sheriff Mayfield, she worked for me for a while as a clerk. Really sloppy worker! Left things all over the office. I had to let her go. I think it was about that time when those records disappeared."

"Well," said the district attorney, "we can explore that connection later. The first question is, can you testify that you remember January Wilson paying the taxes on the Adams farm?"

"I sure can!"

Nicholas looked quickly at his boss. "Is there a chance that we can get that tax sale overturned?"

"It's a matter for Clarendon County, but the Adams's can try," said Scott Barnes.

January Wilson had been standing near and listening. "Of course we'll try! Half an hour ago I wouldn't have thought anything like this could happen, but now I can't wait to tell my mother!" he said.

"Tell her to keep praying," said Nicholas. "I'm pretty sure she's been on her knees today!"

"And she's not the only one!" Catherine pushed through the men gathered at the prosecutor's table to stand close to Nicholas. "With so many unlikely things working out perfectly, it's clear that lots of people have been praying." She took Nicholas's hand. "I certainly have," she said.

"You know," said Nicholas, "when you think about it, it's an amazing thing." The faces around the table looked at him expectantly, but he paused and blushed, shaking his head. "This is way beyond me," he said. "Maybe I can tell you later when I've puzzled over it a while."

+ + +

Nicholas and Catherine left the courtroom with the others who had helped gather the evidence against Conner Mayfield. The men were making plans to return to Riverton when Catherine saw her father drive up in a taxi.

"There's Father," she said, hurrying toward the former governor while towing Nicholas by the hand. "I can't wait to tell him!"

During her breathless summary of the day's events, Governor Heyward listened closely, and then clapped Nicholas on the shoulder as he shook his hand. "Well done, young man! I know your mother will be happy for you. And your father, had he seen this day … Well, this is the kind of accomplishment that fills fathers with pride!"

Nicholas blushed at the governor's compliments. He had a momentary image of his father's dark eyes and black beard, and instead of feeling the fear that Captain Bower always drew from him,

Nicholas experienced a surprising sadness. He remembered Asa Turnbull's funeral homily for his father. "We are all led by our eagerness for praise."

"Not just praise for him! Praise for me, too!" thought Nicholas. "Desperate for it! Driven!" As the sadness subsided, Nicholas said out loud, "Such a loss!"

"No doubt! No doubt!" agreed the governor. "South Carolina has seen too few men like Maximillian Bower."

"What I mean, sir, is not so much the loss of my father's life, but the loss of real living while he was alive. It's as though ..."

"I understand, son. Catherine has told me about your father. I've known many men like him, and for all their accomplishments, they do have a sadness about them."

"Governor Heyward," said Nicholas, "I would like very much to talk more about this with you and there are other things I want to consult with you about, but I know that you and Catherine have a train to catch pretty soon. May I visit your family on Saturday?"

The governor assured Nicholas of his welcome, and as he turned to climb into the taxi, Nicholas and Catherine exchanged secret smiles. "Until Saturday," he whispered. "I love you!"

+ + +

Catherine waved from the seat of the gig as the train brought Nicholas into Walterboro. "You have made me a mad woman," she exclaimed as he climbed up to sit next to her. "Are you going to ask Father today? I thought we were going to wait! I can't eat! I can't sleep!" Catherine turned the horse from the station yard to the tree-lined street leading toward the Heyward's residence. As soon as they were far enough from the station, Nicholas kissed her, wrapping her in his arms until she allowed the horse to stop and retuned his embrace.

"I've missed you so much!" she whispered.

Nicholas smoothed her hair. "I guess I should have talked with you about it before asking to see your father, but after the trial everything felt so right. But as soon as you left, I was terrified. Believe me, I haven't slept much either!"

"There are just so many things we need to decide! Where would we live? Aren't you in a little apartment? When should we have the wedding? And where? Oh, Nicholas! What if Father tells us we have to wait a year while you get established?! Two years! I would go absolutely mad!"

Nicholas laughed. "I sounded just like you when I rode home with Philip and January! Couldn't think of a thing but problems! And you know what January said to me?"

"I can't even begin to guess!"

"Let me not to the marriage of true minds admit impediments."

"Of course! Shakespeare! And what did you say?"

"Omnia iam fient fieri quae posse negabam."

"Translation, please."

"Everything which I used to say could not happen will happen now."

"That's easy to say, but are we really ready to talk with Father?"

"I was ready three years ago! Unless you tell me no, I will speak to him today."

"And if he says no or wants us to wait? Oh, but he won't! He's already told everybody that he likes you!"

"If he says no! If he disappoints us! Catherine, that's what I wasn't able to talk about in the courtroom. We were all talking about God answering our prayers because we won the case. But I've begun to see that God is answering prayers not just when good things happen, but even when we're disappointed."

"Please don't talk like that! I don't want to think about disappointments."

"Oh, I'm not really worried that your father might discourage us. I'm just learning that God answers prayers even when all we can see is trouble. Don't you see? God was there when Conner bought January's horse and put his full name on the bill of sale! I couldn't see it. I was angry at God for letting my friend be so hurt. But God already had planned the reappearance of that paper ten years later in a courtroom!"

"I suppose I can see that. But I still don't want Father to say no!"

"Wait! I'm not finished. You know how I came to the university all wrapped up in Sally Hemphill?"

"Of course I do! Why are you bringing her up?"

"Because when she changed and began to ignore me, I felt abandoned by God. Until he sent you! And you sat on a rock in Tallulah Gorge and changed my life."

"That's better. You may continue."

"All I'm saying is that God was there all along. The bad times as well as the good! He brings out of our disappointments better blessings than we could possibly imagine!"

"Like me?"

"Especially you! Now let me hold those reins. I have a meeting with an important man!"

+ + +

At the evening meal, Nicholas and Catherine struggled to make conversation with her parents. The governor himself seemed nervously cheerful as he persuaded Nicholas to describe for Catherine's mother the strategy that led to Conner Mayfield's eruption in the courtroom. Mrs. Heyward expressed her admiration for such an effective beginning for Nicholas's career as a lawyer. "Do you suppose that you will continue with the district attorney's office?" she asked.

"It is a good opportunity," said Nicholas, "one that will give me plenty of courtroom experience. But I don't think I will make a career as a prosecutor. I'd like to join an established firm, or maybe find a partner or two, and hang up my shingle."

"Would you stay, perhaps, in Columbia, or maybe in Charleston or another large city?"

"I suppose it would depend on a number of things."

"How about a small town?" said Mrs. Heyward. "Walterboro needs a country lawyer. And I'm sure your mother would be happy if you settled somewhere near your family's farm, maybe a practice in Sumter?"

"Mary," said the governor. "You certainly seem to have a keen interest in this young man's future!" Catherine coughed abruptly into her napkin.

"Do mind your manners, Duncan!" said Mrs. Heyward. "I'm just curious about what one does with an Oxford education in South Carolina!"

"And I'm interested in stretching my legs after that fine supper," said the governor. "Claus, let's take a stroll. I'd like to show you my grass."

Nicholas saw Catherine's eyes shine his way as he stood and helped Mrs. Heyward with her chair. "I love you!" she silently mouthed as Nicholas turned to join her father on the piazza.

Stepping out onto the lawn, the governor said, "The challenge I've faced in my years as a planter hasn't been growing rice. When the weather cooperates, I've always been able to produce fine crops. But right here in my back yard, under these big trees, I've had the hardest time getting grass to grow."

Nicholas gazed out across the broad lawn shaded with live oaks and magnolias. "This grass looks perfect to me," he said, "like an artist's low country landscape."

"You're kind to say so. And truth is, I've only recently been able to have a lawn like this. The areas under the trees would support clumps of grass here and there, but it wouldn't flourish or stay green and it certainly wouldn't spread over the shaded soil."

Nicholas listened to the governor's words with the part of his mind that wasn't rehearsing the request he was determined to make. "So your grass was alive, but just barely. And it's as lush as can be now. What made the difference?" he asked.

"You see over there, under that magnolia? See those sprigs of green grass? That's the secret! I found this species of grass that is designed to grow in the shade. You don't scatter it as seed. You put plugs of the new grass right in between what's left of the old, and little by little, the shade-trained grass spreads and takes over."

Nicholas followed Catherine's father as he walked across the rich green lawn. "New grass in between what's left of the old." The governor's words rooted themselves in Nicholas's consciousness while peace shaded the burning question of the day. He now knew how to proceed, and he felt himself relax.

"Sir," he said. "Your grass brings to mind a conversation we had to cut short the other day in Columbia. Perhaps you remember me saying that the greatest loss to me and my family was not my father's death but how little he lived while he was alive."

"Claus, I'm surprised to hear you say that! Your father had a reputation for the most vigorous living! An underage soldier. A wounded hero. College man. A successful farmer and a real community leader. Wasn't it he who reorganized then Clarendon Rifles a few years ago when there was trouble in the county? I don't understand what you mean when you say he didn't live while he was alive."

"I mean that his whole life was a struggle! I think he was driven to do everything he did. He had a desperate hunger to succeed, a constant need for praise, either for his own accomplishments, or for other people's successes that might reflect credit on him."

"As I think I told you in Columbia, I've known men like your father. There's an intensity that grips them and sometimes robs them of their freedom. But what's this got to do with my grass?"

Nicholas said nothing for several breaths. Then the words came. "Men like my father are like your old grass that couldn't live in the shade, couldn't seem to get enough sun or water. Those sprouts struggled year after year and competed heroically and they never really lived. But when you planted the new grass that was developed to live in the shade, the old grass gave way to the new." Nicholas brushed the soles of his shoes across the thick green grass beneath his feet. "Governor Heyward," he said, "I treasure Catherine's praise, and yours, just like plants treasure sunlight. But like your lawn, I've been sprigged with a new kind of life that doesn't require much sunlight and, in fact, does quite well in the shade."

"If you mean that you now know how to live with criticism, may I say that you've chosen the right profession," said the governor.

"It's not just living with criticism. It's knowing that I don't have to prove myself in everything I do."

The governor turned and smiled at Nicholas. "Are you so certain of Catherine's love?"

"As certain as this grass is green. But, sir, if something beyond my imagination should ever cloud her love for me, I would still have no doubts about my worth."

"Now you're speaking of God's love."

"Exactly! The love of Jesus who died for me even though I'll never deserve it." Nicholas felt his mind racing with other ways to explain himself to Catherine's father, but his spirit told him he'd said enough. "And speaking of Catherine's love, sir, may I say something more about that?"

"You don't really think I brought you out of the house just to look at the grass, do you? I wondered when you were going to get around to dear Catherine!" said the governor.

Nicholas felt his face redden. He took a breath and began to speak. "Sir, your daughter is always on my mind, and she has been since that first summer at Lamont. I hope you know that I love her dearly, and would be honored if she would be my wife. And I pray, sir, that this would be agreeable to you and Mrs. Heyward."

"Mrs. Heyward and I would like nothing better than for you and Catherine to marry! Now, let's go in and tell the ladies before they fall out of the window they've been peering through!"

+ + +

On Sunday morning, Nicholas and Catherine walked with Governor and Mrs. Heyward to St. Jude's Church. The night before, they had telephoned Sophie Bower to tell her the news. Once she had shed her happy tears, Nicholas's mother expressed her delight to Governor and Mrs. Heyward and had a long conversation with Catherine, who promised to visit the Bower farm very soon. Since the announcement had been made to both families, Catherine's parents were at liberty to share the news with their friends at church. Nicholas was pleased, but not surprised, at the number of Walterboro citizens who knew his parents. One after another, they shook Nicholas's hand. "A fine man, your father!" they said. "South Carolina lost a treasure when Captain Bower died!" Nicholas nodded respectfully at their words of praise. Then someone took his hand and said, "I am surprised, though, that Captain Bower's eldest son is a lawyer and not a farmer. If you didn't inherit the farm, I hope your legacy is your father's forcefulness!" Nicholas smiled and said, "I have the most wonderful inheritance!"

Walterboro's small wooden church reminded Nicholas of the Riverton church where he'd spent so many Sundays of his boyhood. He felt at home here, comforted by the familiar words of the Episcopal prayer book. But as the worship began, he realized that the peace he felt grew from something more profound than familiarity with words. When the minister read the Ten Commandments and invited the congregation to respond together, Nicholas knew something was different.

"Honor thy father and thy mother," read the minister. The congregation replied together, "Lord, have mercy upon us, and incline our hearts to keep this law." And Nicholas began to weep. There it was again. Mercy. But this time, Nicholas knew mercy as God's gift and not his demand. "Father," he prayed to the man who had given him life and had raised him, "Father, I do honor you! For the times I disappointed you, forgive me. And for the times you did the same to me, I forgive you."

"Are you all right?" whispered Catherine looking over at his tear streaked face. Nicholas nodded and squeezed her hand.

"I'm fine," he smiled. "I'm happy because lots of things are making sense for me. 'Facilius per partes in cognotionem totius adducimur.' We are more easily led part by part to an understanding of the whole."

"Now I'm sure you're OK," Catherine said into his ear as the service continued.

The next scripture reading ended with these words: "And because you are sons, God has sent the Spirit of his Son into our hearts, crying, 'Abba! Father!' So through God you are no longer a slave, but a son, and if a son then an heir."

## EPILOGUE

NICHOLAS BOWER AND CATHERINE HEYWARD were married at Trinity Church in Columbia, South Carolina. They had eight children. Nicholas left the district attorney's office and entered the practice of law with a friend, and eventually, with two of his sons. One of Nicholas's and Catherine's daughters studied at Oxford and later married Oliver Courtenay, Junior, who became the 16th Earl of Devon. Nicholas acquired several large tracts of land in the South Carolina midlands and low country, in addition to the farm near Riverton, and devoted many happy afternoons to shooting doves and quail.

Sophie Bower lived on the farm until her death at age 84. She became an accomplished portrait artist and also wrote the history of Clarendon County. During her research into the history of Riverton's Winter Race, she discovered that Simeon Wilson, the young man who rode to warn the town of the Union Army's advance, was a former slave and the father of January Wilson. In the turmoil of Reconstruction, the name of the local hero had been preserved, but his identity had been lost.

Philip Bower accepted the governor's appointment as interim sheriff of Clarendon County after Taylor Mayfield was removed from office. Philip hired Abel Simmons, a neighbor and recent

Clemson graduate, to manage the farm. After serving one elected term as sheriff, Philip resigned and bought a Ford dealership in Columbia. He married Becky Singleton, one of Mr. Singleton's twin daughters. They had two sons who later bought and operated the cotton gin built by Conner Mayfield.

January Wilson married Sally Hemphill in a civil ceremony in Washington, D.C. His mother, Venus Adams, was present, along with his sister, April, and her husband. Nicholas and Catherine were not able to attend. January completed coursework for a Doctorate in English Literature at Howard University and served for thirty years as professor in the School of Education. When the university received certification to grant doctorates, January was awarded a PhD, posthumously. Sally continued to be active in the Women's Rights Movement. Their daughter, Sophia, was one of the first women ordained to the priesthood of the Episcopal Church. Their son, Nikki, was killed while participating in a civil rights demonstration in 1957.

Conner Hiram Mayfield served 18 years of a 25-year sentence before being released on parole. He moved from South Carolina and was never again seen in Clarendon County.

The horse, Freedom, traveled by train to a farm in Arlington, Virginia, not far from the residence of January and Sally Wilson. He carefully carried the Wilson's children around the paddock until his death at age 22.

# END NOTES

[i] From a letter written to Irvine Furman Belser by his mother, Gulielma Baker Belser, cited on p. 122 of Irvine Belser's book, *Life is a Glorious Adventure*.

[ii] Ibid.

[iii] The honors are those awarded to Irvine Belser on the occasion of his graduation from the University of South Carolina in 1910

[iv] *Life is a Glorious Adventure*; Irvine Furman Belser, 1968; p. 36

[v] Ibid.

[vi] Op. Cit. p. 40

17084243R00214

Made in the USA
San Bernardino, CA
30 November 2014